THE PIECES

James Wilson

SENEX
PRESS

Senex Press
Boston, Massachusetts
www.senexpress.org
'We publish the best books.'

The Pieces will be published with the ISBN
979-8-9863159-2-8

Typeset by Octavo Smith Publishing Services

Printed and bound in Great Britain
by CPI Group (UK) Ltd, Croydon, CR0 4YY

'Edith Piaf famously regretted nothing, but I have a couple of regrets. The first of them is that I once listened to a Bon Jovi album. My biggest regret, though, is that I never saw Adam Earnshaw play "Mr Morris" live.' — John Peel, speaking in 1991

'Like woodsmoke hanging in the autumnal air in the dying light of the Sixties, Adam Earnshaw's enigmatic presence haunts all those who draw in a breath of it.' — Cathi Unsworth, author of *Season of the Witch: The Book of Goth*

'So mind-altering is Adam Earnshaw's music that it could easily join LSD on the list of proscribed substances.' — Mick Farren, *Oz*, 1968

'Psychedelic troubadour Adam Earnshaw looks set to make the tricky transition from underground cult to overground star...' — *Melody Maker*, 1967

'Earnshaw? The guy's a loon who howls at the moon. But I never did like his shoes.' — Dennis Hopper, interviewed in *Time* magazine, 1970

'Some artists burn out, others fade away. Adam Earnshaw did both, disappearing as the sixties trip turned dark and the seventies shadow descended into the black.' — Matthew Worley, Professor of Modern History, University of Reading

'The wisest heads in the music business may not agree on much, but they all say the new platter from Adam Earnshaw is bound to happen in a big way. He's a young man with heaps of talent and a bright future.' — "The Buzzin' Dozen", *Pop Weekly*, 1967

'I met him once. Or I think I did. Was it at the club in the basement of the Pheasantry on the King's Road? Who the hell knows...If you can remember meeting Adam Earnshaw in those days, you weren't really there.' — Lemmy, interviewed in *The Face*, 1983

'The times are undoubtedly a-changing. Nairobi-born Adam Earnshaw is poised to depose Bob Dylan as the Voice of a Generation. I'm tempted to say, "It's All Over Now, Baby Bob."' — *Disc and Music Echo*, 1968

'I'm not really into possessions because I see myself as a kinda wandering minstrel like that Alan-a-Dale guy in *Robin Hood and His Merrie Men*. All the same, if my house was on fire the first thing I'd rescue would be my signed copy of [the Adam Earnshaw EP] *Our Dancing Days*.' — Denny Laine, interviewed in *Record Mirror*, 1969

'I'd trade all my Jeff Buckley gigs for one chance to have seen Adam Earnshaw. He released *Standing Stone* when he was twenty-two, for chrissake. Imagine the possibilities had he lived. Although, who knows, maybe he *did*?' — Andrew Smith, former *Sunday Times* music critic and author of *Moondust*

'Most musicians don't know when to stop, their early brilliance too often blotted out by inferior later works, things simply churned out at the behest of management, record companies and us, Joe Public, ever hungry for more product. Adam Earnshaw, on the other hand, only ever leaves me wanting to hear more and wondering what might have been. But there's beauty in that brevity and the sheer not knowingness of it all.' — Travis Elborough, author of *The Long Player Goodbye* and *Through the Looking Glasse*s

For Paula, Tom, and Kit
With my love

CONTENTS

INTRO

Where are we?

Somewhere in rural America, it looks like. A ragged collage of trees and rock pasted on to blue sky. In the foreground, a single-storey log building, with gaudy beer-ads in the windows and a sign over the entrance: Double D Bar. In the parking lot – a bare scrabble of dust and stone cut into the hillside – a couple of pick-ups, three Harleys, an ancient but still-shiny red Corvette. Their lines are wonky with late-afternoon heat-haze. Just by looking, you can feel the slap of the sun on your skin, smell the mix of fumes and scorched varnish and pine needles.

The camera swivels round. We see a man sitting in a car at the edge of the road. Not young, not old; nothing-coloured hair that needs a cut; standard-issue face lined with tiredness. He stares at the row of parked vehicles, lingering for a moment on the Corvette. After a few seconds he looks up again, eases his car next to the Harleys and gets out. He looks round, pushing his unruly shirt back into his trousers, grabs a worse-for-wear leather satchel from the rear seat and lopes to the door.

Inside it's dark. A hum of talk, indistinct figures hunched over tables. All he can see clearly are the windows, with a couple of old air conditioning units rattling underneath them. He stares at those units, bringing them into close-up. What do they look like? Something weird. Organs, maybe: alien organs, awaiting transplant. We get the idea, anyway: the place is fridge-cold.

'Well, hi there.'

He blinks. A woman looms into view behind the bar. She's big, her bare arms thick with muscle, a bolster of fat under her ribs.

'Hello.'

Only two syllables. But enough to betray his English accent. The people at the tables stop talking and glance towards him. Apart from the bikers – all huge, all winking with studs – there are a couple of college kids with a half-empty pitcher of Bud between them, and an old hick, scrawny as a corn-stalk, sitting next to a stocky seventy-something woman with untidy corkscrew hair. You know what this smells like, too: beer; iced sweat; the lingering ghost of long-dead cigarettes.

'May I get you something?'

'Just a Seven-Up, please.'

She double-takes. 'You're not from round here?'

'Well spotted.'

She laughs. 'Australia?'

'England.'

'Ooookay.' The way you'd say it to a seven-year-old who tells you he's Batman. She opens a chill cabinet, bends down to peer inside, gropes for a green can. 'There you go. You want a glass?'

He shakes his head. 'No, just like that's fine. Thanks.'

He pulls off the tab, puts the can to his lips.

'You're a long ways from home,' says the woman.

'Yes.' He wipes his mouth with the back of his hand. 'I'm looking for someone.'

'In Truscott?'

'Near Truscott. I was hoping maybe you could tell me where to find him.'

She raises her eyebrows.

'Name of?'

'I don't what he calls himself now. Or called himself. He could be dead, for all I know. But his real name was Adam Earnshaw.'

He studies her eyes, searching for a tic of recognition. She shakes her head.

'An older guy. Kind of a recluse. Suspicious of strangers, I imagine. Not ringing any bells?'

'Nope.'

'I've got some pictures.' He opens the satchel, takes out an envelope, slips a handful of photos onto the bar. 'This is what he looked like when he went missing.' He prods it towards her: an over-enlarged snap of a man in his mid-twenties. The man has long fair hair and wears a collarless cheesecloth shirt. He's squinting in the bright light, his heavy mouth in a discontented pout.

'No, I'd remember if I seed him,' says the woman. 'He some kind of a hippie or something?'

'He was a singer.' He separates another sheet from the pile. 'Here. I got a guy to do an impression of what he might look like now. With a beard, and without.'

She stares at the two images. 'Looks like he's been gone a whiles.'

He nods. 'He was playing a gig in St Louis in 1968. And in the middle, he just got up and walked out.'

'Why?'

Our man shrugs. 'There's all sorts of theories. Involving aliens and drug dealers and the CIA. All we really know is that he was acting strangely. The people who were there that night said he seemed to be under a lot of stress.'

'And no one's seed him since?'

'Not for sure. There were a few, you know' – hooking his fingers into inverted commas – 'reported *sightings*. But none of them was ever confirmed.' He pauses. 'Anyway, you definitely don't recognize him?'

'I don't.' She picks up the then-and-now pictures, moves out from behind the bar, and starts taking them from table to table. 'You know this fella?' Some of the customers study the pictures carefully and then say 'No'. The woman with the corkscrew hair barely looks at them before glaring at our man and calling,

'Who sent you here?'

She's square-jawed and big-hipped, with the run-to-fat bulk of an old prize fighter. You wouldn't want to mess with her.

'No one,' says our man. 'It's my own project.'

She glances cursorily at the photos again, then shakes her head.

Our man sighs. His shoulders sag. He repacks his satchel.

'OK.' He pays for the Seven Up, takes another swig, leaves the rest. 'Thanks.'

As he reaches the door, one of the college kids catches his eye. The man hesitates. Did the boy hear what he was saying? Does he know something?

But the next second the boy looks away again, pointing to the pitcher, and muttering something that makes his companion laugh.

Our man steps outside into the heat and stumbles towards his car. As he opens the door, there's a sound behind him. He turns. The corn-stalk hick is hurrying after him, moving in jerky little eddies, like a piece of litter caught in the wind.

'Hey.'

'What?'

'I see those?' He nods at the satchel. 'Them pictures? I didn't get a real good look.'

Our man hesitates, then slaps the satchel on the roof of the car.

'You think you know him?'

'I might.' His eyes narrow to slits. 'Who's asking?'

Our man frowns, giving the odd impression for a moment that he can't remember. Then he says,

'My name's Walter.'

'That supposed to tell me something?'

Walter doesn't answer. The hick grimaces, as if he's trying to suck something from between his teeth.

'OK, Walt. Show me.'

Our man removes the envelope and spreads out the pictures. The old geezer barely gives the snap of the youngster a glance. But when he sees the artist's impressions of the older Adam Earnshaw, he leans close, forehead puckered, jaw working, as if he's chewing something.

'What you say he goes by?' he asks.

'Adam Earnshaw. Well, that's his real name. No idea what he calls himself now. Could be anything.'

'Why you looking for him, anyways?' He screws up his eyes, studying Walter's face. 'Family, is he?'

Our man hesitates. 'I'm trying to find out what happened to him.'

'Why?'

Walter seems surprised. His eyes widen. After a moment he says,

'It's an obsession, I suppose. You could say it's my calling. What I'm here for.'

'So what brought you to these parts?'

'He had friends…Well, a connection…With the area.'

'Kind of left it a long time, didn't you? What makes you think you're going to find him now?'

'Breadcrumbs.'

'Huh?'

'A trail of breadcrumbs.' He reaches into the satchel, pulls out a thick sheaf of paper, slaps it with his hand. 'They're all in here, if you look hard enough.'

The hick screws up his face like Popeye. 'And that is?'

'Stuff I've gathered from different people. I've been through it all with a fine-tooth comb. I am now the world bloody expert on Adam Earnshaw. I know more about the guy than he knows about himself, if he's still alive. OK?'

The hick gives him a sceptical look. 'OK.'

'So if there's anyone on the planet can find him, it's me.'

The hick nods, sucking in his cheeks, deepening the seams in his long face. He sniffs, then leans down to look at the pictures again.

'No, I never seed him before in my life.'

But his expression tells us he's lying – or at least that he knows more than he's saying. When the camera cuts to Walter, we can see that he's sceptical, too. He scowls at the hick, like a disbelieving adult trying to shame a child into telling the truth. But he's not dealing with a child.

'You take my advice, son,' says the old geezer, 'you'll just git back in that vehicle of yours, and keep on going till you hit the airport.'

He turns and shuffles off towards the bar.

For a few seconds Walter stands there, looking from the bar to the line of parked cars and back again. Then, as the hick goes inside, he gathers up his things and gets back into his own car. He puts the satchel on the passenger seat, lays the sheaf of paper on his knee, and starts leafing through the pages.

1

CAT HAYES

God, how the hell did you find me? After all this time? I can't even begin to imagine.

No, that's OK. Don't tell me. I know: weird stuff happens.

So yeah, I'm happy to spill the beans, if you think it'll help. I still owe Adam money, so perhaps this'll sort of settle the account. Just one thing, though, up front: I don't know anything about his disappearance. That happened years later. You'd have to ask someone else about it. All *I* can tell you about is the one time I met the guy. No problem there: it was maybe number three in my list of least forgettable experiences. Actually, come to think of it, I'd say probably number two.

It was the bad bad summer of sixty-five. A lot of crazy girls had taken to the road, me included. One evening I'd parked near Kew Bridge, gone into the Gardens, and scoffed five hundred belladonna seeds. Two hours later, I looked in the make-up mirror my mother had given me. No difference, except my pupils had dilated almost to the size of my eyes.

And then, suddenly, wham! Talking palm trees. Scorpions growing out of my fingernails. The ground trundling under my feet like a treadmill, till I couldn't walk any more, and fell over and dragged myself under a bush. How long I was out, I'd no idea. All I knew was that I eventually regained the use of my legs, and headed towards the gate – although I still had a lot of things that weren't there crawling over me.

I got in the car, and found I could still (sort of) handle the controls. It was a beat-up old Hillman Minx, but my dad had done something to the exhaust that made it sound like a Jag. It didn't go any faster, but boy did it turn heads. I remember laughing hysterically at people's faces as I drove by, and at the same time thinking it was a strange thing to be doing.

Just as I was approaching the Hogarth roundabout I noticed a freak standing with his thumb out on the other side of the road. He was a nice enough looking guy, pale and slim, wearing a cool ex-army fatigue jacket, and with fair hair down to here. (Guess where I'm pointing. OK, I'll tell you: my neck.) It took me a while, but I managed to wobble all the way round without hitting anything, and pulled up beside him.

'What big eyes I've got,' I said, leaning across and lowering the passenger window. 'Where are you going?'

'Staymouth.' I noticed he had a rucksack and a rolled-up tent and a guitar in a sleek black case.

'Where's that?' I said.

He squinted up at the sun, then pointed south-west. 'Over there. About 250 miles, I think. But anything would help. Even just –'

'Get in.'

'You're going that way?'

I nodded.

'You sure?'

I nodded again. He threw his things in the back, then clambered in beside me and slammed the door.

'Thanks. I was beginning to think no one was going to stop.' His voice didn't sound quite British. Not that he had an accent, exactly: more that the words came out a bit jerkily, like they were being slipped into place individually, rather than strung together to make a sentence.

'What's your name?' I said.

'Adam.'

'I'm Cat. Where are you from?'

'A long way away.'

I giggled. 'Mars?'

'Something like that.'

'Yeah, well I know all about Mars,' I said. 'I just spent three days there or something. What day is it today?'

'Saturday.'

'Yeah, three days, then. And I'm not all the way back to earth yet.'

'What were you doing?'

He turned to look at me. I suddenly saw that he was rather dishy (there's a term you won't have heard for a while) in a Cupid kind of way: dark eyes, and a smooth pale face, with light graceful furrows either side of a curvy mouth. God, how I wanted to kiss that mouth, feel the soft pink cushion of the upper lip against mine.

'Careful,' he said.

The car had started to drift into the next lane. As I straightened it, I glanced in the rearview mirror. My dad's face glared back at me. I blinked, and he was gone.

'I was tripping,' I said. 'On Belladonna.'

'Belladonna! That's Deadly Nightshade, isn't it?'

'Only if you have too much. Or eat the wrong bits. Seeds are OK. All they do is take you to Mars. I'd give you some. Only I finished them.'

'I just got here, remember?'

I laughed. It sounded too loud. I yanked at my hair.

'Witches used to use it,' I said. 'In their flying ointment. Rub a bit on, then off you go.' I made my hand into a broomstick. As I whooshed it up to the roof, I caught sight of my dad's face in the rearview mirror again.

'Oh, just fuck off, will you?'

'What?'

'He's talking to me!'

And he was. *You slut. You whore. You don't know what you're doing to your mother and me. You'll be the death of us.*

'Who's talking?' said Adam.

'My dad.'

'Where?'

'There. Next to your guitar. Just make him shut up, will you?'

How many millions of nineteen-year-old boys are there in the world? What would any one of them have done in that situation? You know as well as I do.

But not Adam. Adam says, 'OK.'

He turns and looks into the back. He has this fixed stare and his lips are moving, though I can't hear what he's saying. After a couple of seconds, I can still see my dad but his voice has gone. Then – I swear to God – his face changes. He starts to smile – a big gummy smile, like when I was little. And then he disappears altogether.

OK, I was still tripping. But I know what I saw.

'Right,' says Adam, turning back. 'I don't think you ought to be driving like this. Let's stop at the next café, and I'll buy you a cup of tea.'

It was one of those places you hardly see any more: bacon sandwiches, egg and chips, big white mugs of khaki-coloured PG Tips and Maxwell House. We sat at a Formica-covered table in the window. The air was steamy, and smelt of grease and fag smoke. Unless you count the belladonna seeds, I hadn't eaten anything in God knows how long, but I couldn't face a fry-up. I settled for tea and a day-old Chelsea bun. Adam ordered the same.

'You're not really from Mars, are you?' I said.

He shook his head.

'Where, then?'

'Kenya.' He pronounced it the old way, *Keenya*, then corrected himself. 'Kenya.'

'Is that where they taught you that stuff?'

'What stuff?'

'How to make people disappear.'

He shook his head again. 'He wasn't there.' He touched my forehead. 'Just in here.'

'Still, it's quite a party trick.'

He laughed.

'So how do you like the old country?'

'Well, I'd been here before. When I was younger.' He looked around, taking in the burly lorry drivers, the misted-up windows, the elderly couple – both of them smoking, the man wheezing with bronchitis – traipsing in through the door. 'But I have to say, it's not quite what I was expecting.'

'What, you mean getting picked up by a girl on a belladonna trip?'

He smiled. 'Yeah. What's the idea? You planning to be a witch?'

I shrugged. 'I just couldn't do it any more. Living the way I was. So I threw in my job.'

'What was it?'

'Ugh. Secretary at a cardboard factory. That's why my dad's so angry with me. Well, that's today's reason. And here I am.'

'Flight of the witch.'

I thought about it for a moment. 'Yeah, that's good. So what's this Staymouth?'

'There's a folk festival there.'

'Ah, right. I'm not really that into folk. Well, Dylan's all right, I suppose. Is he folk?'

He said nothing.

'So what sort of stuff do you do?'

'Traditional, mostly. But I write some of my own songs, too.'

'That's far out.' I hesitated. I didn't want to scare him away. 'You mind if I come with you? If I promise to drive better?'

He laughed. 'You sure you want to?'

'Yeah, I'm sure. Long as you can tell me where to go.'

'You got a map?'

'There's one in the what-you-me-call-it.'

'Glove compartment?'

'That's the one.'

'OK.'

Back in the car I got him to take his guitar out and sing to me. He tuned up, then launched into a ballad about a poacher and a gamekeeper and the white doe of the woodland glade. Not my thing at all, I'd have thought; but something about the way he did it – his voice suddenly taking off and lifting high above the melody, like a captive bird finding the door of its cage open and making a bid for freedom – blew across my skin like a breeze.

'Aaah,' I said. 'More please.'

We had knights and serving wenches and a girl in a tower, and something weird about a blind raven. When he started playing *Scarborough Fair* – the first song I actually recognized – I found myself joining in:

Parsley, sage, rosemary, and thyme;
Remember me to the one who lives there,
For once she was a true love of mine.

'Hey,' he said, at the end, 'you've got a great voice.'

'You too. Yours is amazing.'

'You ever perform anywhere?'

'God, no! Well, only in the bathroom. Till my mum tells me to shut up.'

'You want to go on with me?'

'What, at the festival? Have you got a gig there?'

He shook his head. 'People just do it. In pubs and places. Get up and perform. It's called singing from the floor. That's what I heard, anyway.'

I hesitated. It was an insane idea. But then this was the summer of insane ideas. 'Yeah, OK,' I said. 'What the hell.'

'You want to learn some stuff now?'

'All right.'

'Here we go, then.' He started to strum. 'One, two, three, four...'

Six songs, he said: that's what we needed. He came up with a list: *Brigg Fair* and *Lovely Joan* are the only ones I can remember now. We went through them all twice, repeating the fiddly bits until I had them straight. By the end I still didn't know all the words, but I could hum along with the melodies and join in with the refrains.

'Great,' he said. 'You're a fast learner.'

He began to play another song – one I'd never heard before, about a girl called Annabelle. It was slow and lilting, and his voice seemed to inhabit the words, to possess them – or rather, to *be* possessed *by* them, as if, almost against his will, he was confessing something to you.

'That's pretty,' I said, when he'd finished. 'Did you write it?'

He nodded.

'Who's Annabelle?'

'Oh, no one, really.' He laughed. 'Someone I haven't met yet.'

'Play it again. I want to learn that, too.'

He shook his head. 'I'm not going to be doing it there. You hungry?'

'Yeah. A bit, I suppose.'

He peered ahead. 'Pub there. Let's see if they'll do us a sandwich.'

You try it some time: not washing or changing your clothes for three days. Long before we got to Staymouth, I was aware of my own stink.

And though he hadn't said anything, Adam had to have noticed it, too. I couldn't be with him – not the way I wanted to, anyway – until I'd cleaned up.

'You need to go right,' he said, as we reached the outskirts.

'Why?'

'I just saw a sign. *Festival campsite.*'

'I've got to get to the shops first.'

I followed the main road into the High Street and parked in front of the Boots. That got me soap, toothbrush and toothpaste. But when we looked for somewhere to buy clothes, all we could find was a place that called itself a *Ladies' Outfitters*, with a window full of coats and skirts and floral frocks that my mum would have thought too old for her.

'Shit,' I said, pointing at something that looked like a rose-pattern curtain billowing in the wind. 'Can you see me in that?'

I opened the door. He hung back.

'Come on,' I said. 'I need help.'

The woman behind the counter wore bright red lipstick, a white blouse and pearls. You could tell the moment we walked in that we were her worst nightmare – living proof, probably, that she'd been right to back the *Keep the Hippies out of Staymouth* campaign. Her lips moved, but she couldn't even bring herself to say, *May I help you?*

'I need to get some underwear,' I said. 'And maybe a pair of jeans and a t-shirt.'

She put a finger under her nose. I expect it smelt better than I did. 'I'm sorry, madam. I don't think we'd have the kind of thing you're looking for.'

'Can you tell me somewhere that would, then?'

She cleared her. 'Not in Staymouth, no.'

'Well, at least you can sell me some knickers, can't you?'

I glanced at Adam, expecting to find him enjoying her embarrassment as much as I was. But he was staring rigidly at the floor.

I ended up with some underpants, a bra, a plain white blouse with a Peter Pan collar, and a pair of what she called light summer slacks. But when I took out my chequebook, she shook her head.

'I'm sorry, madam. Cash only.'

I looked round. 'Where does it say that?'

'It's at the discretion of the management.'

'What, you, you mean?'

The bitch wrinkled her nose and said nothing.

I had less than ten bob in my purse. Most of last month's paycheque was still in my account, but the banks were closed. I thought about simply grabbing the stuff and running, but she'd be on to the police before we could get back to the car.

'It's OK,' said Adam. 'I can do this.'

'Really?'

He nodded.

He took out his wallet and handed her a note. She held it up to the light, checking that it was genuine.

'You think we're all criminals then, do you?' I said.

She slipped the money into the till and gave Adam his change.

'There you are.'

'Thank you.'

'Serve her right if it *was* a forgery,' I said, as we got into the car. 'I'll pay you back on Monday, all right? Soon as I can get to the bank.'

He didn't reply, but pointed through the window at the way we'd just come. The woman was standing in the shop doorway, squinting after us, and writing something on a slip of paper.

'Shit,' I said. 'What do they bloody want? You give the fuckers legal tender, and they still don't trust you.'

The campsite was a couple of fields a mile or so out of town. Next to it was a sports ground, where you could leave your car if you had one. For a shilling you could also use their changing rooms. From what I could see of the alternative – a line of dripping black hoses fixed to a plywood wall, halfway across the next field – it looked like it would be money well spent.

This is where it starts to get strange. Not dad-in-the-mirror strange: what-on-earth-is-he-doing strange. We got our stuff out of the car and set off to search for a good spot to put up his tent. The closest field was already pretty packed, but there was still plenty of space in the further one. I could have settled for any one of a dozen places, but Adam prowled around like a dog trying to find somewhere to take a shit. Nowhere appeared to satisfy him: every time I said *What about here?*, he'd wrinkle his nose and say, *Let's just look over there.* Only the flood of people pouring in behind and grabbing the pitches he'd already rejected eventually persuaded him to take an out-of-the-way corner under a tree. The roots made the ground lumpy, but (I had the impression that this was the most important thing for him) there was no near neighbour. Even so, he was fidgety and uneasy, and kept looking over the hedge at the distant strip of sea, as if he was thinking of making a break for it.

'You OK?' I said.

He nodded.

'No, you're not. What is it? What's the matter?'

'Nothing.'

'Shall we get this up?'

'OK.' He actually seemed relieved. And he obviously knew exactly what he was doing: within five minutes the thing was standing, poles upright, guy ropes taut, not a crease to be seen.

'Right,' I said. 'I'm going to go and get clean. You got a towel I can borrow?'

From the way he looked at me, you'd have thought I'd asked him to strip naked and do handstands.

'Come on. I can't hang myself out to dry on a clothesline, can I?'

He fumbled in his bag, produced a crumpled green towel and held it out to me at arm's length. 'There you are.'

I plodded off to the rugby club and paid my shilling. The shower felt so great that when I'd finished I started all over again and took another one. Then I sneaked into a cubicle and put on my new clothes. God, it was embarrassing. I stuffed my dirty things into the ladies' outfitters bag and hugged it against me, hoping no one would notice what I had on behind it. Wishful thinking. A guy who was leaving at the same time stopped dead when he saw me, and stood looking me up and down with an amused smile.

'Don't ask,' I said.

'Kind of hard not to,' he said. 'You look like you're going to a Tupperware party. And planning on doing a load of wash while you're there.'

American. That figured. He was tall and broad, not fat exactly, but with a puppy heaviness around the jaw. He had a thick mane of red-blonde hair, like a Viking, and a white tee-shirt stretched thin by the bulk of his chest.

'Yeah, yeah, yeah,' I said. 'I know. But everything else I've got is filthy. And this was all I could find in Staymouth, all right?'

He bent down, appraising the crease of the slacks. 'I think it's kind of a neat look for a music festival. Maybe you'll start a trend.'

'Hilarious. Satire isn't dead, I see.'

He pinched his lower lip. 'Satire? What's that? I don't think we have it where I'm from.'

I laughed.

'Where you headed?' he said.

I pointed towards the further field.

'Me too. Mind if I go with you? Then if anyone gets jealous and tries to tear the pants off you, I can protect you.'

He slung his army kitbag over his shoulder. We set off towards the campsite. 'You just get here?' he said.

I nodded.

'Thought so. I think I'd have remembered if I'd seen you around.'

Was he talking about me, or the clothes? I rolled my eyes. He laughed – a slow deep sound like a big engine rumbling into life.

'I'm Tate,' he said.

He held his hand out. I stared at it for a moment before taking it. There wasn't a lot of hand-shaking in my world.

'Cat.'

'Cat, huh? That's good. Means you get nine lives, right?'

'Boy, I wonder why no one's ever said that to me before?'

'Hey, you're my first Cat, OK? So lighten up. And cut me a bit of slack. I only got off the plane three days ago.'

'You here on holiday?'

'What's that? *Vacation*? No, I'm working. And having fun. All part of the same package.'

'That's nice.' Looking at him again, I saw that he was older than I'd thought: mid-twenties, maybe. I wondered if he was a draft dodger. 'What do you do, then?'

'I'm a promoter. Plus I work for a label in the States. Signing bands. So if you want to know what's worth seeing here, I'm your man.'

'OK. Give me the list.'

'Bill Sweet. Allhallows. The Lakeside Boys. Vera Maxted.'

I hadn't heard of any of them. 'All right.'

'And there's this young guy. Jamie Penhaligon. You know him?'

'Don't think so.'

'You will. He's something else. It's like this Cornish troubadour sets out to serenade the lady in the high tower. And on his way he picks up an Indian sitar player and a dwarf on electric bass. And they do a lot of acid. And *wham!*'

I laughed. 'OK.'

'I get to hear a lot of stuff. And I'm telling you, Jamie's the most exciting thing I've seen in I don't know how long. Just give it six months, a year. Pete Seeger and Ewan McColl'll be wringing their hands, and pretty much everyone else is going to be going, *man, this dude's out of sight*. Ten bob on it, OK?' The *bob* seemed to intrigue him: he rounded his lips for it, like a kid blowing a bubble. 'This time next year. Staymouth sixty-six. You going to be here?'

'Jesus, I don't know where I'm going to be tomorrow.'

'Well, *if* you're here, and if Jamie Penhaligon hasn't charted in the top twenty albums by then, I'll give you half a quid. Deal?'

'That's a lot of *ifs*. But OK. Deal.'

We shook hands again. We were in the first field now. It was teeming: a crazy jumble of tents, dogs, girls with flowers plaited in their hair and lanky sunburned guys looking like characters from *The Hobbit*. Sort of like the freaks I hung out with, but sort of not. A lot more beards and muslin than I was used to.

'Thing is,' I said. 'Folk isn't actually my scene at all. I wasn't planning to come. It just kind of happened.'

'Lucky you met me, then.' He paused. I knew what was coming next. I tried to think of a quick answer, but it was too complicated. 'You here on your own?'

Was I, wasn't I? I'd *brought* Adam, but that didn't mean I was *with* him. All I owed him was the money for my clothes – and I could deal with that by putting a cheque in his tent. No, that would be shitty: I needed to give it to him in person, and tell him I was leaving. Then I'd be free to go with this guy, who was groovy, and obviously liked me, and knew lots of stuff, and was in the music business.

'Long silence,' said Tate. 'I guess that means no.'

'It means I don't know. I need to sort something out.'

He stared at me. I thought he was going to argue with me, but in the end he just nodded and said,

'OK, Cat. You go sort. And maybe catch you later.'

I nodded. 'Where are you staying?'

He pointed. 'There. Just past the entrance. You can't miss it. Big orange American bastard.'

I gave him half a minute start, then followed him into the second field. It was almost full now. As I approached Adam's tent, I noticed a guy and a girl I'd never seen before standing in front of it, but the campsite cacophony of talking, laughter, pan-clattering, guitar-strumming was so loud that it wasn't until I was a few yards away that I realized they were listening to someone singing inside:

> *Remember me to the one who lives there,*
> *For once she was a true love of mine.*

It wasn't the words that melted me, or even the way his voice prickled the hairs on my neck: it was the memory of singing it with him in the car.

I edged past the couple outside and lifted the flap.

'Hi, I'm back. Sorry, did I make you jump?'

He nodded and laid down his guitar. I crawled in and sat opposite him.

'I won't stink the place out now.' I dropped the bag of dirty clothes outside the door. 'I'll put those in the car later. In the morning I'd better take them to a laundrette.'

'Have you ever slept in the car?'

I shook my head. 'Don't think it'd be very comfortable. Why, don't you want me here?'

'It's not that. It's just there isn't a lot of space, is there? And we've only got the one sleeping bag.'

'That's OK. We can unzip it and spread it over both of us. That'll be enough. We'll keep each other warm. It'll be fine. You'll see.'

'Done it before, have you?'

I blushed. Not something that happens a lot. 'Yeah.'

He said nothing. I handed him the guitar. 'Go on. We need to rehearse, don't we?'

That night. That weird night.

We had no food and nothing to cook on – so, after I'd dumped the bag in the car, Adam slung his guitar on his back and we went to a food stall at the edge of the campsite and bought hot dogs dripping with mustard and fried onions. Then we decided to go into town and look for a pub where there was some music. The one we settled on was packed with people listening to four old guys in striped shirts and braces playing (I guessed) Irish music, sad and dancey at the same time, on pipes and fiddles. When they took a break, soaked with sweat, and asked if anyone wanted to sing from the floor, Adam stood up.

'All right, young man,' said the oldest fiddler, wiping his forehead with the back of his hand. 'Ah, young lady, too.' I remember the little smile on his face: *Come on: impress us.*

We began with *Scarborough Fair*. I worried that it might be too obvious, not unusual enough; but the moment Adam started to sing, the whole room seemed to pivot towards him. A magnet dropped into a box full of pins: that's what it made me think of. And long before we'd finished, my nerves had completely evaporated. What had taken their place is a bit hard to describe. You know those dreams where you discover part of a house that you hadn't known existed before? It was sort of like that: Adam had opened a door and led me into something that had always been there but was completely new to me. And *because* it was new, I couldn't put a name to the feeling it gave me. Not *love*, exactly: definitely not just *closeness*. The word that wants me to use it, though I'm a bit hazy about what it means, is *partaking*. Adam and I were sitting there together, *partaking* of each other. That sense is overwhelmingly my most powerful memory of the evening. Everything else – the applause; the people queuing up to buy us drinks;

the chain of hands patting us on the back on our way to the door – is just a collection of dreamlike fragments.

As we stepped outside, the glow of a cigarette bobbed in the darkness ahead of us.

'Hey.'

A bulky figure loomed towards us. The face was just a smudge, but I saw a streak of coppery hair flare in the light from the pub.

'Oh, hi,' I said.

'So folk's not your scene, huh?'

I laughed. 'Not really, no.' I tugged Adam's sleeve. '*He's* my scene.'

'Yeah,' he said, turning to Adam. 'I get that. You're really good, man. No, no shit, I mean it. I couldn't even get in. I was watching you through the window. And you still blew my mind.'

'Thank you.'

'You do anything else? Like, write any of your own material? Or –'

'A bit.'

'Any way I could hear that?'

'Not really, no. Not at the moment, anyway.'

'OK.' He waited for Adam to go on. When he didn't, Tate said:

'Any particular reason?'

'I'm not ready, that's all.'

'Sound pretty ready to me.'

Adam shook his head. 'Sorry, I don't mean to be rude.'

'Uh-uh.' He lifted his big hands, spreading the fingers wide. 'No sweat. That's cool.'

'I'm just not sure. Whether I should be doing this at all.'

'Well, let me help you out, then. You should. What's your name?'

'Adam.'

'Adam –'

'Earnshaw.'

'I'm Tate.' They shook hands. 'Cat tell you about me? What I do?'

Adam glanced at me, then shook his head.

'She should have. I'm a promoter. And I sign acts for Wheatsheaf Records. But listen, I'm not trying to lay anything on you. Everyone needs to go at their own speed.' He stuck his fag in his mouth and rummaged in his pockets with both hands. 'Here. Take this.' He produced a card and held it out. 'When you get to that place on the road, give me a call, OK?'

Adam hesitated. '*If* I get there.'

'Trust me. You will.' He jabbed the card against Adam's arm. Adam took it. Tate touched his finger to the brim of an imaginary hat. 'Catch you later.'

Adam barely spoke on the way back. Finally, as we were approaching the campsite, I said,

'What's the matter?'

'Nothing.'

'Come on, tell me.'

He shook his head.

'You ought to be, I don't know, howling at the moon or something. I mean, that was just great, wasn't it? In the pub?'

He said nothing.

'Well, I thought it was. I was really tripping. And then that guy afterwards wanting to promote you. Maybe we could be the new Sonny and Cher. Or the new Simon and Garfunkel or something. I could frizz my hair.'

I expected him to laugh. Instead he said,

'Who is he? How did he know your name?'

I explained.

'And that's the only time you've ever met him?'

Crazy: the guy was jealous. Any other time, and with any other man, I'd have probably yelled. As it was, still tingling with whatever that feeling was that I'd had when we were singing, I was weirdly touched.

'You don't need to worry about him,' I said, squeezing his arm. 'What kind of a name is Tate, anyway? Makes him sound like a sugar cube. You want to drop acid on him and swallow him whole.'

He smiled, but he still seemed ill at ease when we got back to the tent.

'I'm clean, remember?' I said. 'So you go and take a shower. And I'll get things ready here.'

I had a pee behind the hedge. Our nearest neighbours gave me a cup of water to brush my teeth with. Then I unzipped the sleeping bag and opened it out into a kind of duvet. I stripped to my underwear, bundled my summer slacks into a pillow, and lay down. The smell of the canvas and the dewy grass made me feel like a little girl on a family camping trip.

'You were gone a long time,' I said, when he finally reappeared. 'I was starting to think you'd been kidnapped by aliens. Whisked back to Mars.'

He didn't reply. Crouched with his back to me, he took off shirt, trousers and shoes and stretched out on the other side of the tent, pulling the edge of the sleeping bag halfway across his body. I rolled over, nuzzled his neck, tried to kiss him. He turned his face away. He felt like a plank of wood.

'You need to relax,' I said. I started to stroke his chest. His jaw clenched so violently that I could hear the click of his teeth. An awful thought struck me. 'God, you're not queer, are you?'

'No.'

I ran my hand down his belly, found the elastic of his underpants. He twitched and groaned.

'No,' I said. 'Obviously not.'

'I haven't got anything,' he said.

'I should hope not.'

'I mean –'

'A rubber johnny? That's OK. I've got one.'

That seemed to stun him into silence.

He didn't say so, but it was obviously the first time for him. I was shocked: that possibility had never even occurred to me. But it's the only way to explain the anxiety, the mis-timing, the fumbliness, the impression he gave of not understanding his own body, let alone mine. It was still a few years before feminism made it OK to talk openly about bad sex, but – when the time came – you could easily imagine seeing my night with Adam appearing under the headline *The Worst Fuck of my Life.* There was a moment when I found myself thinking, *shit, Cat. You could have had Tate, and you settled for this.* But it was only one night. And I really liked the guy. So as he knocked and bumped and heaved around like a beached sea-lion, I told myself to hang loose and let it slide. It was no big deal. Just one more thing to put down to experience.

I woke early, shivering. I rolled over, groping for Adam, but couldn't find him. I opened my eyes. There he was – lying on his side against the far wall of the tent, head on hand, watching me. In the murky light his face was just a blur. But I could sense the intensity of his gaze, and it freaked me out. It felt like – I don't know, I was being spied on by a peeping tom or something. I wriggled a bit closer.

'How long have you been looking at me like that?'

'I don't know.'

I could see his expression now: a slight frown. Disapproval? Bafflement? I was lost.

'What is it?' I asked.

He said nothing. I reached out and stroked his wrist.

'Come on. Tell me. And while you're at it, you can warm me up.'

He hesitated, then shunted towards me and took me in his arms, like a mechanical grabber seizing a bale.

'Brrr. That's better. So what's going on? Couldn't you sleep?'

He shook his head.

'Why not?'

He didn't reply. But I knew that if I pressed him, he'd only retreat further, so I just shut up. After half a minute or so he said,

'Last night.'

'What about it?'

'I...I...Was it...normal?'

Seemed an odd way of putting it – but what he meant, presumably, was *was it all right?*

'It was fine,' I said.

'No, but...' He gulped. His scrawny muscles were tight as guitar strings. One more turn of the machine heads and they'd snap...

'Honestly, Adam,' I said. 'Don't worry about it. It was nice.' I touched his nose. 'OK?'

Another pause. 'So what...you know, normally...happens now?'

That threw me. Why should he imagine *anything* happened? Because – this was all I could think of – he thought a one-night stand at a music festival meant a commitment of some kind? That it made us a couple?

'What happens next,' I said, disentangling myself, 'is that I take my stuff to the laundrette. And pick up something for breakfast.'

He didn't say anything, but he wasn't happy. I didn't want him getting any ideas, so I sat turned away from him as I pulled on my clothes. But I could feel his eyes on me: not randy or angry or reproachful, but puzzled, trying to figure what he could do to stop me leaving, draw me back into the conversation.

'You'll have to lend me another ten bob,' I said, crawling free of the sleeping bag, then turning at door to face him. 'To be repaid, of course.'

From the mournful way he glowered at me, I thought he was going to say no. But after a moment he rummaged in his jacket for his wallet and handed me a ten-shilling note. Humming *Scarborough Fair* under my breath, I walked through the campsite to the car park. It must have taken me how long – five minutes, six? I've often thought about those minutes since. I see them as a snippet of film: the train leaves the station, gathering speed, oblivious to what lies round the next bend…

When I got to the car, I saw that someone had put a slip of paper under the windscreen wiper. The registration number was scrawled on the outside. Inside it said: *Please come to the campsite office immediately.*

I went. The office was a two-wheeler caravan with the beds taken out. A sunburned man with a pirate earring was sitting behind a desk. I gave him the note. He frowned at it.

'Is this to do with the parking?' I said. 'Do I need to pay you something?'

He consulted a large memo pad, then shook his head.

'Sorry, love,' he said, returning the note to me. 'Your dad Mr George Hayes?'

'Yes.'

'Bad news, I'm afraid. He's had a heart attack. You need to get back home. It's pretty bad.'

'Jesus. Where is he?'

'Ashford Hospital.'

Half way down the steps I turned and said:

'How'd they know where to find me?'

'You were lucky. They put out an announcement on the Home Service, giving your registration number. And a woman in town heard it. Who'd seen the number and made a note it of it, for some reason. She rang us, and said she thought you were coming here, and we should check the car park. So we did.'

I ran back to the tent. Adam wasn't there. He must have gone off to wash, and taken his jacket with him, so there was nothing to write with.

All I could do was leave his ten shillings under the sleeping bag – together with the note I'd found on the windscreen, so that he'd know to go to the office and find out what had happened. I didn't want him to think – funny how much it bothered me, even then, in the middle of everything else that was going on – that I'd just walked out on him because of the terrible sex.

Then I sprinted to the car, and drove the 150 miles to Ashford Hospital. My foot was on the floor virtually the whole way.

My dad recovered and lived for another eighteen years. I never saw Adam Earnshaw again. Not in the flesh, anyway.

But two years later, late at night, when I couldn't sleep, I turned on the radio and was startled to hear Rufus Strange saying:

'And this is the incredible Adam Earnshaw, with *Flight of the Witch*.'

For a split second, I wondered if it was a coincidence. Then he started to sing, and I knew it wasn't.

> *I'm in a cage*
> *Scrabble on the hamster wheel*
> *Time to pay a call on Belladonna*
> *Belladonna*
> *Belladonna*
> *Lovely lady, help me to fly free*

It was about me, all right. And pretty soon – when we got to *Saw him drooping by the road* – I realized it was about *us*. It was a bit weird to hear it, like opening a newspaper and seeing a picture of yourself. But then I thought, hey, the guy's a musician. That's what musicians do.

But what I still don't understand is: why is it from *my* point of view and not his?

2

RODDY HORNE

How odd. Adam would probably see some mystical significance in it, but I don't have the imagination for that sort of thing, so I'll just put it down to serendipity. Last night, for the first time in years, I had a dream about him: I go into a pub and there he is, standing at the bar. Bulked out now, jowly, throat like a bit of beef, eyebrows starting to run riot. But still recognizable.

'Hullo.' As if he'd been expecting me. He nods at the row of pump handles. 'What'd you like?'

'Bitter.'

He turns to the girl behind the counter. 'Two pints of bitter, please.' His fingers are thicker, and specked with liver spots. But he still thrums them on a beer-mat, nervy as a teenager. 'So. Good week?'

This is a regular rendezvous, then. We must do it every week. Somehow there's been a misunderstanding: 1968 wasn't the end of everything. Adam Earnshaw didn't vanish. He's been here all along.

'Not bad,' I say. 'How about you?'

He nods. 'Some and some.'

A chord, broken for God knows how long, suddenly resolves itself. That old feeling, that first-sip-of-whisky warmth, spreads through chest and belly and arms. *Some and some.* As reliable, those words, as the Pearl and Dean adverts before the main feature. Whenever you heard them, you settled back, enchanted by the sense that you were about to be made privy to something extraordinary.

'Well –' he begins.

And then, maddeningly, I wake up, before I can discover what – in this alternative universe, where Adam Earnshaw didn't disappear at the age of twenty-two – he has actually been doing for the last week. Or the last year. Or the last five decades. Or, for that matter, what *I've* been doing, either. Because maybe in that universe *my* life took a different course, too – maybe my marriage survived, and I stayed in London, and my sister is still here. She has kids. And – come on, let's really push the boat out – they're Adam's.

All morning I found myself haunted by the idea – the fantasy – that perhaps *that's* the reality, and this is the dream. And then – lo and behold – when I turn on my computer at lunchtime, there's your email.

How can I refuse?

Any sudden loss jolts you, rearranges the landscape in unexpected ways. But in Adam's case, the effects were magnified by the uncertainty about what had happened to him. Accidents; heart attacks; overdoses – all horrible, of course, but part of the known world, the dog-eared catalogue of middle-of-the-night fears we have for ourselves and those close to us. You can at least understand the mechanism involved, come to some kind of terms with it.

But when a man simply walks out of his own life? How do you deal with that? How do you *account* for it? I've been trying, on and off, ever since it happened, and still haven't come up with a credible answer. So few people seem even to know who Adam was, let alone have any interest in his disappearance. So – though I confess that I still don't really understand why you're doing it – I'm delighted that you have taken up the torch. I don't know, frankly, how much help I'm going to be able to give you. But I'll tell you what I remember, and hope that – if by some lucky chance, unbeknownst to me, it contains the vital clue – you're eagle-eyed enough to spot it.

At least question one is easy enough: I met Adam on our first day at Oxford. My mother had driven me down from Derbyshire that morning, the boot so full it wouldn't close properly and had to be tied with a bit of rope, one of the back seats piled with books, and a rattly box filled with cutlery, a set of mugs, an old kettle. In the seat next to it sat my sister

Molly, who'd hurt herself falling off her bike and couldn't go to school. Even though her wrist was in plaster and half her face covered in dressings, she'd insisted that she wanted to come, rather than being left on her own at home all day. She'd brought her camera – a brand-new Pentax she'd had for her birthday – and a bag full of extra films. That's what she wanted to be when she grew up: a photographer. Either that or a naturalist. Or a detective. She was a great recorder of things, was poor accident-prone Molly.

We parked in front of the college and asked for directions in the porters' lodge. As we trudged across the quad, Molly trailed in our wake, clutching the camera awkwardly in her bandaged-up hand, *click-click-clicking* anything that caught her attention.

'Honestly, darling,' our mother said, 'people will think we've done something dreadful, and you're a private eye sent to spy on us.'

When we found my staircase, it turned out to be in an out-of-the-way building that must once have been a coach-house. Just inside the entrance was a board. On it – in glossy lettering so fresh you could still smell the paint – was written:

1. *Mr. R.H.M. Horne*
2. *Mr. A.L. Earnshaw*

We traipsed upstairs. As we passed room two, we could hear a soft tapping from inside, as if someone was putting up picture hooks. I unlocked the door to my room and went in. A bed, a wardrobe, a writing-table, a chair – all as characterless as a youth hostel. We stood looking at each other, wondering how on earth we were going to get everything out of the car, and where we could put it all when we did.

'I can carry something,' said Molly.

'No you can't!' *grrrred* my mother. 'Not so much as a paper bag! I absolutely forbid it!' She glanced out on to the landing. 'Let's ask Mr A.L. Earnshaw.'

'Oh, no, Mother, we can't!' I said.

'Yes we can. *I* can. Then you can blame it all on me.'

She strode out and knocked on his door.

'Come in?'

I positioned myself behind her shoulder, squidging my face into a *sorry about this* expression. She pushed open the door. A gust of cool, fusty, empty-room air hit me, strongly scented with sweat and TCP.

'I'm Janey Horne. Roddy's mother. You and he are going to be neighbours. So we thought we'd just look in and introduce ourselves.'

'Oh, oh.' He was standing by the window, as if he thought he might have to make a sudden bolt for it. Next to him were two large bags. On top of one of them was an old black leather-bound photograph album. Towers of books lay on the floor. Propped on the chair by the desk was a guitar case.

'This is Roddy,' she said.

I edged round her and held my hand out. He stepped towards me, moving from silhouette into light. He wore grey flannels and a new herringbone sports jacket so uncreased that it enclosed him like a shell. The collar was speckled with dandruff.

'I'm Adam Earnshaw.'

'And this poor old walking Egyptian mummy,' said my mother, waving at Molly, who had crept out to peer curiously past her – 'is Molly. Who's been in the wars, as you can see.'

'Ooh,' said Adam. He frowned at me, mouthing, 'What happened?'

I told him.

'Ow.' He winced, then turned towards Molly. 'Do you want to sit down?'

'That's very kind,' said my mother. 'But really, it's not as bad as it looks –'

But Molly had already slipped past her and was heading for the chair. Adam pulled the guitar out of the way.

'Here.'

Molly settled herself gingerly, then tilted her head to read the titles of the stacked-up books.

'What we were going to ask,' said my mother, looking at her askance, 'is whether you could do us a big favour, and help ferry Roddy's things in from the car? It's an awful nuisance, I know, but we're parked miles away.'

'Oh, yes, of course,' said Adam.

'Can I wait here?' said Molly. 'If I'm not allowed to be a ferrier?'

'No!' I said. 'For heaven's sake, what a question! Go back into my room!'

'But there aren't any books there.'

She looked up at Adam appealingly. I was surprised: she was fifteen, and starting to feel awkward in front of young men, but here she seemed completely at ease. It was as if her accident had put the growing up process on hold, and returned her temporarily to the un-self-consciousness of childhood.

'That's fine,' said Adam. 'I don't mind at all.'

'Honestly,' said my mother, as we set off for the car, 'it's too bad of us, isn't it, putting you to work like this the moment you get here?'

Adam shook his head. 'Really, it's nice to have something to do. I was starting to feel a bit odd in there. As if I'd walked through the wrong door or something.'

'Well,' she said, 'that's understandable on your first day. But I'll bet you a pound that by the end of term you'll realize it *was* the right door, and you won't *want* to get out. Roddy, you're my witness, all right?'

It took us three round trips to shift everything, my mother rushing ahead to open doors and clear a path for us through knots of dazed-looking freshmen. After we'd squeezed the last load into my room, she turned to Adam and said,

'Well, all I can say is, you deserve a medal. The least we can do is offer you tea somewhere. Is there anywhere round here, do you know?'

He shook his head. 'Sorry, I don't.'

She looked at me. 'How about the Randolph? That used to be the place when Uncle Ralph was here after the war. Is that still going?'

'I don't know.' Actually I did: I'd passed it when I came up for my interview. But I didn't want my first proper conversation with Adam to be filtered through my mother's charm and my sister's moodiness, so I said, 'But you should be getting back, shouldn't you? Father'll worry if you're late.'

'Yes, yes, perfectly right.' She tapped my arm, smiling at Adam. 'What a responsible son I've got. Well, in that case' – taking her purse from her bag and unclipping it – 'get yourselves a bottle of something extra-specially something-or-other to have with dinner tonight.' She handed me a pound note. 'All right?'

I nodded. She waggled a finger at Adam. 'You make sure he does. Otherwise there'll be hell to pay.'

She opened the door to his room and leaned in. Molly sat hunched over a frail-looking book with a faded cover.

'I'm afraid we need to be on our way, poppet.'

Molly got up, her eyes still moving over the open page.

'What have you got there?' said Adam. He bent down to squint at the title. 'Oh, yes, *The Amulet*. Do you want to borrow it?'

She shook her head. 'I've got all of E. Nesbit at home.'

'Ah, a real fan then. Like me.'

She looked up sharply. For a moment, I had the sense that both of them were aware of something that had eluded me, like the sound of a too-high-pitched whistle. Perhaps it was merely that I had outgrown the ability to surrender to the magic of a world in which five Edwardian children could travel through time – and Molly and Adam hadn't.

'Come on,' said my mother. 'Or you're going to get left behind.'

Molly hesitated a second, then closed the book and handed it to him.

'We need a photo,' she said.

'No, we don't,' said my mother. 'You've taken loads already.'

'Yes. Roddy with Adam. To show Daddy.'

She closed the door, told Adam and me to stand in front of it and fired off a couple of shots.

'OK. And now one with all of us.' She got us all to squat down, then balanced the camera on the arm of the chair, screwed in the remote release and hurried back to join us. 'One, two, three – there!'

'Right, that really is enough,' said my mother. She turned to Adam. 'I'm so sorry. You must be heartily sick of us.'

He shook his head, smiling.

'I'll come and see you off,' I said.

We all said our goodbyes. As we were crossing the quad, my mother said, 'Well, they may have put you in a broom cupboard. But at least you couldn't ask for a nicer neighbour.'

'I thought he was a bit odd,' said Molly.

'Didn't you like him?'

'Oh, no, I did. Only –'

'Chaps are always odd. Or chaps that are worth their salt, anyway. You might as well learn that now. Save a lot of trouble later on.'

'Only what?' I asked Molly.

'Why did he have all those children's books?'

When I got back, Adam's door was still open. I gave a token knock and stuck my head in. He was perched on the edge of the chair, looking at *The Amulet*.

'Thanks again for doing that,' I said.

He shook his head. 'Is Molly all right?'

'What, apart from the broken arm, you mean? Yes, as far as I know. Just going through the messy business of growing up, poor kid.'

He said nothing. I nodded at the guitar.

'You a musician?'

'Not really. I just play a bit.'

'What sort of thing?'

'Folk, mostly.'

'That's nice,' I said, though I hadn't heard a folk song since we sang *Bobby Shafto* at the dame school I went to when I was six. 'Anyway, better leave you to it, I suppose. Got to try and find somewhere to shove all my stuff. Don't give you a lot of space, do they? They must be running out of places to put people. This is probably where the grooms lived.'

'Grooms?' He looked round, as if he thought he might see the previous occupant still standing in the window.

'Or a gardener, maybe. Or one of the provost's servants.' I laughed. 'Heavens, you're not afraid of ghosts, are you?'

He said nothing.

'*My* only grouse is that it's a bit of a comedown,' I said. 'I was expecting a proper set, with a glass-fronted bookcase and an oak you could sport.'

He gawped at me.

'Oak,' I said. 'You know. An outer door. So you can barricade yourself in when the townies run amok.'

His eyes widened.

'Don't worry. A minimal risk these days, I imagine. Anyway...' I started to leave, then turned and looked back in. 'Why don't we go over to hall together later, and see about getting this extraordinary bottle of wine?'

I've no idea how much you already know. When I say Gloucester College hall, for instance, can you actually picture it? In case you can't: it's an echoey, high-ceilinged, baroque cavern of a place that looks more like an art gallery than a dining room. Two long tables run almost the entire length, culminating at the far end just short of the dais where the provost and the dons sit, looking down on the *hoi polloi* ranged below them. Wherever you turn, you find yourself under the stern gaze of generations of bewigged Gloucester worthies, whose portraits line the walls on either side. And the white-jacketed college servants exude a damp air of resentment, as if they consider it slightly beneath their dignity to wait on you.

It was all a bit daunting – and, if I'd been on my own, I'd have probably just slipped inconspicuously into a place close to the entrance, where a group of other freshmen were desultorily exchanging names, schools, subjects, jokey comments about the food. But I was aware, even then, of Adam's painful awkwardness – and of the way he kept watching me, as if I were somehow the model of sophistication, and he could learn from my example how to negotiate the treacherous waters of college life. Nervy and excited as I was, I'm afraid I rather let that idea go to my head. Strutting into the middle of the hall, I waved Adam to a seat opposite me, and demanded to see the wine list. I can't remember what I picked now – only that it had a long double-barrelled name, which I rehearsed silently to myself, in the hope that it would come tripping off my tongue as if I'd ordered the damn thing dozens of times before.

But in the event, I don't think Adam even noticed: he was gazing round, trying to take in our surroundings – the plaster swags and festoons draping the walls; the vistas of dark wood, punctuated with a semaphore of winking silver and glass. I met his eye and smiled. He looked away, squinting at something above my head. I turned, searching for what had caught his attention: an apoplectic eighteenth-century provost glowering down at him from an ornate frame.

'God, he's a cheery-looking soul, isn't he?' I said. 'It's a good painting, though. Probably a Ramsay, I'd say. You know Ramsay?'

He shook his head. Out of the corner of my eye, I saw a group of three undergraduates swaggering into the hall, led by a fat chap with baby curls, like a gone-to-seed *putto*. They looked round for a moment, then spotted the empty spaces next to us and descended on them *en masse*, laughing and chattering, as impervious to Adam and me as if we weren't there at all. As they sat down, a pimply-faced fellow further along the table shouted, 'Hullo, Sandy!' and the fat chap bowed stiffly – a Regency wit acknowledging an acolyte.

'Ramsay was a Scottish painter,' I said, determined not to be derailed. 'Very underrated, in my view. Though generally better at his women than his men. And that' – nodding at the provost's neighbour, who stood gazing at the viewer with a fey smile – 'is a Gainsborough, unless I'm very much mistaken.'

'How can you tell?'

'Something about the quality of the brushwork. It's a lot looser, isn't it? You might almost say slapdash, if you were being unkind.'

I was aware, suddenly, that the little group next to us had fallen ominously silent. But I pushed on regardless:

'And those bright summery colours. Like a stage set for the Forest of Arden. Or –'

'Were we misinformed?' said a drawly voice to my left. 'I thought lectures weren't supposed to start till next week?'

There was a titter of sycophantic laughter. I looked round. The fat chap was scowling at me, with an expression that made me think of an overfed eagle chick studying a pigeon that had strayed into its field of vision. His cronies watched with taunting half-smiles, waiting to see how I responded. I did briefly consider a not-particularly-devastating retort – then realized that to engage with him at all would only draw me into a battle that I couldn't win, and humiliate me in the eyes of my new-found friend. So after holding his stare for a few seconds, I turned back to Adam and said,

'The big question is, are you a Gainsborough man or a Reynolds man?'

He shook his head, too mesmerized by fat-chick-chap and his pals to reply. For a nerve-racking moment they were dangerously silent, and I braced myself for a renewed assault. Then, quite suddenly, they started talking among themselves again, and the crisis was past. But – even though for the rest of the meal they completely ignored us – their presence still created a kind of chill, like a draught from an open window, hampering conversation, and turning the probably excellent wine to vinegar in our mouths.

'Who was that?' said Adam, as they finally got up to leave.

'I've no idea.'

'Sandy Mellor,' said the pimply fellow further along the table, disentangling his long legs from the bench. 'We were all at school together. He and I and those other chaps.'

'Lucky you,' I said.

He gave an odd little smile and hurried past us. Adam and I followed him out into the drizzle.

'I don't know about you,' I said, 'but I could use another drink. Why don't we go and find the buttery?'

It wasn't hard: you just had to follow the crowd, down a flight of worn steps, and into a dark cramped quad of old buildings that must have been part of the original monastery. Inside, the air was full of smoke and the smell of beer and damp clothes, and the stone-flagged floor slithery with wet footprints. At the far end a small elderly man with thick-lensed glasses was serving drinks. He looked far too frail to deal with the herd of fidgety young bullocks jostling to get his attention.

Adam and I managed to find an out-of-the-way spot next to a window.

'Got any tickets?' I said.

'Sorry?'

'Buttery tickets.'

I took mine out. He stared blankly at them, as if the drab little coloured squares – 6d, 1/0, 2/6d – were mysterious hieroglyphs from a long-lost civilization. He shook his head.

'Well, you'll need to get some,' I said. 'But I'll do this. What would you like?'

'Bitter, please.'

'OK. You stay here, all right? And defend it with your life.'

I joined the fray, conscious of more and more people piling in behind me. The poor old chap behind the bar worked painfully slowly, drawing pints from the barrel with shaking hands.

By the time I finally got back to Adam, he was no longer alone. Sandy Mellor and his friends had invaded the space by the window, and hemmed him into a corner.

'Excuse me,' I said.

Sandy Mellor turned. I held out a glass and nodded at Adam, indicating that it was for him.

'Ah,' said Mellor. 'Here you are. I think your wife was beginning to suspect you'd deserted her.'

His friends laughed. I pushed my way between them and handed Adam his beer. As we raised our glasses, I could feel Sandy Mellor's gaze on the back of my neck. I spun round.

'What are you staring at?'

'This affecting domestic scene. Mr and Mrs pledging their troths. It's straight out of Dickens. And are we now to be treated to some more gems from *The Boys' Book of Art History*?'

'Oh, fuck off!' I said.

He staggered back, shunting the fellow behind him, and causing a falling-domino chain reaction of *oohs* and spilt drinks.

'Ah!' he said, clapping a hand operatically over his heart. 'I die!'

I touched Adam's arm. 'Come on.'

We started through the crowd towards the door. I felt like a defeated prize bantamweight leaving the ring. Outside, the drizzle had almost stopped, though the occasional cold drop still pinged against our skin. We took refuge by the wall, where we had the shelter of an overhanging eave.

'That was bad luck,' I said. 'Meeting a bastard like that on our first day. But I'm not going to let it put me off. You mustn't, either.'

He said nothing, but stared in through the window. Sandy Mellor was holding forth, jabbing the air with one finger, while around him his courtiers were doubled up with merriment. Something in Adam's face – caught for a moment in the smoky yellow light of the buttery, like an onlooker at the edge of a Caravaggio painting – was heart-breaking. It wasn't just that his pain and puzzlement were so naked: there was also an intensity in his eyes that made me think of a child, arbitrarily sent into the corner and trying to deduce what he's done wrong.

I clinked his glass against mine.

'Forget him,' I said. 'All he is is a common-or-garden bully, pretending to be Beau Brummell. You just have to learn to live with it. Like we did at school.'

'I didn't really go to school.'

'Heavens! How did you manage that?'

'My health. The doctors didn't think I'd be up to it.'

'What, not even a day school?'

'There wasn't one. It was in Africa. And we moved around a lot. And I was an only child. So I had a sort of…Well, a governess, I suppose you'd call her. Only she wasn't really that. Just a friend of my father's who happened to live with us.'

'Well, she must have been good, if you got in here. Was she pretty?'

He thought about it for a moment. 'Yes.'

'Lucky sod. And I suppose no games then?

'No.'

'And no corps? You didn't have to put on a uniform and parade about the veldt, while she stood there with a swizzle stick under her arm and barked orders at you?'

He shook his head.

'Sounds blissful. How much will you give me not to tell anyone?'

He stared at me.

'Don't worry. I'm not being serious.' I clapped him on the shoulder. 'Tell you what, let's guzzle down this indifferent beer, and scuttle back to our cubby holes. It so happens I've got some rather good port.'

We started across the quad. He was biting his lip and frowning slightly, following some private train of thought I didn't want to intrude on. When we were almost at our staircase he suddenly turned to me and said,

'Your family…Do you think they'd adopt me?'

'God, I hope not!' I said. 'My mother's smitten enough with you already. The minute you were in the house, I'd probably be out on my ear. Perhaps I should tell you the place is haunted. Would that put you off?'

He looked away again, saying nothing, his face an affectless blank. And for a moment I found myself wondering whether what I'd heard as a joke had been something else entirely.

An anthropologist – or maybe even an ethologist – would have had a field day with that first term at Gloucester. Social groups eddied together, fell apart, reformed in a different configuration, started to gel. A hierarchy began to emerge; or rather a series of hierarchies – sport; wit; style; intellectual brilliance – each with its own alpha males, its contenders, its hangers-on, its no-hopers.

Within a few weeks, Sandy Mellor had seen off the competition and seized the crown he so obviously craved: *most amusing man in college.* Having established himself, he became slightly less vicious. Occasionally he would still humiliate some unfortunate nobody who'd blundered into his line of fire; more often, he ignored the lower orders altogether, and contented himself with cod Augustan couplets or surreal flights of fancy. His circle now extended beyond the little knot of people who identified with him personally and basked in his reflected glory. Walk into the JCR or the buttery when he was there, and you'd see ten or a dozen chaps – some of whom he didn't even know – orbiting the outer limits of his gravitational field, enjoying the free entertainment.

To begin with, it surprised me how easily he tolerated these semi-detached satellites. Most of them were exactly the kind of careful, clean-cut conformists that you'd think he would have despised. They had no cultural or artistic ambitions, no hankering to be recognized as wits and *enfants terribles.* They worked hard, but were discreet about it, and sociable enough to avoid being dismissed as *grey men* or *boring.* Virtually to a man, they were destined to be successful lawyers, captains of industry, heads of national institutions.

Most prominent among them – almost, you might say, their unofficial leader – was a lawyer called Tim Bruce. He was good-looking, in a loose-limbed, athletic way: broad-shouldered, with a squarish face permanently primed for a smile, and a flop of fair hair, which he wore slightly shorter than the rest of us wore ours. Glance at him in a certain mood, after you'd had a few drinks, and for a brief moment you might imagine that the mist had cleared and you were glimpsing a member of the lost generation of 1914, whose absence – even after fifty years – still seemed to haunt every quad and side-street and meadow.

He was off-handedly friendly to everyone. Once, when I was coming down the stairs from the library, I met him on his way up. We'd never spoken, but he stopped, squinted at the copy of *Historia Ecclesiastica* I was carrying, then laughed and said,

'Ah, the venomous Bede. Poor chap. No wonder you need a break.'

It was unforgettably odd seeing him and Sandy Mellor together. They were so obviously polar opposites: confident good health on the one hand, self-destructive decay on the other. Sandy appeared to recognize the difference himself. You'd have predicted that it would simply aggravate his insecurity and aggression, but instead it seemed to make him uncharacteristically wistful and self-deprecating. On one occasion, Tim walked into the buttery to find Sandy, red-eyed, Turkish cigarette in hand, hunched over his fourth glass of madeira.

'Gosh, Sandy. Are you all right? Not overdoing it, are you?'

Everybody watching held their breath, bracing themselves for the waspish retort. But Sandy just pulled a face and said,

'I don't know, Tim. I think perhaps I'm beginning to feel my weight.'

I was on the very outer fringe of Tim Bruce's world, of so little significance that Sandy had nothing to gain by publicly attacking me again. Adam was more marginal still. As far as I know, I was the only real friend he had: his circle otherwise seemed to consist of a couple of scarcely-visible misfits – a young, agonisingly shy historian called Mark Davenant, and a smelly chap with a limp whose name I can't remember – who scuttled about in the shadows, like mice trying to escape the attentions of the college cat. Although I sometimes heard Adam going out in the evenings, I found it hard to believe that it was to carouse with them – and, indeed, when I was out and about myself, I never saw him with them, or with anybody else, for that matter.

It puzzled me, not only that he accepted being relegated to this social limbo, but that pretty much everyone else in college seemed content to leave him there. For me, he was a source of endless fascination – like one of those Italian seventeenth century landscapes, where a path tempts you to follow it, across the pasture dotted with cattle, through the trees, over the river, and up to the mysterious castle shimmering on a distant crag. I couldn't understand how other people, looking at the same scene, appeared to see only a dull rectangle of canvas, not worth a second glance. So let me briefly try to explain what *I* found so appealing about him. No, *appealing*'s not the right word. So *enchanting*.

Firstly, there was his innocent delight at finding himself where he was.

Part of the attraction, it's true, is that, whenever we were out together, I was flattered by the way he deferred to my superior knowledge of art and architecture – *You mean that's really by* Hawksmoor? But he was as much a revelation to me as I was to him. Often, when you were walking with him, he'd stop suddenly and stare, with the wonderstruck look of a man seeing something for the first time. Usually, he'd say nothing; but once, I remember – we were at the end of the Broad, gazing back past the sober Clarendon Building, the blousy curves of the Radcliffe Camera, the higgledy roofline of the old shops beyond – he murmured:

'How did they do that?'

'They didn't,' I said. 'Well, not *deliberately*. There wasn't one overarching imperial plan, like in Haussmann's Paris. Just hundreds of individual visions. All of which somehow contrive to co-exist harmoniously.'

Contrive to co-exist. That was a very nineteen-year-old me sort of phrase. Just thinking about it now makes me blush.

'Evolution,' said Adam slowly.

'That's it. No grand design. Just different organisms developing in symbiosis.'

He stretched out his hands, forming them into a kind of loose arch. I could see immediately what he was trying to suggest: a shell. 'And we're part of it. Part of the process. Actually in*side* it.'

I didn't realize, at that point, the full significance for him of the word *inside.* But I was already beginning to understand how aware he was of time, the way he experienced it as a fourth dimension, that trembled just beyond – and occasionally even crossed – the threshold of visibility. The past was a constant presence to him. And not just the collective past: our individual pasts, too. His memory was prodigious, and he would frequently startle me by recalling some detail of my own life – a snide remark I'd made about someone I'd only met once; what I'd eaten for breakfast some morning weeks before, when we'd gone to George's in the covered market – that I'd forgotten myself.

One day, when he'd been complaining about one of his tutors – a cocky young chap called Stuart Dixon, who he said was killing his love of literature – I asked him why he hadn't decided to read History instead of English.

'I don't need to *read* History,' he said. 'History's just here, isn't it?'

And – though much of the time he seemed lost in a different reality – he could also be astonishingly alert to the here and now. On an autumn walk through Christ Church meadow, we saw a woman two or three hundred yards away coming towards us, clutching her coat round her, and stumbling in the buffeting wind. To me, she was no more than a blip on my internal radar screen; but Adam suddenly started running towards her, with an ungainly, unsteady, side-to-side lope. By the time I caught up with him, he'd led her to a bench, where she sat hunched forward, head drooping, elbows on knees.

'What's wrong with her?' I said.

He tapped his chest. 'Quick. Go to the porter's lodge. Get them to call 999.'

He stayed with her, one hand on her shoulder, until the ambulance arrived.

'Well, that was pretty amazing,' I said, after, they'd gone. 'You probably saved her life. How did you know?'

But he just shrugged, as if I'd asked him how he knew it was raining.

And then there was his music. Every day, you'd hear him practising in his room, sometimes for an hour or two at a time, stroking the strings with his fingertips and singing in a breathy stage whisper to keep the volume down. I didn't much care for folk music then – I still don't, to be honest: however unfairly, it conjures up a charmless picture of self-righteous chaps with beards and earnest long-haired girls singing about mining disasters and damsels in distress – but there was a quality to his voice that intrigued me. You must know what I'm talking about: the way it suddenly seemed to split open the walls that imprisoned it, and soar into the stratosphere. And sometimes, too, amid all the traditional airs, you'd catch a snippet of something more original. Once, as I was passing his room, I heard him singing the same line – *Ratty peeping through the reeds* – again and again, tinkering with the tune each time, gradually turning it into the sound of water running over stones. Finally I knocked on the door and went in.

'What is that?' I said. 'Something from *Wind in the Willows*?'

He nodded.

'Did you write it?'

'I'm *trying* to write it.'

He put down his guitar and looked away. But I didn't take the hint. I was intrigued: it seemed such a peculiar thing for a nineteen-year-old to be doing.

'Honestly, you're such a dark horse!' I said. 'People would be astounded if they knew you could play like that. Why don't you do something in the JCR one evening? Nothing formal. Just a sort of impromptu concert.'

He shook his head.

'Well, all I can say is I think you're missing an opportunity. You know, to put yourself on the map, make people sit up and take notice. It wouldn't do you any harm to start getting a bit of a reputation.'

But he wouldn't budge. In desperation, I began looking for other ways to introduce him into a wider circle. One evening, he and I were drinking in the buttery together, when I happened to overhear Tim Bruce – who was standing a few feet away, at the edge of a large group – saying,

'No, I've never been to Africa at all. Can't say I'm terribly tempted, from all I've heard.'

I was slightly fuddled after my second pint of bitter, and – in a reckless moment – found myself leaning over and blurting,

'Adam grew up in Africa. Did you know that?'

'Mm? Sorry?' Tim was surprised at the intrusion, but still managed a smile.

'Adam here. Have you met?'

'No, I don't think so.'

'Well, any questions about it, he's your man.'

'Right. Hello, Adam.' He held his hand out. Adam hesitated, then took it.

'He's also a jolly good musician,' I said. 'Though he won't thank me for telling you.'

'Why not?'

'Too shy and retiring.'

Tim nodded. His gaze panned from my face to Adam's. 'What sort of thing?'

Adam said nothing.

'Folk,' I said. 'See what I mean?'

Tim laughed. 'Ah, a man of many talents. So whereabouts in Africa?'

'Kenya, mostly.'

'Very beautiful, I'm told,' said Tim. Behind him, his companions stirred and turned towards us. I suddenly realized that I'd cast my net too wide, and – in addition to Tim himself – unwittingly managed to catch Sandy Mellor and two of his sniggering friends.

'Your people still live there?' asked Tim.

Adam nodded.

'Bit difficult, I'd imagine. Since independence.'

Adam shrugged. I could see Sandy smirking at him, one eyebrow raised. I touched Adam's shoulder and spun him round.

'Sorry,' I muttered. 'Didn't mean to interrupt.'

'That's OK,' said Tim. 'Nice to meet you, Adam.'

He turned back to the others. A few seconds later, I heard a ripple of laughter as Sandy Mellor embarked on a monologue – about what, exactly, I couldn't tell, except it didn't seem to have anything to do with Adam. I breathed a sigh of relief. No harm done, after all. We'd got away with it.

But as it turned out, life was not so forgiving. In the way of these things – flip a coin, and once in a while you'll get seven heads in a row – in the week following that first meeting we found ourselves constantly bumping into Tim Bruce. He'd always stop and chat with us for a minute or two, in that easy, leader-of-men way that – like his broad cricketer's shoulders and blue eyes – seemed a kind of natural endowment, one of the catalogue of blessings showered on him at birth by a benign fairy godmother. But the third or fourth time we saw him, he made more of a point of it, hailing us from the other side of the quad, and then hurrying towards us.

'Hello, Roddy.' He was wearing his gown, and carrying a ring-binder. He smiled and pointed a friendly finger at Adam. 'I was hoping I might run into you today. A question. Poor Tom's?'

I had no idea what he was talking about. I assumed it was because I didn't move in the right social world. So I was surprised when Adam – even more of an outsider, I supposed, than I was – replied,

'What about it?'

'You know it, I gather. So you can tell me. What's the form there?'

Adam frowned. 'It's just a club, Tim.'

'Well, all right. But I mean, what about clothes, for instance?' He tugged at the front of his shirt. 'Something like this OK? Or –'

'Yeah, of course.'

'No need to wear a CND badge?'

Adam shook his head.

'Well, that's good. Don't want to stick out like a sore thumb.'

'When are you going?'

'This evening.'

Adam blinked. I could see his throat working.

'What's Poor Tom's?' I said. 'A folk club?'

They both nodded.

'Doesn't quite seem your natural habitat, Tim.'

'Oh, I don't know.'

'Something to do with a girl, is it?'

Most people would have blushed. Tim took it effortlessly in his stride.

'Yes, as it happens. Well, thanks, Adam. That's put my mind at rest.'

He half ran up the steps towards the porter's lodge. As we started to follow him, we saw Sandy Mellor at the top, obviously waiting for him. Something in Sandy's posture – stiff and dangerously still, his brow slightly furrowed – made me think of a dog sizing up a rival. As Tim approached, Sandy raised a hand to stop him; but Tim just quickly muttered something in passing and kept going. I slowed my pace, hoping that Sandy would move before we reached him. But he stood his ground, watching our progress with an insolent lift of the lip that half bared his teeth.

'Prepare yourself,' I said. 'I think we're going to have acid flung in our faces.' I waited till we were almost at the last step, then waved and called,

'Hello, Sandy.'

He took no notice of me. His whole attention was fixed on Adam. His face was pink and pimply with heat.

'Ah, boy,' he murmured, when they were no more than a few feet apart. He clapped his hands. 'Go up to my room and get my cigarettes.'

Adam stopped and stared at him. Unhurriedly, Sandy felt in his pocket and after a few seconds produced a packet of Sullivan Powell Turkish Number Ones.

'Ah,' he said, holding it up. 'Here they are after all. That's a relief. Means I don't have to worry about you pilfering anything.'

He slipped out a cigarette, lit it, then turned and lumbered away towards his room. I tugged Adam's sleeve.

'This way, sir, if you'd be so good.'

I half dragged him past the porters' lodge. Adam didn't speak till we were in the street. Then he said,

'I don't understand. First I was a woman. Now he's talking to me as if –'

'There's no logic to it. All it is, is, the last he time he didn't know you grew up in Africa. Now he does. So that's become your weak point. Just forget it, OK?'

He shook his head.

'I suspect the real problem,' I said, 'is that he doesn't like you being on such good terms with Tim Bruce.'

'What's that got to do with him?'

I glanced at him. He looked genuinely puzzled. How, I wondered, could he be so dense? And then I remembered: this was a chap who'd never been envious or resentful of a brother or a sister, never had to endure the hideous, *Lord of the Flies* jostling for position at school.

'Come on,' I said. 'Let's go and get lunch somewhere in town. My treat.'

Breakfast in hall, the following day. I still remember those breakfasts, even now. The textures, as much as anything: the limp cold toast; the red tinned tomatoes, slithery as sea creatures; eggs swimming in fat; sausages that simply disintegrated at the first touch of the knife. And the noise: the clatter of plates and pans and cutlery, amplified by the cave-like acoustic of the place, making anyone with a hangover screw up his eyes and pinch his temples in pain.

Adam and I were sitting opposite one another, drinking the last of our coffee, when Tim Bruce slid on to the bench next to me.

'I've got to admit, Roddy,' he said, nodding at Adam, 'when you told me he was a musician I took it with a pinch of salt. I mean, we all knew those fellows at school who taught themselves three chords and thought they were going to be the next Mick Jagger. But I've heard the evidence with my own ears. And I'm bound to say you were absolutely right.'

He held his hand out. Adam shook it.

'You were terrific last night. Honestly.' He laughed. 'I couldn't believe it was the same bloke I see skulking around college.'

Adam flushed. 'Thank you.'

'And in case you're thinking, what does *he* know, the girl I was with was impressed, too. *Wow! Didn't it just blow your mind, Tim?* Her very words. And she's an old hand at this kind of thing. She's the one who told me about you.' He turned to me. 'You ever seen him?'

I shook my head, staring at Adam.

'Well, you should. He's *far out*.' He laughed. 'Another Mel-ism.'

I drained my coffee and stood up. 'OK. Well, I'm off.'

I expected Adam to come with me, but he didn't. I didn't see him again till that evening, when we more or less collided on the staircase.

'There you are, you bastard,' I said. I grabbed his sleeve to stop him sloping past. 'Why didn't you tell me you were going to be playing at Poor Tom's last night?'

He said nothing.

'And that wasn't the first time, I take it?'

He shook his head.

'And not once did it occur to you to mention to me that you were performing there?'

He shrugged. 'It's just a completely different thing. Nothing to do with my life here at all.'

'So what, you're a schizophrenic, are you? Sometimes you get headaches and have to sing folk songs, and then afterwards you forget all about it?'

Why was I so harsh? Jealousy, I suppose: I was meant to be his closest friend, and here he was striding off into pastures new without even telling me.

He shook his head, flushing. 'It's just I thought I was going to find England here.' He lassoed the college with his hand. 'That first day, meeting your family, I imagined it would all be like that. But –'

'Whoa, whoa, whoa, whoa, whoa,' I said. 'Like what?'

'Just…slipping into something familiar. But it wasn't.'

'And Poor Tom's was?'

'The *music* was. And the stories.'

And he barged past me and went into his room.

Tim Bruce's new-found interest in Adam subtly changed the dynamics of our lives. People in college started to acknowledge us, buy us drinks, even invite us (though Adam never went) to the occasional party. Sandy Mellor's persecution continued; but it was no longer a public sport, carried out in the amphitheatre of the buttery or the quad. Instead, it became a kind of private vendetta, pursued in dark, un-overlooked corners, like a child's campaign of cruelty against a cat. On Guy Fawkes's night, for instance, with firework fumes and drizzle thickening an already dense fog, he and his two staunchest cronies suddenly loomed out of the murk in front of the buttery, blocking our way. The weather gave them an eerie, demonic look: three jeering gargoyles erupting from a wall.

'Ah, boy.'

He and Adam stared at each other. I glanced round. Not another person to be seen: just swirly grey muzz. We might have been standing in the middle of a moor.

'You've been neglecting your duties,' said Sandy. 'Too much singing to Massa on the stoop.' He held his beer mug away from his body, then leaned forward and pointed to his knee with his other hand. 'Look at the state of my trousers.'

'God, you're amusing, Sandy,' I said. I touched Adam's arm. 'Come on.'

I tried to go round Sandy, but he sidestepped into my path again. Then, to my astonishment, he handed his glass to one of his friends, unlaced his shoes and started unbuckling his belt.

'Here we are,' he said, holding out his trousers to Adam. 'Off to the cleaners with you. Chop chop.'

The two friends were shaking with silent laughter. Adam seemed dumb-founded. But the sight of Sandy standing there, trying not to shiver, resisting the urge to cover up his pale lardy legs even though – at any moment – a college servant might walk by and report him, drove home to me, for the first time, the price *he* was paying for his need to keep endlessly raising the stakes. More and more, he could only undermine Adam's dignity at the expense of his own.

*

Some time around the sixth or seventh week of term, Tim Bruce accosted me one morning outside the library.

'Ah, Roddy. The very man. Have you got a minute?' He glanced behind him, checking that we were alone. 'This is just between ourselves, all right?'

I couldn't imagine what he could possibly have to say to me in confidence, but I nodded.

'As you may or may not know,' he said, 'Adam's going to be playing at Poor Tom's on Thursday. And a few of us are planning to go along and hear him.'

'Ah. Are you sure that's a good idea?'

'Why shouldn't it be?'

'Well, you know how funny he is about his music. He'd probably run a mile if he knew.'

'That's why we're not telling him. Interested in coming along?'

I thought about it for a moment. It seemed slightly underhand. I could imagine the startled rabbit look on Adam's face as he came on and saw us all there. But then I thought, so what if he *is* startled? Serve him right for being so bloody secretive.

'Yes,' I said. 'All right.'

It was no wonder that I'd never stumbled on Poor Tom's: it was tucked away in a side street in St. Ebbe's, in a wonky little stone building that had obviously started life as a shop. A poster in the window advertised forthcoming events. I was surprised to see that two or three of them featured *Adam Earnshaw* – though he always appeared towards the bottom of the list, dwarfed by the bigger names at the top.

There were five of us. We waited in the street for the last straggler to arrive, then joined the desultory queue, gave our half-crowns to the toothless woman at the door, and squeezed along a narrow passage to a room at the back. There was a makeshift bar to one side, and a stage area – stool, microphone, amplifier, but no performer yet – defined by a circle of light at the rear. Behind us, a constant stream of people kept trickling in, forcing our little group into a tighter and tighter huddle. The air was heavy with the rasp of smoke, the smell of sweat and soap and deodorant and damp cloth.

Charmed Tim Bruce somehow found a way through the crowd, and passed back a chain of drinks for us. He'd just returned, sipping at his own glass, face beaming *mission accomplished*, when the room suddenly fell silent, and everyone turned towards the stage. A moment later, Adam shuffled on, guitar in hand, staring at the floor, as if he had to monitor the progress of his own feet to avoid stumbling. As he sat down, pinged the strings with shaking hands, fiddled with the machine heads, a gush of fear surged through me. Even if, on this occasion, Tim was responsible for my being there, Adam was still ultimately *my* friend. If he was too nervous to play, I would share his humiliation, and feel that I had somehow failed to protect him.

He adjusted the microphone, bringing it to the level of his face. I could hear the dry click of his mouth as he tested the volume.

And then, all at once – like a dancer abandoning his whole body to the rhythm of the band – he was picking his way through the opening bars of *Scarborough Fair*, moving at a cracking, pony-trotting pace, much brisker than the version Simon and Garfunkel released the following year. The audacity of it took my breath away. But his fingers travelled so deftly over the frets that my anxiety soon started to dissipate; and when he began to sing, and I felt the people around me draw together, as if someone had suddenly closed a giant zip, it melted away altogether.

It wasn't the best performance I ever heard Adam give: at that point, he still hadn't got the technical mastery and perfectly judged projection that we all remember from his brief golden age a couple of years later. And he was still only singing traditional music, so we had none of the sense you got from his own material of glimpsing another reality. But, as he worked through his five-song set, moving with a kind of animal instinct from melancholy to spritely back to melancholy again, you could feel the audience pulled, almost forcibly, out of their lives and into his. They were so entranced that there was a pause of five or six seconds at the end before the spell broke, and silence gave way to applause.

Adam was already on his feet, bobbing his head nervily like a toy duck, when Sandy Mellor appeared out of nowhere, barged his way to the front of the crowd and flung a handful of coins into the pool of light.

You could hear the gasps, and a couple of incredulous sniggers. The meaning was so obvious that for a moment no one moved. Then Adam edged forward, squinting into the darkness. Sandy tried to beat a stately retreat, but found himself floundering against the close mesh of humanity. Adam stared at him.

'Why are you so unpleasant to me?' he said.

'Unpleasant?' snarled Sandy. 'Isn't that what one's supposed to do with nigger minstrels?'

It was as if someone had pressed a switch, turning his polarity from positive to negative. People shrank away, opening a space around him that – despite the density of the crowd – no one seemed to want to fill.

Adam held his hand out, fingers spread, and peered into Sandy's eyes. After a moment he nodded and said,

'Ah, I see. I see.'

Sandy cast about desperately for his friends, pleading for a lifeline; but they turned their backs on him, and started – heads lowered, apparently deep in conversation with each other – towards the door. Sandy rounded on Adam again, a harried mammoth preparing to make its last stand. But something he saw in Adam's eyes seemed to deter him, and after a few seconds – without a word – he spun back and followed his pals out into the night.

It wasn't till next morning at breakfast that I had the chance to quiz Adam about it.

'Did you really see something? At Poor Tom's? When you were looking at Sandy, and you said, "I see"?'

'Oh, yes. His father.'

'Sorry?'

'That's what I saw. The reason he's like that. It's because of his father.'

'Why, what did his father do?'

'I've no idea. But it's always something to do with the father in the end, isn't it?'

I made my own enquiries. Sir Nigel Mellor, it turned out, was a businessman, who'd made his fortune out of a brand of cooking oil called Sizzle. His knighthood had been awarded for *services to politics*. It didn't take much rooting through back issues of *Private Eye* to discover that he'd been one of the largest donors to the Conservative Party in the 1959 general election.

I didn't tell Adam, for some reason, but I couldn't resist mentioning it to my other friends. I swore them to secrecy, but within a few days – as I must have realized, at some level, it inevitably would be – it was all round the college. Soon, Sandy had only to walk into hall or the buttery for a chorus of voices to start murmuring, 'Sizzle, Sizzle, Sizzle'. He took it with the sulky glower of an *ancien regime* aristo on his way to the guillotine. But by the end of term, it was noticeable that he had almost completely disappeared from public view.

Throughout that Christmas vacation I was conscious of an odd nagging unease about Sandy. I'd glimpsed his vulnerability, his reckless tendency when cornered to hurl himself on the rocks; and I had a troubling vision of him sticking a shotgun muzzle in his mouth, or kneeling with his head in a gas oven.

So, despite everything, it was a relief, when I lurched into the porters' lodge at the start of Hilary Term, to see him standing there, checking the contents of his pigeonhole. He'd lost so much weight that for a moment I wasn't certain it *was* him.

'Sandy?' I said.

He turned, gave me the tiniest nod, then stalked out into the quad.

For the rest of our time at Oxford, he was a diminished, rather solitary figure, who made no attempt to recover his lost reputation. Instead, he worked hard, got a respectable degree, wangled a place on the BBC graduate trainee course, and ended up as a well-regarded radio producer. When, years later, I bumped into him by chance in Langham Place, Sandy claimed not to remember Adam Earnshaw at all.

And that, it occurs to me now, *is* Adam. A kind of quantum particle, that erupts out of nowhere into our three-dimensional world, alters lives in a way that appears to defy the normal laws of cause and effect, and then vanishes back into the void.

That doesn't explain the *how* of his subsequent disappearance, I'm afraid – but it does perhaps help make the *why* a bit easier to understand.

3
TATE FINNEGAN

Jesus, man, you don't give up, do you? And I'm getting tired of saying no. OK: here's the deal. I have a one-hour layover. So I sit here in an out-of-the-way corner at LAX and talk about the guy for one hour. I send you this as an audio file. You take out the *ers* and *ums*. You clean up the grammar, so I don't look like a dumb fuck. You don't change anything else. And if you publish it, I get to OK it first. And my decision is final. All right?

All right. Sorry if I came on too strong there, everyone's nightmare obnoxious loud American. Truth is, you've been shafted as many times as I have, you get to be quick on the draw. It's just like *wham, bam, don't fuck with me*. But now we have the hard-nosed shit out of the way, I'll quiet down. That's a promise.

And by the way, before we go on: you've given me nothing, so I don't know what your angle is here. But when you say listening to *Standing Stone* changed your life, made you feel you had to find out about the guy who recorded it, I can totally dig that. You're obviously a man with taste. And there aren't too many of us now, so we better all hang together.

OK. Let's free associate here.

Adam Earnshaw. Yeah. Staymouth Festival, 1965. Les Cousins, a couple years later. *Annabelle, Dancing. Standing Stone. Sleeping Giant.*

Shit, no, I try to do all that, I'll miss my connection. Here's a better idea: the day I signed him. That kind of says it all.

So: London. Mid-sixties. I'd been there once before when I was still at college, when I parlayed my experience of getting blues artists like Bill Sweet and Charley Gibb to appear on campus into doing a vacation job for a New York douche bag who called himself a promoter. He didn't know anything about the blues, but he was smart enough to realize there was an audience for it over in England, and wanted someone to do the heavy work for him. I booked the hotels, handled the transportation, made sure the guys showed up sober enough to play and didn't quit half way through to lay one of the chicks trying to get in their dressing-room. You have to remember, these dudes grew up during segregation. They'll have known people, heard about them, anyway, who were lynched just for *looking* at a white woman. And suddenly they're in England, and it's raining white chicks that want to fuck them. So it's hard for a guy like Bill Sweet, he's already almost sixty, it's hard for him not to want to get all the candy he can before they close the store.

And London back then, let me tell you, was really something else. It was like you were living in a movie: one part of it was colour – crazy colours, the brightest you ever saw – and the other was black-and-white, and you never knew which was coming next. So you'd be walking along this street full of guys in scarlet and gold-braid uniforms and girls in psychedelic mini-dresses, and then you'd turn a corner, and, wham, you're in a scene from *Oliver Twist*, scruffy urchins with pinched faces, geezers in striped aprons serving jellied eels, old warehouses black with soot – except there's a big hole in the middle, where a building was destroyed in the Blitz that they still haven't gotten around to replacing yet. To a middle-class kid from New Jersey, it seemed totally far out. Being there was just one long trip, no chemicals required.

And then there was the music. The folk scene in New York was pretty hard-line: no electric guitars; no original material, unless it was straight down-the-middle political. Pete Seeger and Alan Lomax couldn't ship you off to the gulag if you didn't fit the bill, but they could stop you playing any of the best places in Greenwich Village. Some of the less traditional acts got out from under and moved to Boston, which was more relaxed – but still, a lot of the time, just felt like an outsized college town. London was the best of both: a big city, but an *everybody welcome* attitude.

There *were* commissars, of course – people like Ewan McColl and Mayburn Ellis – but the scene was too new, and moving too fast, for them to control it. What you had instead was a bunch of wide boys (one of those great English expressions I'd never heard before I got there) running around like crazy trying to make a quick buck from all the talent that seemed to be crawling out the woodwork. A lot of them were drunks, misfits that'd never gotten over the war, ten-time losers who saw this as a last spin of the wheel. I took one look at them and figured I could do better. Hard not to, if you still had all your limbs and knew something about music.

In May 65, after graduating from Yale, I go back to New York and begin the big hustle. I've only been there a couple weeks when serendipity does its thing: the douche bag's brother-in-law, Pete Grimaldi, decides to start Wheatsheaf Records. A quick perusal of the charts convinces him he needs a London office – not just to promote new releases and organize tours, but to sign British acts. Bingo. By mid-July, I have a tiny apartment in Notting Hill, a broom-closet with a phone and a trial-size desk in Wardour Street, and a pocket-book full of cards saying: *Tate Finnegan. Wheatsheaf Records.* Days, mostly, I did paperwork, and tried to figure out how to play the music business executive without being a total asshole. Nights, I went to clubs, listened to everything – and I mean *everything* – from the embarrassing to the amazing, and worked the room like a small-town mayor running for re-election, trying to pick up what was humming on the grapevine. There was this older German woman, Judith someone, you'd see sometimes. She was kind of a mom figure for a lot of the kids, and she knew everybody. *What they are,* she said, *the true musicians, is outsiders. But at least they have a voice. And they use it to win our love for the outcasts, who can't speak for themselves.*

That sounded good to me. So I'd hang out with her whenever I could. And one evening, must have been the end of November, I guess, I was there at the Troubadour when this really cute chick called Trudy came up and started talking about this guy she'd seen a couple days before.

'His name's Adam Earnshaw,' she said. 'He's amazing. You ever hear of him?'

Judith whatever-her-name-was hadn't. But weirdly, for once, I had.

'Yeah,' I said. 'Blonde guy with a guitar. Looks like nothing at all until he opens his mouth. Then this voice comes out gives you goose bumps.'

She stared at me. That was the idea, of course. She was petite, with big possum eyes. To use another good English expression, I fancied her something rotten.

'Who are you?' she said.

I handed her my card. She read it. 'Well, you know your stuff, I'll say that,' she said, looking up. 'Where'd you hear him?'

'Oh,' I said. 'Staymouth Festival. He was singing with a girl. In a pub.'

Trudy didn't like the girl bit, you could tell. 'Really?' she said. 'I thought he only sang solo. At this club in Oxford, Poor Tom's. You know it?'

I shook my head.

'I was there last weekend,' she said. 'It's a bit of a dive. But this woman told me he never goes anywhere else. Hates any kind of publicity, apparently. Just slinks in, does what he does, slinks out again.' There was a beer-spill on the table. She doodled in it with her finger. 'Well, that was her story. Probably she was just shitting me.'

'Not necessarily,' I said. 'I should go down and check him out. You want to ride shotgun?'

She shrugged. 'It was kind of a strange weekend. I'm not sure I'm ready for Oxford again yet.' She did another doodle and squinted at the result. 'So who was this girl?'

'What girl?'

'The one in the pub with Adam Earnshaw.'

'Her name was Cat.' Which I remembered only because I'd fancied *her* rotten.

'What was she like?' said the girl.

'A voluptuous vixen, who made Adam Earnshaw the envy of every man in the goddam bar.'

She half-smiled. 'You're shitting me too,' she said.

'I am,' I said. 'Anyway, you have my number. I'll call the place up, and if he's playing Saturday, I'll go then. Ride leaves at 2.00, if you're interested. And you ought to be. You know what I drive?'

She shook her head.

'Well, you'll find out Saturday,' I said.

Only she didn't. I laid my plans and waited and waited, but she never called. Finally I thought, what the fuck, I'll go anyway. Just hearing her talking about Adam had piqued my interest again. Plus, I might see Cat there. Plus, it was a chance to drive my new car.

I guess maybe that calls for a footnote. I don't know where you're from, how old you are. If you're American, east coast, my age ± ten years, I don't need to explain. If not, here's the story. Growing up where I did – New Jersey, remember, late 50s – pretty much the first life-lesson you learned was that when you saw a car cruising around with big chrome teeth and fins the size of airplane wings, it was 100 to 1 the guy behind the wheel was a grade-A asshole. Stingrays and Starlights, they were a little bit different, more of a grey area, could go either way. But the really cool dudes, the dudes you wanted to be like when you were older, *they* all drove MGs, Jaguars, maybe once in a while a Mercedes coupe. Sleek, gorgeous, 28-carat *class*.

Yeah, yeah, you don't need to tell me: owning a shiny British sports car didn't really fit with the whole hippie radical freak thing. Plus Ralph Nader wouldn't have approved. But a couple weeks before I shipped out for England my grandfather died and left me some money. Not enough to buy me a title and a fine stately home. But enough for a brand-new Austin Healey 3000 Mk III, two-tone, with blue leather seats and a silver *whoosh* on either side, graceful as a dolphin's back. It was the most beautiful thing I ever saw. For a few days after I got to London, I contented myself with peering through the showroom window, drooling. Then I broke down and ordered me one.

So that morning I went into the garage, rubbed her down, polished her till I could see my own crazy hair in the paintwork. 'We are going on an adventure, baby,' I said. 'We arc going to take Oxford town by storm.'

I drew up a contract for Adam Earnshaw, just in case, leaving a couple spaces blank to give me haggle room. Then I dressed for the part: cowboy boots, purple bellbottoms, a sheepskin Afghan that bulked me out to the size of an AWA wrestler, skimpy round shades that turned my eyes into a couple of dark holes. A few miles short of Oxford, I stopped, snuck my slab of righteous Acapulco gold from its hidey hole under the seat, and made myself one of those giant British joints, more engineering than recreation, a cardboard subway tunnel wrapped in skins. It must have been at least six inches long. When I'd finished, I lit up, patted the dash and said,

'Right, momma. We are *ready*.'

I've put on hundreds of shows in my life, maybe thousands. I can't say that was the best, but it has to be one of the most memorable. It was a grey late-fall day, but not raining. I put the top down, so as to give the good folk of Oxford the full package. In the background, all those towers and spires draped in mist. Closer to, crowds of young Brits thronging the sidewalks, all – to a man and a woman – turning their pasty faces to stare as I went by. When I finally pulled up outside the little hotel I'd booked, a guy standing by the door looked like he'd just seen a lizard slither out of a television screen.

'It's OK, man,' I said. 'Don't blame your dealer. I'm for real.'

I checked in to my room, then moseyed out again to get the lay of the land. The dope probably had something to do with it, but it was quite a trip. A Brit in America has to acclimate to the distances, all those miles of nothing between where you started from and where you're going. For a Yank in the UK, the problem is acclimating to *time*. The effect of all that brick and stone, the sagging arches, the centuries of architectural history – Tudor mullions, Georgian sashes, pointy Victorian gothic – crammed into one blackened wall, is weirdly disorienting. You walk past a building you know must have been pretty much the same when Columbus was getting the *Nina*, the *Pinta* and the *Santa Maria* ready for their big adventure, and it's like, *no, that's not possible, the world ain't like that.*

And the way I looked, I have to say, it wasn't just a one-way traffic. Even without the car, I was still turning heads. Give it maybe a couple years, and half the freaks in Oxford would be Tate clones; but in 65 I was still a visitation from the planet Zog. The girl who told me the way to Poor Tom's couldn't so much as meet my eye.

Even with her directions, it took me forever to find the place. When I did, I knew at once I'd made a big mistake. I guess when Trudy had said *Oxford*, even when she'd told me it was a *dive*, I must've envisioned – without really thinking about it – a fancy night-spot full of braying public schoolboys, as I'd just learned to call them. What I actually saw was a shabby storefront with unwashed windows and a door that needed a lot of paint. A handwritten poster scotch-taped to the glass said: *Tonight 8.00 p.m. The Strawberry Line. Carrie Bateman. Adam Earnshaw.* Going in there dressed the way I was would be like riding a Sherman tank into a Quaker meeting.

I went back to the hotel and toned myself down: blue jeans; *Marty's Bait Store* t-shirt; army surplus jacket. Then I excavated the remains of the giant joint from my pocket, lay down on the bed and took a dope-fuelled tour of the stars.

I didn't want to show up in the car, but I wanted it close by, just in case. So a little after eight I parked in the next street, then walked the rest of the way to Poor Tom's. I hung around outside for a few minutes, then attached myself to a group of five or six kids who were going in together. They looked like a cartoon from the *Beano* (something else I'd just discovered) – a girl with a doughy face covered in spots, who could've been played by a cinnamon Danish; a guy with a huge overbite and peg teeth – but I figured there was safety in numbers. Easy in, I thought, and then – if you don't like what you see – easy out again. Adam Earnshaw never even need know you were there.

The dimly lit little room was already half full. I bought myself a pint, then stood at the back, checking out the talent. There was no sign of Cat – or of anyone else interesting enough to lure me out of the shadows. Almost immediately, the lights went up on the tiny stage area, and the noise subsided to a few desultory coughs and whispers.

The way the bill was laid out, I was expecting Adam Earnshaw to open. Instead first up we had the Strawberry Line: two guys and a girl doing *a capella* sea shanties. They weren't terrible, but you knew within three bars they weren't going anyplace. It sounds harsh, but listening to them made me angry. I'd heard a hundred bands like them, all destined to sink without a bubble. And the beer wasn't that great. And Trudy had stood me up. And the only girl in the place who even looked at me was the cinnamon Danish. It suddenly hit me that I'd seen Adam Earnshaw just once, for maybe ten minutes, through a window. If it turned out he wasn't as good as I remembered, this was going to be the biggest fucking waste of time and money ever.

Next on was Carrie Bateman. You'll know the type: more hair than face, with a big Gibson acoustic and a quavery voice. She did OK versions of three or four traditional ballads, and a song about nuclear war called *Autumn Leaves*, that I guessed she'd penned herself. Better than The Strawberry Line, no question, but the only thing that really stood out about her was a noticeable lisp. Cute, I suppose, if hearing *misty willows* pronounced *mithty willowth* is your thing, but not *that* cute. So I couldn't figure out why more and more people seemed to be squeezing in to hear her, till by the end of her set there was hardly room to breathe. Guys, I wanted to say, if you think this is good, you need to get your asses up to London, check out the real thing.

And then I got it. *Thank you very much. Good night.* Applause – but only on the scale from polite to warm. She gives us a shy wave and walks off, hair swirling. The room goes spooky-silent. Even before she's slipped behind the curtain, the audience have forgotten about her: their attention is on something else, something they haven't seen yet. You can feel the expectation: it's right there, prickling your skin. There's what seems like an unbearable wait. And then, all around you, people start breathing again. Someone is shuffling into the light.

For a couple seconds I wasn't sure it was him. The face was familiar, but it seemed more defined than I remembered, the lines deeper. Something – the mix of dope and alcohol, probably, plus the pie and beans I'd had for supper – gave me the way-out notion that maybe he was a dog. That would explain it, because it meant that while I was only four months older than I'd been when I saw him, he'd aged almost two-and-a-half years. The idea of it seemed hilarious. I began to laugh. People turned and shushed me. It was too damned loud, I knew it was, but I couldn't stop myself. Adam Earnshaw started to play. I put my hand over my mouth – but I was still heaving like I was doing the shake, and you couldn't do the shake in a place like that without the whole room knowing about it. The guy next to me had to whip his drink out of the way. In the process, he knocked into his girlfriend, and made her spill hers. He turned red and said, 'What's so fucking funny?'

All I could do was shake my head. And then Adam began to sing, and *boom*, I wasn't laughing any more.

You've heard him, of course, but did you ever see him? If the answer's no, it's hard to convey the power of his voice. I'm not just talking about the range here – the way it seemed to be cruising easily along the deck, and then, with a surge of the jets, suddenly launch off into space. When you heard it live, there was another quality, a kind of intensity that you could *feel* in the vibration of the air, like he was directing the words to you personally, responding to some secret need in you that *he* knew was there but nobody else could see. I knew a lot of the songs he sang – *Matty Groves*; *John Barleycorn*; *The Sprig of Thyme*; *The Blue Cockade* – but before that night they'd always seemed remote and quaint, echoes of a lost world, with nothing to say to a kid who'd grown up in Jersey, watching *Leave it to Beaver* and Lucille Ball on the TV. Suddenly the lives of all those soldiers and servants and maidens were tangled up in *my* life. *Spencer the Rover* – you know that one? There's this one verse that goes:

> *The night fast approaching to the woods he resorted*
> *With woodbine and ivy his bed for to make;*
> *There he dreamt about sighing*
> *Lamenting and crying.*
> *Go home to your family and rambling forsake.*

That just blew me away. By the time we'd gotten to the third line, I was in tears. That was me: a traveller in a strange land, thousands of miles away from his folks. I looked around: everyone else was choked up too.

I had to have the guy. He was even better than I remembered. But I'd already tried to sign him, when I saw him in Staymouth, and he hadn't seemed that thrilled. Plus, London was full of A&R men, most of them with bigger chequebooks than I had and the ethics of a tarantula. And as soon as word got around they'd be down here like dogs out of the trap, so I needed to figure out an offer he couldn't refuse – and fast.

At the end, I waited for a few seconds, listening to the applause, feeling the waves of love pulsing from the audience on to the stage. Then, as he stood up, bobbing his head like a pigeon (that's something needs to be fixed, I thought), I hurried to the door. No point being part of the crowd: you couldn't do a deal surrounded by adoring fans. The name of the game was to wait until I could talk to him alone, then get him in my headlights and switch on the brights.

Outside it was beginning to rain. I crossed the street and stood in a doorway. People started to spill out of the club and gather round the entrance, buttoning their coats, squinting suspiciously at the sky. After a few minutes Adam appeared, blinking in the fuzzy glow of the streetlamps. Next to him was the lispy girl, pressed close against him, touching his arm. Shit: what if they were a couple? How to say, *hi guys, I'd like to sign one of you, but not the other*?

The hum of voices erupted into a drunk party gabble. Words began to detach themselves and float my way: *Out of sight…Incredible…Amazing.* Adam looked kind of uncomfortable, still bobbing his head, and moving jerkily through the crowd as if some crazed Parkinson's sufferer was pulling his strings. But unlike the night I'd caught him in Staymouth, he could at least make eye contact, and mutter *Thank you. Thanks. Glad you enjoyed it.* He even managed to smile a couple times. That seemed like progress.

I had my speech all ready now: *Excuse me, ma'am, could you spare us a moment?* But as I started to move in, another guy suddenly appeared out of nowhere and hopped past me, like a sparrow beating a starling to a crumb.

'Ah, ah,' he said, pitter-pattering into Adam's path and heading him and the girl to a standstill. 'That was marvellous. Can we talk?'

He was half my size and twice my age, with thick-rimmed glasses and a brush of silky white hair. There was something familiar about the face – wide mouth; quivery upper lip; grey skin, like unfired clay – but in the dim light I couldn't be sure if I'd actually seen him before or simply recognized the type: the old-guard purist who'd come to folk through the WEA and the Communist Party. Either way, it made me nervous. One accidental collision with my shoulder, I knew, could have him on his knees, scrabbling myopically in the gutter. But that didn't seem like the smartest way to open negotiations, so I decided to wait my turn, like a good boy.

'You may possibly have heard of me,' the little guy murmured, with a smile that said, *I'm just being modest. It's a dead certainty you'll have heard of me.* 'My name's Mayburn Ellis.'

Fuck, that explained it: I'd never met the dude, but I'd seen photos of him, hanging out with Pete Seeger and Bert Lloyd back in the 50s, when they'd been pretty much the Lenin, Stalin and Trotsky of the movement. Other people were pushing between us now, so I couldn't hear what he was saying, but it wasn't too hard to guess the drift. *This is the People's music. We need sturdy young chaps of your stamp to carry on the tradition. Chaps strong enough to resist the wiles of record producers like that ghastly American fellow, Tate Finnegan, who want to turn it into bourgeois entertainment.*

There was nothing I could do except clench my fists and pray to the god of art. Maybe the god of art heard me, because after five minutes or so – instead of all heading off together to get a drink, like I'd expected – they shook hands, and Ellis hurried away alone. Adam and the girl stood talking for a moment, then suddenly kind of toppled towards each other and hugged. It was long and lingering, that hug: from where I was standing, I couldn't see what his hands were up to, but hers were doing a lot of work on his back and shoulders. Two bodies that already knew each other intimately – or one that was crazily trying to find out as much about the other as possible? For present purposes, it didn't much matter: whatever the relationship, people only hug like that in public if they're about to go their separate ways. And sure enough, after thirty seconds or so, the girl disentangled herself, and – with a last bush baby smile through the hanging vines of hair – set off towards the centre of town. Adam waited a moment, then turned and headed in the opposite direction, with just the guitar slung over his shoulder for company.

Bullseye.

I gave him a twenty-yard lead, to avoid freaking him out, then started to follow. The idea was to wait till we were out of earshot of the club, then catch him up and hit him with my spiel. Pretty soon, though, I realized this wasn't a great plan. By the time we reached the end of the street, it was just him and me and the drizzle, hemmed in by two rows of deserted buildings with boarded-up windows. The whole thing looked like a scene from an Ed Wood movie. If I sprang on him now, he'd probably think I was Jack the Ripper.

What saved me was the English weather. As we turned the corner, the rain suddenly got serious, strafing the blacktop like a Bonnie and Clyde shootout. He grabbed his guitar to his chest and hunched forward to protect it.

'Hey!' I called.

He stopped and looked back.

'You want a ride?' I said. 'Car's right there.'

He hesitated, then nodded and started plodding back towards me. We met half way, at the end of the street where I'd parked. When I stopped by the Austin Healey, his eyes widened.

'Is that yours?'

I was surprised. I'd figured he wouldn't know the difference between a Ford Popular and a Ferrari.

'Yep,' I said. 'That's my momma.' I opened the passenger door for him. 'Momma, meet Adam Earnshaw.'

'God, it's beautiful.'

'You an auto freak?'

He shrugged. 'I don't know. Yeah, maybe. All we ever had was an old Land Rover. So –'

'Get in.'

He opened the door, ogling the blue leather, then pulled the front of his wet jacket. 'I'm wet,' he said. 'I'll spoil it.'

'No, you won't,' I said. 'Momma won't mind, will you, momma? I'll give her extra hay. Come on.'

We ducked inside at the same moment, slamming the doors in unison.

'Remember me?' I said.

He slitted his eyes, trying to see me in the darkness.

'Here.' I switched on the interior light. It didn't seem to help him much.

'Tate Finnegan,' I said. 'I saw you back in August. At Staymouth.'

'Oh, yeah, yeah, of course,' he said. 'You gave me a card, didn't you? I've still got it somewhere.'

I took out my pocket-book. 'Well, here's another one. In case you can't find it.'

'What happens when I get the full set?'

I pinched myself. What was going on here? Had the guy actually made a *joke*?

'You get a record deal,' I said. 'Only you don't have to wait that long. We can do it now, if you want to. I have a contract with me. It's in the trunk.'

He stared at the card, as if what it said and what I'd said didn't quite add up.

I patted the steering wheel. 'So where are we going?'

'Back to college, I suppose. Gloucester College? You know where that is?'

I shook my head. 'You'll have to give me directions.'

'It isn't far.' But he sounded sad, as if that was a bad thing rather than a good thing.

'You want to take a ride in momma first?' I said. 'See what the lady can do?'

His eyes scanned the dashboard, the rearview mirror on its slender column, the perfect geometry of clock and speedometer and tachometer and fuel gauge, all lined up like the instruments on a Spitfire. He nodded.

'What's the quickest way out of town?' I said.

'I don't know. Woodstock Road, probably.'

'Show me.'

It's hard to believe now, when the whole of southern England is pretty much one giant gridlock, but there was hardly any other traffic on the road that night. We blitzed north, past a blur of monster Victorian houses – looming gables; lights in weird places on the walls – like illustrations from a fairy story. In no more than a few minutes, we'd reached the ticky-tacky sprawl at the edge of the city, and could see a black billow of Oxfordshire countryside ahead. I pulled over on to the side of the road.

'So,' I said. 'The music.'

'What?'

'Where's it come from?'

He said nothing.

'This lady I was talking to,' I said. 'You know what she said? She said, the thing about people like you, musicians like you, is you're outsiders. But at least you have a voice. And what you do is, you use it to speak for the outcasts. The dudes who can't speak for themselves. You dig that?'

He looked at me. 'What dudes?'

'Shit, man, I don't know. I guess she means kids. Freaks. Junkies. You know.'

'And the ones *most* people can't see at all.'

Was it a question, or a statement? Either way, I didn't know what the hell he was talking about.

'Yeah,' I said. 'Maybe.'

He switched off, *bam*, and went quiet on me. Wherever he was, it was some place I couldn't follow him. After a minute or so I said,

'Ready to head back?'

'If you want to.'

'I'm just the chauffeur, man. I can drive all night, if that's what does it for you.'

He craned his head to look through the windshield. 'Why don't we go to Minster Lovell?'

'What's Minster Lovell?'

'I've never been there. But it's meant to be beautiful. And it can't be that far. It's only just beyond Witney.'

He pointed to a signpost. It said, I don't know, I don't remember exactly, Witney twenty miles or something.

'Well, we could,' I said. 'But we won't see a whole lot if we go now, will we?'

'It might be better in the dark.'

'You think? OK, let's make a real night of it then, why don't we? Get Mary Jane along for the ride.'

'What?' He glanced over his shoulder, as if he expected to see someone in back. I was confused. Was he joking again, or did he actually not know what the hell I meant? I reached under the seat for my stash. He watched in silence as I rolled a joint, lit up, took a couple tokes.

'Here you go,' I said, giving it to him.

I pointed the Austin Healey at Witney and gunned the engine. The noise – that deep brandy-and-cigars purr – was enough to make you shiver. I glanced over at Adam. He was pale and intent, a kid on a fairground ride, one hand holding the joint like he wasn't sure what to do with it, the other balled up on his knee. All righty: this was going to be the journey of the guy's life – a sneak preview of what was in store for him if he signed with me.

'Don't bogart that, man,' I said.

'What?'

I waggled my fingers at him. 'The j-stick.'

'Oh.' He hunched forward, drew on it furtively, like a twelve-year-old who didn't want Mom to see him trying his first cigarette, then handed it back again.

'Thanks.'

That was a strange trip. At first, we were in a rocket, hurtling silently through space, dodging the stars that zoomed toward us and then vanished into the void. And then, suddenly, after five miles, ten, maybe, we weren't moving at all, but sitting in a movie theatre, and watching the changing horizon, the sweep of oncoming headlights, projected on to a 360 degree screen. At some point I heard myself saying,

'You know what we need here? Popcorn.'

There was a pause, like the time-lapse in a transatlantic phone call. Then, dreamily, Adam said,

'OK, I'll go out and get some before the main feature. And a couple of Kia-Oras.'

You're probably thinking, that should have really blown my mind. But I was so stoned, at the time it just seemed funny. I started to laugh, the way I had at the club. Adam joined in. One of us would stop for a second or two, then the other one would set him off again. We carried on that way till we reached Witney. And then suddenly Adam was jabbing his finger and saying, 'Look! Look! There! *Minster Lovell, 2½.*'

That seemed to break the spell. Neither of us spoke for a minute or two. Then, like he thought we'd gone too far, and he wanted to bring some decorum back into the conversation, he said,

'Why are you here?'

'Same reason you are, man. I'm watching a movie.'

'No, I mean...' He pointed down towards the ground. '*Here?*'

'Girl named Trudy told me where you were playing. Said you were hot shit. So I came down to see you. And I'm glad I did.'

'No, but...*England*,' he said.

'Oh, well, that's a long story. It has something to do with music. Something to do with the draft. Plus there's some personal stuff in there, too.'

'But is this where you're from? Your family, I mean? Originally?'

'On my Mom's side, yeah. That's the Tate bit. Pretty much went over on the *Mayflower*.'

'Really?'

'Yeah. Well that's what I heard, anyway.'

'That's incredible.'

I was surprised, I remember – but not surprised enough to try to find out just *why* he found it incredible.

'And Finnegan…' I said. 'Well, you know what kind of a name that is.'

He nodded, closed his eyes, leaned back. He was quiet a long time. Then, slowly, like he was under hypnosis or something, he said, 'Two astronauts. They get in a spaceship, fly to the furthest reaches of the galaxy, land on a planet no one's ever seen before. They put on their spacesuits, open the door. And the moment they step outside, they realize they're home.'

An occupational hazard of dope smoking is that you hear a lot of bullshit. If anyone else had said that to me, I'd have laughed. But loaded as I was, I still had enough low animal cunning left to know that wouldn't be a smart thing to do to someone I was hoping to sign. So I just nodded and murmured,

'Very true.'

I don't think he heard me. He was too busy looking out the window. We'd just turned a corner, and there, looming through the naked branches of a clump of trees, was a ragged black hole torn out of the sky.

'Jesus!' I said, hitting the brakes. 'What the fuck is that!?'

'Minster Lovell Hall.'

'What happened to it?'

'It was abandoned, I think. In the eighteenth century.'

'Yeah, I'm not surprised,' I said. 'I'm ready to abandon it now. I've seen as much as I want.'

'Oh, no, let's go and look at it,' said Adam.

'It's raining, for fuck's sake.'

'No, it isn't.' He opened the door, put out his hand. 'Well, not very hard.'

I've been back to Minster Lovell a couple times since, and on a summer day, no question, it's romantic, in a National Geographic travelogue kind of a way – ruins; cute houses; a pub called the Old Swan; meadows leading down to a meandering river, with a name so beautiful you think somebody (probably J.R.R. Tolkien) must have made it up: the Windrush. But that night, jazzing on dope and beer and adrenalin, and with zero idea of where the hell I was, I had no desire to improve my acquaintance with the place. Any moment, I thought I might see Dracula landing on top of one of the busted towers, and I wouldn't know if he was really there, or it was just another scene from the Acapulco gold picture show.

'Do we *have* to do this?' I said.

'Yes. Come on. There's magic here. I can feel it.'

'Yeah? Well, tell you the truth, I'm not that crazy about magic.'

'You will be, Tate. Just give it a chance.'

It was the *Tate* that did it. Up till then, I wasn't sure he'd even registered my name. Now all at once it was like he was acknowledging that I was a person, that there was – or might be, anyway – some kind of a bond between us. It bumped me back to why I was there: not just to get stoned with a guy I'd given a ride to, but to sign an act to Wheatsheaf Records.

'OK,' I said, and I got out. Adam waits for me to come round to his side of the car. Then he puts a hand on my arm and says,

'You don't need a magician. Or a spell or anything. It just kind of seeps into you.' He shivers, as if he's not too wild about the idea himself. 'I've been in places like this before, and that's what happens.'

I followed him across I don't what you'd call it, a lawn or a field or something: that time of night, in the November spritz, it just looked like a pool of ink. The ground was squelchy underfoot, and we'd only gone like fifty yards when I started to feel my boots leak. I was cold – and yeah, OK, I was scared, too. It would've been hard not to be. I'd seen *The Hound of the Baskervilles* on TV when I was a kid, and every step I took I expected to find myself sinking into the Grimpen Mire.

A voice suddenly floated out of the darkness: 'Hello?'

I nearly had a fucking heart attack, only just managed to stop myself screaming. Then I heard it again, and realized it was Adam. I started to laugh. I couldn't help it. It was just pure relief.

'You shithead!' I yelled. 'Don't do that to me!'

'Sssh!' He was up to the building now, peering through a gap in the broken walls.

'You see something in there?' I called.

He flapped a hand, telling me to be quiet. OK, I thought, I am going to give the guy a taste of his own medicine. I tiptoed up behind him, took a deep breath and went '*Whoooo!*'

He barely moved.

'No,' he said. 'That's all wrong. You have to show some respect.'

'To who? What the fuck are you talking about?'

'The people here.'

I looked over his shoulder. All I could see was darkness, torn open here and there by weird-shaped holes and the remains of windows.

'Are you trying to freak me out?' I said.

He said nothing, but slipped through what was left of an arch and began picking his way between the stumps of pillars and old heaps of rubble. From the way he moved – nodding, stopping – you'd think he'd just arrived at a party. I pretty quickly figured that whatever was happening – or he *thought* was happening – in there, he wasn't shitting me. That left two possibilities: either he was stoned out of his head, or he was a crazy man. Oddly, the crazy option didn't bug me too much. Probably something to do with reading R.D. Laing, you know, *the world's so fucked up, the only sane people are the insane.* That seemed to make a kind of sense with Adam. And if that was his secret, the price he had to pay for his gift, so what? Crazy could be cool. Think Van Gogh. Think William Blake.

When he came out again he looked like he'd just been laid by the foxiest chick on the planet.

'Everything OK in there?' I said.

He nodded.

'Well, that's good, man,' I said, patting him on the back. 'Glad it worked out for you.'

'That stuff,' he said. 'The stuff we've been smoking. It's –' He shook his head wonderingly.

'Only the best,' I said.

'Normally I'd have been terrified out of my wits,' he said. 'But –'

He broke off, and drifted off someplace I couldn't join him. And that's where he stayed, all the way to the car, while I was trying to think how the hell I could get the train back on the track, and persuade the guy to do a deal with me. Neither of us spoke till I'd turned around, and we were heading out on to the road again. Then, out of the blue, he said,

'So, where do I sign?'

'Pardon me?'

'This contract of yours. Where is it? I'm ready to sign.'

Hey, I did it. Well, I almost did it. I was going to tell you the end of the story, how I took him back to his college and he climbed in over the wall like a naughty kid. But they just called my flight. So I guess you'll have to imagine that part for yourself. Think moss, rain, leather soles on wet stone.

OK. I'm out of here.

4

STUART DIXON

That's a rather odd pair of choices you give me: email, or record something and send it. In my world, if you wanted information from someone, you normally did him the courtesy of at least *offering* to come and see him in person. But perhaps I'm out of touch, and the triumph of technology has sent the last vestiges of good manners gurgling down the plughole.

In any event, yes: I did teach Adam Earnshaw in his first year, the English Literature *1830 – 1910* paper. I wish I could tell you that he was an outstanding student, but he wasn't. The only reason I remember him after all this time is that he was just plain *odd*.

To begin with, it really didn't strike me: he was just one of a more or less indistinguishable job lot of freshmen, all of whom started out as short-haired, tweed-jacketed chrysalises, and in the space of a few weeks turned into sub-Carnaby Street butterflies, complete with fashionably dishevelled Beatles-era mop-tops. It was only when I tried to engage with him that I began to notice the signs: the inaudible mumbling; the gnawed fingertips; the way his eyes flickered about when he walked into the room, unable to settle on anything for more than a couple of seconds. At first I just put it down to shyness. It was only several weeks into term that I realized the *real* problem was my approach to literature.

Roland Barthes was just getting into his stride at that point, and I'd been over to Paris a couple of times to hear him. Not just semiotics, but a lot of the ideas he went on to write about in *The Death of the Author*. I thought my students should at least know about him – and most of them, the brighter ones, anyway, found him exciting. But when I broached the subject with Adam Earnshaw, he just froze. I asked him what the matter was, and, painful stammering phrase by painful stammering phrase, it all came out. He loved the books – George Eliot; Thackeray; Hardy, even: the solid England they evoked – but the criticism completely confounded him. It wasn't just Roland Barthes, it was more or less the whole of the twentieth century. Nietzsche. Modernism. The unsustainability of the omniscient narrator.

I don't know what your background is (you're remarkably unforthcoming about it, I notice), so perhaps I should take a moment to join up the dots. Nietzsche signed God's death certificate – and all at once we found ourselves in uncharted territory, a place where no human culture had set foot before. It's the job of the novelist – the serious novelist – to *map* this frightening new landscape for us. The godlike view – the Olympian, George Eliot view, which allows the creator to look down on the world she has made and understand it in its entirety – is no longer available to us. The only possible truth now is partial, fractured, subjective.

And that's what seemed to drive Adam Earnshaw mad: the loss of the Olympian view. He felt there still had to be one, ultimate perspective from which everything made sense. And when I insisted that there wasn't, that from now all great art must be created in light of our godless condition, and follow its implications to their logical conclusion, it seemed to reduce him to – well, to despair.

What I remember best is the last time I spoke to him, our final tutorial. When he came in that day he was completely different: animated, smiling, talkative, even. For a minute or two I wondered whether he'd suddenly discovered drugs – which had just started to be the likeliest explanation for that kind of abrupt change of mood. And then, out of the blue, he produced a copy of Wilkie Collins's *The Woman in White*, and asked if I'd read it. Well, I had, but I didn't see it had any bearing on the texts or the ideas we'd been discussing. It's just a piece of superior hokum, really – full of evil baronets and sinister Italian counts and fainting heroines. The narrator is an impossibly gentlemanly drawing master called Walter Hartright. All that sets it apart from scores of Victorian sensation novels like it is the unusual structure, because – instead of telling the whole story himself – Hartright keeps handing the microphone to a range of other characters, so that they can relate particular episodes in which they were involved.

And this is what Adam Earnshaw latched on to. He thought that, by allowing Hartright to marshal all these different points of view, Collins was effectively offering a solution to the problem the Modernists struggled with fifty years later. I had painstakingly to explain that there was no comparison at all – that, unlike Woolf and Joyce and the rest, Collins hadn't used the form to reflect the loss of certainty, but merely as a cheap trick to entertain his readers, the way a filmmaker might use cuts and cross-fades. Perhaps I was a bit harsher than I should have been. But the idea that the answer to all the formal problems of modernism could be found in a mid-nineteenth century pot-boiler was just laughable.

His whipped-dog expression that day is my abiding memory of the man. After that, I have no clear recollection of him at all. Although I should add that when I heard, a couple of years later, that he'd disappeared, it surprised me that I didn't feel more surprised. In fact – just as you realize that some students were always destined to be bankers or civil servants – I could see that vanishing without trace was really the perfect career choice for him.

5
MELANIE NORRIS

Adam Earnshaw. God, that's going back. A real blast from the past.
But what I don't get is, why are you asking me? Did someone tell
you him and me were a thing? Cos if they did they were wrong. I didn't
even know him that well. Though in a funny way I suppose you could say
he changed my life.

Anyway. I don't mind. But if you're going to understand, you have to
know a bit about me first.

You ever been to Cowley? If not, you've probably seen places like it:
street after street of little three-up-and-two-downs, all just the same. Back
in the 50s and 60s, when I was growing up, it was still a motor town. The
BMC factory was its heart, the reason it was there at all in the first place:
the moment you stepped outside, you could feel it pulling at you, hear it
humming from those rows and rows of long buildings like a giant radiator.
Everyone's dad worked there. Mine was in the paint shop. He was a big
bloke, arms like beer kegs, a sloping belly that always made me think of
one side of a railway cutting. Once, when I was really little – we must have
had a lot of snow that winter – I remember imagining sliding down it on
a sledge. He smelt permanently of sweat. You don't meet fellows like that
any more. Well not much, anyway. But then, there were loads of them.
You just thought it was normal. Natural man-smell.

Outside, it was the works. Inside, everything revolved round him.
He'd have his tea, then – most evenings – meet his mates down the pub.
Sometimes we'd nag Mum to let us watch the telly while was out, but
whenever she did, she'd sit by the door, and as soon as she heard his footsteps, it was *off to bed with you, quick!* If he caught us in the living room

when he came in, there'd be hell to pay. There was something wrong, every night. And if it happened to be you, you knew you'd get a clip round the ear.

Here's some of the things he didn't like. Lip from my brother and me. Toffs. Bosses. Students. Vicars (limp-wristed soapy sams, the lot of them). Blacks coming over here, trying to get their dirty hands on our women and our jobs. The royal family. (Though that didn't stop him getting up and standing to attention with tears in his eyes whenever they played the national anthem. You just take things for granted when you're young, don't you, so I never asked him about it. But now I think he was probably remembering people who'd been killed in the war.)

Mum wasn't a hater, like him. She wasn't much of a liker, either, I suppose cos she was so worried the whole time. When I was a kid, I thought every mum must be like that: thin, stringy-haired, with a noisy tum that made her wince with pain and spend hours in the toilet. Even now, it still surprises me when I meet one who laughs a lot and enjoys her food.

School was all right. Most of the lessons were a bit boring, and a few kids – the clever ones, mainly, the Einsteins – got picked on. But you get that anywhere, don't you? And having an older brother meant that I was usually left alone. I had a best friend called Karen, and we'd go round together in break, and hide next to the gym, listening to her tranny. At first, pretty much all we could get was the Light Programme, so the main thrill was just knowing we were breaking the rules. But then the pirates came along – Radio Caroline, Radio Stella, Radio London – and that, whenever it was, 64 maybe, 65, was really the first crack in the wall. The first time I realized there *was* a wall, and I was trapped behind it, and there was a whole other world beyond it.

Not long after, Terry, that's my brother, left school and got a job at a printers. To get to and from work he bought this second-hand scooter with a CND sticker on the front. Dad didn't hold with nuclear weapons – the only people they helped, he thought, were the arms manufacturers and their capitalist cronies – but he told Terry that CND were a bunch of layabouts, and if people saw that sign outside the house it would give them the wrong idea about us. Terry wouldn't remove it. Dad started to undo his belt, but Terry stood his ground. They stared each other for God knows how long, then Dad looked away and slowly re-buckled his belt. That was the second crack in the wall. I knew then that just because Dad said something, that didn't mean it was necessarily so.

Terry began going out in the evenings, saying he was meeting friends. Usually he was home before Dad, but one night he didn't get back till after twelve. I was already in bed, but I could hear him and Dad shouting at each other in the hall. After a few minutes Dad clumped upstairs, effing and blinding and muttering something about the war. Not long after, Terry knocked on my door. He was red in the face and I could smell the drink on him. He sat on the end of my bed and told me that he'd been at a folk club in Oxford, where he'd met some students who'd made him see, in a blinding flash, what a shitty dead-end life he was going to have if he didn't leave, right now, tonight, and start living the way *he* wanted to. If I don't, he said, in thirty years I'll be just the same as Dad: a stupid angry ignoramus (I'd never heard that word before: I guessed he'd picked it up from one of the students), doing a useless meaningless job, living in a hamster cage, moaning about West Indians, and bullying my wife and kids.

I was shocked, of course, but I was excited, too. This – by a long way – was the biggest crack in the wall so far. It wasn't just that I couldn't have imagined either of us ever saying those things about Dad. It was also that Terry had got the idea from talking to *students* at *Oxford*. Oxford – the university, anyway, and there wasn't much else as far as I could see – was enemy territory, full of stuck-up posh boys. Not only Dad, but every-one I knew thought that,. And now, all at once, here was Terry, turning everything on its head. Maybe Oxford wasn't, after all, holding us back. Maybe it could actually be a way out for us.

Silly little girl: that's what I'd say if I could go back now. But I just have to remember: I was only sixteen. Please you remember it too.

Terry's plan was to go and stay with a friend until he could find a place of his own. He wouldn't tell me who the guy was or give me his number. But he said if I'd meet him at the folk club in Oxford – Poor Tom's – the next weekend, he'd bring me up to date, let me know what he was doing.

It took some organizing. Specially after what happened to Terry, I knew Dad would never let me go on my own, so I got Karen to ask me over to hers for the night. She didn't have a Dad – her Mum told her he'd died when she was a baby, and that's why she didn't have brothers and sisters, although later on Karen found out they hadn't even been married, and he'd gone off to Canada with another woman. Her Mum wasn't like mine: she liked me to call her Barbara, not Mrs Brewer, and sometimes when we were in Karen's room listening to music she'd come in and listen too. And she had a job, which most mums didn't when I was little, so usually Karen had to make her own tea. And she was out a lot at other times too. I wouldn't have thought of it then, she seemed much too old, but now I wonder if what she was doing was trying to meet another fellow. Anyway, I think when Karen and I said we wanted to go to a folk club together, she was actually quite relieved, cos it meant she could have a drink with *her* friends, without feeling guilty about it. Only thing was, we had to promise to be back by ten. She even gave us ten bob, so we'd have enough for the bus and the entrance charge and a couple of glasses of orangeade. She winked when she said *orangeade*.

Poor Tom's wasn't what I'd expected at all. I thought we might have to argue with the woman on the door, but when she asked how old we were and we said eighteen, she just nodded and let us in. Inside there was no stage, no bright lights, no people dancing, like they did on *Top of the Pops*: just a dingy smoky room at the back of an old shop. Christ, said Karen, grabbing my arm, where've you brought me? The Black Hole of Calcutta? I can't see a bloody thing. She sounded different. More grown-up. If I hadn't have known, I'd have thought it was her Mum talking.

A bleeding Jesus (that's what my Dad would have called him) was sitting in a pool of light at one end, singing in a whiney voice about a plough-boy who went for a soldier. The rest of the place was dark, except when somebody struck a match – and that just made it worse, because the flare would dazzle your eyes. We blundered around, squinting into everyone's faces. There were all sorts there. A group of fellows I'd seen around Cowley; dopey-looking girls who smiled back through curtains of hair, like you'd suddenly popped up in a dream they were having; a couple of bald chaps old enough to have fought in the war. And mixed in among the rest – you couldn't miss them, even though they tried to keep their voices down – four or five posh boys from the university. When I peered at them, they didn't do what posh boys had always done before: glance at my clothes and hair, then turn away like they were stepping over a piece of dog shit. One of them even gave me this jaunty little salute, finger to forehead, and said good evening.

We found Terry standing at the end of the bar, staring at the bleeding Jesus and jigging his head in time to the music. He was smoking a big droopy fag that didn't look like any roll-up I'd ever seen. It took a lot of nudging and tugging at his sleeve to break the spell and get him to notice me. When he did, it was like he'd forgotten the arrangement we'd made and was surprised to see me – and even more surprised to see Karen. I explained that she was my alibi. He said I should leave home, like him, and then I wouldn't need an alibi. And Karen said, how could she, you thicko? She's still at school, isn't she? Or are you so stoned out of your head that you forgot?

That first evening we didn't do much – just drank the two half-pints Terry bought us, and listened to him talking about the music. This was the real thing, he said, not the fake rubbish you heard on telly and radio, which was nothing more than a way for the record company bosses to get their hands on our money. But people were waking up, finally realizing the whole system was just designed to oppress and exploit them. The revolution, when it came, and it wouldn't be long now, would start in places like this. I told him he sounded a bit like Dad, and he said that was totally different, Dad was just an angry old man, trapped inside his own head, who blamed black people and students for his problems, cos that's what he was conditioned to think, when really they were on the same side he was. The only way to be free, *really* free, was to change your consciousness, and that meant turning on – and Dad would never do that, not to save his life.

I liked the word *revolution*. But it wasn't the politics made me decide to go back. And it wasn't the music, either – or at least, not to begin with, though I liked some of it, specially the sea shanties. No, what did it was the atmosphere. It was the only place I'd ever been where, the moment you were in there, all the barriers disappeared, wham, like that, and everyone was just the same, and nobody judged anybody else. Sort of how it would be if you were a nudist, I suppose, and you could walk around everywhere without any clothes on and wouldn't have to be ashamed about it.

After the second or third time, when Terry turned us on, and people, complete strangers, were passing round joints and laughing together, it got even better. Soon it had become this regular thing for us: every Saturday I'd stay over at Karen's and we'd take the bus down to Poor Tom's and get stoned, and feel, yeah, this is it, something new is happening here, a new way of living, and we're part of it. I kept worrying that one weekend Dad would finally guess what we were up to and tell me I couldn't go, but he never did. I think now that maybe he'd been more shaken by Terry leaving than he let on. He still grumbled, but he didn't throw his weight around as much as he had before. And even though from time to time he'd raise his hand and say *shut it, girl!*, like he had when I was a kid, he never hit me again.

The big moment came after we'd been going there a couple of months. I shouldn't blame Adam Earnshaw for it, it wasn't his fault, I'm sure he had no idea. And there was a lot of other stuff going on that evening, too – another guy, and some Moroccan hash that Terry had got from somewhere that sent me way up, the highest I'd ever been. But looking back from here to there, I can see that the night I first heard him was a fork in the road for me, and that if he hadn't been singing I probably wouldn't have gone the way I did.

He was the second act, and when he came on – stooping like an old man, and not looking anyone in the eye – I didn't pay him any attention. But the instant he launched into *Scarborough Fair*, it was suddenly like he was singing just for me, that's how it felt, beaming the words direct into – well, I don't know what you'd call it, my soul or something. I'd heard the song before, but now, suddenly, I was *in* it. *I* was *the one who lives there*. It was *me* who had once been a true love of his.

I know. Sounds bonkers. But I was very, very stoned.

I looked at Karen. She was staring at him, mouth drooping.

God, I said, who is that? She shook her head. No idea. But he's really groovy, isn't he?

She used words like that. Words she'd picked up from watching Cathy McGowan on *Ready, Steady, Go!*

And then this college boy standing next to us – he's a real dandy, all dolled up in a velvet jacket and a silk scarf – he turns to us and says, that's

Adam Earnshaw. So we say, yeah? Where's he from? And the guy says, he's in my college. Gloucester College. Usually he plays during the week. You should come then. As a treat for the rest of us. And Karen giggles and says, what do you mean? And he says, well, you're a couple of very pretty girls, aren't you? Can I get you a drink?

Even then, I knew how corny it was. You heard stories about it all the time in Cowley: how some snotty college boy had got a girl drunk, taken advantage of her, then dumped her, leaving her up the spout. In the back of my head Mum's voice was playing, like a recording, don't do it, he's not your sort, men are only after one thing. But she – this is what I told myself – was talking about the bad old days, and this was now, and everything had changed. We were listening to the proof at that very moment, weren't we – a college boy sitting not ten feet away, singing to *me*, as if all the old differences between us had just melted into nothing.

So instead of telling velvet man to get lost, we both said yes, we'd have a half, and he said really, just a half?, and my name's Jonty, by the way. And then, a few minutes later, he said he was going on to a party after, and it should be good, and would we like to come? And Karen and me looked at each other, and I said, it's a shame, maybe another time, we have to get back. Hang on a minute, said Karen, have you got a tanner for the phone? He gave her one, and she slipped out. When she came back she said, that's all right, we can come. And when I prodded her and said what do you mean, she leaned across and whispered that she'd rung her Mum, and told her we'd met a friend from school, and we'd be staying over with her.

The party was in this humungous old house in the Banbury Road that had been divided into flats. I'd never been in such a big room: there must have been forty people there, most of them boys, just a half a dozen prim girls standing around looking like tourists who didn't understand the local customs, but there was still space to walk about. In one corner was a record player, booming out something with a lot of bass that I hadn't heard before. A few guys and a couple of girls were dancing, if you can call it that: the way they jerked their arms reminded me of the little pipe-cleaner men my granddad used to make for us when we were small.

A fat bloke with a red face – it's weird how clearly I can still see him, like someone stamped him onto my brain – was sitting opposite the door when we walked in. Ah, Jonty, he said, in this horrible drawly voice. You're indefatigable. Up with the owl and off to market, while the rest of us are sunk in hoggish sloth. And what an eye you have. Only the freshest produce, every time. How ever do you do it?

I didn't know what he was talking about. But you didn't need to, to tell he was being rude. If I hadn't been stoned I'd have turned round, right then, and walked out again. But it was like the hash had put this kind of balloon around me, protecting me.

Oh, fuck off, Sandy, said velvet man. Behave yourself, or I shan't introduce you.

The fat bloke laughed. It sounded phlegmy, like something bubbling on the stove. Forgive me, he said, but I have to wonder if that's a price worth paying? I assume you propose to keep one for yourself, and offer the other to, who shall we say? He glanced round, then nodded at this fair-haired chap who looked like a cricketer. Ah, yes, he said. Of course. Tim Bruce. So what would an introduction gain me, beyond ten minutes conversation about dog-racing? Not behaving myself promises to be far more diverting.

You could see the cricketing chap prick up his ears. Did I hear someone taking my name in vain? he said, coming over and smiling at Karen and me. Don't pay any attention to Sandy. He's drunk. And he's very little better when he's sober. Can I get you a glass of wine?

He was different, I could tell that at once – not only from the fat bloke and velvet man, but from all the other boys I'd met, too. When we got in a muddle about what wine to have, he didn't just laugh at us, but helped us to find something we'd like. He asked questions like he was actually interested in the answers. When Karen went off to dance with velvet man – I saw them out of the corner of my eye, and wanted to shout, that's it girl, you show them how to do it – Tim Bruce stayed and talked to me. He wanted to know where I lived, where I went to school, everything about me. When I said what my Dad did, he went, Oh, really? My parents have got a Morris Oxford Traveller. Perhaps your father painted it. Wouldn't that be funny? I'll look next time I'm home, and see if I can find his signature.

What? I said. I'm only joking, he said. He looked over at velvet man. So how did you and Karen meet Jonty? So I told him and he said, I've never been to Poor Tom's. Is it good? Yeah, I said it's far out. We saw this amazing singer there called Adam Earnshaw. Adam Earnshaw? he said. Honestly? Yeah, I said. Why? Oh, he said, the coincidences are coming thick and fast tonight. Adam Earnshaw's in my college. I don't know him terribly well. Seems a quiet sort of a chap. But from what you say, I must obviously get along there and hear him. Would you like to come with me one evening? And I said, Yeah. All right.

After that, things start to move more and more in-and-out of focus. We danced for a bit, and then he asked me if I needed to be anywhere, and I said no, and he took me into a smaller room and we lay on a mattress on the floor. The lights were off, but we could see another couple under the window, and hear the noises they made trying not to make a noise.

I don't know if it was that, or because he was too drunk, or just (though this idea wouldn't have occurred to me then: he seemed like the most confident person I'd ever met) that he was nervous, but whatever the reason we didn't do it that night. In the morning he said he was sorry, and hoped he hadn't been a disappointment to me, and it wouldn't happen again. And I said it was all right, and I hadn't been expecting anything. And I kissed him, and told him I liked him very much. He said he had to get back to college, but he'd see me at Poor Tom's the next weekend, and find somewhere we could stay afterwards.

Karen was still asleep somewhere in the house, so I left without her. As I closed the door behind me I heard bells from a nearby church. And I remember thinking, right, Mel, the wall's down. It was like I could actually see it, the place where it'd stood, and everything it had stopped me from reaching. And now here I was, stepping out over the rubble into that new world.

First thing we decided to do, Karen and me, was get fixed up. Easy enough, if you were a posh Chelsea bird and could go to the Brook Street Clinic. But for us it was the FPA, where they weren't supposed to give you a prescription unless you were married. So we went shares on a cheap wedding ring from Woolworths. She used it first, then came back out into the waiting room and gave it to me. The receptionist noticed what was going on and winked at us, and the doctor, this older Scottish woman in glasses who'd probably never had sex with anyone in her life, stared at the ring like she knew she'd seen it five minutes ago, and got really sniffy with me when I told her what I wanted. But in the end she gave it to me – though even then it cost me two bob or something a month, until Tim said *he'd* pay.

This bit's hard. I'm not going to give you all the gory details. Just enough for you to get the general picture.

Nearly a year: that's how long it lasted. Well, *lasted* isn't quite the word. What I mean is, it was almost a year from the day me and Tim met to the day we finally said goodbye. But in between there were different stages, lots of ups and downs.

Stage one – that would have been the few weeks following the party in Banbury Road – was pretty much one long up. We went to Poor Tom's together, and Tim really started to get into it, and asked me all kinds of stuff about the different acts, where they came from, the sort of folk they sang. And when I told him, he'd squeeze my hand and say, well, all I can say Mel, is thank God I've got you here, to explain it all to me. Cos if I didn't, I'd be absolutely lost. One evening he went up to Adam Earnshaw after the gig and said, Adam, I want you to meet Mel, I've told you about her, remember, she's a big fan. And we had a drink with him, which was exciting – though he kept looking at the clock, like he had to be somewhere else, and left after about ten minutes. I wondered if it was me, if he'd thought I was boring. But Tim said, no, he's like that with everyone. Premature evacuation. Actually, he lasted longer tonight than he does usually. He must like you.

Afterwards, we'd go to this place he used to borrow from a friend – a third year, who had a room in a house in Jericho, and most weekends was in London, visiting *his* girlfriend. I don't know if I was Tim's first, but he was mine – and you know what that's like, when you really like the other person, and you both start to figure out what it is you're meant to be doing.

And sometimes we'd just talk – though mostly that meant him talking and me listening. Once, when I teased him about studying law, he got very up himself – I'd never seen him like that before, and I never did again. A lot of people, he said, thought the only reason anyone became a lawyer was to get rich. But what they didn't understand – and he wanted *me* to understand this, too; it was important *everybody* understood it – was that the law was the basis of a civilized society. Without a system of rules like that, we wouldn't be able to sleep peacefully in our beds, earn money, buy and sell things, bring up our children, walk safely in the street. It was all very well being an idealist, but if we lived the way the hippies wanted, we'd soon be back in the jungle. Oh, back in the jungle, eh? I said, in this fake posh voice. Well, we couldn't have that, could we? And he stared at me for a moment, like he was really angry, and then he laughed.

Sometimes he'd go out and buy the Sunday papers, so we could look through them in bed while we were drinking our coffee. And he'd pick out a few stories to read, and explain them to me. I really ought to know a bit about what was happening in the world, he said – and that was something he could help me with, the way I helped him with folk music. And then suddenly he'd say, *now, to business.* And he'd put the papers down, and I'd hear them slapping on to the floor as he rolled towards me, and we'd do it again.

So where did it start to go wrong? If I'm honest, I don't think it did, not exactly: it's more that it never really started to go right. Or maybe I should say, it *couldn't* go right, because it was never going where I thought it was. We had fun together, lots of good scx; he bought me meals, told me how pretty I was, said what a lucky chap he was to have me. He'd laugh at my silly jokes, pat my bum or ruffle my hair and say, very good, Mel.

But there were too many missing pieces. Stage two, I suppose – the longest stage – was when I seemed always to be reaching out for those slippery bits, hoping to get my fingers on them so I could start putting them into place. It was useless: didn't matter how I approached it, what I said, he would just turn into a jellyfish every time. His parents were coming up to Oxford to see him. Maybe I could meet them, then? Hm, probably not the right time: they'd be going out to lunch for a family discussion. Fair enough: how about a drink with his friends? No, they were all busy at the moment, preparing for exams. All right: then why didn't he take me to his college May Ball? They wouldn't be doing exams then, would they? That's months away: let's talk about it later. Only we never did.

When he came back for his second year everything was different. I'd left school by that point and got a job – more just a tea-maker and general dogsbody than anything else – in a BMC showroom. Tim had been abroad somewhere and got a nice tan. And he had a car now, too – an old Riley

Pathfinder, like the police used to use when I was a kid. The first time he took me out in it, soon as we started off, it was like someone else was behind the wheel – a man I didn't really know. Before, most of the time, I could tell just by looking at him what he wanted: sex, a cup of coffee, something to eat. But now, sitting there in his Riley, weaving through the traffic, there was something new pushing him, something I didn't recognize at all. What is this? I said. You Inspector Bruce of the Yard all of a sudden, hot on the trail of a tasty villain? But he didn't even answer.

He dropped me off at a bus stop a safe distance from Cowley. Next weekend, he said, as I was getting out, instead of Poor Tom's, why don't we go down to Dorchester and stay in a place I know there? It's a pretty spot, and the food's good. Only thing is, they're a bit old-fashioned, so we'd better be Mr and Mrs. Have you got a ring you can use? Course I have I said. How'd you think I got the pill?

All that week I told myself stories. He's grown up over the summer. He's had time to think, and realized you're the girl he wants to be with. He's driving you down to Dorchester so he can propose. In the bedroom, or over dinner, he's going to take the ring off your finger and slip on the one he's bought. Here, darling. Let's be Mr and Mrs for real.

I know, I know. Half of me feels exactly what you're probably feeling, hearing this. And the other half's back in my seventeen-year-old skin, all trembly and weak-kneed and ready to blush at the drop of a hat.

It was a romantic old stone pub, with dark polished beams. There was a log fire in the dining room, and candles, and lots of brass winking at you out of the darkness. I think the owner – an old bloke with a floppy bow tie and hands blue with cold – who served us himself, thought maybe we were on our honeymoon. He kept calling me Mrs Bruce, the way you'd call someone who's just got a knighthood, *sir*. Here we are, Mrs Bruce. Have we finished, Mrs Bruce? Once when he did that I smiled across at Tim, but he didn't smile back.

It wasn't till after breakfast the next morning that I finally gave up hope. I didn't cry, not at that point, I just went very quiet. In the car on the way back, it took Tim about ten minutes to notice. Then he said, what's the matter, Mel? Didn't you enjoy yourself?

And then the tears came. And everything else, too. *Marriage?* he said.

We never talked about *marriage*. You can't ever have thought that was on the cards. And I said, why not? And he blew out his cheeks and ran his fingers through his hair and said, Oh, God, I'd no idea. Honestly. I'm sorry.

After that, all I wanted to do was get home as quick as possible. He must have felt the same, cos he put his foot down and swung the Pathfinder along those tight little roads like a rally car. Neither of us spoke another word till he stopped at Carfax and said, All right, I'll let you out here. Sorry it had to end like this. But no hard feelings, eh? And he leaned across and said, Just a kiss, for old times' sake?

I grabbed my bag, got out of the car and slammed the door.

You know what I'm going to say, said Karen.

I did. She had a boyfriend at the works now, and they were planning to get married as soon as he'd finished his apprenticeship, and she'd been telling me for months I was living in cloud-cuckoo-land if I thought I'd ever be more to Tim than a bit on the side, and I should dump him before he dumped me.

But I love him, I said. No you don't, she said. You love the car and the posh food and the idea of living in a big house and having enough money to buy all your clothes at Bazaar. No, I said, it isn't just that. Yes, it is, she said. Trust me. I know. I knew the first time I saw you with him. You need to forget it. The longer you leave it, the harder it'll be to get your feet back on the ground.

But I couldn't forget it. I hung around his college, half hoping to get a glimpse of him, half dreading it. Once I actually did see him, coming out with a smart-looking college girl. I tried to hide behind a car, but he spotted me. So – what else could I do? – I went over and said hello. Oh, hello, he said. And then turning to the girl, Carol, this is Mel. She's a big fan of Adam's. Probably lying in wait for him, hoping to get his autograph. And he laughed, like seeing me hadn't affected him at all.

For a few days after that, I thought I was going to die. I stopped eating. I called in sick at work and just lay in my room, crying myself stupid. The second day my Mum came up and said, what's wrong, Mel, you're not pregnant, are you. I told her, no, it isn't that – but it was a real struggle not to add, but I wish it *was*, cos then he'd *have* to marry me.

Then one night when I couldn't sleep it all got too much. I went in the bathroom and counted the aspirin in the big bottle we kept there. There were 27. I didn't know how many it would take, but I was pretty sure that wouldn't be enough. As I was closing the cabinet again, I suddenly caught sight of myself in the mirror on the door, and it really shocked me. What the hell was I doing, standing there at three in the morning, looking like something they pulled out of the sea and thinking about killing myself?

The next day, I went round to see Tim. I'd never been to his room in college before. He'd always said it would be *a bit difficult*. So I'd no idea how to find it. I hung around the entrance, but I didn't have the nerve to ask anyone. And then suddenly I heard this voice behind me saying hello Mel.

I turned round. It was Adam. He was with a chap called Roddy, a sort-of friend of Tim's that I'd seen a couple of times at Poor Tom's. Adam asked me what I was doing there. When I told him, Roddy looked really uncomfortable, like he knew what had happened and didn't know what to say to me. Sorry, he said, I've got to go, and shot off. But Adam put his hand on my arm and said, come on, I'll show you where Tim lives. It was up a poky old staircase, a lot shabbier than I expected. But it turned out Tim wasn't in. So Adam said would I like to come and wait in his room?

It sounds daft, but it was almost a surprise to find he actually *had* a room. You kind of expected him to sleep out under the stars, or in the back of a lorry somewhere, with his guitar at his side. We went outside again and up another staircase. His room was tucked away on the top floor, like someone had added it on at the last moment. There was a bed, a desk stacked with books, a little table with a kettle and mugs on it, and two chairs either side of a gas fire. Next to one of them were an open notebook and a pen, like he was in the middle of working on something. Adam still wasn't a star exactly, but for a guy who'd made a name for himself locally and was about to release his first EP, it all seemed a bit ordinary studenty.

Sit down, Mel, he said. You're busy, I said. I don't want to – You're not, he said. Not what? Not whatever it is you don't want to be, he said. It's fine.

I sat down. You want a cup of tea? he said. No, I said. He nodded and sat in the other chair. So, he said. Tell me. And I don't know why, but I did. It all just came pouring out. The only other person I'd talked to about it was Karen, but then I'd kept my armour on, to protect myself when she said, well, what did I tell you? But now there was nothing to hold me back, and I heard myself saying things I never expected to tell anyone. And then I'd break down and cry, sniffing and shaking like a little kid, until I could get my breath back enough to say the next thing. After a minute or two he came over and knelt down next to the chair and put his arms round me, which only made me cry harder. And we stayed like that for I don't know how long, while I sobbed and stuttered and hiccupped my way through to the end.

When I'd finished he said, I'm sorry. He squeezed me, then got up and went back to his own chair. Tim's been in a bit of an ostrichy mood all week, he said. But he wouldn't say why. So I could only guess. Now I know.

Do you think he's missing me, then? I snivelled. *Yes*, was what I was expecting. *I'm sure he is.* Instead, he thought about it for a bit, then shook his head and said, I don't know, Mel. I'm as lost as you are. We're both in the same boat. Well, not the same boat. Adjacent boats. But we've pitched up on the same beach. He laughed. That took me by surprise. No, sorry, he said. Forget the boats. Situation. We're in a similar situation. We've both ended up in a world where we feel we ought to belong. Or at least ought to understand the language. Only we don't, do we? We're strangers.

Before then, I'd never thought much about Adam and girls. I'd seen him once or twice with another singer called Carrie Bateman, but I'd no idea if she was his girlfriend. I didn't know if musicians even *had* girlfriends and boyfriends, the way the rest of us did. But now this really way out idea suddenly hit me. It sounds crazy, but I was so confused and torn up that at the time, sitting opposite him in his room, it seemed to make a kind of sense. What if the whole problem had started that first evening I heard Adam at Poor Tom's? What if I'd been right then, and he *had* been singing to me, because he could see we were meant to be together? Only I was stupid and didn't understand, so I took a wrong turning and ended up with the wrong guy instead. And perhaps what *this* was, was life giving me another chance.

Why are you a stranger? I said. Oh, he said, cos I grew up in Africa. I always thought of England as home, thought I'd *feel* at home when I got here. But I don't. It's as if the home's still here, but everyone around me now thinks they're living somewhere else. I didn't know what he was talking about. He must have seen, cos he sort of shrank into himself, like a tortoise that's stuck its head out too far. Anyway, he said, I'll talk to Tim, and see if I can get him to explain. And then I'll write to you. He picked up the notebook and turned to a new page. Here, he said. Put your address in here.

That was a weird few days. I was like this table tennis ball, held up on a gush of water. At some point, I knew, the water'd be turned off, and I'd end up on the ground somewhere. But where? Where did I *want* to end up? With Tim again, business as usual, *look, I'm sorry, I've been a bastard, forgive me*? Or with Adam, *Mel, ever since I first saw you, I knew…?*

The truth is, I couldn't decide. You probably think that makes me a bitch. But really it just makes me stupid. Cos I honestly convinced myself that in some mysterious way life would make the right decision for me.

I went back to work, but my boss must've thought I'd been replaced by a zombie. All the time I was there my chest felt tight, like I had asthma. I only started to breathe properly again after I got home and checked the post. There was always this strange mixed feeling when I saw there was nothing for me. Part of it was disappointment, of course. But the other part was relief, because it meant the moment of truth had been delayed, and I wouldn't fall to earth for another night.

By the weekend, I still hadn't had a letter. On the Saturday, it bucketed down all day, so I stayed in my room, listening to Radio Stella and trying not to think. It was already almost dark outside when I heard someone ringing the doorbell. I thought it might be Karen, so I went down to answer it. Standing on the step, his coat pulled over his head, was Adam. Hello, he said. I was going to write, but then I thought it would be better to do it in person. Do *what*? I thought. But before I had time to ask my Dad came out into the hall. Who is it? he wheezed. No one, I said. Just a friend. What, Karen? he said. No, not Karen. I caught the smell of him as he walked up behind me. Oh, I see, he said, peering out. This is him, is it? Your fancy man? Finally gracing us with his presence? He's not my fancy man, I said. His name's Adam. What? said Dad. You think we're stupid, do you? Didn't realize something was going on? Sorry, said Adam, but you're making a mistake. Mel's not my girlfriend. We – No, said Dad. I dare say she isn't. More like your tart. Your bit of rough, is that it? Oh, for God's sake, Dad, I said. Come in, Adam, quick. He's not coming in here, said Dad. Course he is, I said. Look at him. He's soaked. He'll catch his death. I don't care if he does, said Dad. I won't have him in my house. Oh, for fuck's sake! I said. And I grabbed my coat and stormed out, slamming the door.

Sorry, I said. Sorry about my dad. I hate him. Adam shook his head. It's hard for him. No, it isn't, I said. It's hard for *us*. Me and Terry. Specially me. What's his name? said Adam. Jim, I said. Why'd you want to know that? But he just shook his head again.

The pubs weren't open yet, so we went round to Karen's. She wasn't in, but her Mum was. She looked at Adam a bit oddly, and it wasn't just his wet clothes: she obviously thought the same as my Dad, only in her case she didn't mind about it. Quick, she said, into the bath with you. You can change in Karen's room, I won't peep, promise. Then I'll put your things in front of the fire, and Mel can bring them up to you when they're dry.

And that's how Adam and me ended up sitting side by side on Karen's bed, him all pink from the hot water, and dressed only in an old terry towel bathrobe of Barbara's that didn't come down as far as his knees. Sorry, he said. I should have written after all, shouldn't I? And that's when I knew it wasn't going to be, *Mel, I knew from the moment I saw you…*

Doesn't matter, I said.

Only I did speak to Tim, he said. Finally. He didn't want to talk about it. But I cornered him. And – I wish he'd had the guts to come and explain to you himself. But he didn't. So –

So no, *look, I'm sorry, I've been a bastard*, either.

I told him how upset you were, said Adam. And Tim just went, you think I don't know that? Of course I bloody do. I can't sleep for thinking about her. But how's it going to help the poor kid if we just keep going over and over it? Least said, soonest mended. It's hard, but that's life. She'll understand soon enough. That it was for the best.

There were tears in Adam's eyes. I reached out and took his hand.

I told Tim *I* didn't understand, he said. But he said that was because I was a boy from the bushveld. *You'd* know because you grew up here, where these sorts of things are perfectly normal, happen all the time.

What sorts of things? I said.

Adam hesitated. Then he said, I'm telling you this because I've realized – I've realized – the only way we can get our feet securely on *terra firma* – you and me – He stopped and shook his head, like he'd lost his way. Relationships, he said. Between men like him and girls like you. That's what he's talking about. And what makes it so awful is that he's a nice chap, he isn't a monster. So he has to persuade himself it's all right. Both sides get something out of it, and no harm done. The fox enjoys the hunt as much as the hounds. Only it doesn't, does it? What? I said. The fox, he said. Enjoy it.

I started to cry. But at the same time I felt weirdly calm, like something that had always been a blur had at last come into focus. I reached inside the bathrobe and touched his shoulder. He put his hand over mine, squeezing it through the cloth.

Why don't we? I said. What? he said. You know, I said. He thought about it for a bit. Then he shook his head. I don't think that would be a good idea. Why not? I said. Don't you like me? Of course I like you. But that would just make things even more complicated, wouldn't it? I burrowed my face in his neck. I'd like to, I said. I want to. He stroked my hair. I know. But –

Don't let me interrupt anything, said Barbara outside the door, but your clothes are dry. Adam and me looked at each other and laughed. Or cry-laughed. I was cry-laughing.

The first time as tragedy, the second time as farce, he said. Or is it the other way round?

I've been wondering what he meant ever since.

6
DANNY PACK

What are you? One of those sad nerds that comb through the credits on old album covers, thinking that's cooler than standing on a station platform, jotting down engine numbers? I can't think of anyone else would be interested, not after this long.

But yeah, since you ask: I do remember him. I was the engineer on *Our Dancing Days*, back at the start of 1967. Can't say it's among my most treasured memories. But then again, the guy was a musician. And in my experience, without exception, musician = tosser.

Anyway, I'll give you ten minutes. That's about as much wistful song-smith as I can stand now. It'll be a bit of a jumble, but you'll just have to take it or leave it.

Bah, bah, bah. Right…Adam Earnshaw…

Thin, pale, worried-looking, like he was constantly thinking he might have left the gas on. A man of few words, most of them *no* or *I need a smoke*. But when you penetrated the miasma of dope fumes and *aren't-I-mysterious* silence, you'd find he was just as up himself as the pretentious young fucks droning on about candy floss typewriters and ships made of caramel. Head full of giants and pixies and God knows what. And he was so fucking *solemn* about it all.

One thing I will say for him, though, fair's fair, credit where credit's due: he always turned up sober and on time, carrying a clean hankie and ready to rock. And believe me, when you've dealt with as many tripped-out primadonnas and cleaned up as much vomit as I have, that makes him an 11/10 star.

So yeah, he was a soppy git, but not the kind of complete arsehole who makes going to work a nightmare. That distinction went to Tate Finnegan, who'd hired me to do the recording. The idea was to produce a limited-edition EP – goopy *Annabelle, Dancing*, and five folk covers – and, as Tate put it, slip it quietly into the bloodstream, and let it start to find its own cult audience. What made Adam's live act so mind-blowing, he said, was its intimacy, so he wanted the sound to be close up, as if the listener was right there with him, sitting just the other side of a table. OK, I said, I'll see what I can do. So I softened the acoustics, fiddled with the position of the mike – till eventually it was about six inches from Adam's face – and kept the levels down.

But was that enough? Not for Tate Finnegan, it wasn't.

Adam did the first track in a single take; but when I asked Tate if we should move on, he said no, he wanted me to play it back to him again. He listened for about ten seconds, then shook his head. It still wasn't *intimate* enough. I told him we couldn't make it any more intimate without getting inside the listener's skull. OK, he said, do that.

So I went back into the room and continued fiddling. And that was where the trouble started. Whenever I made a change, I'd ask Adam to play and sing a few bars so we could check the effect. Always the same five lines:

> *Annabelle*
> *Tripping through the daisy ring*
> *Taking wing*
> *Sweet and wild*
> *Fairy child*

He was fine the first few times – I wasn't: I was going daisy-ring crazy – but then he said, if he did it any more, he wouldn't be able to perform properly. You couldn't chop a song up like that: it was a complete thing in itself, a journey, and you had to be able to *live* it as you sang, or it would sound false.

'What you talking about?' said Tate.

'It's like an actor,' said Adam. 'You wouldn't ask him to say *To be or not to be* again and again and again, and then expect him to deliver the whole speech, would you?'

'What,' said Tate, 'you think you've written fucking *Hamlet*, do you?'

Tate Finnegan was a funny bugger: he loved swaggering round London playing the brash American; but he also carried a pair of invisible kid gloves, which – when he was trying to get the best out of some opinionated, insecure young musician (and what other kind was there?) – he could slip on at a moment's notice. So I was surprised that on this occasion he didn't bother to disguise how pissed off he was. Maybe he felt Adam had wrong-footed him, somehow, made him feel stupid. Anyway, he told me renting the studio and paying for me was costing him big bucks, and we couldn't afford to fuck around. And he stomped out to lunch, saying by the time he got back, he expected the problem to be fixed.

After he'd gone I said, why don't you give that stuff a rest, play something else? So Adam did, just in time to save my sanity. Not a folk standard, like he was doing for the album: a song about a girl on belladonna who picks up a hitchhiker in her car. I couldn't really get my head round it – it was full of wacko lyrics and strange chords – but at least it wasn't *Annabelle, Dancing*. What the hell was that? I said when he'd finished. Just something I wrote. What's it called? Doesn't have a name yet. You got any others? A couple. Well, play them, all the way through. I won't interrupt. Forget I'm even here.

I set the tape running, then sat back. He finger-picked his way through a long introduction, then launched into a melancholy slice-of-life ballad – I've forgotten what it was about exactly: I was too busy concentrating on the quality of the sound – with a disturbing, syncopated rhythm that made you feel you were being hypnotized. Song two was equally unsettling: a series of unexpected lurches that seemed to leave you dangling vertiginously over a sheer drop, before the boat righted itself and threw you back down on the deck.

Such was the dynamic range that, by the end, I'd finally figured out what I had to do. Using coats and blankets stretched over a framework of mike stands, I improvised a kind of tent round Adam, to squeeze out the last traces of echo. When it was all in place I got him to play *Scarborough Fair* for me. There, I said, that should satisfy him. If it doesn't, I'm going to look for a new job.

Adam laughed. Can I have the tape of the other songs? The ones that won't be on the album? So I asked him, Has Tate heard them? He shook his head. Don't you want him to? I said. Not at the moment. Why not? I said. But he just shook his head again. So I gave it to him.

I was right: when Tate heard the result, he said yeah, man, you did a great job. And several people when the record came out told me they felt as if Adam was singing to them inside their own heads. *Annabelle, Dancing* turned out to be a surprise sort-of hit, got a lot of airtime on the pirates. But, for all the hard work, the EP only sold a few hundred copies. I don't know if Adam was disappointed, or relieved not to have the attention. Both, I'd guess.

So there you go. Me and Adam Earnshaw. The end.

Happy trainspotting.

7

RUFUS STRANGE

Kudos, as they say now. I'm well impressed. Getting my real name – well, that's probably not too hard, given the number of trivia-lovers there are out there, sitting on their fairy hoards of obscure music trivia. But then tracking me down, finding my email address: that's something else. I don't know how you did it – but good job.

The name, by the way, just in case you're thinking, *what kind of an arrogant pillock would call himself Rufus Strange?* – that wasn't my idea, it was the Major's. As far as I can remember, he did the same thing to pretty much all the Stella DJs. How it worked was, they'd call you in for an interview – just you and the Major and the station manager – and if you got the job, the Major would light up a Players and peer at you through the smoke and say, *we'd like you to start next week. The only trouble is the moniker.* And that was that: take it or leave it. So I took it. And I'm glad I did. You wouldn't think it to look at him – you know, very proper, suit, tie, moustache – but he had a real fingertip feel for the music, the Major. Nineteen sixty-five, sixty-six, sixty-seven, he could see the way things were going. And he wanted a show that would do for Stella what Peel was doing for Radio London. Ta-taa! Introducing *Strange Sounds!* Lasted almost thirty years, that show, first on Stella, then on Radio One, then on Magenta. It *was* me, professionally speaking. So if you use any of this stuff, here's my only condition: you call me Rufus Strange, rather than you-know-who.

OK: time to board the magic carpet. A wave of the wand, a rub of the bottle and here we are: the Bankside Hall, autumn – can't remember the exact date – 1966. Still almost a year to go before the Marine Broadcasting (Offences) Act, which will finally put the kibosh on pirate radio – but it's already visible on the horizon, and I'm doing everything I can to make sure I still have a job when it's come and gone. So that's me there, hurrying up the steps, a weeny bit late, hoping to get a scoop with a just-starting-to-be-talked about singer called Adam Earnshaw. As I reach the top a couple of girls waiting in the queue recognize me. One puts her hand over her mouth. The other says,

'Oh, my God! You're –'

'Yep,' I say. 'I am. Would you ladies like a photo?'

It's an unwritten clause of the Stella contract: *signed photos shall be carried at all times, and handed out at every possible opportunity.* And it's also the quickest way to get rid of the girls – short of ignoring them completely, and watching my ratings start to tumble.

'Yes, please,' says girl two.

Here's the problem: the signed photos are at the bottom of my bag, under my Uher tape recorder and the jumble of bits and pieces that accompany it on its travels. As I crouch down and rummage around trying to find the bloody things, the mike and the battery box spill out, dragging after them a tangle of wires like the entrails of a run-over rabbit. The girls giggle.

'You did that on purpose, didn't you?' says number two. 'Captain Clumsy.'

As at least a couple of the geeks will be able to tell you – better that, I suppose, than collecting an arsenal of semi-automatic weapons and massacring their classmates – Captain Clumsy was my Radio Stella nickname. (If you want to know why, Google +"Radio Stella" + "Rufus Strange" + "Denny Wright".)

I force myself to laugh. I've got the pics now, but they're caught under the tape recorder, and as I try to yank them out one of them starts to tear.

'Oh, Garibaldi,' I groan. No, I don't know either: it was just something my grandmother used to say. Not as satisfying as *Fuck!*, but I'm on duty here, and the rule is, *Absolutely No Swearing.*

I grab the Uher, but it slips from my fingers and lands with a thud on the nest of cables, quickly followed by my glasses. The girls are shrieking now. One of them calls, *Look, it's Captain Clumsy!* A crowd starts to gather, tittering and whispering. What if they *all* want photos?

'Please,' I say, pointing at the auditorium. 'I think you'll find the entertainment's over there.'

More laughter, more curious onlookers. I start to panic. Then a deep, volcanic eruption voice says,

'Come on, people. Give the guy a break.'

I look up and see Tate Finnegan looming over the heads of the mob like a storm cloud. It's embarrassing, because I'm there at his invitation. But it works: within seconds, the crowd has dissolved.

You ever meet Tate Finnegan? If you did, enough said. If you didn't, here's the thumbnail sketch: six-foot-three-or-four, fifteen stone, bull shoulders, long copper-red hair. Today he's wearing plum-coloured velvet trousers, cowboy boots, a silver-and-gold wristwatch the size of a small clock, and a blue frilly shirt with a backstage pass clothes-pegged to the breast pocket.

'Give you a hand here?' he says, squatting down and retrieving the tape recorder.

'Just a minute.' I finally manage to extricate two photos. The girls have retreated, but they're still watching. I stand up and give them a picture apiece.

'Oh, great, thank you,' says the first one, giggling. 'Sorry about all the trouble.' Now that she's uncovered her mouth I can see she's rather pretty, with pouty, Marianne Faithfull lips and big, *come-on-surprise-me* eyes. She shifts from one foot to the other, looking at me the whole time. 'What are you doing after?'

'Putting on my water-wings and swimming back to the good ship Stella.'

She laughs. 'What, tonight?'

'Maybe not tonight.'

Tate hands me the Uher. 'Who knows what the evening may bring, ladies?' he says. 'So if you'll excuse us...'

The girl pulls a face, points towards the entrance. 'Well, we'll be waiting,' she says. 'Over there. After the concert.' She turns to her friend. 'Won't we?'

'Yes,' says girl two.

'Very good.'

'I'm Dilly. And this is Bub.'

'Bub.' Tate glances at me. 'That some kind of an English name?'

'I never heard it before.'

'Dilly and Bub. That's what I call standing out from the crowd. Well, enjoy the show.' He touches my elbow, nudges me away. 'Seems like *you're* taken care of, anyway,' he murmurs, glancing back at the girls. 'Shit, wish I'd had a camera to film that.'

I laugh. 'Christ, what a terrible idea!'

He shakes his head. 'For educational purposes. To show Adam. He still doesn't dig it.'

'What?'

'All this, man.' He looks round, drawing in the foyer, the box office, the crowd. 'It's a fucking licence to get laid.'

I laugh again. But it's awkward: I've met Tate two or three times, but we're not *friends*. It's more a *you-scratch-my-back, I'll-scratch-yours* arrangement: I give his acts airtime, and in return he lets me have advance copies of new tracks and exclusive access to his artists. Which I really need, if I'm going to establish myself firmly as the where-it's-at DJ for underground music, so enabling me to jump ship (so to speak) from Stella to the BBC when the pirates are closed down.

'*A fucking licence to get laid*? Well, that's one way of putting it. But if the Major heard me say that, he'd fire me.'

'If you said it on air, maybe.'

'Or if someone told him I'd said it.'

He stops, turns to face me. 'What is this? You seriously think I'm going to blow it on you? Go to Do Right John behind your back, and say *your boy Rufus likes ass*?'

'No, of course not. But you do have to be careful in this business. One mistake, one story in the papers the advertisers don't like, and –'

'Oh, come on! He knows anyway. So do the advertisers. So does everyone. It's the way the scene works. Getting to check out the chick menu is all part of the package.'

As always, the layers of deception here make me giddy. A = what the Major officially knows. B = what he thinks he'd find out if he investigated. C = what he'd *actually* find out – and would undoubtedly destroy my career, and probably land me in jail. But I'm an old hand at diversionary tactics.

'*Check out the chick menu!*' I splutter. 'Where does all this stuff come from?'

'Fuck, man, I don't know. Maybe I made it up. But you know what I'm saying. I mean, sure you dig the music, we all do, it's great. But you're not going to puke about on the ocean, are you, for, I don't know, three weeks or something, putting discs on a rocking turntable and telling housewives what cleaning product to buy, unless you know there's a big slice of Dilly and Bub waiting to meet the boat when you come off on furlough?'

'Fair point.'

'Yeah. It's obvious. Except to Adam Earnshaw.'

'Perhaps he just isn't interested.'

'You mean he's a flit?'

I clear my throat. 'Some people are.'

He shakes his head. 'Not Adam. I seen him eyeing up the sweet meat, when he thinks no one's looking.'

'He's shy, then.'

'That's a concept I'm not familiar with. You want to explain?'

We both laugh.

'Maybe he *has* a girlfriend,' I say. 'And you just don't know about it.'

'I thought of that. There's this singer called Carrie Bateman he hangs out with sometimes. You heard of her?'

'No.'

'Big goopy chick. Off with the fairy folk most of the time.' He pulls a wad of folded paper from his pocket, waves it in front of me. 'But she's not on the guest list. So he didn't ask her tonight. What does that tell you?'

I shrug.

'What it tells me is, she's not his old lady. Or he wants to scope out the scene, if he can figure out a way to do it.' He jabs me with a huge finger. 'Which is where you come in, my man. Help give the guy step-by-step instructions. Nothing's going to make him normal, whatever that is. But at least if he got laid, maybe he'd be less hung-up.'

We're at the stage door now, and he gets me past the hulking security guy with a gruff *This gentleman is a guest of mine.* Ahead stretches an airless, dusty-smelling corridor, lined with identical grey doors. From the far end I can hear a man and a woman rehearsing a mournful dirge.

'That Stevie and Maeve?'

He nods. 'They'll be fine. They've done this before. But Adam…The most he ever played is sixty people.' He stops, touches my arm. 'I'll tell you up front,' he says, 'this isn't for the housewives, but I'm kinda, you know' – waggling his hand like a banking plane – 'about him.'

'Why? You think he isn't ready?'

He stares at me. I stare back. For a second it's like peering inside a VW van painted with brilliant psychedelic designs and seeing a guy in a suit poring over a calculator.

'OK. Well, I think someone's fucking with his mind. Specifically, I think Mayburn Ellis is fucking with his mind. You know Mayburn Ellis?'

'I know who he is.'

'Well, he's been sniffing around, pissing against my picket fence when he thought I wasn't looking.'

'What, trying to steal your acts?'

'Trying to steal Adam Earnshaw.'

'But he's not a producer, is he?'

'Doesn't matter. I'm the anti-Christ. He's just trying to save the guy for the true church.'

'Is that really still going on?'

'The People's Republic of Folk? Sure.'

I shook my head. 'Why would anyone sign up to that now? It's like saying, yeah, OK, I'll spend my whole life in the station. Instead of getting on a train and going somewhere else.'

'Hey, that's good.' He takes a pen from his pocket and draws a little symbol on the back of his hand: two wobbly railway tracks crossed by four sleepers. 'Fact is, I don't know what's going down,' he says. 'I'm figuring maybe it has something to do with class. That make any sense?'

'*Class*?'

'Don't look at me like that, man. I'm just a dumb Yank, walking around, knocking into china. You're the one that's meant to know about this stuff.'

'Why?'

'Cos you're a Brit. Race, no sweat: race I can handle. But not class: we don't specialize in that shit. So you have to help me out here. All *I* know is, a lot of the time I feel the guy's only half here. It's like some dick has taken up residence in his head, and every time Adam goes out on stage, the dick starts whispering, this ain't the real thing. *Real* folk singers play working men's clubs in Hull.'

'And you think the dick's Mayburn Ellis?'

'Maybe. Anyway, see what you can find out.'

He leads me along the corridor and knocks on the second-to-last door. There's no reply. He waits a second, then turns the handle and goes in.

'Hey, man. Visitor for you. Rufus Strange.'

Adam sits in the corner, an animal cowering in its cage. I'd seen pictures of him, of course, but they hadn't prepared me for the real thing. The image in a photo is – by definition – always fixed: Adam in the flesh, by contrast, appears provisional, a work in progress. As he gets up to greet me, arms swinging, as if the puppeteer can't be bothered to tug the strings, he seems unable to settle on a persona: in the course of only a few seconds, his expression moves from sulky to tentative to anxious.

'Hi, Adam,' I say. 'Nice to meet you.'

He nods, but says nothing. We shake hands.

'Well,' says Tate, 'I'll leave you gentlemen to it.' He taps his watch. 'Twenty minutes. OK?'

'OK.'

He shuts the door behind him. I'm used to dressing rooms tricked out like a whore's boudoir and littered with whisky bottles, wine glasses, half-smoked joints. This one's as bare and dingy as an office. The only light comes from a single bulb hanging from the ceiling. There are just two chairs, and the functional little table's empty except for a water jug, a tumbler and a smeared coffee mug that's left a brown ring on the Formica. Lying on the floor beside him is a battered satchel that – to judge by its appearance – he's probably had since he was ten.

'I enjoyed *Our Dancing Days* a lot,' I say quickly, hoping he won't pick up the lack of enthusiasm in my voice. 'It's a great record.'

Bad start: he obviously can't handle compliments. 'Thanks,' he mumbles, looking straight past me. 'So how does this work?'

'Well. You've heard *Strange Sounds*, have you?'

'Not...Well, I have. A bit. But the reception in Oxford isn't very good.'

'Really? OK, I'll talk to the station manager. Maybe they can boost the signal. Anyway…Let's sit down. I'll explain.'

He nods. I shunt my seat over, so that we're facing each other across the coffee mug.

'Three times a week,' I say. 'Eleven till one in the morning. That's when we're on. So the graveyard slot. But it turns out there are more ghouls out there than they expected. Over a million, at the last count. The Major was really surprised. There's probably the occasional retired postmistress among them who can't sleep. But most of them – judging by the letters I get, anyway – are freaks.'

He nods, but he doesn't seem that impressed.

'A million freaks,' I say. 'That's a lot of people going down the record shop every Saturday, standing in the listening booths, trying to find something more interesting to spend their money on than The Shadows or Gerry and the Pacemakers.'

'Yes.' But his eyes are wide, as if the thought frightens him.

'And it's my job to help them. Introduce them to sounds they might want to buy. So every Friday, there's a section of the show called the Secret Garden. Where we feature someone like you. Someone they won't have heard before. We do a short interview, you know, nothing too heavy, just ten, fifteen minutes. And then we break it up with three or four tracks.'

'And advertisements?'

'Well, yeah, of course. The advertisers are the guys who pay the bills.' I wait for a nod or a smile or a *yes*. Nothing. 'That bother you?' I say.

'Some and some.'

I laugh. 'I take it that means yes.'

'Well, do you think music should be used to sell things?'

'In an ideal world? Strictly off the record: probably not. The world we're in? Yeah, if it means people can hear stuff they wouldn't be able to hear any other way. If someone can come up with a better system, that's fine by me. But in the meantime…'

'What about the BBC?'

I shake my head. 'You know what the BBC's like.'

'Not really.'

That stops me. 'Where were you when the rest of us were listening to Uncle Mac and Three-Way Family Favourites?'

'I don't know. Africa, I expect.'

'Oh, yeah. Africa. You grew up there, didn't you? Tate did mention that. Sorry.'

'So what's Three-Way Family Favourites?'

'It's what it sounds like. Danny Kaye by way of Vera Lynn. Then there's *Pick of the Pops* on Sunday. *Top of the Pops* on the telly. And that's it. Nowhere to hear your kind of music at all. Nowhere to hear the Beach Boys, even. Or the Byrds. That's why the pirates are so successful they're having to close us down. We play stuff people actually want to listen to. OK. End of lecture.' I slide the Uher out, plug in the battery pack, start setting up the mike. Then I open my notebook. 'Look,' I say. 'I'm a clever devil. Prepared a list of questions, and everything. Ready?'

I reach for the switch. He puts out a hand to stop me.

'Yeah, can we wait a minute? It's just I have to...You know...get my head...'

'It's OK, man. No need to get uptight about it. It isn't a big deal.'

Even as I say it, I can hear how bogus it sounds. Why can someone like Tate Finnegan get away with talking like that, when I can't? Maybe it's that he actually *thinks* that way, while I still have to translate. Result: instead of relaxing, Adam's frowning at me, trying to figure out whether I'm being serious.

'By which I mean,' I say, suddenly putting on my Peter Cook posh drawl, 'there's absolutely nothing whatever to worry about. The natives are perfectly friendly.'

The effect is instantaneous. He laughs. 'That's amazing, being able just to slip into a different voice like that.'

'I don't know. A certain vocal facility' – switching to my old-geezer-in-the-pub character – 'gives you a bit of a leg-up, I suppose, in my line of business.'

'And do you – I don't know – do you feel you actually *are* those people? That they're sort of different versions of you, all living inside your head, and when you talk like that they come out, and you start seeing the world through their eyes?'

Does he know about me? Has he guessed somehow? It would be easy enough to put him down: *Hm, that's a very Oxford student kind of a question.* But that would slam the door shut before I've even managed to get it open. And he doesn't seem unsympathetic: just curious.

'You know what?' I say, reverting to my normal voice. 'The honest truth is, I think it's just a classic case of little-guy-in-the-playground syndrome. There I am, eleven years old, we've just moved to Harlow, most of my friends are still back in Poplar, I should have gone to Grammar School but I screwed up the 11+ and pitched up at the Secondary Mod instead. And it's heaving with scrappy little tykes looking for an outsider to pick on.' For a fraction of a second I'm teetering on the edge of adding, *And telling you what they'd like to do to queers with a rusty breadknife.* No, it'd be madness. I bring myself back to heel. 'So it's a question of survival,' I say. 'How do you avoid them picking on *you*? If you're a five-foot-eight shrimp like me, beating the shit out of them isn't an option. So you make them laugh.'

He nods.

'Anyway,' I say, 'this isn't getting the baby bathed.'

'So is that why they gave you the job?' he says quickly, watching surreptitiously as I reach for the tape recorder again.

'Is what why?'

'Because you can do voices?'

'They gave me the job,' I say, switching back to Peter Cook, 'because, ahem, I am *in the groove.* Now come on.' I point a finger at him: *We're meant to be talking about you.* 'And clock's a-ticking.' I shift the mike so it's half-way between us. He stares at it as if it's the barrel of a gun.

'OK?'

He says nothing. There's a ready-rolled joint in an Old Holborn tin in my pocket. The plan had been to sneak it into the toilet during the interval and get myself into the mood for the after-show party. But desperate times call for desperate measures. I pull it out, light up, take a couple of tokes, hold it towards him. He hesitates, then grabs it greedily and draws in a deep, ragged lungful. I flick the *on* switch and test for level.

'Strange dudes and strange ladies,' I say. 'Here I am backstage at the Bankside Hall, sitting in the dressing room of His Serene Majesty, Adam Earnshaw. And if you're not familiar with Adam Earnshaw, then take my word for it, you're in for a treat. He's certainly one of the most exciting folk acts I've heard in a very long time. Only *folk* doesn't really do it justice. Hang around, and you'll see what I mean.'

As I pause, Adam frantically waves a hand at me: *stop*. I switch off. 'What?'

'*His Serene Majesty*?'

'We can change that, if you want. I'll re-record. But we need to get on with the questions.' I turn the machine back on. 'One, two, three: So, Adam, the first time I heard your name must have been three or four months ago. A Strange Person in Oxford told me I needed to get down there to see a new folk singer who was taking the local scene by storm. *I don't know how he does it*, she said. *But when you hear him singing* Spencer the Rover, *say, it's like you've gone to the pub with Spencer's best friend, and he's telling you the story.* Let's get a taste of what she's talking about...' I pause the tape. 'Then we'll put in a quick track here. Maybe just thirty seconds or so, so people can hear that tingle-the-nerve-end voice. Then –'

'Look, I'm sorry,' he says. 'I've never done anything like this. I just...I mean, what you're saying...It doesn't sound like me...'

Keep cool, I tell myself. I glance at my notebook, then shove-halfpenny it away across the table. 'We'll forget about this, OK? Let's just say we're in your pad, my pad, wherever, sitting at the kitchen table, having a conversation. All right?'

He nods. But I can see the Adam's apple working in his throat.

'Hang loose, my man,' I say, Peter Cooking it. 'It'll be a blast.'

Bingo: a smile. I re-start the tape.

'So let's begin with Africa,' I say. 'With Kenya. What's the deal with that?'

'It's where I grew up.'

'Sure. But then when you come to England – to Oxford University, no less – and start singing, it sounds like you've spent your whole life here, roaming our green and pleasant land, picking up songs in out-of-the-way pubs or plucking them from the hedgerows. So what's going on?'

He shrugs.

'People can't see you do that,' I say, imitating him. 'You have to say it.'

'I don't know.'

'You've no idea?'

'Not really, no. Well…'

He trails off. I yell:

'Fuck, shit, cunt.'

He looks startled. That was the idea, of course.

'I just did that to show you,' I say. 'It doesn't matter what we say here. Anything you don't want to air can be edited out. So forget about the audience. This is just you and me having a chat. OK?'

He nods.

'OK. So if you were living in Africa, where did it come from, the music?'

'Well…' He takes another drag on the joint. 'When my grandparents were still alive, sometimes I used to spend holidays in England with them.'

'Where was that?'

He laughs. 'Salisbury. And we'd drive out to the country sometimes, the Marlborough Downs, places like that. And *then* the music – well, it seemed like the perfect soundtrack to the landscape. Didn't you find that? When you were growing up?'

'The soundtrack to Harlow was Frank Sinatra and Alma Cogan. On a good day, maybe Buddy Holly.'

He laughs again. It's an unexpected sound, like the gush of water when you unblock the sink. Must be the Mary Jane.

'But even then,' he says. 'Didn't you feel…Under the streets, the houses, the crescents, there was something there –'

I'm not sure where this is going. 'You ever been to Harlow?' I say.

'No.'

'You're making it sound like Bath. Harlow's a giant slab of concrete.'

'Under the concrete, then.'

I hesitate. Oh, what the hell. 'You mean, what, *spirits* or something?'

He doesn't answer at once. While I'm waiting, I try to figure out what I should do if he says *yes*. There's a tiny group of people out there, at the freakiest fringes of my audience, who'd say *right on*. But for every one of them, there are ten others who'd think it was mystic horseshit. I could see the beef-red Major sitting opposite me, thumping the desk with his rolled-up *Daily Mail*, then unfurling the front page to reveal: *Radio Mumbo Jumbo*.

'You think that's all Mumbo Jumbo, do you?' says Adam.

'Fuck, what made you say that?'

He blinks, as if he's having trouble focusing, then waggles the joint between his fingers.

'Ah, the good old Mexican red, eh?' I say. 'In case you're listening, Major, Mexican red is a high-quality form of cannabis, a narcotic substance currently much in vogue among the young.'

'You want to hear something?' says Adam.

'What?'

'Two songs.'

'Sure.'

I'm hoping he'll do something live, but instead he reaches into his satchel and brings out an EMI box.

'Here.'

I take off the interview tape and loop up the one he's given me. 'Can you tell me anything about them?'

I'm expecting *Elves and goblins*. Instead he replies,

'One's called *Oxford Blues*. The other's *Mr Morris*.'

'That's it?'

He nods. I press *play*.

If you're familiar with those two tracks from *Standing Stone* – as I guess you must be – it'll be hard for you to imagine their effect on me that first time. I was just totally freaked: not only by the spiky chord sequences, the sense of being led across a swaying rope bridge, and then – miraculously – delivered safe to the other side, but also by the strangeness of the lyrics, the particularity and detail of the world they conjure up. And – most striking of all – by the odd, unexpected light that each song casts on the other.

'Wow,' I say, as the tape finishes. 'That was…' I shake my head. 'Explain.'

'Just some new material I've been writing.'

'I've never heard anything…I mean, that Cubist thing. Getting the girl's point of view. And then her dad's in the next track. Incredible. Has anyone else ever done that?'

He starts to say something. I hold my hand up.

'No, hold on. Let me get the interview tape back on. In the meantime, here's another question. Not for the Major's ears. You ever done acid?'

He jerks back in his chair, shaking his head.

'It's OK,' I say, waving at the switched-off Uher. 'It's just that some of what you were saying, about, you know, spirits and –'

'I see enough stuff as it is.'

There's a knock. Tate's huge head appears round the door.

'How's it going?'

Adam smiles. 'Yeah.'

'Cool,' says Tate. He glances at me. 'Yeah?'

I nod. He turns back to Adam. 'We have to go. You're on in ten minutes.' He taps his throat. 'Don't forget.'

'OK,' says Adam. He drops his gaze, like a child weary of being told to stand up straight.

'Right. We're out of here.' He steps aside to let Adam pass, then turns to me and mouths:

'So?'

'It was great. But we ran out of time.'

'He say anything about Mayburn Ellis?'

'No, we didn't get that far. But if you could just maybe give us another fifteen minutes or so? Afterwards, I mean? He might be a bit more in the mood then.'

'I'll try, man. But hey, you know.' And he starts hustling Adam towards the stage.

I still have the tape of Adam's songs. I almost call after him. Then I think, if he hasn't told Tate about it, I'll only end up embarrassing him. So I slip it in my bag and head back to the foyer.

I had a reserved seat close to the front, between the guy from the *NME* and a weird-looking dude – pale and podgy, with a pustule-dotted face and chaotic teeth –who introduced himself as Tristram Orr-Molton. He wore a bottle-green Carnaby Street jacket and a silk scarf tied like Beau Brummell. I asked him if he was a journalist, and he said, no, he was a friend of Tate's. His voice was soft and lispy, the upper-class vowels planed down to a neutral mumble. I couldn't imagine what such a complete herbert was doing there. In the two years he'd been in Britain, Tate had managed to get to know an astonishing number of people – but seeing this guy made me think that he should have exercised a bit more quality control.

I don't remember much about the concert itself. Or more accurately, I remember it as something far off, that barely touched me – as if, instead of sitting fifteen feet from the stage, I was watching it from half a mile away, through a telescope. The foreground of my attention was occupied by someone who wasn't there at all: the Major. I could see him sitting at his desk, poring over my receipts, totalling train fare, taxi, subsistence, then looking up and saying, *It may have escaped your notice, but Radio Stella is a commercial enterprise. The BBC might be prepared to pay good money for ten minutes of unusable tape, but I'm not.* Ninety per cent of my mental energy was focused on what, if anything, this late in the day, I could do to save my interview. The remaining ten per cent tracked Adam's progress as he worked his way through his set: five folks classics, punctuated by *Flight of the Witch* and *Annabelle, Dancing.* It was neither a triumph nor a disaster – or, rather, it was both a triumph *and* a disaster. Which one you experienced depended pretty much on where you were sitting: if (like me) you were in the first dozen or so rows, you felt the magic; any further back, and – to judge from the near-silence behind me – you were beyond its reach. The effect was like seeing someone sticking a frozen pie in the oven and taking it out too soon: the top inch has warmed up nicely, but the filling's still a lump of ice. At one point Tate went on stage himself and fiddled with the sound system, trying to extend the range – but if it made any difference, I couldn't hear it.

After Adam, there was Stevie and Maeve. I'd seen them before, and I wasn't much of a fan: the flashy guitar-work, the crude jokes, the air of sweaty intimacy – as if, at any moment, they might take their clothes off, and expect you to do the same – all made me feel queasy, like being trapped in the Stella studio in a gale. It didn't help that the guy next to me kept tittering and squirming in his seat, as if he was trying to dance sitting down. When I guessed we were only a song or two from the end, I got up and slipped away, attracting a volley of odd looks from the ranks of adoring fans. I didn't really care. Even if someone recognized me, *Rufus Strange walks out of Stevie and Maeve gig* wasn't much of a headline. And my only hope, I knew, was to grab Adam before anyone else did.

I was out of luck. The Neanderthal on the stage door didn't remember seeing me earlier, and obviously decided that I was just a chancer trying to crash the after-show party. I asked him to look on the guest list. He didn't have it. I played a snippet of the interview, in hope of convincing him, but he'd never heard of *Strange Sounds*; and the way he scowled at me, holding my gaze longer than he needed to, said he strongly suspected Adam was just a guy I'd picked up in a pub somewhere.

I turned away, blushing – then had to wait helplessly, listening to the muffled noise of the concert trundling towards its climax, before watching the audience pour out into the foyer, and guests with passes and invitations surging past me. By the time Tate finally came to my rescue, I'd missed my chance: as I followed him backstage, I could hear the sea-sound of the party in full swing.

The place was packed: a swirl of interstellar dust, revolving in slow motion round some invisible object. Tate had shoved his way to a side door, and was talking to a couple of the silky-haired dolly birds who were ferrying in the drinks. I started towards him – but then I noticed creepy Tristram Orr-Molton hovering at his elbow, ogling the girls as frankly as if they'd been pictures in *Mayfair*, so I abruptly altered course.

Adam, I assumed, must be somewhere in the centre of all this; but when I fought my way through, all I found was Stevie and Maeve, bottles in hand, holding forth to a jittery throng of journalists and hangers-on. It was only when I reached the far side that I saw him, standing beyond the centripetal pull of the crowd, talking to a couple of people: a fair-haired, square-shouldered guy who looked more like a cricketer than a musician; and a wiry little weasel of a man with shrewd brown eyes and a heavy duty moustache. It didn't appear a particularly animated conversation. This, I thought, was my chance.

'Hey!' I called, hurrying towards them. They all turned. 'That was great,' I said. 'Magical.'

'Thank you,' said Adam, staring at my feet.

'See?' said the sporty guy.

Adam shook his head. 'People weren't listening. I could tell…'

'Of course they were!' I said.

'Exactly what I've been telling him,' said sporty guy.

'They were coughing and whispering.'

'Well, I didn't hear them,' I said. Though I had. 'But anyway, you can't expect to have five hundred people sitting together in the same place and not get a bit of that.'

'Good point,' said sporty guy. He held his hand out. 'I don't think he's going to introduce us, is he? I'm Tim Bruce. We're at university together. And this' – pointing to the man with the moustache – 'is Peyton Whybrow. And *he* was at university with Tate Finnegan, have I got that right?'

Moustache man nodded. There was something careful, almost furtive, about him. Stick him in a big felt hat, in fact, and you could have been looking at one of the Gunpowder Plot conspirators. 'Freshman year roommate.'

I told them my name.

'Oh, yes, the Radio Stella chap!' said Tim Bruce. 'Of course. Adam said you might be here.' He tapped my bag, which the weight of the Uher had half-pulled from my shoulder. 'You have to take this everywhere you go? Like a ball and chain? To make sure you don't abscond from the prison hulk?'

'Something like that.' I looked at Adam. He appeared completely disengaged from us: unsmiling, resisting the draw of my gaze.

'I have to say, I find it rather fascinating,' said Tim Bruce. 'This whole pirate radio thing.' He turned to Peyton. 'Have you heard about it?'

'Yeah.' His voice was soft and fastidious, with a languorous southern drawl. 'Kind of an interesting phenomenon.'

'I mean,' said Tim Bruce, 'the idea that you could make a successful business out of buying up an old rustbucket, anchoring it just outside British territorial waters, and beaming a mixture of pop music and advertisements to the mainland. When I first heard about it, I thought it sounded pretty far-fetched. But obviously I was wrong. Otherwise you wouldn't have people falling over each other to join the club, would you?'

'Club's not going to be around too much longer, as I understand it,' said Peyton.

'No,' I said. 'Doesn't look like it.'

'And that's kind of interesting too. Your government figuring all they have to do is kill the pirates, and it'll be 1960 again.' He shook his head.

'Genie's out of the bottle, man. No way you're going to wave a wand and send it scooting back.'

I laughed. Peyton said, 'You be interested in doing an interview?'

'For who?' I said.

'I don't know. I've had a couple pieces in underground papers over in the States.'

'On music?'

'On everything. Everything that's going down. The empire's in its last days, and my job is to chronicle them. Tell the people what's really happening. That's the way I see it. Only there's already a lot of competition back home. So Tate thought I ought to check out the scene here. Pretty much virgin territory, he said.' He smiled, his moustache parting like a pair of curtains. 'And *he* seems to be doing OK, doesn't he?'

He glanced across the room at Tate. Tate caught his eye and beckoned.

'England. Land of Opportunity,' I said.

Peyton laughed. 'Yeah. Plus: the land where they don't send you to fight in Vietnam. Excuse me, will you, I better see what he wants. But I'd still like to interview you.'

'Odd guy,' I said to Adam, hoping to draw him into the conversation. But without even looking at me, he turned and hurried off after Peyton.

'Don't worry,' said Tim Bruce. 'It isn't you. It's me. I'm in his bad books at the moment.'

'Why?'

'A girl.'

'Oh, I see, right. The usual, then.'

He shook his head. 'Well, the usual in 1870, maybe. He's cast me in the role of Sir Jasper Stonyheart.'

I was obviously meant to laugh, so I did.

'My theory is that it's the music,' said Tim Bruce. 'Everyone has to be a character from a folk song. So I'm the wicked squire and she's the serving wench.'

I laughed again. '*Is* your girl a serving wench?'

'No, of course not. But that's the part he's given her.'

He stopped a passing dolly bird, took a glass of bubbly, raised his eyebrows at me, hand hovering above the tray.

'Yes, please.'

He gave me a flute. 'Anyway,' he said. 'This Major of yours. Is he going to knuckle under?'

'What?'

'When the Marine what's-its-name Act comes into force. Is he going to close the station? Or –'

'*If* it comes into force,' I said. 'We don't know for sure it's going to. But yeah, *if* it does, he'll bitch about it, but he'll give in in the end. He's done all right out of it. And he isn't going to find himself on the wrong side of the law.'

'No, I can see. It's tough.' He gazed past me dreamily, his mind on something that wasn't in the room.

'So what does Adam think you ought to do?' I said. 'About this girl?'

'Oh, marry her,' I expect. 'Make an honest woman of her.'

'For the obvious reason?'

He frowned. 'Oh God, no, not that. We've been careful.'

'Did you *tell* her you'd marry her?'

He flushed.

'Yeah, OK,' I said. 'None of my business. I'm just curious.'

I could see him wrestling with the conflicting impulses to justify himself and to preserve a dignified silence. After a few seconds, dignified silence threw in the towel.

'As it happens, I didn't,' he said. 'The idea wasn't even mentioned. The whole thing was just a bit of fun. We met at a party, and one thing led to another, and that was that. Both of us knew the score, right from the start. Or at least we did until Adam stuck his oar in, and convinced her I'd been playing fast and loose.'

'OK. Sorry I asked.'

He nodded abruptly, finally snapping the subject shut. 'I can't help feeling a bit sorry for your Major,' he said. 'Being picked on like that. Seems rather typical of this country, doesn't it? Find out what the public want, then stop them getting it. And punish the people who've been giving it to them.'

'You don't need to worry about the Major. He won't starve. The *rest* of us, maybe, but you can bet on it that he'll have salted enough away for a comfortable retirement.'

'No, but it's the principle of the thing. Once upon a time people with enterprise were rewarded for it. Now they're seen as the enemy.' He laughed. 'Only don't tell Adam I said so. Yet more proof that I'm a heartless capitalist bastard.'

'I don't need to tell him.' I tapped the Uher. 'I'll just play him the tape.'

His eyes flicked to my bag.

'And next week it'll be all over the airwaves.'

He must have figured out that the machine wasn't running, or that he was too far away for the internal mike to have picked him up. Either that, or he had the nerve to play along.

'Well, OK,' he said, laughing. 'I can't imagine your listeners are going to be particularly interested. But if it helps to sell another Picnic Bar or packet of fags…'

He stopped suddenly, shifting his gaze to something behind me. I turned. Tate was locomoting towards us, clearing people from his path with some invisible cowcatcher, flanked by the two girls who had accosted me in the foyer. They were trembling with cold or excitement, blinking in the garish light, glancing around with lowered eyes for famous faces.

'Hey,' Tate said. 'Mind if I butt in?'

Tim stepped back to let him pass – but then, instead of moving away, stood eyeing the girls, calculating his chances, wondering whether being at Oxford was negotiable currency in a room full of musicians and record industry executives.

'Look what I found,' said Tate, touching the girls' shoulders. 'You forget or something?'

I hadn't: I'd just hoped he had. 'No, of course not...'

'I thought you Brits were meant to have manners. Unlike us watermelon heads from across the pond. But no American would keep two ladies waiting out in the cold like that.'

'That's all right,' said one of the girls. Shit: what the hell were their names?

'Hey, ma'am!' called Tate, waving at the nearest waitress. 'Over here, if you please.' As she approached, he airlifted a couple of glasses from the tray and gave them to the girls.

'Thanks,' said the second one, giggling. 'Cheers.'

Bub and Dilly: that was it. But which was which?

'So,' I said, 'how'd you enjoy the show?'

They hesitated, looked at each other, both started to speak at once.

'One at a time,' I said. 'Bub first, then Dilly.'

'It was amazing.'

Gotcha. *B for Big Eyes.* 'And Dilly?'

'Yeah. That Adam. I never heard him before. But –' She touched her throat and shivered. 'He just made me...'

'You want to meet him?' said Tate.

They both squealed: 'Yes!'

'All right. Only tippy toes, OK? He's kind of shy.'

They nodded. They had the dazed wide-eyed look of four-year-olds watching the lights on the Christmas tree blink on.

'OK. Let's go get him, Rufus, my man.'

I grabbed his arm. 'Perhaps not the greatest idea. I don't think it's really Adam's scene.'

'Yeah, well we're here to show the guy what he's been missing, right?'

I glanced at the two girls. They were watching us, curious but baffled, as if someone had bewitched them and they couldn't understand their own language. How to explain what I *really* meant – that I needed more interview time with Adam, and that, in any case, in light of what Tim Bruce had told me, I didn't think the best approach was just to fling a couple of strange girls at him? And then there was the other thing, the thing that I couldn't say to *anybody*, but that sucked the strength from my thighs. I leaned closer to Tate, pointed to the corner. 'Can we –?'

'Christ, man, you can't go on doing this,' he said. 'These ladies been waiting long enough. Now we need to quit bunny-fucking and show them some appreciation.'

I looked across the room. Stevie and Maeve were standing with their backs to us, talking to a couple of West End dandies with paisley shirts and shampoo-ad hair. Beyond them, detached from the conversation, and frowning nervously at us through the gap between their heads, was Adam. And Peyton, who I'd hoped might have been a civilizing influence, had vanished. I had a vivid picture of him sitting at a candlelit desk, writing his report of the evening with a quill pen.

I turned to the two girls. 'And here we are,' I said, in my Peter Cook drawl, 'in the, er, *with it* environs of London's Bankside Hall. At the excruciatingly trendy – not to mention *fab, gear* and *out of sight* – after-show party for Adam Earnshaw and Stevie and Maeve. And with me are those two doyennes of the popular music scene, Dilly and Bub.'

They were both laughing. One of them spluttered:

'Are you recording this?'

'Absolutely.' I held out a non-existent mike. 'Dilly, for the benefit of our listeners at home, and particularly for Mrs Muriel Hogtrouser of Bognor Regis, perhaps you could tell us a little about yourself?'

'Well...'

I don't remember what she said, only her manner: shy, half-smiling, on the verge of laughter, as if the tape were really running, even though it was perfectly obvious that it wasn't. Mostly I was concentrating on where I could go with this, whether I might be able to spin it out long enough to make the girls forget about Adam Earnshaw altogether, and settle for an innocent bit of fun with a madcap DJ, followed by a night of passion with an American record producer. I could sense Tate at my elbow, shifting from one foot to the other, but reluctant to interrupt what – for our two guests – was all part of the floor show.

'Thank you,' I said. 'And now you, madam.'

God, the power of radio. Instead of dissolving in giggles as I'd expected, Bub kept up the make-believe, recounting the details of her completely ordinary life with a kind of girl-next-door jokiness that she hoped would make the audience-that-never-was like her. Out of the corner of my eye I saw Tim Bruce laughing. But now, all of a sudden, he seemed different: not a self-confident, public-school pain in the arse, but a Botticelli angel sent to save me.

'At this point in the proceedings,' I said, when the girl had finished, 'I'd like to introduce our Managing Director, Mr Tim Bruce.' I took his elbow, nudged him towards them. He shook his head, but he was smiling: *honestly, whatever is the guy going to get up to next?*

'Are you really?' Bub asked him.

'No.' But taking it in his stride, all loose-limbed charm. The girl blushed under his gaze.

'Mr Bruce is exactly the sort of plucky young fellow this country needs,' I said. 'A chap who doesn't consider *success* a dirty word. Which raises the interesting question of what he *does* consider a dirty word?'

The girls sniggered.

'What I *actually* am,' said Tim Bruce, shrugging it off with a captain-of-games grin that said, *it's childish, but I'm not offended*, 'is a friend of Adam Earnshaw's.'

'You telling the truth now?' said Dilly.

He nodded. 'I was lucky enough to hear him when he started at Poor Tom's. And you're absolutely right. He is extraordinary.'

'OK,' said Tate. 'Cabaret's over. Let's go meet the guy himself.'

He put one arm round Bub and the other round me and started shunting us across the room. I felt like a man being hauled off to face the firing squad.

'Did I hear you say you're from Sheen?' asked Tim Bruce, easing himself into the space between me and Dilly.

'Yeah, that's right.'

'Whereabouts, exactly? I probably know it. I've an aunt who lives in Richmond.'

That's my boy, I thought. *Keep it coming.* That was my only hope now: that one of them would decide she had a better chance of fun with Adam's charming Oxford friend than with Captain Clumsy. Otherwise…God, the thought of it. I had to lower my head to keep myself from fainting.

'Hey, what's going on here?' said Tate.

I looked up. Stevie, Maeve and Tristram Orr-Molton were still talking, but Adam had vanished.

'Where the fuck he go? To the john or something?'

Flushed, insolent Stevie smiled. 'He didn't confide in us. We're not on bowel and bladder terms.'

Tristram Orr-Molton quivered, flashing a lot of gum.

'I don't think so,' said Maeve. 'He said he was tired. I got the impression he was splitting.'

'Sorry, man,' I said.

Tate shook his head, glowering at me. 'Well, ladies,' he said. 'Looks like we're going to have to make our own entertainment.'

'Motion seconded,' murmured Tim Bruce.

'How about you?' said Bub. 'You going to third it?' She giggled, brushing the back of my hand with hers. 'Three of you and two of us. How does that work?'

My mouth was dry. I looked round frantically for another drink – and did a double-take. Adam was making his way through the crowd towards us. He smiled and waved.

'We thought you'd taken off,' said Tate.

'Yeah, well I'm not staying,' said Adam. 'I just came back for this guy' – putting an arm round my shoulder. 'We've got a bit of unfinished business to attend to.'

'Yeah?' said Tate. 'Well, we have some unstarted business over here –'

'No, honestly,' I said. I hoisted the Uher. Exhibit A.

Tate frowned. He didn't like it. But what could he do? He was a record producer – and if the choice was between two nobody girls and getting airtime for one of his acts, there was really no contest.

'Thanks, Adam,' I said, as we hustled towards the exit. When we finally reached the corridor, he turned to me and said,

'Well, Tate told me what the plan was. *There's a couple chicks waiting out there. And I'm going to go get them. And then my man Rufus is going to show you what to do with them.* And I thought that sounded like a nightmare. For both of us.'

For both of us. Had it been that obvious?

'Too damned right,' I said. 'You saved my life.'

I held his gaze, searching for a reaction. What would it be? Pity? Embarrassment? Disgust?

He said nothing, but smiled.

'So can we finish the interview now?'

He shook his head.

'Five minutes. Please. I just wanted to ask you a bit about your new –'

'I can't. I'm sorry. I'm completely done in.'

I was so frustrated I almost wept. But how can you argue with a man who's plucked you from the flames?

'All right,' I said. 'Well…Good night, then. And thanks again.'

He clapped my back. 'Good night.'

*

For the rest of that week I worked fifteen hours a day, trying to salvage enough from the evening to make a full episode of *The Secret Garden*. The only way I could do it was to flesh out my interview with Adam with everything I could lay my hands on: African drumming; Kenyan bird-song; spooky effects – owls; wind soughing in the trees – to conjure up the old England he sensed lying beneath the streets. And – after a good deal of soul-searching – I decided to sneak in Adam's rogue tape and play *Oxford Blues* and *Mr Morris*. I briefly considered okaying it with Tate, but then thought, why give him the opportunity to say no, when the tracks didn't come from him in the first place? As for Adam – I suspected he was half-*hoping* I'd play them, but could never actually come out and say so. In any event, whatever they thought, they'd both know there was no point in suing a pirate station for breach of copyright.

When I delivered the finished product to the Major, I felt I might – to all intents and purposes – have just offered to walk the plank.

But the weird thing is, he loved it. He seemed *awed* by it. *The best thing you've ever done. Takes radio* – I don't know where he got this from: the station manager, probably – *to a whole new level.*

And when, a few months later, I was offered a job at Radio One, they said it was *The Secret Garden with Adam Earnshaw* that had clinched the deal.

8

CARRIE BATEMAN

Well, Mr Whoever You Are, you've certainly put the cat among the pigeons. I've been sitting here for hours, looking out of my kitchen window at a field full of sheep, and wondering what I could tell you that might help. Because I'd be so happy if I could remember something that turned out to be the vital clue, let you finally bring closure after all these years. Closure for all of us.

Only I can't think where to start. So I'm finally going to do what I did when I was finding it hard to write lyrics: trust the subconscious, and just put down five things, any five things, whatever jumped into my mind, dee dee dee dee dee, like that. Place names, that's the way I thought of them. And then what I had to do was look at the map and see if I could figure out the route, spot the roads running between them. Join the dots.

So here goes:

Fairy tale.
Hard to breathe.
Crooked house.
Crazy girl.
Danse macabre.

OK, well that's clear enough: the weekend Adam and I spent in Essex. So perhaps the answer's there. Let's hope.

Weirdest first. *Hard to breathe.* Where did that come from? I wasn't ill. I don't suffer from asthma. But it's true, when I think about it, a lot of that weekend feels oxygen-starved. I can see myself walking around on eggshells, sucking in little sips of air, terrified of making a noise, or of missing a whisper or a creak that I should have heard.

Part of the reason – the easy to explain part – was that we were visiting Mayburn Ellis. If you were around back then, you'll know what I'm talking about. If not, you'll just have to take my word for it: for a folkie in the mid-sixties, being invited to stay with Mayburn Ellis was a big, big deal. You felt like a silversmith, taking your wares to be assayed. If he approved them, tested them with his teeth and gave them the Mayburn Ellis hall-mark, then – so far as a lot of people were concerned – they were the real thing. The grapevine would start to buzz. And all at once, at a stroke, you'd find yourself a *bona fide* member of that magic circle that included the Watersons, Anne Briggs, Shirley Collins.

The second reason, the harder to explain part, is that I was going there with Adam Earnshaw. On the face of it, there was nothing remarkable about that: we were just two young singers that Mayburn Ellis had heard at Poor Tom's in Oxford and thought were worth encouraging, the way he'd encouraged scores of people before us. That was the story he'd told us, and I wanted to convince myself it was true. But try as might, I couldn't do it. The fact was that I'd been playing for three years, since I was sixteen – not just in Oxford, but at festivals, and a few gigs in London – and in all that time I'd never once set eyes on Mayburn Ellis. Now, just two months after Adam starts at Poor Tom's, the man suddenly shows up out of the blue, all smiles, and tells me he likes my music.

Or I should say, *our* music. That was the giveaway. I remembered the look on his face as he stood talking to us outside the club: the way the eyes behind his bottle-bottom glasses moved between us, trying to figure out exactly what our relationship was. It didn't take him long to decide that we were a couple. At which point it's easy enough to imagine him thinking: if I want him, I'm going to have to take her as well.

And this is where it gets even more complicated. Because – although a lot of other people back then seemed to have reached the same con-clusion – Adam and I *weren't* a couple. There'd been times over the past few months when it had felt as if we were tantalizingly close – when we'd be casually sitting over a drink at Poor Tom's, say, and catch each other's eye, and it was as if we'd both for a moment seen a half-open door, and glimpsed a different kind of relationship beyond it. But always, the next instant, he'd suddenly veer off again, like a nervous animal. It must be the sex, I decided: he'd had a bad experience with some other girl – and the only way to deal with that was to get him into bed somehow, and show him there was nothing to be frightened of with me. But time, I knew, wasn't on my side. He'd already signed to a label, and was starting to get gigs at places like the Bankside Hall. If something didn't happen now, he'd be out of my reach. So I'd leaned on him to come that weekend – hoping that forty-eight hours away from the familiar old more-than-friends, not-quite-lovers treadmill would do the trick.

It was pretty much the bleakest time of year, just a couple of weeks before Christmas. On the train down, Adam was working on something, jotting words in a notebook with a chewed pencil; but he could never concentrate for more than a few minutes, and kept looking up to frown out of the window at the Essex countryside – ploughed field after ploughed field, patches of brown corduroy stitched together by leafless hedges. Occasionally he'd start absently nibbling at his thumb, like an anxious child. The second or third time he did it, I leaned over and tapped his knuckles.

'Hey, stop that! You're a guitarist, remember! You need that nail!'

He winced, as if I'd physically hurt him. I flicked the pencil.

'Those lyrics you're writing?'

He snatched the notebook up and stuck it in his pocket.

'All right. I was only asking. What's the matter? You still belly-aching about coming?'

He nodded.

'You should be excited,' I said. 'There's lots of musicians who'd give their eye teeth to be asked to stay with Mayburn Ellis. Not that I really know what an eye tooth is.' I pulled back my lip. 'Have I got any? Can you see?'

Not a hint of a laugh. 'I won't have any idea what he's talking about,' he said.

'He'll be talking about music. People he likes.'

'*Which* people?'

'Well, *you*, for a start. And then the obvious ones, I expect. You know: Ramblin' Jack Elliott. Alex Campbell. Martin Carthy. People like that.'

'Who?'

'Ramblin' Jack Elliott. Alex –'

'Never heard of any of them.'

I was a bit short-sighted. I had glasses, but I didn't like to wear them in public. So to see him properly, I had to lean in really close.

'Are you kidding me?'

His face was deadpan. But that didn't mean anything. People were always shitting me about stuff. Maybe it was the long hair, made me look dopey.

'Cos if you are...' I bunched my fists and pummelled the air between us.

'I'm not.'

'But surely, I mean, you must listen to records, don't you?'

He shook his head.

'How'd you learn what you know, then?'

'My mother, mostly.'

'So where did *she* learn them?'

'Books. We had loads of them. You know: *Eighty English Folk Songs,* that kind of thing. When my father was away, we'd sit at the piano together, and she'd play them. And then, when I was older, my grandparents gave me a guitar, and I'd go in my room where no one could hear me and figure out how to do them on that.'

'Didn't your parents *like* hearing you, then?'

He shook his head. 'Well, my father didn't, anyway.'

'Oh, God! Poor you! Mine loved it: I was a regular little show-off.'

He shrugged. 'I was always a disappointment to him. When I was a kid, he thought I should have been striding around outside, speaking Kikuyu and learning how to identify animal tracks. Not just hiding myself away, filling my head with wistful Edwardian claptrap.'

'Kikuyu?'

'That's where we were most of the time. In Kenya.'

'Oh, right, so your dad was a District thingummy jigger or whatever they're called, was he?'

'He's a physical anthropologist. You know. Bones.'

I nodded. 'So why *weren't* you striding outside?'

'I wasn't very strong.'

'We should get you a cape and a silver-topped cane,' I said.

'What?'

'Like Adam Adamant.'

'Who's Adam Adamant?'

'It's this TV programme.' I leaned close again. 'Oh, come on. You must have seen it!'

'Where? I haven't got a television.'

'Well, it's about this guy, this Victorian hero, who's frozen in a block of ice by his enemies. And then years later he's discovered on a building site and brought back to life, you know, *now*, in the middle of modern London, with Georgy girls and Carnaby Street and everything...'

'Yeah, that's not quite me. My world goes up to about 1914. So I can just about deal with motor cars. But when it comes to wireless sets and votes for women...'

He couldn't be serious, of course, but it didn't sound like a joke, either. I followed his gaze into the ghost world of the window and caught a reflected eye. He started to laugh.

'I'll be all right,' he said. 'As long as he plays nothing more recent than Harry Lauder.'

'On a wind-up gramophone. With a big horn.'

'What other sort is there?' He reached into his pocket, pulled out a pouch of Golden Virginia and unrolled it on the table. Inside were a packet of Rizla papers and a little broken Oxo-cube of hash in a plastic bag. 'What do you reckon?'

I glanced across the carriage. Immediately opposite us was a red-faced, irritable-looking man in a worn tweed jacket. He was pretending to read a newspaper, but his eyes kept surreptitiously darting towards us. I shook my head. Adam shifted, clocked the tweedy man.

'Yeah, OK,' he said. 'Better not chance it. Shame.' He started to chew his thumb again.

'No, no,' I said, knocking it away. 'None of that.'

'Ellis'll think I'm a fraud,' said Adam.

'No, he won't. Or if he does, he'll think I am, too. I mean, when it comes down to it, we're all frauds, aren't we? How many real-life ploughboys and dairymaids do you think there are on the folk circuit?'

'You mean you're *not* a real-life dairymaid? I'm not sure how much more of this I can take.'

'Don't make fun of me!' I flicked his wrist with the end of my hair. He caught it and held it for a moment.

'I could have sworn,' he said. 'That fragrant odour you give off, spring flowers and newly-mown grass…'

It wasn't the first time he'd talked to me like that. But before, he'd always turned away afterwards, as if he'd gone too far – touched me where he shouldn't have done, or walked in on me when I was getting dressed. Now, he went on looking at me, conscious of his power, deliberately observing its effect.

'Oh, you!' I said, tugging my hair free and spreading it across my face to hide my blushes.

He smiled. If you've only seen him in photographs – scowling Mr Angst, gazing past the camera at the storm clouds gathering behind you – you won't know what that means. You have to imagine the familiar image melting away, and his whole attention suddenly switching to you – eyes half-closed, skin stretched taut across his forehead – as if, for an instant, a frame had formed around your face, and he could see nothing outside it. It was irresistible.

'So what *are* you, then?' he said, after a moment. 'A swinging chick, or whatever the phrase is?'

I shook my head. 'Can't I just be myself? I don't even know what a swinging chick *is*. What she's supposed to do.'

'Pretty much anything, I think.'

I started to blush again.

'I mean, you know, after gigs, you see them, don't you?' he said. 'Just standing there, all lined up. Letting the guys know they're available.'

'Has that happened to you?'

He paused for a second. 'Yes. Sort of. Once or twice.'

I laughed. 'Well, take me next time. I'll protect you.'

He didn't reply.

'What, you think nice girls don't, is that it?'

He flushed, but said nothing.

'That's a bit old-fashioned, isn't it?'

He shrugged. 'Folk singers are meant to be old-fashioned, aren't they?'

'And how many folk songs are about nice girls who *did*? And ended up with a broken heart, or a little bundle, for their trouble?'

He considered for a moment, then smiled and nodded. 'Yeah, all right. Fair point.'

'Well, you'll be safe with Mayburn Ellis, anyway,' I said. 'All he'll expect you to do is buy a copy of *The Industrial Worker*. Or several copies.'

Adam said nothing. His gaze drifted to the window again. It was dark now, nothing to be seen but a solid mass of black, relieved here and there by little clusters of houses, or the moving thread of a car's headlights. I plucked up my courage and laid a hand over his. He didn't look at me – but nor did he withdraw his hand. We sat like that for several minutes.

It's OK, I told myself. *Just try to relax and enjoy the moment. You're not there yet, but you're making progress.*

Fairy tale. Easy to see where *that* came from, at least: Dunstead. If you've been there, you'll know what I'm talking about. It's one of those places that look like they haven't changed since the year dot: a jumble of impossibly quaint timber-framed houses, without a single straight line between them, squeezed around a wonky old covered market with a roof like a witch's hat. That evening it seemed specially magical: everything remote, flat and monochrome – a woodcut illustration from one of the bedtime stories my mother used to read me when I was a little girl.

As we emerged from the station an old Morris Minor beetle-crawled towards us. Its headlamps were just a couple of smudges, too feeble to penetrate the falling snow. The driver's window wobbled open, and Ellis's face appeared.

'Sorry. Have you been waiting long?'

'No,' I said. 'We've just arrived.'

'The old girl wouldn't start,' he said, slapping the metal scuttle. 'This weather doesn't agree with her.'

We dumped our bags in the boot and got in. Adam scrambled quickly into the back, leaving me with the responsibility of having to make conversation. Resignedly, I settled myself in the passenger seat. Even through my jeans, the plastic felt cold and clammy.

'She doesn't get a lot of use,' said Ellis, as we juddered back on to the road. 'I've never really understood about cars, I'm afraid. Why some people seem to worship them. As far as I'm concerned, they're just a way of getting from A to B. And if there's any choice in the matter, I'd always prefer Shanks's Pony. Or the train.'

'Well, I can't even drive,' I said. 'So –'

'Good for you.' He glanced in the rearview mirror. 'Ah, here we are. Case in point. A self-important chap in a great big Rover thinks I'm not going fast enough. Well, I'm sorry, old chum, you're just going to have to put up with it.'

We slithered down the steep High Street, past a couple of pubs and a still-open shop, sparkly with Christmas decorations. Mayburn Ellis stared straight ahead, with a *come on, hate me* smile. At the bottom, he said,

'Stick your hand out, would you? The trafficators are frozen.'

I rolled down my window and put out my arm. The Rover honked. As we started to turn, the driver revved the engine, swung out abruptly, and roared past us in a hiss of slush. Mayburn Ellis clicked his tongue.

'Can't be terribly good for his blood pressure, can it?'

We inched down a narrow street, lined on both sides with terraces of little stucco-covered cottages. Half-way along, Mayburn Ellis pulled over and put the trembling car out of its misery.

'We are arrived, as the French say.'

I peered out. All I could see was a couple of unlit windows in a sea of white plaster, and a heavy panelled front door. A sign above it said: *The Old Bakehouse.*

'This is nice,' I said. 'Charming.'

'Oh, I'm not sure about that. I don't think the people who built it were very interested in charm. A roof over their heads and a fire to warm themselves by, that's what *they* worried about. Anyway, let's get inside.'

He got out and started briskly towards the house. He seemed to have forgotten about our bags, so we retrieved them ourselves. As I slammed the boot shut, I said,

'Do you want me to lock this?'

He looked back, his hand on the doorknob, silhouetted by the light from the house.

'Good Lord, no. We don't do that here.'

We followed him into a square room smelling of wood smoke. Beams shouldered the weight of the low ceiling and made odd irregular patterns in the walls. A log fire burned in the red brick ingle. An arch at the back led into an inner hall, where – half lost in shadow – you could see the first few steps of an oak staircase. Next to it was a closed door, surrounded by an aura of bright light. The kitchen, presumably.

'My wife's in America,' said Mayburn Ellis. 'Doing fieldwork in the Appalachians.' He took off his duffle coat and hung it on a peg behind the front door. Underneath he was wearing a fisherman's sweater and a blue shirt with a turned-up collar, as if he'd just got in from a week on the trawlers. 'But our daughter's here. Traipsing round West Virginia recording old songs is a bit beneath her dignity now.' He took off his steamed-up glasses and wiped them on a corner of his shirt. 'Lily! We're back!'

Crazy girl. Here she is, making her first appearance. She's fourteen or fifteen, pale-skinned, her features blurred by puppy fat. She's wearing a mini-skirt that shows her heavy thighs, and her dark hair's cut in a modish Vidal Sassoon bob, which – instead of making her look older – only emphasizes her childishness. She bounces in from the hall, then lingers inside the door, shifting from one foot to the other, unsure where to put her hands.

'This is Adam and Carrie,' said Mayburn Ellis.

'Hello, Lily,' I said.

'Hi.' She wriggled her fingers and tried to smile, but there was a dark mole in the corner of her mouth that obviously made her self-conscious.

'Can you show them up to their rooms? I'd better go and have a word with Iris.'

Rooms. That answered one question that had been nagging me: was Mayburn Ellis radical enough to put an unmarried couple he didn't know in the same bed? I felt a surge of disappointment – but also, mingled with it, a tiny shot of relief.

'You have to watch out,' mumbled Lily, not looking at us. 'It's a bit higgledy.'

She switched on the upstairs light and clumped up ahead of us. As we came out on to the landing, I whispered to Adam,

'So where's the crooked man?'

It really *was* the crooked house: floor heeling like the deck of a galleon; doors crammed in at weird angles wherever they could be fitted between the misshapen beams; a narrow archway – so low that only a child could have got through it without bending double – opening into a poky corridor on a lower level, with a lopsided room at the end.

'You're in there,' she said to me, pointing to a door straight in front of us.

I waited for her to lead the way, but she didn't move. I squeezed past her and lifted the latch. Inside were a bumpy old bed, a chair, and a chest of drawers. Behind me, Lily was saying,

'And you're down here. Come on, I'll show you.'

I plonked my bag on the faded candlewick counterpane, hung my sweepy-flowy earth-mother dress on the back of the door, put the rest of my clothes in the drawer. By the time I'd finished, Lily and Adam still hadn't resurfaced. I went out on to the landing and ducked through the archway. The door at the end of the passage was half closed. Through it I could hear someone – Lily, presumably – talking in a stage whisper: a rush of words, a little gap, then another rush, like the scuffling of mice under the floorboards.

'All right if I come and have a look?' I called.

Silence. I tiptoed down the corridor and knocked.

'Come in,' said Adam.

It was a long thin room, hardly wider than the passage. Adam stood at the end of the bed, still holding his bag. Lily had positioned herself between him and the door. She barely glanced at me before turning back to Adam and saying,

'That's where I heard you. On *The Secret Garden*.'

'Really?' said Adam.

'*Oxford Blues*. And the other one. *Mr Morris*.'

She hummed a few bars of something I didn't recognize. I caught Adam's eye and smiled. He looked away.

'Well,' he muttered, staring at the floor. 'That's flattering. I'm –'

'I love it,' said Lily. I could feel the warmth pulsing off her like an over-worked car engine.

'Do you think maybe we should go down?' I said. 'Your dad must be wondering what's happened to us.'

Lily hesitated, eyeing Adam, trying to figure a way of being shot of me and getting him to herself again. It took her a second or two to realize there wasn't one.

'All right,' she said, turning towards the door. 'Only don't tell him, will you? Mayburn. My dad? That I listen to Rufus Strange?'

'Oh, that's top secret, is it?' I said.

She nodded. As we emerged on to the main landing, she pointed to the room next to mine.

'That's why I put that on the door.'

There was a sheet of paper taped to the slatted wood. I went over and read:

Ministry of Lily. Keep Out. Authorized Personnel Only.

'Right,' I said. 'We have been warned.'

Mayburn Ellis was waiting for us at the bottom of the stairs. 'Ah,' he said. 'There you are. Supper's ready.'

He ushered us into the kitchen. It was full of the steamy school meal smell of mince and carrots and mashed potato. On the far wall was a cream-coloured Aga. In front of it stood a white-haired woman in an apron, holding an oven cloth. She smiled and nodded as we appeared.

'This is Iris,' said Mayburn Ellis. 'Iris is our *bonne*, as the French say. Our *good*.'

Iris blushed and laughed. 'Nice to meet you,' she said in a soft East Anglian accent. 'I expect you're hungry, aren't you? All the way from London, on a day like this.'

'Oxford,' I said.

She nodded. I don't think she knew what that meant. For her, London was the furthest point on the map, the limit of the known universe.

'You sit yourselves down,' she said. 'And I'll serve up.' She bent over and nudged a Pyrex dish out of the oven. 'Careful now. You don't want to touch this. It's pipping hot.'

'You joining us, Iris?' said Mayburn Ellis.

'Better not.' She smiled at me, one woman to another. 'My man. Jack. He'll be wanting his tea.'

'All right. See you tomorrow.' He waved her out of the door, then collected a kettle from the Rayburn and filled a huge brown teapot. There was a theatricality about the way he did it, as if he was determined that we shouldn't miss the significance. Forget the fleshpots of Soho: here was a man of the people, who ate cottage pie and mushy vegetables, and drank tea with it rather than wine. I looked at Adam. His face was a puzzled blank. A five-year-old child, that's what he made me think of, trying to unravel the mysteries of the adult world.

'Help yourselves,' said Mayburn Ellis.

'Shall I?' I said. 'Everyone want to pass me their plates?'

Mayburn Ellis put out four striped mugs and sat down. 'So,' he said. 'Welcome to Mother Maggot's.'

'Mother Maggot's?' I said. 'What's that?'

He opened his hands, embracing the whole cottage.

'I thought it was the Old Bakehouse?'

'According to the post office it is. But I prefer Mother Maggot's. In honour of the last person in Dunstead to be burned for witchcraft.'

'What, she lived here?' I said. 'In this house?'

He nodded. 'She was a wise woman. If you had a sore throat or a bad leg, you'd come and get a potion or a poultice from Mother Maggot.'

'I wish you wouldn't talk about it,' said Lily.

'When she was small,' said Ellis, smiling, 'Lily thought she saw her. Didn't you, Lil?'

'I saw something,' said sulky Lily. 'A figure. Like a witch in a swirly dress.'

'Well, perhaps,' said Ellis. 'But it wasn't a ghost. Probably just the wind blowing a curtain. Anyway, Mother Maggot wasn't a witch. There were no spells involved. Primitive medicine, that's all it was, for people who couldn't afford a doctor. Herbs and plants you could find anywhere – on the village green, in the woods and hedgerows. But the local bigwigs, the vicar and the squire, they didn't like it. Because of course *they* thought the woods and the hedgerows belonged to them. So they said she was consorting with the devil.'

'God,' I said. 'Poor woman.'

'And here we are, three hundred years later. We've had the enclosures, the industrial revolution – and now late capitalism. And still we're fighting the same battle. Between private property and the common good.'

Lily made an odd snorting noise. I glanced at her. She was looking at Adam, rolling her eyes.

'Only now,' said Mayburn Ellis, 'it's harder to see the line of the trenches. Because they're clever, these gentry. And they've got new allies to help them. Radio. Television. The gutter press. Which is why what *you* do' – squinting at Adam through his heavy glasses – 'taking the music direct to the people, is so important.'

There was a clatter, loud enough to stop him in his tracks. I turned: Adam had dropped his fork, and was staring at his plate.

'Hm,' murmured Ellis. He couldn't quite bring himself to ask, *Is something the matter?* but it was there in his eyes.

'Sorry,' muttered Adam.

'So that's the purpose of this little convocation,' said Ellis. 'To exchange views. And see if perhaps we can agree to work together.'

He waited for Adam and me to respond, to pledge allegiance to the cause. When neither of us did he went on:

'It's a desperate situation. You probably don't realize just how quickly it's all changed. When I started out, fifteen, twenty years ago, we were poor as church mice. We met in scout halls. We made our own instruments. No one got a penny. But we all knew why we were doing it: to keep something alive. Something that wasn't yours or mine but *ours*. The voices of all those thousands of Mother Maggots, testifying to the hardship of the working-class experience. And as a result, the music was pure.'

His ashy face was tinged with pink, and there was a catch in his voice I hadn't heard before, like an idling engine suddenly rammed into gear. My scalp tightened. No one I knew on the circuit would have talked like that: it would have been too embarrassing. But that only added to the power.

'And then, of course,' said Mayburn Ellis, 'folk started to become, dread word, *fashionable.* And all at once the vultures in their Mayfair offices began to take an interest. Because fashion means money. Something you can *sell* to people. *Profit.* It's the enclosures all over again: take something that belongs to everybody, and turn it into private property, with a big *Keep Out* notice to deter the *hoi polloi* who used to graze their sheep there.'

Lily sniggered. She was ogling Adam again, her smile on a hair trigger, waiting for him to say something. But Adam was still staring at his plate.

'You'll gather that Lily doesn't agree with me,' said Mayburn Ellis. 'But that, I'm afraid, really only proves the point.'

'What, so I'm stupid then, am I?' said Lily.

Mayburn Ellis shook his head. 'But you're up against powerful forces, old thing. When I was your age, we had fascism. It was easy to see that that was wrong. It's a lot harder with Pye Records. Or Radio Stella.'

'Well, I like Radio Stella,' said Lily. She hesitated. 'And I like Adam Earnshaw too.' And suddenly, gazing straight ahead at an invisible audience, she began singing:

> *Dad's gone down the Leg of Mutton*
> *Pint of Watneys, talk about the blacks.*
> *Shivering Mum has got her coat and hat on*
> *Mick and Jen are upstairs in the sack*
> *Outside –*

She faltered, unable to remember the rest of the words. Adam flushed.

'Ah, so is that the sort of thing you're doing now?' said Ellis, with a fixed little smile.

Adam nodded.

'Well, it's a…It's an interesting tune.' In the silence that followed, you could hear what he'd left unspoken: *But it isn't folk music.*

'There's a sort of companion piece to it,' said Adam. 'This time from the father's point of view.'

'Hm. Well, I'm afraid, you see' – the smile becoming archer – 'from *my* point of view, that's all part of the problem. That kind of cleverness. And the idea that seems so à la mode at the moment, that it doesn't matter who you are, what your background is, your experience is just as valid as anybody else's, because there are two sides to every question. Whereas in fact there's only one. The side of history.'

'So everyone who writes their own material is betraying the cause?' I said.

'Not necessarily,' said Mayburn Ellis. 'They may just be self-deceived.'

'But what if they're simply expressing something new, that Mother

Maggot couldn't even have dreamed of? I mean, there aren't any traditional songs about nuclear war, are there? That's why I had to write *Autumn Leaves*.'

I knew he'd heard *Autumn Leaves* – I'd sung it the evening he came to see us at Poor Tom's – but he didn't bother to acknowledge it. My hunch had been right, obviously: the attraction was Adam, not me.

'No, of course,' said Ellis. 'There are some very fine anti-war songs. I'm not talking about that. What I'm talking about is narcissism. Self-pity. Drugs. *Petit bourgeois* existentialism. Things that have nothing to do with the great shared inheritance of folk music at all.'

I could sense Adam next to me quivering like a deep freeze, sucking the warmth out of the air. I was angry too. But at least Ellis hadn't succeeded in separating us. He might have ignored me – but he was being even harder on Adam.

'Surely,' I said, 'there's room for both? I mean, yes, it's important to keep the old songs alive. But if drugs and existentialism are part of your life, why shouldn't you sing about them too?'

Ellis smiled at Adam. 'Silence, I note, from the honourable gentleman opposite. Perhaps this isn't the moment. You're tired from your journey. I propose that we reconvene tomorrow, and continue the conversation then.'

Danse macabre. Not, on reflection, the most important thing about that night. But it does capture a mood, the sense of three daddy-longlegs shadows following each other round the house in an awkward *ronde*.

When Adam and I got upstairs, I whispered,

'Are you OK?'

He nodded and hurried towards his room.

But it was obvious that he wasn't. I'd never known him so quiet and uneasy. The reason, I could only assume, was Mayburn Ellis's outburst at supper. I imagined Adam lying there, still in his clothes, rigid with misery. I longed to put my arms round him, tell him it was OK – but I worried that if I walked in on him now he'd feel I was taking advantage of him, using his unhappiness as an excuse to force the pace in our relationship.

I got into bed, read *Siddartha* till I found I was having to go over the same sentence two or three times before I could understand it, then turned the light out. Instantly Adam's miserable face doodled itself on the darkness. I put the lamp back on, picked up my book and repeated the process. Same result. After I don't know how long I got up, padded out on to the landing and peered through the archway. There was a strip of light under his door. A thick haze of spicy-smelling smoke had seeped into the corridor. He must have rolled himself a bomber.

There was a noise behind me: the faintest click, but enough to startle me. I spun round and caught the Rorschach ink-blob of Lily's head poking out of her room. She started to retreat, but stopped when she realized I'd seen her. We stared at each other for a couple of seconds. Then I waved at the bathroom and muttered,

'Sorry, were you going in there?'

She shut the door abruptly. To be on the safe side, I went into the bathroom anyway, waited half a minute or so, then flushed the toilet. As I came back out, I noticed that her door was ajar again – just far enough for her to be able to squint through the crack. I returned to my room, shivering – not just with the cold, but with the eerie, neck-hair prickling sense of being spied on. I turned the key in the lock and crawled into bed.

I must have fallen asleep then, because the next thing I remember is coming to abruptly. The clouds had cleared, and an emaciated moon had turned the room into a jumble of black shapes. For a second I couldn't identify what had woken me. Then I heard it: a muffled knocking, followed by the squeak of the door-handle as someone twitched it repeatedly back and forth. The girl, presumably. I hoisted myself up and tiptoed to the door.

'Lily?'

'It's me. Adam.'

I unlocked the door and opened it. He was leaning against the wall, head down, as if he was frightened he might faint.

'Can I come in?'

I saw a slab of grey shifting in the gloom behind him.

'We're being watched,' I whispered. 'Quick.'

He slipped into the room. He was wearing pyjamas and clutching a blanket round his shoulders like a cloak.

'Was that Lily?' he said.

'Yes. She gives me the creeps. What's the matter? Can't you sleep?'

He shook his head.

'Nor me. I saw your light was on. I almost came and knocked on *your* door.'

He didn't answer. He was shaking. In the dim moonlight his face and feet were the colour of putty. I hugged him.

'Oh!' I said. 'You mustn't let it get to you. It was horrible, I know, what Ellis said, but he didn't know what he was talking about. Chances are he hasn't even heard any of your recent stuff – well, he couldn't have done, could he, unless he listens to Rufus Strange? So he probably didn't realize how rude he was being.'

He shook his head again. 'Can I sleep here? On the floor?'

'If you want. But there isn't a lot of space. You'd be more comfortable on the bed. It's more than big enough for both of us.'

'OK.' He swaddled himself in his blanket and stretched out gingerly on the far side of the mattress. I got under the covers and lay down next to him. His breathing became slower and more regular, and I thought he was falling asleep – but then suddenly he kicked violently and started whimpering like a child.

'Shush.' I tentatively reached for him and pulled him towards me. Holding him, feeling him palpitating like a panicked bird, I realized this wasn't wounded pride. It was something more visceral, more basic.

'It's OK,' I said. My tongue wanted to add another word. But *Adam* would have sounded clinical – and *sweetie, darling, baby* all assumed too much.

He muttered something I couldn't make out.

'What?'

He shook his head.

'No, tell me.'

'You'll think I'm mad.'

'No I won't.'

'The woman. I heard her.'

'What woman?'

'The one he was talking about.'

I racked my brains. 'Iris, you mean?'

'The woman who lived here.'

'Mother Maggot?'

He trembled, as if even hearing her name unnerved him. 'I couldn't stop thinking about her. And then I heard her.'

I was out of my depth. 'Heard her doing what? *Saying* something?'

'Like this.' He made a long groaning sound, like someone on her death-bed fighting for breath. It was scary and comical at the same time.

'Oh, God,' I said, trying not to laugh. 'That's awful. It was probably just Lily playing some stupid game.'

He shook his head.

'Or the wind. A house like this, there must be loads of nooks and crannies it can get in.'

There was a sudden creaking outside on the landing. I leapt out of bed and yanked open the door – just in time to catch a glimpse of Lily scuttling back into her room. I closed the door again and turned the key in the lock.

'It wasn't the wind,' he said. 'It was her. The old woman.'

I climbed into bed again and took him in my arms. He felt slack, as if my disbelief was driving him away.

'Well,' I said, 'I don't know. I never had an experience like that. But if you did…Well, you did.'

'She sounded so frightened,' he said.

I pulled him over, cradling his face on my shoulder, and stroked his hair. For a minute or two he lay still. Then – almost as if he was unaware he was doing it, like a baby blindly trying to find the nipple – he started to nuzzle my breast. I unbuttoned my pyjama top and laid his head on the bare flesh. He winced and moaned, screwing up his eyes.

'No,' I said. 'It's all right.'

I kissed his forehead. He started and blinked, frowning round at the twilit room as if he'd never seen it before.

'I don't where I am,' he said.

'You're with me. With your Carrie.'

He looked into my face, as if he was trying to match it with the name. Then he nodded and closed his eyes again.

I kissed him properly. 'Come on,' I said. 'It's OK. It's OK.'

I don't know if you've ever heard my album? If so, you'll remember the last track is *Perma*. It was my attempt to write about that night with Adam. It's always difficult – love and sex have been done to death: flowers, trapped sparrows, lightning bolts. If I were doing it now, I'd scour the churned-up mud, looking for a still-fresh idea that all the other poets and songwriters had somehow passed over. But at the time, the image seemed right: the warmth spreading through us, opening us to each other – and then, quite suddenly, the feeling that we'd reached a limit, come up against something hard and unyielding.

> *Here at last – the ice-melt sun*
> *Seized-up tundra starts to thaw*
> *Seized-up river starts to run*
> *Till you delve beneath the earth*
> *And bruise your fingers on the frozen core*

I'm not talking about agony aunt stuff here – premature ejaculation, or erectile dysfunction. It was nothing to do with the mechanics. What I'm talking about is something harder to define: for a few miraculous minutes, we were together – and then all at once we weren't.

Even so, afterwards, I didn't let him go, but grappled him to me, murmuring,

'My darling, oh my darling, oh my darling.'

Just before dawn he rolled out of bed and tiptoed back to his room. This time, thank God, there was no sound from Lily. Even teenage voyeurs have to sleep sometimes.

I waited till I heard Ellis stirring, then got dressed and – after a decent interval – made my way down to the kitchen. Even before I opened the door I caught the salt-sweet smell of frying bacon. As I walked in, a wall of heat walloped me in the face. Iris stood by the Rayburn like a boxer, fists gloved in oven mitts. Mayburn Ellis and Lily were at the table, sitting at right angles to each other.

'No Adam yet?' said Ellis, looking up and pushing his newspaper out of the way.

'I haven't seen him. But I don't imagine he'll be too long.'

He nodded. Off-hand, barely registering what I'd said.

'Well, tea's in the pot,' he said. 'Help yourself. Sleep all right?'

I nodded.

'Good.'

No, there was no undertow there: he must not have heard anything in the night. But Lily, of course, was a different matter. Her gaze felt like the sun burning through a magnifying glass: at any moment, I thought, my cheek would start to smoulder. I struggled not to meet her eye, but after half a minute or so the pull was too strong and I gave in. The instant I did, she blushed and looked away, licking her lips. Iris picked up the atmosphere immediately – as she brought over my bacon and eggs, she flicked a sharp, curious bird-glance from me to Lily and back again. If I didn't do something to defuse the tension, even self-absorbed Ellis couldn't fail to notice it.

'So,' I said, 'how's the Ministry of Lily this morning?'

She harrumphed and got up. 'Dad. Mayburn. I'm going upthtairth to my woom.'

The little bitch: she was mocking my lisp. I glanced at Ellis. He frowned at her for a second, then returned to his newspaper. After she'd left, without looking up, he murmured,

'Difficult age.'

'Yes,' I said. 'I remember it well.'

Without so much as a nod he turned the page and went on reading. In silence, I picked my way through breakfast. It seemed to take twice as long as it should have done, and I was painfully aware of every click and squeak of my knife and fork. When I'd finished, I said,

'I'll just pop up and see what's happened to Adam.'

He turned another page. 'OK.'

I hurried out into the hall, closing the door after me. As I got to the landing I heard, leaking from Lily's room, a driving drumbeat overlaid with twanging guitars. Through the almost-shut door I could see part of Adam's leg, with one hand slapping the knee in time to the music. I crept closer. Lily was saying something, though I couldn't make out what. Adam laughed. Behind them, Bob Dylan was singing about Johanna.

I knocked. Dylan droned on for another couple of lines, then stopped with a click. A moment's silence. Then – as if she'd briefly considered pretending that she wasn't there, before seeing it was pointless – Lily called:

'Who is it?'

'It's me. I was looking for Adam.'

'Just a sec.' The ping of a mattress springing back into shape. A moment later she appeared in the doorway, tucking in her blouse over the rubbery little ring of flab round her belly. Piled up on the bed was a stack of LPs. Next to it perched Adam, looking at the *Blonde on Blonde* cover.

'Hello,' I said.

He nodded. Not coldly, exactly – but not with the sudden melting, the secret spark of recognition you expect to see in the face of someone you've just slept with for the first time. Or that you *hope* to see, anyway.

'Aren't you coming down to breakfast?' I said.

'I'm not hungry.'

'Oh, so poor old Iris has been slaving over a hot skillet for nothing, has she? Must be a good half a pig going to waste down there.'

I glanced at Lily, trying to include her in the joke. She glowered back, arms crossed defensively in front of her. Somehow – even though I was younger than Adam – he still seemed to her to be on the right side of the invisible membrane separating the teenage from the adult world, while I had mysteriously managed to pass beyond it.

Adam waved towards the stack of albums. 'Lily's been showing me her record collection. Playing me a few tracks.'

'Ah, right,' I said, turning to her. 'So you're a Dylan fan, are you?'

She nodded, still looking at Adam. Then – without warning – she started to sing:

> 'The ghost of electricity howls in the bones of her face
> Where these visions of Johanna have now taken my place.'

I couldn't help laughing. She scowled.

'That's great,' I said quickly. 'You've got a really good voice. Is that what you want to do? Be a singer?'

She shrugged.

'Seriously,' I said. 'You should think about it. You obviously love music…'

She turned to Adam and rolled her eyes.

'Lily doesn't feel there's a lot of point making plans,' said Adam. 'Because sooner or later we're all going to blow ourselves up.'

She flushed and gaped at him, mouth sagging. *You shouldn't have told her. That was between you and me.*

I caught Adam's eye. 'Can we have a quick word?'

He got up. I backed out on to the landing, drawing him after me.

'You sure this is a good idea?' I murmured.

'What?'

I nodded towards Lily's room. She was still peering at us round the door. As I watched, the tip of her tongue slipped out furtively and started feeling for the mole at the corner of her mouth.

I touched his arm. 'Let's go for a walk.'

He glanced back at Lily, then nodded.

'I'd better just make your excuses downstairs,' I said. 'Meet you outside.'

Mayburn Ellis still appeared to be lost in his newspaper – but the air of studied calm was wearing thin, and he couldn't resist looking up sharply as the door opened, and frowning when he realized I was alone.

'I've seen Adam,' I said. 'He's feeling a bit queasy, I'm afraid. So we're just going to pop out. See if some fresh air does the trick.'

Iris shook her head. 'Shouldn't do that if he's poorly,' she said. 'He'll catch his death. What he wants is to stop in bed. And let me bring something up to him.'

'I don't think it's as bad as that,' I said – and scuttled out again, before the next question completely derailed me. Adam was waiting by the front door, shivering. He hadn't shaved, and the charcoal fuzz of his beard made his skin seem paler than ever.

'OK,' I said. 'Let's go.'

In a rare moment of trendiness, I'd bought one of the first Afghans at Granny Takes a Trip, and Adam wore an ex-army greatcoat that had been made for someone twice his size, and sagged off his shoulders. In a place like Dunstead, I thought, the sight of us might raise eyebrows; so instead of heading back towards the high street, I took Adam's arm and set off in the opposite direction, where the houses gave way after a couple of hundred yards or so to trees and open fields.

It was a still cold morning, stingy with coal smoke – and so quiet that I worried he must be able to hear the nervous grumbling of my stomach. We set off in silence – Adam withdrawn and preoccupied, me waiting for an acknowledgement – a kiss, a hug, a *darling*, even a joke – of our new intimacy. After a couple of minutes I realized it was a lost cause. *He's still not used to it*, I told myself. *You just have to bide your time, It'll come – if not now, then later.* Finally, to cover the sound of another seismic upheaval in my belly, I said,

'What I couldn't say in there is that I don't think you're doing her much of a kindness. Lily.'

He shook his head. 'I just feel sorry for her. She's so angry.'

'Angry? Lily? You're kidding me!'

'Well, you would be, wouldn't you, if you were stuck in this place with that –' He pulled off a glove and spider-walked his fingers up his arm.

'Oh, come on! I know he's a bit annoying. But –'

'He's a tyrant! It's no wonder the poor girl's been driven half-mad.'

'What do you mean, *half*?'

He shook his head, reproaching me for my cruelty. 'Remember what he said about her not going to America? Well, that's complete bollocks! She wanted to go. It was him: he wouldn't let her. Because it would have meant spending Christmas with her cousin Prissy. Who lives in an ante-bellum mansion in Kentucky and has her own car. A Corvette, no less.'

I laughed. 'I've no idea what that is. You're a bit of a secret car-lover, aren't you?'

He made his hand into a shark-shape and sliced it through the air. 'Not the sort of thing Ellis would approve of at all. And the whole family are staunch Republicans. They're even building their own nuclear fallout shelter. The ultimate heresy, apparently.'

'Well, I'm sure she appreciates it, you taking an interest. But don't overdo it. There really is something a bit dangerous about her.'

'Yeah, did you notice her arm?'

'What about it?'

'She cut it.'

'What, an accident?'

'No, she did it deliberately. She showed me. Three long gashes. Like this.' He tensed his fingers and clawed at the air.

Common enough now, of course. But back then, I'd never heard of it before.

'God!' I said. 'Why?'

'Every single little thing about her, she's told it's wrong.' He was so furious, suddenly, that his voice sounded as if it was coming apart at the seams. 'The way she looks. The way she thinks. The music she likes.' He mimed the slash of a blade. 'She calls it cookie-cutting. It's the only thing that makes her feel real.'

'Jesus! Well, that just proves my point.'

He shook his head. I was baffled. Why had the ungainly little drama queen affected him like this?

'Honestly,' I went on. 'I suspect you don't realize how impressionable girls are at her age. Even perfectly normal girls. And she is not a normal girl. You probably think she's just a kid. But she doesn't feel like a kid, I promise you. When *I* was fifteen I had a crush on a sixth-former called Dan. And I can remember, it was agony. I was completely out of my tree. I wrote songs about him. I couldn't sleep. So I used to just lie there, imagining him getting a ladder and climbing up to my window to carry me away.'

He said nothing. I glanced at him. He was slouched forward, hands in his pockets, scowling at his own feet.

'I'm not criticizing you,' I said. 'I'm just saying be careful.'

'I'm sorry,' he mumbled, without looking at me.

'No need to apologize. You don't want to give her the wrong idea, that's all.'

'No,' he said. 'I mean about last night.'

It was like when you're slicing an apple and you suddenly find the knife has slipped and you've cut your own finger. It took me a moment to recalibrate.

'I was frightened,' he said. 'I didn't know what I was doing.'

'Really?' I squeezed his arm. 'You could've fooled me.'

He shook his head. 'I was out of control.'

I laughed. 'Yeah. So was I. That's the idea, isn't it?'

He clapped a hand over his forehead and groaned.

'Did you really think?' I said. 'That you heard that woman in your room? Mother Maggot?'

'Yes, of course I did.' Not turning, his eyes fixed on the road.

'OK,' I said. 'I just thought maybe you were a bit shy. Too embarrassed to say what you really wanted. And if that had been it, I wouldn't have blamed you. It's nothing to be ashamed of.' I pressed close and murmured in his ear: '*I'd* been waiting for...I can't tell you how long...Years. Well, months, anyway...'

He stiffened, tortoising back into himself.

'What's the matter?' I said, more quietly. 'Didn't you enjoy it? Making love?'

He didn't reply.

'Well, I did. I thought it was lovely.' I stroked his hair. 'Don't worry. First times are always a bit...You know...Aren't they? But it'll get better. Promise.'

'You're very sweet.'

The sort of thing your uncle might say. I was so stung I couldn't reply. He walked on, his mouth moving silently, giving the odd impression that he was counting his footsteps. Finally he muttered,

'You didn't happen to notice the times of the trains back, did you?'

My throat ached. But I forced myself to say, 'No. But Ellis'll know. Or he can phone the station for us.'

'I don't want to have to ask him. I just want to say, OK, that's it, 'bye.'

'What, *now*, you mean? Today?'

He nodded. 'You don't have to come with me. But I can't spend another night here.'

'You can sleep with me again.'

He turned on his heel and started hurrying back towards the village. I trotted to catch up with him.

'I'm not staying here on my own,' I said.

He shrugged: *it's up to you.* I almost snapped, *Well, thanks a lot,* but stopped myself. No point being the Dame of Sarky, as my mum would have said.

'What are you going to tell Mayburn, then?'

He tossed his head, like a horse refusing the bit.

'Oh, let's just forget the whole thing,' I said. 'Run away together. Somewhere where there are no promoters, no record producers, no priggish old Marxists telling us what we can and can't write songs about.' I touched his arm. 'We could get a smallholding. Or join a commune or something.'

He shook his head. 'That's what you do when you've given up.'

'Only when you've given up the rat race,' I said.

But he'd returned to his own train of thought, and it had already carried him far away.

Ellis was standing in front of the living room fire when we got back. He was trying to look relaxed – feet splayed; hands spread towards the heat – as if he'd just stopped for a moment to warm himself, and a minute later we wouldn't have found him there. But you could tell from the sharp way he swivelled towards the door as we came in that he'd been waiting for us.

'Hello, you two,' he said mildly. 'Sorry to hear you aren't feeling well, Adam. Has a turn in the bracing air of Dunstead helped? Iris swears by its curative properties.'

Adam hesitated, then blurted, 'Look, I'm sorry. I'm going to have to leave.'

'Why? There's a perfectly good doctor in Dunstead –'

Adam shook his head.

'Oh, dear,' said Ellis. 'I can see…' He pursed his mouth ruefully. 'I've never learned the courtier's art of dissembling, I'm afraid. So I probably expressed myself too freely last night. On the subject of modern music. I ought to have started the other way round and told you I think you have a really exceptional gift for making the *old* music new again. I assumed you knew that, of course. But I should have spelled it out, instead of simply taking it for granted.'

'No, honestly, it's fine,' said Adam. He paused. 'Anyway, I'm going to go and pack.'

I started after him, then stopped. I couldn't leave Mayburn Ellis just standing there. He looked old, suddenly – stooped, glasses slightly misted, upper lip pouched into a sad camel grimace.

'I'm sorry,' I said.

'No, no,' he said, drawing himself up again. 'It just goes to show the power of the enemy. How successfully they've managed to get their poison into the bloodstream.'

'Really,' I said. 'It's just Adam.'

He shook his head. 'Adam's a product of his time.' He hesitated, then dropped his eyes, dismissing me. 'Anyway...'

I turned and hurried to the stairs. As I reached the landing, I saw Adam standing with his back to me. He was speaking – or listening – to Lily. I caught a quick glimpse of her – excited, bright-eyed, the mole on her mouth newly covered by a splodge of make-up. Then she noticed me, and retreated into her room.

'What was she saying?' I asked.

'How she wishes we weren't leaving,' he said, without looking at me, and trudged off to pack.

And that's it. Crazy girl. Hard to breathe. Crooked house. Fairy tale. *Danse macabre.* End of the line.

Six months later I was living in Shropshire in a willow-and-canvas hut, with half a dozen assorted dropouts and a herd of goats for company. Up until the very last moment, I'd hoped that Adam might go with me. But, in the end, he went to spend the summer with a couple of other musicians instead. The idea was that they'd help him to complete his new album. But even so it was more than another year before *Standing Stone* finally appeared.

When, not long after that, he vanished...Well, I was upset, of course. But it didn't really come as much of a shock. I think unconsciously I'd been half-expecting it. It was as if for years you've been trying to finish a jigsaw puzzle, find a home for one troublesome piece that doesn't seem to belong anywhere. And now you're down to the last space, and it doesn't fit there either – so you finally realize it must be part of a different picture altogether, and throw it back in the box.

But still...I hope you find him.

9
STEVIE RAMAGE

Here's a weird thing. For a while, back in the sixties and early seventies, you're a part of the scene. A *big* part. Then, quicker than you'd think possible, *diminuendo*: bye bye record label, *don't call us, what did you say your name was?* For a while you're too dazed to do anything – but eventually you start to pick up the pieces, get yourself clean, trade the big house in the downs for a crap-hole in Hastings, learn to talk about child custody and who gets the record collection without throwing bottles. And then you sit there, reading everything you can get your hands on, scouring the classics and the OED for abstruse bits of vocabulary, so that when somebody finally breaks radio silence, you'll be ready for them. No namby-pamby *If you can remember it, you weren't there* for you, no *We thought we could change the world*. No, sir: you've got the full force of the English language at your command, and by God, you're going to use it.

Finally, after forty-something years, it happens: an eager young researcher, keen as mustard, gets in touch. Only – here's the rub – it isn't to ask about you, your music, the people you played with: it's to pick what's left of your brains about a spaceman called Adam Earnshaw, who drifted into your life for a couple of months in 1967, before drifting out again *en route* for oblivion.

But *sailor fucking vee*, as my dad used to say. It's not such stuff as dreams are made on, but what the hell – any excuse for a meander down memory lane. If nothing else, it'll be a day out for all those words. Don't say you weren't warned.

So welcome to *Wind in the Willows* with sex and drugs.

Our Mr Toad – inspired casting – was a pudgy young scapegallows called Tristram Orr-Molton. His dad had died when he was nineteen, leaving him a three-hundred-acre estate in Wiltshire, Sibley Park, and several million in the bank. Estate duties took a large slice, but there was still plenty more where that came from. The sixties were in full shameless swing, and Tristram – as any red-blooded scion of the aristocracy would – wanted in. But nature – unlike fortune – hadn't favoured the poor sap. After generations of inbreeding, the best it could come up with was a charmless moonchild, five-foot-eight in platform heels, with terrible skin and a bad crop of teeth. His only hope of joining in the fun, it seemed, was to follow the age-old traditions of his class: debauching a servant or two in the laundry, and then buying one of those girls in pearls they advertise in *Country Life*.

So Tristram devised a plan. Actually, I suspect it wasn't him who devised it, but an American record producer he'd got to know called Tate Finnegan, who ran the Wheatsheaf Records office in London. The idea, anyway, was this: behind the big house – a honey-coloured gem by Robert Adam – were a more-or-less disused stable block and two empty cottages. Why not (thought Tate/Tristram) turn the stables into a recording studio, and offer the cottages to musicians looking for a country retreat, where they could commune with nature and lark about like water babies while developing new material? That way, Tate would get product to feed into the sausage machine; and Tristram could finally abandon his embarrassingly unsuccessful attempts to gatecrash the scene: the scene would come to him instead.

So first up, in May 1967, were Maeve and me. It was a shotgun wedding: work on the studio had barely begun, and our little sawdust-smelling gaff was festooned with bits of paper saying *Wet Paint*. But it was a space where we could compose and rehearse – and Tate lent us a state-of-the-art reel-to-reel Ferrograph, the size of an ice-box, on which to produce demos. He was in a hurry: our first album had done OK, and he wanted to get the next one out before the DJs and the promoters had forgotten who we were. And we weren't coming up with the goods fast enough.

The main reason – let's not beat about the bush here – was lust. Maeve was the most sexual lady I ever met, and even though we'd already been together for eighteen months, we still – in the odd moments left to us between partying and performing – couldn't stop ourselves tearing each other's clothes off. Tate figured that – safely tucked away at Toad Hall, where the arrival of the post was a major event – we could indulge in as much priapic frolicking as we wanted, but still have time over to pen the requisite number of tracks.

He hadn't counted on the grounds. Up till then, our repertoire had been confined to fucking in the bedroom, the bathroom, the kitchen, the living-room, and – a couple of times – the back of a car, while the driver pretended not to notice. Now, in addition to our little John-and-Jane play-house, we had woods, a *faux*-gothic folly, a yew-maze, and a boating lake with an irresistible island in the middle of it to choose from. For the first couple of weeks, we were out pretty much all day, every day, making that crazy old beast with two backs in every crease, hollow and cavity we could uncover. *Bliss was it in that dawn to be alive/But to be young was very heaven!* Sometimes we'd get back to find a plaintive note from Mr Toad, asking us to pop in for drinks one evening. But we blithely ignored him, and carried on rutting for England.

Then things started to get freakier. One Sunday, in a Ratty and Mole moment, Maeve and I decided to commandeer the little rowing boat and head over to the island for a picnic. As prescribed by Kenneth Grahame, we started proceedings with a largish joint, then continued on the way across with a couple of bottles of Chablis that we trailed behind us through the weedy water. By the time we'd tied up and spread out our blanket beneath a motherly willow, we were pleasantly twisted, and reckless with it. We took our clothes off and fucked under the startled gaze of assorted birdlife, then cracked open Ratty's hamper and feasted on smoked salmon and olives and cheese, stopping every couple of minutes to giggle at the sheer stupidity of it all. Then we fucked again, and fell asleep, spreadeagled in a tangle of arms and legs.

Maeve woke me. She was shivering, shielding her tits with one arm and trying to tug the blanket out from under us with the other.

'There's someone there,' she said.

'Where?'

She nodded towards the bushes.

'How could there be?' I said. 'We've got the boat.'

'I saw the leaves moving.'

'The god Pan. Hoping to learn some new tricks.'

'Honestly. Go and look.'

The branches shook, and we heard a twig snap. I grabbed an empty wine bottle and hurled it. Crashing foliage, followed by a gratifying yelp.

'Hey! No need for that!'

I jumped up and plunged into the bushes, just in time to catch a glimpse of floral-pattern shirt melting into the leaves.

'Oi!' I called.

The shirt stopped, then slowly turned. Mr Toad, hugging himself like a school-kid who's been nabbed nicking Smarties.

'You spying on us?' I said.

He shook his head. 'I was a bit worried, that's all. I saw the boat was out, and you seemed to have been here an awfully long time.'

'How the hell'd *you* get here?'

'I've got a… You know…A little rubber dinghy. My new toy. So I thought I'd come and make sure you were all right.'

'Well,' I said, parting a couple of branches and waggling my cock at him. 'As you can see…'

'Right…Yes…Well…That's good…Sorry to have…'

He spun round and lumbered off through the undergrowth, as fast as his stumpy legs could carry him.

You'd have thought that would have been it: he'd been caught red-handed, and – if only to preserve what was left of his self-respect – wouldn't run the risk of a repeat performance. But that was Mr Toad for you: no shame. Over the next few days we noticed him hanging around more and more – coming out into the stable yard, apparently by chance, at the same moment we did, and giving us a friendly *fancy seeing you here* greeting, as if the incident on the island had never happened; or following at a safe distance when we ventured into the grounds, trying – by the way he sauntered back and forth, studying the flowers – to give the impression that it was nothing to do with us at all. He never burst in on any of our *al fresco* trysts again, but the possibility that he might was a powerful bromide. After a couple of miserable humps, when the fear of Toad made us feel like a pair of fumbling teens grabbing a quickie behind the bike sheds, we decided the game wasn't worth the candle, and abandoned our outdoor activities altogether.

But even that didn't deter him. Deprived of the opportunity to trail us through the grounds, he simply switched tactics and began to lurk outside our door instead. One morning, when I went out to pick up the milk, I found him standing there, clutching a copy of the *Daily* something-or-other.

'Oh, hullo,' he said, with odd expression – one eye half-closed, the other bulging, as if he couldn't completely agree with his own slyness. 'Did you see this?'

He shoved the paper under my nose. It was open at a racy story about a chart-topping rock god who'd been caught in a drug-fuelled three-in-a-bed romp.

'No,' I said, 'Can't say I did.' And I beat a sprightly retreat, clutching our pint of gold-top.

That afternoon I phoned Tate Finnegan.

'Hey, man,' he said. 'Shit, this must be synchronicity. I got this big sheet of paper in front of me, different coloured pens, high priority down to what the fuck, Mr Fucking Efficient. And guess what's top of the list?'

'Call Stevie Ramage?'

'You got it. So how's it going? How's the music?'

I lied.

'Well, that's good. Working out OK for you, then?'

'Yeah. Except for one thing.'

I told him about our island adventure.

He laughed. 'You have to be more entrepreneurial, man. Next time, sell him a ticket.'

'That won't do it. He doesn't just want to be in the audience. I think he's hoping to join the band. That's what he's hinting at, anyway. Him, me and Maeve. One big happy family.'

'Oh, fuck.'

'Oh fuck is right. Can you get some women down here? The other cottage is empty. Stick a couple of chicks in there and let him sniff around them for a change.'

For the first and last time in all the years I knew him, Tate was silent.

'Preferably someone who isn't too choosy,' I said. 'How about Blind Maggie Whelan?'

He cleared his throat. 'Listen, man, this isn't for public consumption, but Maggie isn't really blind. Just incredibly near-sighted.'

'I wasn't being –'

'OK, OK, I'll talk to the guy, get him off your ass. But hey, listen, I need *you* to cut *me* a huss too, OK?'

'Finish the album?'

'Goes without saying, man. No, here's the deal: you remember Adam Earnshaw?'

'Of course.'

'I won't shit you. The dude's crazy. Not don't-leave-the-breadknife-out crazy, just voices-in-the-head, where-the-fuck-am-I? crazy. I knew that when I signed him. It's what it says on the package. And that's cool. Only now the guy's started to come totally off the rails.'

'Why, what's he done?'

'He's meant to be a folk artist, right? But now it turns out, what he *really* is, is a singer-songwriter.'

'Nothing odd about that.' I said. 'Everyone's doing it.'

'Yeah. Only instead of telling me about it, he slips a couple tracks to Rufus Strange, who plays them on *The Secret Garden.*'

'Yeah, that is a bit cheeky.'

'I'm telling you, I almost told him to walk. But the thing is, they're good. Really good. So instead I said, write me ten more like that, and we'll put out an album. And he said OK. Since when I've had six months of nothing.'

'Ah.'

'When I asked him about it, he said, *I just think I need to get away for a bit.* So that's when I thought of you and Maeve. The thing is, the guy's a backed-up sewer pipe. Fuck knows what's in there, all kinds of junk. So what I want you to do is take him under your wing, work with him, see if you can get him unblocked.'

'Does he have a girlfriend? Or three?'

'Uh-uh. I made some introductions, laid Tate Finnegan's *How to Score Big* course on him, but he just disappeared up his own ass.'

'Maybe he's queer.'

'I keep having this conversation. No, he isn't a faggot. Women scare him, that's all. There's a chick keeps calling the office for him. Whenever I mention it, he looks like I told him he has terminal cancer.'

'Sounds like a suitable case for treatment.'

'What, acid, you mean?'

'Something like that.'

'Uh-uh. There's enough pretty colours and talking eyeballs in his universe already.'

'So what you want me to do?'

'We put him in the other gingerbread house. And a couple hours a day you hang out with the dude, jam with him, listen to his problems, knock lyrics around, whatever it takes. And then when the album's laid down, I slit open a vein and you and me, we become blood-brothers.'

Needless to say, it wasn't what I wanted. But a man in my position didn't say no to Tate Finnegan, unless he was planning to go and jump off a cliff afterwards.

'OK,' I said. 'Long as he brings a chastity belt for Maeve.'

I'd met Adam Earnshaw only once before, when he'd opened for us at the Bankside Hall. He'd seemed pretty out of it then – but I figured that was just nerves, exacerbated by reckless over-medication with Tate's Acapulco gold. But when he got out of the car at Toad Hall, blinking in the sunshine, as if he'd lived the last six months under a rock, before realizing his wallet was missing and ducking back in to scrabble around for it, I began to wonder whether *out of it* was his natural condition. If so, this was going to be a tough gig.

As the car drove off, he stared mesmerized at the big house, taking in the beauty of the stone, the musical regularity of the windows, the oil-on-water gleam of the glass, the filigree slenderness of the frames.

'Yeah, beautiful, I know,' I said, grabbing a bag and one of his guitars. 'But that's not for the likes of us. We're in the nymph and swain quarters round the back.'

You'd have thought that would at least have got a smile: the guy was studying English at Oxford, for God's sake. But no: not so much as a twitch. He picked up the rest of his luggage and we trudged in silence across the stable yard, like a couple of Arctic explorers too exhausted to speak. I opened the door to the empty cottage and shooed him inside. He stood in the little front room, gawping round at the bare brick walls, the space-pilot Swedish chairs, the jazzy black and orange rug.

'Come on,' I said. 'Let's get this stuff upstairs.'

I led him up to the main bedroom, which provoked more gawping – as if the last things he'd expected to see there were a bed and a chest of drawers.

'How old's this place?' he asked.

I shrugged. 'Same age as the house maybe? Eighteenth century?'

'Am I going to be staying here on my own?'

'Yeah. But don't worry.' I tapped the wall above the bedhead. 'Maeve and I are just through there. So any time you feel lonely, all you have to do is knock. Only pick your moment, won't you?'

I don't think he knew what I was talking about. On the way downstairs, I started to plan a phone call to Tate: *Look, I'm sorry, man, but the guy's catatonic. You're going to have to find somewhere else for him.*

'Right, then,' I said, when I reached the front door. 'I'll leave you to it.'

'OK.' He hesitated. 'And thank you. For having me here.'

'I didn't have much choice about it. Tate said he'd spoil my pretty face if I didn't.'

I waited for the blank stare. Instead, he laughed suddenly and said,

'Yeah. And he threatened me with the same thing, *whhhhht*' – making a razor with the edge of his hand, and slashing his cheek – 'if I didn't come.'

OK, I thought: that's a bit more like it. We'll put the phone call on hold, and see how we get on.

'Actually,' I said, 'why don't we just pop next door now, and you can say hullo to Maeve?'

'OK.'

She was waiting for us in the living room, one hand nervously brace-leting the other wrist.

'Here he is,' I said.

She smiled. 'Hi, Adam.'

For a moment he froze, not knowing what to do. Then he bowed stiffly, like Mr Darcy asking Elizabeth Bennett to dance.

'Hullo.'

Her eyes filled with tears. She could never hide her feelings, and any sign of awkwardness or vulnerability always touched her.

'You know what?' she said. 'I'm going to give you a great big hug.' She lunged forward and embraced him. 'Welcome to Toad Hall.'

He was taken aback, but laughed, and managed to get his arms round her, though he couldn't quite shape them to the curves of her body.

'Why Toad Hall?' he said.

I explained. He listened, nodding and smiling. When I'd finished, he said,

'*Wind in the Willows* used to be one of my favourite books. Well, it still is.'

'Mine too,' said Maeve.

'Though I think it would be fair to say that in the version you both so fondly remember,' I said, 'the peeping Tom theme is rather underdeveloped.'

'Oh, I don't know,' said Adam. 'I bet you there's a critic somewhere who could find it.'

Maeve laughed. 'Why don't we go into the kitchen, and I'll make some tea?'

'That'd be nice,' said Adam. As he followed us through, he pulled a Golden Virginia pouch from his pocket and waved it, pointing first at me, then at Maeve.

'Do you?'

Maeve nodded.

'Would this be a good moment?'

'It's always a good moment.'

He sat down, took out a packet of skins. 'Small, regular or large?'

Maeve glanced across at me from the sink. 'Oh, large, I think, don't you?'

'Depends what you've got in there, old son,' I said. 'If it's Tate Finnegan's VSOP, then –'

'It isn't. But it's good stuff.'

'Ah, it comes from this simply marvellous little man you've got in Oxford, does it?'

'Doesn't everybody's?'

Maeve laughed. What the hell did Tate mean, the guy was scared of women? He was certainly having no trouble charming the knickers off my wife. I started thinking about making that phone call again.

'Here,' he said, rolling the joint tight and holding it out to her. 'You want to do this?'

Giggling, eyes closed, she ran her tongue along the gum strip.

I can't remember how long Adam stayed that evening. Tea turned into what Maeve – in winsome mode – called *drinkies*; and drinkies into supper: a huge mound of spaghetti Bolognese, topped off with another joint. Even what we talked about – after the second glass of wine, at least – is a bit of a blur. But one moment, a brief video clip, has stayed with me: Maeve leaning over to give him a refill, and inadvertently – I'm pretty sure it was inadvertent: the dope/alcohol combo always made her a bit maladroit – brushing his cheek with one of her braless tits. I was watching him, eagle-eyed; and was startled to see that – instead of smiling, or catching her eye, or surreptitiously touching her in return, as I'd expected – he hunched up, ramming his hands between his knees. And it struck me, in a sudden dope-fuelled flash of understanding, that he was relaxed with Maeve, not because he wanted to be her lover, but because he knew – or thought he knew – that being her lover wasn't an option.

We went to bed that night with a muzzy sense of relief: we'd broken the ice and everything was going to be OK. But it turned out to be not that simple. True, there were days when – after a few exchanges – you'd find Adam suddenly tuning to your wavelength, and blossoming into an animated companion; but there were others when without warning he'd revert to the boggle-eyed alien who'd emerged from the car that first day, and nothing you could say would seem to reach him. About a week after he arrived, for example, there was a letter for him mixed in our post. It had been addressed to him c/o Wheatsheaf Records, and must have been forwarded on by Tate's snotty Brummy sidekick Roy Batley, who'd decorated the envelope with little doodles of eyes and skulls. When I gave it to Adam, he gulped and took a step back.

'Don't worry about Roy's artwork,' I said. 'He's just trying to freak you out.'

That didn't seem to help. He licked his lips and ripped open the flap with trembling hands. Inside was a single sheet of paper. He scanned it quickly, then let it go. It fluttered on to the table.

'Bad news?' I said.

He didn't reply. I looked down and read, in childishly big handwriting:

> *In the witchy night*
> *All I do is think of you*
> *Your hair, your eyes, your voice, your smile*
> *Your touch*
> *Jesus Jesus Jesus Jesus Jesus*
> *I take the blade*
> *And carve your name*
>
> *lil*

'Who's Lil?' I said.

He said nothing. I'm not sure he'd even heard me.

'Well, sounds like you're well in there. Why don't you ask her down, and we'll show her a good time?'

He stared past me, as if he was planning his escape.

'What is it?' I said.

'I'm worried about her. *Worried* understates it.'

'Why? She pregnant, or something? Does she needs money?'

Without saying anything, he pushed me out and shut the door. After that, for more than an hour, we heard intermittent thumps and clunks from his house, as if he were packing. I kept peering out of the window, half-expecting to see him leaving. But then the noises subsided; and when I went round that evening to ask if he wanted to come over for something to eat, his stuff was still strewn about the place as usual.

'Oh, right,' he said. 'Thank you.'

'You OK now?'

'Some and some,' he said.

But, despite his unpredictability, we soon settled into a sort of artists' colony routine: work on our own stuff in the morning; meet at lunch to discuss progress; go our separate ways again in the afternoon, and then foregather at Maeve's and my place to play one another – if we felt like it – what we'd done, after which we'd embark on the preliminaries (usually a fat joint and a bottle of wine) to a boozy supper. That was the idea, anyway: in practice, none of us was particularly good at sticking to the timetable. Adam would often lurch into lunch tangle-haired and bleary-eyed, without even having had time to shave; and in the afternoons, when he'd gone back to his house, Maeve and I tended to resume our extra-curricular activities. But a certain competitive playground spirit – *I can jump higher than you can* – kept us all more or less on our toes. In Adam's case, I think, that often meant sitting up working half the night. I remember once going down at two in the morning to terrorize a couple of squalling cats in the stable yard and hearing a gentle babble of notes from his living room, like the sound of a far-off brook.

He was a good guitarist – oh, a pox on envy, I'll admit it: a *very* good guitarist, just the wrong side of great – with crystal sharp fingering and a knack for finding interesting chord progressions. But Tate was right: he was blocked, in a way I couldn't really figure out. He wouldn't play us the two songs he'd already sent Tate, and when I asked him why, he said he didn't want to be defined by them: he was trying to develop a new voice. At suppertime he'd come in with some pretty little fragment he'd written, and Maeve and I would say, *Yeah, that's really nice, keep going with it*; but then the next day he'd show up, not with a development of the same piece, but with something completely different. So he had a growing repertoire of promising snippets, but no way of turning them into a whole garment – because, of course – for most of us, anyway – music doesn't work like that: it isn't tailoring, it's gardening.

At first I thought the problem might simply be isolation, a lack of exposure to the ways other people were responding to the challenge of hammering out a new form. He liked Delius, Vaughan Williams, George Butterworth; he had a reasonable knowledge of traditional English folk; but rock-and-roll, jazz, the underground scene, barely featured on his map at all – except as a windswept expanse of *terra incognita* marked *Here Be Dragons*. So I sat him down and played him Dylan and the Band – he'd heard a bit of *Blonde on Blonde* for some reason, but nothing else – the Byrds, the Mothers of Invention, the Lovin' Spoonful. He listened politely, but said nothing. When I pressed him, his only response was,

'It's a different language. I'm still trying to learn *mine*. What the rules are. What I can and can't say.'

And then there were the lyrics. They were just ditties, really, no more than a verse apiece, that he'd patch on to the little scraps of music. But, short as they were, they were always weirdly memorable. While most of us were writing songs about free love, drugs, youthful disappointment, most of his seemed to be snapshots from the lives of imagined characters: a girl trying to get home through an almost impenetrable forest; an elderly college servant who finds he's become invisible.

One evening, after supper, I said,

'You know what I think? I think that's what's holding you back: writing about other people. Why don't you tell us what it's like being Adam Earnshaw instead? See if maybe that gets the juices going?'

He said nothing, but picked up his guitar again, hunched forward, closed his eyes – we were all pretty stoned by this point – and played *Spencer the Rover* from start to finish. It was a beautiful performance, but – even though I should have been too out of it to care – it really pissed me off. What were we supposed to do – roll on our backs and kick our legs in the air, overwhelmed by the guy's soulfulness? It didn't help that that was exactly the effect it seemed to be having on Maeve, who looked on, head swaying in time to the music, tears trickling down her cheeks.

'There,' he said at the end. 'See, that *is* about me. When I got to England, that's what I thought I was: Spencer the Rover, coming home.' He began picking at the strings again. 'But *this* is what I actually found.'

He started on a song I'd never heard before: I realized afterwards, when the album finally came out, that it must have one of the tracks he'd already sent to Tate:

'*Rainy Friday, Mr Morris*
Takes his lunchbox, leaves the assembly line
In the street the kids are drifting
Going nowhere
Blowing like litter
Don't they know we fought a war for them?'

Three more verses in the same vein – with no chorus, so the whole thing had a kind of unchanging assembly line feel.

'Who's Mr Morris?' I asked, when he'd finished.

'A chap who works at Cowley. Though that isn't his real name.'

'Oh, so you know him personally, do you?'

'Only slightly,' he said, impervious to the sarcastic edge in my voice. 'I went to his house once.'

'What on earth was a nice posh college boy like you doing there?'

He shrugged. 'It's complicated.'

'No, come on.'

'His daughter. She'd broken up with someone. I was trying to comfort her.'

Maeve sniffed. Oh, Jesus: not just John fucking Keats: Sir Gala-fucking-had, too.

'I don't think he was terribly pleased to see me,' said Adam. 'He pushed me out in the rain and slammed the door in my face.'

'Why?' said Maeve.

'*I don't want no bleeding long-haired layabouts in my house.*'

He began to giggle. I joined in. Maeve hesitated, then clambered on the bandwagon. Soon, thanks to the benign influence of Mary Jane, we were all shaking with silent laughter.

Fanfare. Stage left, (re-)enter Mr Toad. For some reason, Adam's arrival seemed to have deterred him from making a nuisance of himself – either Tate's warning must have had the desired effect, or else the prospect of *four* in a bed was too kinky even for his tastes – so we haven't seen much of him recently. But then *ba-boom*, I open the bedroom curtains one morning, maybe three weeks into the new regime, and there he is, talking to Adam in the stable yard. A double surprise: I've never known Adam a) to be up this early before; or b) to exchange more than three words with Tristram Orr-Molton. But now they're chatting away like old friends, not about some tabloid sex scandal, evidently (there isn't a newspaper in sight), but – to judge from the way they're pointing and squinting at the house – about architecture.

At lunchtime, he says he won't be in for supper that evening. It takes a bit of thumb-screwing to extract the reason: he's going over to Toad Hall instead. Tristram's going to give him the guided tour, and tell him the history of the place, before a light collation in the blue parlour or wherever.

'That's a bit of a turn-up,' I said after he'd gone. 'What do you reckon? You think Tate's wrong, and he's queer after all? And old Toady's so desperate he'll settle for any port in a storm?'

Maeve shook her head. 'Adam isn't queer.'

The next day he came into lunch jittery with excitement.

'How'd it go, man?' I said. 'You have a good time?'

He nodded. 'It's a beautiful house. But it must be a bit freaky. For him, I mean. Living there all by himself.'

'Apart from the servants,' I said.

'One elderly housekeeper. And his sisters, when they can be bothered to come and see him.'

'I shouldn't worry,' I said. 'I don't think you need shed any tears for Mr Toad. He's not exactly on the breadline. No one's dropping napalm on him. Or lining him up against a wall with the other counter-revolutionary elements. Not yet, anyway.'

'Still, he can't really escape, can he? It's what he is.' He hooked his fingers into chord-shapes. 'I've been writing a song about it.'

'Really?' said Maeve. 'You going to play it to us?'

He nodded. 'Soon. Soon. When I've finished.'

'Oh, OK. Some time in the next millennium then,' I said.

But when he showed up that evening he was carrying his guitar and a couple of sheets of paper covered in messy writing. He sat at the kitchen table and went through the lyrics once or twice, mouthing them to himself and changing the occasional word with his leaky Bic. Then he nodded and said,

'Ready?'

'You bet your sweet ass,' I said.

Adam straddled his chair and launched into a spidery, Bach-on-the-harpsichord introduction. Then he began:

'You are what you are
Flesh and bone
Lights and liver
Heart and soul
But I am a house
Glass and stone
Lake and river
Trunk and bole.'

Eight lines: the most he'd ever managed to write since he'd been with us. But instead of stopping there, as I'd expected, he went on to give us three more verses: a complete song. I couldn't really follow it: there seemed to be no clear thread, just a series of more or less vivid images spliced together like random frames from a film. But the oddity of the lyrics was balanced by a conventional AABA structure, so the effect was of a cluster of brilliant stones held gracefully in place by a silver loop.

'Yeah,' said Maeve, when he'd finished.

'Yeah what?'

She shook her head – amazed? Baffled? 'Just…Yeah.'

'Well, I'm pleased with it,' said Adam.

And he was off. For months he'd been snuffling round inside his pen, while Maeve and I hovered about by the gate, trying to find a way of coaxing him out to join us. Now, suddenly, he'd somehow wriggled under the bars on his own and was streaking away from us across open country. Over the next couple of weeks, while we produced one-and-a-half tracks, he wrote half a dozen. They were all as freaky, in their own way, as *I Am a House*; but taken together they gave you the dreamlike sense that you were watching some odd-shaped new species struggling out of the chrysalis and testing its wings. We recorded them on the monster Ferrograph in a single session, and he posted them off to Wheatsheaf. The next day, I had a call from Tate Finnegan:

'Hey, Stevie, what the fuck you do?'

'Sorry, you'll have to narrow the field a bit. Do when?'

'I just heard Adam's tape. You put acid in his Cheerios?'

'No.'

'A chick then?'

'In his Cheerios?'

Tate groaned.

'No chick,' I said.

'Well, something happened. It's tits. Most of it, anyway. Four tracks. That's a bon-a-roo strike rate.'

'What, better than ours, you mean?' I'd never heard him so excited. I should have kept my insecurity to myself, but it seeped out.

'I didn't say that, mano. I'm just telling you, whatever you been doing to the guy, you and Maeve really put him through some changes. So thank you.'

'Nothing to do with us. It's the strange allure of Mr Toad.'

'Excuse me?'

'Mine genial host.'

'Oh, Tristram. Why you call him Mr Toad? No, don't tell me. How's he doing? Still trying to stick his dick in?'

'No. I don't know what you said to get him off our backs, but it seems to have worked.'

'I just mentioned the magic words: *Love-in.*'

'*Love-in?* Mr Toad?'

'Yeah. Conjures up kind of a freaky picture, doesn't it? He doesn't actually know what a love-in is. Fuck, *I* don't know what a love-in is. But the *idea* of it turns him on. So that's what I said. He keeps his dong clean with Maeve – and as a reward, we ship in a whole load of Carnaby Street chicks and have a love-in.'

'What, you're getting up a *charabanc* party, are you?'

'*Share a bang?*'

I laughed. 'So when are you thinking of?'

'Soon. Hey, what's the joke? Did I miss something there?'

'When's soon?'

'I don't know. Couple weeks. This some English humour thing?'

'Play on words.' I said. 'So what about Adam? Does he know? About the love-in?'

'Not yet, bud.'

'He'll run a mile.'

'Chance we have to take.' His voice was tugging at the leash. He was obviously impatient to get off the phone all of a sudden.

'OK,' I said. 'So is that it?'

'Pretty much – Oh, except when do I get to hear some of *your* stuff?'

'We're working on it.'

'OK, man. Later.'

Two bits of information to process: your record producer a) loves your work, and b) wants to organize a party. Which makes the bigger impression? If it had been me – or you, probably, or pretty much anyone else – the answer, no contest, would have been (a). But for Adam, it was the other way round. Being told his music was tits was a sideshow. The prospect of a love-in at Sibley Hall, by contrast, was so terrifying that it immediately seemed to take over his life. He stopped writing new material, and became even more fidgety and withdrawn. He couldn't function without a joint in his hand. And his joints weren't just take-it-or leave it accessories, to help the time pass more pleasantly; they were built like dreadnoughts, with enough dope to flatten a shore battery.

The next day, as I was walking past his open window, I overheard him talking on the phone. The near-desperate tone in his voice made me stop in the lee of the frame and listen. He was pleading with someone called Roddy, but I couldn't figure out what exactly he wanted: at one point he said he needed *a lifeline*, a minute later a *Get-Out-of-Jail* card. It wasn't until he mentioned the date that I realized: he was begging for an invitation for the day of the party. A moment later he let out an agonized groan. Clearly Roddy whoever-he-was was otherwise engaged that weekend.

At supper that evening I asked Adam, 'What do you think's actually going to happen at this love-in?'

He shook his head.

'Well, I'll tell you. Nothing. All it is, is a way to keep Mr Toad sweet. There'll be girls, music –'

'Figs and pomegranates,' said Maeve. 'Served by scantily clad Nubian beauties.'

I looked at her so sharply that she winced. 'No there won't. It'll just be an old-fashioned English garden party. Strawberries and cream. And Mr Toad prancing about the place playing the lord of the manor, making sure everyone has enough champagne. Blink, and you'll think you're back in 1913.'

Adam shook his head. 'It's just the crowd. I don't know how to deal with all those people.'

'That's a bit of a drawback for a musician.'

'I don't mean when I'm performing.'

'Perform, then.'

I expected him to throw up his hands and burst out, *God, no, I couldn't.* But instead he looked past me, eyes widening, picturing the possibility to himself.

'You'll have the girls fighting to get to you,' said Maeve.

He appeared not to have heard – though that didn't stop me kicking Maeve under the table. But later, when she was in the kitchen, he asked,

'So do the girls fight to get to *you*? When *you're* playing?'

'My dear sir, may I remind you that I'm a married man?'

'Yeah.' He pondered, unsmiling. 'Is that how it happened, then? Maeve was one of them? And she just pushed all the others out of the way?'

I shook my head. '*I* saw *her*. Performing at The Troubadour. And the instant I did, I thought, right you are. That's the one. I'll have her.'

'How did you know?'

'No gentleman should ask a question like that. But since you did, it was the prodigious stirring in my loins.'

'I'm sorry, I –'

I clapped his shoulder. 'I'm joking. You're way too uptight, man. Take a deep breath and relax. You don't need a wife. What you need is to get laid. So if you see a lady who turns you on, just magic her away, whispering sweet nothings, and...'

Mistake. He looked as if I'd smacked him in the teeth.

'Or alternatively,' I said, backtracking, 'you can just play your music, if that's all you want to do.'

He sighed with relief, like a kid who's been told he doesn't have to go to school.

*

The love-in. Mr Toad's love-in: MTLI. Do people still have parties like that? I don't see how they could. Back then, Big Brother was still securely tucked away between the covers of *1984*; now he's escaped into the ether, and the second you let your guard down, you find some fucker with a phone has snitched the moment for eternity, and you're riding a shit storm of illiterate abuse online.

Not – just to be clear – that MTLI was an *orgy*. To me (and OK, yes, I am speaking from experience) orgies always have a residual tincture of puritan earnestness about them: they're regimented affairs, patrolled by grim-faced pleasure police determined that everyone should fuck till they drop, or else...But the love-in was just *free*. A lot of people made out, but quite a few didn't – and either way it was fine. The point was simply to do your own thing, knowing that – whatever that was – there was a safety net of love and acceptance waiting to catch you if you fell. No, not a net: that sounds too harsh and scratchy. A *web*, fine enough to mould itself to your shape, but infinitely strong.

It was more than a month past the solstice, but the summer was still set in a good-tempered pattern of long easy days, and nights smelling of tobacco plants and roses. In the lead-up to the party, Mr Toad was in his element, showing an unsuspected vein of officer material running through his normal gawd-help-us-ness. Marquees mushroomed on the lawn behind the house; half a dozen extra boats were ferried in to swell the little fleet on the lake; on the day itself – under Toad's personal supervision – a galaxy of Japanese lanterns was hung from the trees on the island. And in the final hours, when the caterers' vans arrived and started to disgorge their cargo of food and drink, Toad was there in the stable yard, stick in hand, directing operations with all the aplomb of a subaltern sending his chaps over the top.

For Adam, all this bustle wasn't exciting: it was the harbinger of impending doom. Like a condemned man blocking out the sight of the gallows, he kept his curtains drawn even during the day, and set foot outside only to scurry the few paces – gaze averted – to our door. Once, he even failed to turn up for lunch, and I wondered if, after all, he'd decided to do a runner. But when I squeezed my ear to the wall I could hear the sound of him playing, repeating the same tricksy chord sequence again and again, till it started to drive me crazy. So I assumed he'd just forgotten, and left him to it.

But when the day arrived, Maeve and I weren't so *laissez-faire*. To get him confident enough to play, but not so zonked out that he fell on his face or began eating his guitar, demanded a carefully calibrated regime of alcohol and Mary Jane. We started around five o'clock by blowing one of his big boy sticks, followed – an hour or so later – by a stiff gin, to which I heroically refrained from adding a tab of acid. By the time the *loveinistas* started to show up, he was borderline mellow, and even managed to make a joke or two.

Sadly, there was no *charabanc*, just a succession of cars – most of them sporty little numbers driven by blonde and smiling Simon Dee lookalikes, each with a girl at his side, and sometimes a couple more wedged in behind. They climbed out in slow motion (or was that just Adam's big boy messing with my head, and throwing in some extra frames-per-second?) and seeped round the edge of the house, in a slow pageant of paisley and muslin, ruffs and kaftans, scarves and stripy blazers.

There was no sign of Tate Finnegan, but it didn't seem to matter: the party just eased into life, as if it had been going on all day, and was resuming after a break. Maeve and I waited for a few minutes, then drifted out to join the fun. I've no idea what was happening in her head, but I know what was going on in mine. Remember: we'd been on our own – apart from Adam and Mr Toad – for almost three months. We were just as crazy about each other as ever – but, whatever Paul Newman may have said, when you've eaten steak at home every day for eleven weeks, the idea of going out for a burger and onion rings is pretty appealing. So, as we started to mingle, I did a rough headcount. Yep, Tate had done his stuff: there seemed to be perhaps five more unattached females than unattached males – enough to give Adam and Toad (and me, if I got lucky) a clear shot, but not so many that it looked weird. And, as promised, all the girls – as well as most of the men – were astonishingly beautiful, with the unreal perfection of models got up for a photo-shoot. To a real, honest-to-God Hashbury hippie it would have looked more like a fashion show than a love-in, but Mr Toad didn't know the difference.

He, poor clod, was in seventh heaven, greeting every girl he could get near to with a kiss, and bobbing his head to the guys like a strutting pigeon. He sported a flounced mauve shirt, and – thanks to a last-minute trip to the barber – a new hairstyle that, from a distance, made him look like the fifth Monkee. He bounced around tirelessly, herding people towards the drinks table, serving the women himself, then trying manfully to keep them talking, until they made their excuses and started edging away. I lingered nearby, occasionally – if I saw something specially tempting – moving in to pick up the pieces. But this was just the research stage of the evening. The night was still young, and Maeve was watching me, so I simply concentrated on squirrelling away a list of names – predictably, they turned out to be pretty much a job lot of Tessas and Suzies and Janeys and Flicks and Belindas – for future reference.

Somewhere around the second or third drink, as I was tacking gingerly towards a temporarily-detached Flick or Suzie, the crowd suddenly fell silent, and I saw everyone looking at the lake. The next moment I knew why: the sound of a flute – sensual, languid, and at the same time neck-hair-stirringly wild – was floating towards us from the island. But whoever was playing it remained hidden by a screen of trees – so it was as if the landscape itself was serenading us, inviting us to abandon ourselves to antic play.

Somebody knocked against my elbow. I turned.

'Ah,' I said. 'Tate. The spaced man cometh. Where have you been?'

'Had to give these folks a ride.' he said, nodding to the couple next to him. One of them was a guy with a big moustache called Peyton Whybrow, that we'd met once at a concert, and seemed to have become Tate's *numero uno* hanger-on. The other was probably the most gorgeous girl I've ever seen: poised and slim, wearing a mini-dress stamped with off-kilter green and red squares that set off the perfection of her lightly tanned arms and legs. As she looked up at me, her blonde hair slipped back from her face, letting the light catch her pearl-pink mouth and wide-set tawny eyes.

'Yes, I'm sorry,' she said, laughing. 'It's all my fault. Peyton was ready on time. It was me. I let the side down.'

Rrrrgh: that voice, and the whiff of freesia on her lustrous skin. I'd been ogling girls like her since I was fourteen, knowing that – whatever happened – they'd always be out of reach. Someone like me could turn up at her house in an Aston Martin, and still be expected to use the tradesmen's entrance. So had *Tate* managed to get in the front door, the rich American from outside the class labyrinth? I doubted it somehow. There was a sort of formality between them that suggested they didn't know each other well. Besides, Tate didn't really have girlfriends. And I couldn't see this lady settling for being just another of his endless succession of one-night stands.

'You know Sadie?' he said.

'No. But if I don't by the end of the evening, it won't be for want of trying.'

She laughed again.

'Sadie what?' I said. 'I'm sure you must be famous.'

'Long.'

'Where's Maeve?' said Tate.

'I don't know. We're not actually stapled together. We do both talk to other people sometimes.'

He frowned. Clearly – if he had anything to do with it – Sadie Long was not for me. He nodded towards the island. 'Pretty smokey, huh? Delia on her flute?'

'Smokey indeed,' I said. 'Your idea?'

He nodded. 'I had Tristram take her over there ahead of time. So it'd be a surprise.'

Sadie Long squeezed his arm. 'It's lovely. What made you think of it?'

'Adam Earnshaw. I was listening to those tracks again. And it hit me, *kapow!* That's the key. That-is-the-key. The god Pan, playing in the middle of the English countryside.'

'The key to what?' said Sadie.

'The place he's been hiding all this time. Where is Adam, anyway?'

'I don't know,' I said.

He sucked his teeth. 'I was counting on you, man.'

The Adam obsession was starting to piss me off. 'We're not nursemaids,' I said. 'We did our best. But you can take a horse to water –'

'Yeah, yeah, yeah. When'd you last see him?'

'Couple of hours ago.'

'Couple of *hours*?'

'Yeah. At our place.'

'Oh, shit.' More teeth-sucking. He seemed genuinely perturbed, like a mother whose kid's gone missing in a shopping centre.

'OK,' I said. 'I'll see if I can flush him out.'

I dodged through the crowd, glancing right and left. Adam was nowhere to be seen. As I came out into the stable yard, I saw that his curtains were still drawn. I knocked at the door.

'Yes?'

He was crouched on the sofa in the gloom, cradling his guitar on his knee, wearing a crumpled T-shirt and a pair of old-fashioned cotton trousers with turn-ups. I wondered if he realized how uncool he looked. Or was it maybe deliberate – a way of signalling *I'm not like the rest of you: I play by different rules*?

'You coming out?' I said.

'Are you ready for me?'

'We've been ready for hours. Everyone's wondering where you've got to.'

'But I mean, do you want me to play now?'

'In a bit. Come and say hullo first. Join the party.'

'But we agreed, didn't we? That I was just going to play.'

'I thought we agreed that you'd make your mind up when the time came.'

'Well, it's come. And I have.'

I shrugged. 'OK. But you're not going to play in here, are you? So let's go.'

He checked the tuning on the guitar, then got up and followed me outside, blinking in the light from the low sun. My calculation was that, once we'd hit the party, there was a fighting chance he'd get snagged up in it, have a drink or three, start talking to someone, wow her with his heroic tales of singer-songwriting derring-do, sneak off into the bushes to get his reward, mission accomplished. Just as long, I hoped, as that someone wasn't Sadie.

But it soon became obvious it wasn't going to happen. Adam plodded through the crowd with downcast eyes, mumbling *sorry* if he collided with an arm or a shoulder, but otherwise refusing to engage with anyone at all. Beauty and delight on every side, and the daft git wouldn't even look at it. And everyone else was too far gone by this point, too involved in their own schemes and machinations, their own dance of evasion and pursuit, to pay any attention to a bashful newcomer. So we pushed ahead, unaccosted and unnoticed, moving inexorably towards the lake. When we finally came out by the shore, I said,

'We should find Tate.'

'Just let me play. Where should I go, do you think? Here?'

'Shit, man, I don't know!'

He flinched, stung by my anger, struggling to understand it. And then suddenly he heard the sound of the flute – a sobbing, ethereal warble, wafting across the surface of the water – and his expression changed. Eyes wide, ear cocked to catch the music, he gazed towards it with a kind of religious awe.

'What is that?' he whispered.

'The god Pan.'

He looked sharply at me. 'Really?'

I shook my head. 'You are the most gullible fucking human being I've ever met.'

Even as I said it, I was shocked by my own cruelty. But the cumulative effect of the last hour or so had been to put me into a lethally foul mood. First there was Adam himself: his unreasonableness; his self-absorption – and Tate Finnegan's apparent assumption that they were somehow my responsibility, as if my only role in life was to run around making sure the bugger didn't fall off his tricycle. Then there was the by now indisputable evidence that the whole evening had been planned, not – as Tate had said – to thank Maeve and me for taking care of the man-child, but entirely for the man-child's own benefit. And now – the final straw – here was Adam's epiphany at the sound of the flute. It felt like a real slap in the face: the crass, bull-in-a-china-shop American, who had spent a fraction of the time with Adam that Maeve and I had, clearly understood his character better than we did.

To add to my bewilderment, the man-child – normally so painfully over-sensitive – didn't seem to credit my rudeness at all.

'I'm going in one of the boats,' he said excitedly. 'I'll play out there. Out on the lake.'

He hurried out on to the landing stage, dropped into the furthest dinghy and cast off with a few quick twists of the wrist.

'Careful,' I said. 'You'll drift away.'

'It's a lake. No current. And there isn't a breeze.'

'Even so…'

He lifted one of the oars. 'Well, then I'll just row back again.'

'You sure? Have you ever done it before?'

'Of course. Lots of times.'

He manhandled his way past the rest of the little fleet, till his dinghy was lying fifteen or twenty yards offshore. Then he settled himself on one of the thwarts, picked up the guitar, and started to play. To begin with it was barely audible: a faint pricking in the air, like far-off wind chimes, that seemed to come from the landscape itself. Gradually it grew louder, entering into a long-distance conversation with the flute, weaving in and out of the melody. A small group standing near the shore turned and smiled, nodding along with the languorous rhythm for a moment, before looking away again.

And then the beat quickened, the strumming grew more urgent, and – without warning – Adam launched at full volume into *Spencer the Rover*. The impact was like a gunshot. A girl just behind me gasped. The whole crowd was stunned into silence. After a second or two, a few voices started to erupt again. But it was an unequal struggle, a collision between two incommensurate worlds, and the chatter soon petered out.

People started to press towards the lake: desultorily at first, then – swept by a kind of herd instinct, like cattle jostling each other to get to food – faster and more insistently. And, jealous and irritable though I was, I could understand their response: even in the open air, and with no amplification, Adam's singing seemed to take the top layer of your skin off, leaving the nerve-ends exposed. You either had to surrender to it, or move out of earshot. So I stayed where I was, letting it go to work on my emotions – and, at the same time, in some mean little corner of my soul, hoping that Tate Finnegan had been called away for some reason, and couldn't see his protégé bringing a crowd to its knees.

No such luck. Adam had barely finished his second song – a long, mournfully drawn out rendering of *Matty Groves* – when Tate bulldozed his way into the space next to me.

'Whoa,' he said. 'You found him.'

I turned. Shit: there was Sadie Long, holding his arm, looking as impressed as everyone else. Her eyes were unnaturally bright, and she'd donned a daisy chain tiara, which gave her the air of a little girl at a kids' birthday party.

'See what I mean, Sade?' murmured Tate.

She nodded. They watched in awe as Adam made his way through *Scarborough Fair*. Then, as the applause started to subside, and Adam was tuning up for the next song, Tate called,

'Hey, Adam! How about one of the new ones?'

Adam stared at him.

'Come on, man! These are good people. You're among friends.'

Adam hesitated, then nodded, and mumbled, 'This is called *Cookie-cut Kid*.' He played a brief intro, and then, looking up at the summer stars, began to sing:

> *Peace and justice*
> *Ban the bomb*
> *Victory to the toiling poor!*
> *But when she sleeps*
> *Lily dreams*
> *A pair of six-guns in her drawer*

The music was a rollercoaster, switching from bombastic to ethereal and back again – and of course, after the episode of the crazy letter, I was intrigued by the mention of *Lily*. But I soon became less interested in following the song than I was in watching the reaction of the audience.

Looking back, it's hard to explain. All I can suggest is that you try to imagine yourself there: a soft, fragrant evening in the grounds of an English country house; a ceaseless flow of drugs and alcohol; and, all around you, beautiful beyond belief in their peacock finery, the cream of a generation – *your* generation – whose time had come. There was lust in the air, understated but unmistakable, like a lingering scent; and – for most people – the near-certainty that it would be satisfied before the night was out. And, as Adam played, the lone flautist, realizing her performance duties were at an end, downed tools, and began lighting the Japanese lanterns one by one – making the island a glowing backdrop that turned us into children again and summoned us to a magical adventure. The cumulative effect was like an acid trip: a blurring of boundaries; a melding of souls in a single ecstatic consciousness.

By the end of *Cookie-cut Kid*, a cluster of barefoot girls had lined up on the landing stage, teetering on the edge, trying to get as close to Adam as possible. Half-way through *Mr Morris*, one of them lost her balance and fell in. For a moment the cold stunned her; then she started to splash about, laughing and shouting, *God, this is great!* Almost immediately, a couple of other girls held their noses and leapt in to join her. More laughter, more splashing. Then all three of them waded out to Adam's boat and clung to the gunwale, listening goopy-eyed, like a shoal of mermaids mobbing a sailor. And after he'd finished – with the spine-tingling *I Am a House* – they drew the dinghy in triumph to the shore, where Tate helped him out on to dry land.

'That was am*a*zing,' murmured Sadie Long, so close I felt the warmth of her body.

What could I say? I nodded.

'Tate says you and Maeve have been helping him.'

'We've tried.'

'I think you're being modest. If what we've just heard is anything to go by.'

'Well, thank you. But, believe it or not, that's not our only claim to fame.'

'Oh, no, I know. I saw you once. At the Bankside.'

I moved nearer, till our hands were touching. 'I wish I'd known. It might have changed my life.'

She drew away, laughing, and looking towards the lake. Tate was leading Adam towards us, along an avenue of awe-struck admirers. And *click*: I suddenly saw it, in the Polaroid image of their three faces: Tate, a man on a mission; Adam in a daze, with no idea where he was being taken; and Sadie the smiling prize at journey's end. *That* was why Tate had brought her: as Adam-bait.

'Here he is,' said Tate.

As he stopped, a phalanx of girls, led by the three mermaids, broke ranks and surged forward. Tate slipped an arm round Adam's shoulder.

'Excuse us, ladies, would you?' he said. 'The guy's wiped out. Even geniuses need a break sometimes.'

The girls backed off.

'Meet Sadie,' said Tate.

She held her hand out, lifting her face to him. 'Hello.'

Adam stared at her. What else was he going to do? The adrenalin was pumping through him: he'd just given the performance of a lifetime to an adoring crowd, and now this. His sense of reality, shaky at the best of times, must have been struggling to keep up. He glanced behind him, as if to make sure the magical island was still there, then turned back and took her hand.

'Hello.'

'Thank you so much,' she said.

He shook his head.

'No, really. Your music's extraordinary. I've never heard anything like it.'

Adam looked round. The mermaids were still there, but further off people were starting to turn their attention to each other – laughing, kissing, embracing, hands moving lightly over bums and breasts. Two or three couples were stretched out on the grass, impervious to everyone around them. Some were drifting away towards the shrubbery at the side of the house, in search of greater privacy. For a moment I thought Adam was going to make a run for it. But then he glanced at the island again, and that seemed to steady his nerve.

'Well, thank you,' he said, forcing himself to meet Sadie's gaze. Out of the corner of my eye I could see a relieved Tate bowing out, happy to let events take their course.

'I mean, *A pair of six-guns in her drawer*,' said Sadie. '*I* could never have come up with something like that. But when *you* use it, I know exactly what you're talking about. That longing just to flounce in and blow everything away. How do *you* know so exactly what it's like to be a teenage girl?'

OK, OK, I thought. *Tate played the song to you before, didn't he? So you had time to prepare?* But the idea never even occurred to Adam. He flushed with surprise.

'I don't know,' he said. 'No one's ever…Most people…Well, they aren't that perceptive…'

'I don't think it takes much perception,' said Sadie. 'That's what's so great about it. It's completely original, but the moment you hear it, you realize –'

A male voice, startlingly loud, stopped her in her tracks. 'Right, right, right, right, right.' And – like a dancing girl bursting out of a cake – Mr Toad appeared, elbowing his way through the mermaids with a bottle in one hand and a clutch of champagne flutes in the other.

'A celebration,' he said. 'A *coupe* of Pommery for the undisputed star of the evening.' He bowed in mock obeisance. 'Needless to say…Words fail me…Anyway…' He sloshed champagne into the glasses and passed them around. 'A toast? To Adam Earnshaw.'

'To Adam Earnshaw.'

'And what,' said Toad, sidling close to Sadie, 'did you think?'

'I was just saying. I thought it was wonderful.'

'It was. It was. Really far out.'

'Adam,' said Sadie – without so much as glance at Toad – 'was just about to tell me how he does it. The way he manages to get inside other people's lives.'

'Yes, fascinating,' boomed Toad.

'At least, I hope that's what he's going to do.' She leaned forward and whispered in Adam's ear. He listened, forehead puckered, then nodded. 'We're going to go somewhere a bit quieter,' she said, straightening up again and sliding her arm through his. 'See you later, everyone.'

It was brutal but effective: even Toad wasn't dense enough to think he might have been invited too. Like the rest of us, he just stood and watched as she led Adam across the lawn and into one of the empty tents.

'The Marquee de Sadie,' I murmured.

Tate appeared not to hear me. 'Beautiful,' he said, as he watched them sauntering inside. He waited a second or two, as if to make sure that Adam didn't come out again. Then he turned to me and said,

'So where the fuck is Maeve? I didn't even say hi to her yet.'

I don't really know what happened that night. I can only surmise, from what I saw, some time around noon the next day, in the stable yard: Sadie Long, pink and dewy as a rose petal, with newly washed hair, wearing jeans and a crisp white blouse, saying goodbye to dishevelled, stubble-jawed Adam, still in his t-shirt and ludicrous trousers. They hugged, they kissed, then hugged again, chins on each other's shoulders, while she gently stroked his back. Then she extricated herself and walked towards the front of the big house, stopping at the last moment to turn and wave.

'So how was it?' I asked, when Adam came in to lunch. He'd showered and shaved, thank God, and changed his clothes. 'You have a good time?'

He nodded.

'*Really* good?' said Maeve.

He nodded again – and, to my amazement, smiled.

'Pity Sadie didn't stay a bit longer,' I said. 'So –'

'She couldn't. She's got something on this afternoon. In London.'

'What sort of thing?'

'With a photographer.'

'Ah, so she's a model, is she?'

He shook his head. 'I shouldn't really talk about her. We told each other... You know... Things.'

And that was the end. For the next few weeks he was still officially res-ident at Toad Hall, but he was gone for days at a time. And when he *was* there, he didn't leave the house. Whenever I went past his window, I could hear him playing and singing, trying out words and snatches of melody.

And then, without warning, he moved to London.

Bye bye Adam.

10

RACHEL LAKE

Oh, my goodness. This is really creepy. Like someone coming back from the tomb and tapping at my window.

Who – well, who are you? And how on earth did you even get my name? I can't believe Sadie would have given it to you. We haven't spoken for years, but I'd imagine the last thing she'd want is for me to have a chance to tell my side of the story. But if it wasn't her, I can't for the life of me think...

Anyway, forget that. It doesn't matter. I'll do it. I *want* to do it. I want to tell you about Adam.

Sadie and I – you'll know this if it *was* her who told you – were at boarding school together. I was gawky, short-sighted and given to breaking things. She, right from the start, was popular, effortlessly good at sports, the star of every end-of-term play, and – apart from a brief run-in with acne when she was fifteen – goddess-beautiful. Half of us had an aching, life-swamping crush on her. In my case, at least, it was chaste and barely conscious. When I closed my eyes to go to sleep, I saw her, laughing and bright-eyed, hair streaming in the breeze, in a snazzy open-topped sports car. Next to her in the driver's seat was an indistinct figure: Simon Dee, perhaps, or Paul Jones from Manfred Mann – or me?

But of course it was hopeless. For our first four years, she barely acknowledged my existence. Not that she was ever cruel to me – or to anyone else, for that matter: I simply didn't feature on her map. It was only when we were in the upper sixth, and she was made head girl, that we suddenly became friends. Even now, in that not-so-tiny bit of me that's still a teenager, I can feel the thrill of it.

So what did she see in me? A lot of the other girls wondered that. The answer, I think – though it took me a while to figure it out – is actually quite simple: a way to nourish some part of her that most people never even glimpsed. You can't blame them: our whole culture conditions us, doesn't it, to look at girls like her as nothing more than specimens of physical perfection. The last words likely to spring to mind, when you encounter her staring out at you from the colour supplement fashion pages, are *bookishness* or *thoughtfulness*. And yet she *was* bookish and thoughtful – and even, at moments, oddly melancholy, as if she'd plumbed the depths of her own nature, and was disappointed to find them so shallow.

So it seemed quite natural, when we left school, and she decided to move to London, that she asked me to go with her. I was to be her haven, a refuge from the relentless hustle of establishing herself as a model and trying to break into acting. 'I'm just froth on a choppy sea,' she told me once, after a gruelling ten-hour shoot that had left her with sore muscles and swollen feet. 'It's only when I'm with you that the water's calm enough to see anything beneath the surface.'

My parents, needless to say, took a bit of persuading. You realize – when it's too late to tell them so – just how hard it was for their generation. My mother had gone to finishing school, and – if it hadn't been for the outbreak of war – would have been presented at court, like *her* mother before her. Instead she found herself in the ATS, working as a driver for Staff Officers – one of whom was my father. She was married at nineteen, had her first child when she was twenty-two, and the second – me – three years later.

By the time *I* was nineteen, the world had become unrecognizable to them. What were they going to do with me? There was no question of *my* being a debutante, of course. My mother – a keen reader of Dorothy L. Sayers novels – had, I think, some fuzzy idea that I might go to Cambridge and become a Girton bluestocking. But I failed the entrance exam – and the new concrete universities that were springing up all over the country seemed dangerously left-wing and subversive. The thought of sending their daughter to one of them, and seeing her brain-washed into Marxism and passed from bed to bed by a lot of long-haired revolutionaries, was too awful to contemplate.

So, in the end, the prospect of my sharing a London flat with my former head girl seemed better than any of the alternatives. My mother managed to reconcile herself to it by visualizing our existence there as a kind of school story: we'd continue to have all that fifth-form fun – practical jokes; cocoa at bedtime; midnight feasts – while simultaneously teaching ourselves the crucial domestic skills that would equip us for marriage. Poor woman: she wasn't a fool, and I can see now – with horrible clarity – that at some level she realized she was duping herself. That must be why, the whole time we were there – although she sometimes met me for tea at Fortnum's or Harvey Nichols – she never came to the flat. She knew only too well that the Angela Brazil schooldays fantasy couldn't survive an encounter with the real thing – and that, once it had gone, she'd never sleep easy again.

My father – always less confident than Mummy that I'd find a husband – suggested I should take a secretarial course. But, even if I wasn't Oxbridge material, that seemed a bit dowdy and unambitious – particularly if my glamorous flat-mate, the while, was scaling the heights of the fashion industry. So eventually, via a connection of a friend of a wartime colleague, he got me a job teaching English to foreign students, in a shoestring little outfit on the fringes of Kensington.

Somewhere like the Maurice School of English would be inconceivable now. Health and Safety would condemn the building in seconds flat, and the owner – and principal – find himself charged, not only with running his business in a death-trap, but with sexual harassment, false advertising and employing unqualified staff. Dr Maurice himself was an exotic creature, part of the huge flood of displaced persons that had spread across Europe at the end of the war. He was small and dapper, with a taste for bow ties and double-breasted suits. He seldom left the office without a black Malacca cane, which was as reliable a guide to his mood as a cat's tail: if he stopped swishing it suddenly, you knew you were in trouble.

None of us ever discovered what he was originally called, or where he was from – or why, when he came to this country, he had decided to reinvent himself as Bernard Maurice. It seemed an odd choice, as if he'd just rattled through a drawer full of British Christian names and plucked out two at random. At the start of every term, he would address the students, stick whisking at his side. A lot of them were would-be playboys from the Middle East, who frowned suspiciously as Dr M went into his carefully enunciated *spiel*:

'A language is not merely a collection of words, my friends. It is a key – yes, a *key*, to the soul of a people. And here at the Maurice School we pride ourselves on giving that key to those who study with us, so they can open the beautiful treasure-chest of English culture.'

In practice, that meant hiring people like me – well-bred girls (he was a tremendous snob, and an inveterate name-dropper), whose lack of experience meant he could get away with paying us a pittance, but who could introduce the students to the niceties of upper-middle-class behaviour. Occasionally, out of the blue, he would add an injunction of his own. They were generally so bizarre that, if I hadn't seen for myself the earnestness with which he delivered them, I'd have thought he was being satirical: *A gentleman, no matter what the circumstances, always wears a tie.* Or, *It is unusual for a lady to smoke after she is married.*

I soon learned to do a fair impression of Dr M's voice, and would entertain Sadie for hours by repeating some of his more outlandish pronouncements. They quickly turned into standing jokes, part of the lubrication that kept our life together running smoothly: if one of us, say, came in with a packet of Dunhills, the other would invariably burst out, *Ah, still not married yet then, I see?* But as the weeks went by, it dawned on me that I was hearing a lot less about Sadie's life than she was about mine. Sometimes, when I got in, I'd find a note saying she wouldn't be back that night; but when I asked her the next day where she'd been, she'd just shrug and say, *oh, you know, out and about* – and then instantly change the subject. Normally I played along with her; but on one occasion – when she'd come in looking uncharacteristically dishevelled, and with dark smudges under her eyes – I said,

'No, come on. Out and about with who?'

'Oh, a chap I know.'

'What's his name?'

'Simon.'

'Simon what?'

'Antrobus.'

'And?'

She laughed. 'And nothing. He's just a chap. Tell me about Dr M. I need cheering up.'

I assumed this was just her natural sweetness (and she *was* very sweet): she obviously had a boyfriend, and – in order to spare my feelings, since I didn't – decided to mention him as little as possible. It was only one afternoon a month or so later that I finally started to glimpse the truth.

I'd gone to work as usual that morning, but at lunchtime I suddenly developed a vicious sore throat, and persuaded Dr Maurice – it wasn't hard: among his other oddities, he had a morbid fear of infection – to let me leave early.

When I walked into the flat, it was the warmth that struck me first. The only heating in the place came from old-fashioned gas fires, so in winter it usually felt as cool as a larder when you first got in. For a second I wondered if I was running a fever. Then I noticed that the ceramic elements in the fire were still clicking, as they did for a few minutes after it had been turned off. And there was a heavy smell in the air, so insistent that it felt like an alien presence: a compound of Sadie's freesia scent and a rich, game-soup reek of sweat.

I glanced into the hallway. Sadie's door was half open, and through the gap I could hear someone whispering, and the muffled groan of the mattress. I knew I was being unreasonable, but I felt hurt and betrayed. I was still a virgin; and though I knew, of course, that Sadie wasn't, I'd always assumed she wouldn't rub my nose in it by bringing her sex life home. I'd been hoping to retire to bed that afternoon with a hot honey and lemon, but my room was next to hers, and I didn't want to disturb them – or hear something that would disturb *me*. I was too unwell to go out again, so I just retreated to the sitting room and, muzzy-headed as I was, dozed off in a chair.

I was woken by a voice. I couldn't tell what it said, but when I opened my eyes I saw a man standing a few feet away, gazing down at me. He was huge – built like a centaur, with a mane of red-gold hair. His shirt was unbuttoned, showing a rippled wedge of chest, and he was unhurriedly fastening the buckle of his belt. Not remotely the way I'd visualized Simon. But what did I know? I'd never met anyone in the fashion world.

'Ah,' I said, getting up, and holding my hand out. 'Mr Antrobus, I presume?'

'Antrobus? I thought it was meant to be Dr Livingstone?'

Another surprise: he was American.

'Well, yes,' I said. 'Originally. But –'

'It's a joke,' said Sadie, appearing in the doorway behind him.

'A joke?' said the big man. 'Why? Who's Mr Antrobus?'

She shook her head, smiling. She had nothing on but her dressing gown – the same one, tartan with a silky sash, she'd had in sixth form. She hunched forward, hugging it to her.

'No, come on,' he said. 'You have to explain.'

She shook her head again. 'Rachel, this is Tate.'

'Hey, Rachel,' he said. 'So you tell me. Mr Antrobus?'

I glanced at Sadie. Her face had become inscrutable.

'My lips are sealed,' I said.

'What is it with you people?' said Tate. 'You lost the empire, so all that's left is the jokes? And you're sure as hell not going to let any damn foreigner get his hands on *them*?'

Sadie laughed. 'Shall I put a kettle on?'

He shook his head. 'Not for me. I have to make tracks.'

'OK.' She watched him to the door, gave him a chaste little wave, then turned to me and said,

'Why did you come back early? Aren't you feeling well?'

I pointed to my throat.

'Poor you.' She started towards the kitchen. 'Can I get you anything?'

'I just need to lie down. Sorry I put my foot in it. Calling him Mr Antrobus.'

She shook her head. 'Oh, don't worry. It doesn't matter. Gosh, you do sound hoarse, though. You should gargle with salt water.'

'I will. So what happened to Simon?'

'Nothing.'

I glanced towards the door.

'That's different,' she said. 'Tate's just Tate. I met him at a party. He's a record producer. He knows all kinds of people. And he's a lot of fun.'

We stared at each other. After a couple of seconds she looked away again, shaking her head, as if the effort to explain was too much for her.

'Right,' she said. 'One salt water coming up.'

I was puzzled and unsettled. She seemed to have split into two people: my best friend, and someone I didn't know at all. I wanted to quiz her further, force her somehow to resolve the contradictions; but every time I tried, she simply side-stepped the issue.

Then things started to get even more complicated. There were phone calls for Sadie from men I'd never met and she'd never mentioned. The most persistent of them was a chap called Roy. One evening, just as I was about to go to bed, I heard the doorbell. When I answered it, I found a young guy outside. His shirt and bellbottoms were sodden, his hair rumpled and dripping water, his eyes rimmed with red.

'Where's Sadie?' he said. He had an accent of some kind. Midlands, maybe?

'She's not in, I'm afraid. Are you Simon?'

He frowned. 'Who's Simon?'

'Oh, no, sorry, I know. You're Roy, aren't you? The one who keeps phoning?'

'Where is she?'

'I've no idea. She didn't tell me.'

'You're trying to stop me seeing her, aren't you, you bitch?'

'What? No, of course I'm not.'

He lunged towards me, one hand on the handle. '*Where is she?*'

'I've told you, I don't know.'

His breath stank of alcohol and something chemicaly I couldn't identify. I leaned against the door, trying to push him back. He jammed it open with his foot. For God knows how long we stared at each other, like a couple of boxers before a fight. Then suddenly he seemed to realize what he was doing and, without a word, turned away and clattered down the stairs.

Shaken, I poured myself a brandy, took it to my room and locked the door. An hour later, I heard Sadie come in. I was too frazzled to talk to her that night, but over breakfast the next morning I told her what had happened.

'Oh dear,' she said. 'What did he look like?'

I described him. She clicked her tongue.

'Yes, that's Roy.' She leaned across and took my hand. 'Oh, I'm so sorry you got mixed up in all this, sweetie.'

'Well, it was a bit…But I'm worried about *you*. Knowing someone like that. He seemed really unstable.'

'He is.'

'Have you told the police about him?'

She shook her head. 'I'm not sure that would help.'

'But if he's dangerous –'

'What could they do, except issue a court order, telling him to keep away from me? And then the papers would get hold of it.' She laughed. 'You don't want to see your flatmate plastered all over the front pages under an unflattering headline, do you?'

'Why wouldn't *he* be plastered all over the front pages?'

'I'm more photogenic. And I'm a girl.' She reached for the coffee pot and started to refill our cups. She was trying to seem unperturbed, but her hand was trembling so much that a little black moat formed in my saucer. 'Don't fret about it, sweetie,' she said. 'I'll deal with it. It's his background, I'm afraid. If one tries being civilized about it, he doesn't understand. So obviously I'm going to have to be a bit fiercer with him. I won't have him coming here and frightening you.'

I was desperate, of course, to ask what he'd done – but if she'd wanted to tell me, she'd have done it already. And some frightened little corner of me – the lover of familiar routine and shared jokes – urged me to let sleeping dogs lie. If I really knew what she did with all these men, it would finally destroy the innocent fiction that allowed us to live together.

Roy never reappeared. But, though I tried as far as I could to forget about Sadie's love-life, it kept sending me reminders of its existence: cards; more phone calls; deliveries of flowers from men I'd never heard of. And as she began to have more success as a model, the strain of juggling so many different relationships, of arranging exits and entrances with the split-second timing of a French farce, started to show. One evening – this must have been June or July 1967, a month or so before her first big *Sunday Times* job – I got home to discover her slumped in the sitting room in tears. I was shocked: I'd never seen her cry before. I sat on the arm of her chair and hugged her.

'What is it? What's happened?'

She shook her head.

'Tell me.'

'Simon. He's left me.'

'More fool Simon. Why? Did you have a row?'

She wiped her nose on the back of her hand. 'He saw me. With Tate Finnegan.'

'What, he didn't know about Tate?'

She shook her head again.

'Well, I'm sorry.' I said. 'But it's not as if he's the only one, is it?'

'He was my boyfriend.'

'Well, maybe Tate could be your boyfriend. He seems nice.'

She put her face in her hands and started to howl. I held her tighter and stroked her hair. Gradually she became quieter, and her breathing grew more regular.

'That's better,' I said. 'Now tell me what happened.'

But she was asleep.

A few weeks later, Adam Earnshaw entered our lives.

I didn't witness his first encounter with Sadie: that was at a party in Wiltshire, organized by Tate Finnegan. But when she came home the next day, I could tell that something monumental had happened. She moved slowly, as if she had just woken up, and was still brushing away the last tatters of sleep. She had a dreamy smile, and kept gazing off into the distance at nothing at all. When I asked *Did you have a good time?* she seemed not to hear me.

'Ground Control to Planet Sadie,' I said.

'Hmm? Oh, yes, sorry. Yes, it was lovely, thanks.'

'When do I get the blow-by-blow account?'

'It was indescribable.'

'Well, have a go. I've been stuck here pretty much the whole weekend, preparing lessons for a lot of rich dullards. *My name is Rachel. What's your name?* So –'

She fluttered her fingers. 'Japanese lanterns. Fairy music…And I met someone extraordinary.'

'Well, that's good. Who?'

'You might have heard of him. Adam Earnshaw?'

I shook my head.

'He's a singer.'

'What kind of singer?'

She strummed an invisible guitar.

'Pop?'

'Tate calls it freak folk. It is a bit strange.' She began to sing:

> *'I am a house*
> *Glass and stone*
> *Lake and river*
> *Trunk and bole.'*

She laughed. 'Well, you can't really tell from that. But when he does it, it's as if someone's stuck a needle under your skin.'

I was surprised. I'd never seen her respond so powerfully to an individual song before. Normally, all music was pretty much generic to her: provided it had a rhythm she could dance to and a tune she could hum along with, she liked it.

'That doesn't sound very comfortable,' I said.

She shivered. 'No, it's not.'

'And does he like you?' I asked.

She gave a Cheshire-cat grin.

'So are you going to be seeing him again?'

'That's the plan. In fact, he's meant to be coming here next weekend, if that's OK?'

'Of course. As long as Tate doesn't mind. I mean, he might find it a bit odd, mightn't he? Given that he introduced you in the first –'

'It was Tate's idea.'

Two evenings later, when she came home from work, she handed me a paper called *The Scene.*

'Have you seen this?'

I shook my head.

'It's new. Tate knows the chap who started it. And one of the writers. Take a look at page five.'

I looked at page five. Most of it was taken up with an article titled *A Midsummer Night's Dream*, by someone with the unforgettable name of Peyton Whybrow. I glanced up at her quizzically.

'It's about the party,' she said. 'Go on, read it.'

It was nicely written, full of vivid descriptions and witty asides. But when it got to Adam's performance, the style became plainer and the tone more serious. One phrase stood out: *Like seeing a door open into another dimension.*

Countless times during the next few days, when I was thinking about something else entirely, I found Adam Earnshaw – the *idea* of Adam Earnshaw – suddenly materializing in my mind. It was obvious – given his effect on cool-as-a-cucumber Sadie – that he must be quite exceptional; and by the end of the week I was preparing myself to meet a demi-god: fabulously beautiful, with a hypnotic gaze, and a tendency to speak in oracular pronouncements that would have me scurrying for my notebook.

The reality…Well, of course you know. But oddly enough – you might not guess this from the photos – he *was* beautiful, in a little-boy-lost kind of way. He came into the flat tentatively, head lowered, but watchfully reading the signs, as if he wanted to make sure he was welcome before committing himself to staying. When Sadie stood on tiptoe to kiss him, he gave a startled blink, then realized what was required and put his arms round her.

'Here he is,' she said, extricating herself. 'Adam, this is my flatmate, Rachel.'

He mumbled something that was probably *hello.*

'I'm glad to see you brought this,' said Sadie, patting the guitar case on his shoulder. 'But' – stepping back, and appraising his rumpled T-shirt – 'I think we should go shopping tomorrow. I want to buy you a present.'

He stared at her, like an explorer who's strayed unprepared into a native village. You could tell what was going through his mind: *Is that the custom here? Should I have brought* her *a present?*

'But now, anyway, let's have a drink.' She turned to me. 'Wine, sweetie?'

I glanced at the front door. 'Maybe I should –'

She touched my arm. 'No, no. Stay, please.'

I knew her well enough to see she meant it. Which surprised me – because in all the time I'd lived with her, she'd done everything in her power to keep me and her men friends firmly segregated. What was it about Adam that had changed her mind – made her pick up needle and thread, all of a sudden, and start stitching the two sides of her life together? All I could think of was that – improbable as it seemed – one meeting had been enough to convince her that she wanted to marry him.

'Shall I get it?' I said.

'Would you mind? There's some Rioja open. You'll see.'

I went into the kitchen, found the bottle and grabbed a fistful of glasses. When I re-joined Adam and Sadie, they were squeezed together on the tiny sofa, and Adam had an open tobacco tin on his knee. He lifted a giant skin, made of four or five papers gummed together, and waved it at me.

'OK if I – ?'

'Yes, sure.' I poured the wine, handed them a glass apiece, then sat down opposite them and watched him assembling the joint. I'd seen people smoking dope before, but the mechanics were still a bit of a mystery to me.

'Well, cheers,' said Sadie.

'Cheers.'

Without looking at either of us, Adam took a big gulp of Rioja, then started trailing strands of Golden Virginia into the skin and breaking chips of resin into it. Sadie turned to gaze at him – not critically, exactly, but with a kind of bafflement. Like many people – as you've probably discovered by now – she struggled to understand why someone so gifted and attractive should behave like a self-conscious teenager in a roomful of adults. But that's because she had never, in her entire life, felt out of place. I had – and I could recognize a fellow-sufferer when I saw one.

'Sadie sang me a bit of one of your songs,' I said. 'It was very…intriguing.'

Sadie laughed. 'I mangled it, I'm afraid. Why don't you play it? Let her hear the real thing?'

His eyebrows shot up, as if she'd just suggested he should strip naked and dance on the table.

'It doesn't have to be now,' I said. 'But at some point, if you feel like it.'

He nodded abruptly, then busied himself with sealing the skin and twisting the paper at the end into a little pig's tail.

'No need to be shy about it,' said Sadie, stroking his arm. 'It's fantastic.'

He stuck the joint in his mouth, lit it, drew in a lungful of smoke and held it for a few seconds. As he exhaled he looked at me and said,

'What do you do? Are you a –' He flicked his eyes towards Sadie.

I was stung that Sadie hadn't told him even that much about me. 'No,' I said, laughing. 'I don't think I'm quite what they're looking for.'

'Don't be so hard on yourself,' said Sadie. 'You're lovely.'

'*Men don't make passes at girls who wear glasses.*'

'That's not true. You'd get plenty of passes, if you only gave the chaps half a chance. Wouldn't she, Adam?'

'Oh, bah, humbug,' I said, swiping it away with my hand. But too late: he'd started to redden – and that, to my embarrassment, made me blush, too. For a moment we sat there, our bodies signalling their unease to each other, like a couple of traitors trading secrets in the night. Then I said:

'No, my life's very dull, I'm afraid. I work in a language school.'

'It's not dull at all,' said Sadie. 'Tell him about Dr Maurice.'

'Really,' I said. 'Compared with the fashion industry…Or music…'

Sadie shook her head. 'Honestly, you two – you're as bad as each other.'

Adam leaned forward slightly. Something in my face had caught his interest.

'Is that not what you want to do, then? Teach English?'

'I'm not sure what I want to do,' I said. 'At one stage I thought about trying to be an academic. But I'm not bright enough.'

Sadie clicked her tongue. 'Oh, for heaven's sake! What do you mean? You're very bright!'

'What subject?' said Adam.

'I don't know. English, I suppose. That was always my strong point. Well, my strongest.'

He took another drag, then handed me the joint. I'd never tried one before – but it couldn't be that different, I thought, from smoking Dunhills, so I gingerly poked it between my lips. It was odd tasting his saliva on the tip, and, as I inhaled, the heat burned the back of my throat; but I managed to avoid making a fool of myself by choking.

'Name an author,' said Adam.

'What kind of author?'

'One that you like.'

I was in the middle of a Georgette Heyer regency romance at the time. I frantically tried to think of someone more respectable.

'Thomas Hardy.'

He nodded noncommittally. I handed him the joint back. He took another toke, then passed it to Sadie.

'How about you?' I said.

He shrugged. 'I tend to like writers I shouldn't.'

'What do you mean? There's no *should* or *shouldn't* about it.' I winced at my own hypocrisy. 'Surely it's just a matter of taste, isn't it?'

'My tutor wouldn't agree with you.'

Sadie gave me the joint. She'd only had it for a second or two. She couldn't have taken more than a small ladylike puff. 'Have you read *The Woman in White*, sweetie?'

I had, but I wasn't sure I should admit it. 'Why?'

'Adam recommended it. So I bought a copy.'

He turned to her. 'And?'

'I love it. The different voices. And the atmosphere. The way' – walking two fingers along an invisible path – 'it treads that line between the everyday and the uncanny. I took it with me to the photo session I did yesterday. And there I was, lost in the churchyard at Limmeridge, when the girl arrived to do my make-up. And I almost said, no, come back in ten minutes, I have to find out who the figure by the grave is!'

'It's –' said Adam.

'Shush! Don't tell me! I want it to be a surprise.'

He smiled – eyes half-closed, face radiant, as if a ray of light had suddenly angled through the window and caught him. After a second, he leaned over and kissed her. She pushed him away, laughing – but with one hand still on his shoulder, as if she couldn't bear to lose contact with him completely. He stared at her intently – then, with his finger, drew something in the air in front of her eyes.

She giggled. 'What are you doing?'

'If someone looks closely enough at those pictures, they'll probably be able to see the ghostly imprint of poor Anne Catherick' – pointing at her pupils – 'just there.'

What a creepy idea, I thought. Let's hope it's just the dope. But Sadie seemed enchanted.

'I think they'll see an imprint of *you*,' she murmured.

He moistened his lips. I could feel the dryness in my own mouth.

'Because that's all I've been thinking about the last week.' She craned her face up, neck as graceful as a flamingo's, and kissed him.

They appeared to have forgotten that I was there. I left the joint in the ashtray and tiptoed to the door.

Outside, it was one of those blowsy, over-ripe late summer days that seem to swaddle you in heat. I headed for the park, trying to blinker out the troubling fly-on-the wall images of Sadie's bedroom – curtains closing; sheets drawn back; puddles of sloughed-off clothes on the floor; the dim dazzle of bare flesh – that kept invading my mind. I could feel the wine weighing heavily on my legs, but the dope seemed to have had no effect on me at all. Typical, I thought, with a jab of self-pity: yet more evidence that the grown-up world still isn't ready for me – or that I'm not ready for it.

I found a patch of grass in the shade of an oak and went to sleep. When I woke up again, shivering, the sun had almost gone, leaving nothing but a red gash on the horizon and a twilight chill in the air.

The Sadie and Adam show. What, ultimately, to make of it? I didn't know then, and I'm not much the wiser now. The nearest I can come is to see it as a kind of Escher drawing, in which A and B are both true – but at the same time contradictory.

A, in this case, is that she adored him. After she took him shopping that first weekend, she came in beaming like a mother who can't wait to show off her baby. She made him change into his new threads – deep-collared shirt; embroidered waistcoat; denim bellbottoms – and then, as he modelled them for us, stood shaking her head and whistling softly, as if she couldn't quite believe how perfect he was. It was an expression I saw on her face time and again when they were together. One glance, and you knew that she was smitten.

So it wasn't much of a surprise when, not long after Adam's arrival in our midst, she accosted me one morning as I was leaving for work and said,

'Can I just ask you something, sweetie? How would you feel if Adam moved in for a while? We'd be very quiet. Keep out of your way.' She laughed. 'And if he leaves his socks lying around, I promise I'll pick them up.'

'Maybe it would be better if I moved out?' I said.

'No, no. It'll only be for a few weeks. Just till he goes back to Oxford. His family's in Africa, and he's left the place he was staying in the country, so he hasn't really got anywhere else to go.'

A few weeks turned out to be a bit of an underestimate: in the event, Adam was with us for a couple of months. The effect, for me, was like a river suddenly being diverted: before, I'd been mid-stream, and now I found myself stranded on the bank, with only the occasional eddy coming my way. But Sadie was right: Adam was – as far as he could be – an unobtrusive presence, so at least I was spared the usual annoyances of chipped cups, dirty dishes, vanishing loo rolls.

And while it was hard to avoid feeling that Sadie had turned her back on me, there was something fascinating in seeing the way she set her stamp on Adam. The clothes were a part of it – but only as a sort of declaration of intent, a down payment on what was to follow. Next came the hair. The bird's nest straggle disappeared inside a modish barber's on the King's Road, and re-emerged as a glossy helmet, neat as a Renaissance courtier's cap. To a casual observer, he suddenly looked, not just like a different person, but like a different *kind* of person: assured, comfortable in his own skin, and completely at home in the moment in which he found himself. I often wondered whether this transformation altered his own perceptions as profoundly as it had other people's – whether, looking in the mirror, he saw something so unlike what he was used to that it changed his understanding of who he was. Perhaps that had been Sadie's calculation: alter the appearance, and everything else will follow suit.

Certainly, in only a week or two, you could see it starting to have an effect on his behaviour. I first noticed it one evening when he and Sadie were getting ready to go to a party. It was at the house (very grand, no doubt) of the fashion editor at one of the swankier women's weeklies – the mere idea of which, I'd have thought, would have been enough to reduce him to panic. But, while he was even quieter than usual, he got dressed up meekly enough, and waited patiently by the door until she appeared in a breath-taking shimmer of gold-and-red silk, smelling like a bunch of spring flowers.

'Wow, you look fantastic,' she said, fingering the back of her head to make sure her hair was still in shape.

'So do you.' No hesitation, not – as far as I could detect – the least hint of irony.

'Well, thank you.' She whirled round, saw his guitar leaning against the sofa, whisked it up. 'Why don't you bring this?'

He stared at her.

'Really,' she said. 'I'm sure people would love to hear you play.'

You idiot, I thought, *don't you remember what happened when you asked him to sing for me?*

But then, to my astonishment, he said, 'OK', and slung the case over his shoulder.

At the time, I wondered if he was simply so nervous that he felt he couldn't say no. But a couple of days later, the same thing happened again. And over the next few weeks, it became a regular feature of their social life. As the summer headed bleary-eyed towards its end, and Adam started to make a name for himself playing at clubs like Les Cousins and Troubadour, the coolest people in London – socialites; models; film-makers; actors; fashion journalists – began competing with one another to get him to sing at their own private parties. Once, when I found myself alone with him in the kitchen, I said,

'Aren't you starting to get tired of it? I mean, doesn't it make you feel a bit like a...' I was going to say *performing monkey*, but stopped myself at the last moment, worried that it would sound rude.

'Yes,' he said – and startled me by tugging on an invisible chain and doing a grotesque little shuffling dance. 'But that's OK. It gives me something to do.'

I laughed. 'You could try talking to people.'

His eyes widened.

'That's not *such* an outlandish suggestion, is it?' I said. 'Why don't you practise on me?'

He rolled the idea round in his mouth, feeling its shape with his tongue.

'Come on,' I said. 'Tell me something about yourself.'

It sounded ludicrous, like one of those early evening Sunday television shows where a young person was solemnly questioned about his views on drugs and sex. We both laughed.

'No, but honestly,' I said. 'I'd like to know. You're a bit of a man of mystery, as far as I'm concerned.'

He tilted his head and looked directly into my eyes, giving me the eerie sense that he'd spotted something there I was only half-aware of myself. Eerie, but –for an instant – oddly exciting too. Then, abruptly, he turned away again.

'Not much of a mystery,' he said, picking up his guitar. 'Anyway, I need to go.'

For the next few weeks I barely saw him. Dr M, determined to extract every last pennyworth of value from his overheads, had accepted far too many students for our short summer courses, so – like the rest of the staff – I seemed to be at the school from dawn to dusk, trying to sort out the chaos. And Sadie appeared to be pursuing a similar policy with Adam, getting as much social mileage out of him as she could before he had to go back to Oxford, which meant they were generally out when I got home. And on the occasions when they weren't, they were in Sadie's room, with the door firmly closed.

The first time it happened, I was almost distraught. It had been a nerve-shredding day, during which I'd only managed to keep myself going with the promise of a hot bath and a cup of tea when it was all over, and the last thing I wanted to do was listen to the sound of their lovemaking. For a start, it was embarrassing: they must have heard me come in, so when they finally emerged, there was bound to be an awkward she-knows-that-I-know-that-she-knows moment. But there was something else, too, darker and more troubling, that I didn't want to acknowledge at all.

How to describe it? Voodoo, that's the nearest I can come to it: the sense that I was in the presence of voodoo. Something or someone had cast a spell on them, powerful enough to transform Adam from pure spirit into a groaning hog, and reduce Sadie, the soul of coolness, to a frenzied whimpering. The thought of it repelled me – but I found it impossible to turn away. The effect on my own body was simply too potent: the surge of heat to my head and groin; the almost unbearable sensitivity of nerves that – for most of my life – lay dormant and unnoticed. Even when I returned to work the next morning, I couldn't put the memory of it out of my mind. What if, one day, the same enchantment fell on *me*?

To begin with I resisted putting it to the test – but then, the second or third time I heard them, I felt so over-wrought that, all of a sudden, I couldn't hold out any longer. Without giving myself time to change my mind, I hurried into my room and locked the door.

God, what am I doing? I've never so much as mentioned this to anyone in my life. But now I've started, it's such a relief.

Such an almighty relief.

Sadie's and my beds were on opposite sides of the same wall, so – when I lay down – all I had to do to hear what was going on was press my ear against the plaster. The squeak and thud of the mattress was absolutely regular, one two *three*, one two *three*. I flipped up my skirt, and felt a rush of liberation as the air touched my bare skin, like a small child being undressed for bed. One two *three*, one two *three*. I moved my fingers down – was it *his* back I was stroking, or *my* belly? – and abandoned myself to the relentless rhythm.

It was a fumbling, ungainly muddle: a collision between physical hunger – my hands standing in as best they could for the bits and pieces of the male body, which I still couldn't picture with complete clarity – and the equally urgent need to imagine it being satisfied by someone else. How about bearded Robin from the language school? *Everyone else gone home? It's awfully hot in here, isn't it? Why don't you take that off?* God, no, what a disgusting idea. Or Dr Maurice himself? *A glass of champagne, Miss Lake? I wouldn't normally, of course. But a young woman of such rare sensibility as yourself.* Yuck, no, even worse. All right, then: Paul Jones. But I couldn't even *visualize* him, let alone spin a remotely plausible story to explain how he and I could have ended up in bed together.

I cast about, ransacking my memory, but – whatever I did – the only face I could see was Adam's. As he started to grunt like a long-distance runner nearing the finishing line, I felt his mouth against mine, heard him whispering in my head the little speech I'd hastily scripted for him: *I've always loved you, Rachel. From the very first moment I set eyes on you.* And as the answering *Aagh!* forced itself up through my body, I found myself murmuring, *oh, Adam, Adam, Adam.*

Afterwards, needless to say, I felt guilty, unclean, ashamed of my lust and my treacherous imagination. I wasn't just a voyeur and a sneak: I was, to all intents and purposes, an adulteress, too, spiriting my best friend's boyfriend from under her very nose into a parallel universe. I must never, never, never do it again.

But my resolve lasted exactly four days. And after that, with indecent speed, I started to make excuses for myself. If they were in bed when I got in, it was OK – as long as I was discreet about it – to lie in my own room and join in. It wasn't hurting them, was it? There was no reason why they should ever know about it. Even for me, in fact – except in those moments when I was actually doing it – it felt oddly unreal, like a kind of vivid dream, for which my conscious self wasn't responsible, and which had no bearing on the waking world.

Odd the way memory alters the proportions of things, shrinking this, extending that, like a distorting mirror. The phantom threesome period of my life *feels* as if it drifted on for months, but when I look back and do the calculations, I realize it can't actually have lasted for more than a few weeks. Some time around the beginning of October Adam returned to Oxford, and we moved on to a new phase altogether – the second storey in the Escher drawing.

At first, Sadie behaved as you'd expect, moping about the place, waiting for hours at a time by the phone for him to call, and then – when he did – trailing it through into her room and talking in a muffled mumble until his supply of two-shilling pieces ran out. Sometimes I'd get home to find her slumped in a chair, legs up over the arm, reading – or maybe re-reading – *The Woman in White.*

'You all right, sweetie? Shall I get some supper?'

She'd shake her head. And then, half an hour later, go to bed with a mug of Horlicks.

But then, quite suddenly, she started to change. I first noticed it one evening when she was booked to do a sunset shoot on Waterloo Bridge. While she was out, in an effort to cheer her up, I took a photo of Adam from her dressing table, set it up in a corner of the sitting-room, and arranged a line of joss sticks and candles in front of it. I lit them ten minutes before she was due back, then hovered by the door, listening for the sound of her coming into the building. It was a long wait. By the time she finally reappeared, the candles were just puddles of wax and the place smelt like an opium den.

'Where the hell have you been?' I said. 'I was about to call the police.'

She shrugged. Her face was flushed, her eyes unnaturally big. 'With some people.' She sniffed. 'What have *you* been doing? Having a dope party?'

I nodded towards the corner. 'I made an Adam shrine.'

'Oh, yes, I see.'

No giggle, not even a smile.

'Sorry,' I said. 'I hoped you'd like it.'

'That was a nice thought. Thank you.'

And she slipped past me into the bathroom and began running a bath.

I was puzzled by her response, but attributed it to tiredness and the mix of drugs she'd taken. But then, a few days later, as I was walking into the flat, I heard the phone ringing. When I picked it up, it was not – as I'd expected – Sadie, telling me she'd be late, but Adam.

'Oh, oh, Rachel.' He sounded surprised, embarrassed even. 'I thought... Is she there?'

'I've only just got in. Let me check.'

I knocked on her bedroom door. There was no reply.

'No, sorry. Shall I give her a message?'

'That's all right. I just thought this was when I was meant to phone. But it doesn't matter. I'll try again.'

'I'll tell her. How are you? When are we going to see you again?'

'Don't know. That's what we were going to talk about. Next weekend, maybe.'

But he didn't come the next weekend. Instead Sadie said she had to go back to visit her parents. Rather than spending the whole two days on my own, on the Sunday I arranged to meet some other friends for a picnic. Going home that evening, I saw, as I turned into the square, a car pulled up in front of our building. I've never been interested in cars, but this one instantly caught my attention: it was silver, and long and curvy like a fish. As I reached it, the passenger door suddenly opened, bashing my elbow and nearly knocking me over.

'Oh, sorry...Oh, hullo.'

She turned and said something to the driver, then got out, clutching her overnight bag, and slammed the door.

'Aren't you going to introduce me?' I said.

She shook her head, blushing. The silver fish eased away from the kerb.

'Oh!' I said. 'I'd have liked to have met him.'

'He had to be somewhere.'

'Well, all I can say is, I wish *my* father had a car like that.'

She laughed.

'How were they?' I said. 'Did you have a good time?'

She nodded. 'How about you?' she said, slotting her key into the lock. 'What have you been up to?'

On the way upstairs I told her. But she listened like an automaton, her eyes always somewhere else. When we were inside the flat, she said,

'You didn't really think that was my father, did you?'

I shrugged. 'Well, you had been home for the weekend, hadn't you? So it seemed like a reasonable –'

'My father doesn't drive an E-Type.' She sank into the armchair, pincering her forehead with her thumb and fingers.

'Who was it, then?'

'A friend.'

'Someone I know?'

She shook her head.

'Was he staying there too, then?'

She opened her hands, trying to let go of the burden of being Sadie. 'Just please don't say anything to Adam about it.'

'Oh, he'd understand, wouldn't he? The chap was only giving you a lift.'

She said nothing. She didn't look at me. She was frozen, a bound animal frightened that the slightest movement would only pull the ropes even tighter.

'Tell me,' I said.

'Everything's so bloody complicated. I love Adam. Of course I do. But he's there. And I'm here. So –'

'So you're sleeping with other men.'

'Sometimes. Why shouldn't I? We don't own each other. And he's sleeping with other girls.'

'Really? Has he said so?'

She shook her head. 'He's too…considerate. But it's obvious, isn't it? I mean, he's not a monk. He has, well, strong desires. Sometimes I wonder what I've unleashed. And somewhere like Oxford, he'll have his pick, won't he?'

'And that doesn't worry you?'

'I don't think it's any of my business. As long as he still loves me when we're together.'

'Well, if that's really what you feel, I think you should talk to him about it. Then you won't have to go through all the palaver of pretending you've gone home for the weekend, or you've been booked for a late-night shoot, or –'

'I'm not sure that's a good idea. It's one thing to know perfectly well what's going on. It's another to spell it out…' She looked up suddenly, saw the expression on my face. 'What's wrong with that? All it means is we don't hurt each other.'

'You think that's how most people behave?'

She shrugged. 'It's how I behave.'

'Do you imagine your mother slept with every man she met?'

She tensed. 'I don't sleep with every man I meet. And it was different for them, wasn't it? They didn't have the pill. And they had a war to fight, poor loves. And Victorian grandparents.'

I was shocked. My parents had never talked much about relationships, but – by a process of osmosis – I had absorbed from them the idea that you waited until the right man came along and then married him. In my generation that had been modified to *If you really love someone, it's all right to go to bed with him even before you're married.* Sadie had taken it one stage further: *While you're waiting for the one you love, it's all right to go to bed with other men.* But now she'd found the one she loved, and she was *still* sleeping with other men – and, on top of everything else, lying about it.

Three or four times over the next few weeks Adam phoned while she was out, and I wondered whether I should tell him – or at least hint at – the truth. But, in the end, the responsibility always seemed too great, and – well-brought-up girl that I was – I concealed it in conversational wrapping-paper instead: *No, I don't know when she'll be back; she's probably working late; yes, she's fine as far as I know, but I've not seen a lot of her lately.*

And then, one Friday towards the end of October, just after I'd got home, I heard the buzzer. Scared that it might be another disgruntled lover, I cracked open the door without removing the chain.

'Oh, hullo, Adam! How are you?'

'Some and some.' He was wan and dishevelled, wearing jeans and a Humphrey Bogart overcoat with holes in it. When he saw me, he grimaced and tried to run his fingers through his hair, but it was going to seed again, and they got snagged up in the tangle.

'Sorry,' I said, 'I wasn't expecting you.' I unhooked the chain and ushered him into the hall. 'Sadie didn't say anything.'

'I didn't tell her I was coming.' He dropped his bag and leaned his guitar against the wall. 'Is she in?'

'No. But she leaves me a note sometimes. Let me just see.'

I went into the kitchen. No note. I fussed about, pretending still to be searching, trying to figure out what I should do. All I could think of was to write my own note and then slip out when I had the chance and stick it on the door.

I scribbled *Adam's here* on a bit of paper and folded it inside my hand.

'Anything?' he said, as I went back into the sitting room.

'No, she's probably just working late,' I said, and immediately wished I hadn't. On the phone, I could get away with it; but now I had that familiar unsettling sense that he could read my mind, and see that I was trying to divert his attention from a different thought altogether. 'You really should have let us know,' I went on. 'She'll be so sorry not to have been here.'

He waved towards the armchair. 'OK if I just –?'

'Yes, of course, if you want. But honestly, I've no idea how long she's likely to be.'

He sat down, elbows on knees, hands dangling between his legs. I edged towards the fireplace and grabbed the roll of Sellotape from the mantelpiece.

'Shan't be a sec,' I said.

I went out on to the landing and taped the sign to the door. When I returned he'd unrolled the Golden Virginia pouch on his lap and was making a joint.

'You want some tea or something?' I said. 'Or a drink?'

He shook his head.

'Or I could make you a sandwich, if you like. You look as if you could use it. Don't they feed you at Oxford?'

He shook his head again. 'Give me a word.'

'What?'

'Any word.' He sealed the joint and lit it. 'First one that comes into your head.'

'Confusion.'

He took a lungful of smoke. 'Ditto.' He paused. 'Come on. Your turn.'

Where was this going? I felt I was at the entrance to an unlit tunnel, and didn't want to be drawn in further.

'Earls Court Station,' I said.

'No, the word you're *really* thinking of.'

'I don't know. Love.'

'Strange.'

'Meeting.'

'Missing.'

'Out.'

'Split.'

'Peas.'

'Queues.'

'Waiting.'

'Wishing.'

'Longing.'

I thought it sounded neutral enough, but the instant I'd said it I knew, from the way his eye recalibrated on my face, that he saw, down to the smallest sordid detail, how I'd imagined myself in bed with him. I started to blush. He handed me the joint. This time, as I inhaled, I felt an almost immediate effect: a sense of being cut free from the clutter of my earth-bound life – achy after-work legs and tired feet; social awkwardness; the weight of my guilt and shame – and starting to drift up, up, up towards another plane.

'That's it,' said Adam. 'We've reached the level.' He sliced his hand from right to left, cutting a line in the air. And though he didn't say it, I knew that meant: *We can talk now.*

I took another drag and handed the joint back to him. 'I don't know where she is.'

He sucked in smoke, then let it out again slowly, watching the shapes it made through half-closed eyes.

'Have you met him?'

Five minutes before I'd have said *Who?* But that kind of pretence was impossible now, part of the discarded baggage I'd left behind me. 'No.'

'You know his name?'

I shook my head.

'Or is there more than one?'

'I've honestly no idea, Adam. She's never brought anyone here. Not when I've been around. But there are other men, I think. Well, no, I know. She told me.'

'Men she knew before? Or men she's met since?'

'She didn't say.'

He took a toke, gave me the joint, then leaned back in his chair.

'You ever read *The Story of the Amulet*?'

'No.'

'Yet one more on the long list of books' – clapping his hands over his ears and giving his neck a sharp twist – 'that seem to have screwed my head on the wrong way. Edwardian magic. Four kids buy an ancient Egyptian charm in a junk shop. Half of it's missing, but the piece they've got allows them to travel through time looking for the other bit. And eventually they find it.' He placed his fingertips together, making an upside-down heart. 'Journey's end. Home at last. And that's what I thought Sadie was.'

He noticed my frown. 'You haven't the first idea what I'm talking about.'

'Not really, no. Sorry.'

'It doesn't matter. No, it *does* matter.' He swiped his hand through the air again. 'That evening, the evening Sadie and I met, I just had this feeling. For years, I'd been knocking and knocking, waiting for a response. And now, finally, the door was starting to open. And the universe was saying, *come on in. You've arrived. This is the path you must follow.*' He turned his palm into a door and swivelled it.

'You mean you actually *heard* something?' I said. 'Like a big voice?'

'I *experienced* it. And suddenly I knew exactly where I had to go and what I had to do. I went down to the lake, and I got in a boat, and I started to sing, completely abandoned myself to it, let everything, life, whatever you want to call it, sing *through* me. The best performance I've ever done. And then at the end, there she was.'

'Yes, I can imagine.' And I could: not as a logical sequence of events, but as a sort of picture: an old master, with Adam and Sadie in the centre, surrounded by a crowd of onlookers, their faces half lit by the Japanese lanterns.

'And I thought, this is it,' he said. 'The other half of the amulet. She wasn't what I'd expected at all. But that wasn't the point. She was my destiny.'

'What *had* you expected?'

'I don't know. Something out of my grandparents' generation, probably. Not someone so –' His throat tightened. 'I've done my best. Honestly I have. I've tried …' He mimed moulding a lump of clay, squeezing it, wringing it.

'I'm sorry,' I said. 'It's always going to be hard for anyone who falls in love with Sadie. You can't…I mean, she's so gorgeous, isn't she? Of course other chaps are going to want to, you know…It's inevitable. But you mustn't think she doesn't love you. She does. I've never seen her as happy as she is when she's with you. It's just…Well, she doesn't feel she's doing anything wrong. And she can't see why anyone else would – or at least, not anyone of our generation. So she takes it for granted that you're doing the same – that you've got other girls in Oxford.'

He started to sob. The only time I'd seen a man cry before was when my father told us that my grandmother had died – and he'd fought it every inch of the way, biting his lip, freezing his face into a mask to stop the flow of tears. But to my astonishment, Adam – normally so affectless, except when he was singing – shook and wailed like a small child. I knelt on the floor and put my arms round him.

'And maybe she's right,' I said. 'I mean, it's as if, I don't know, someone's shaken the kaleidoscope, and suddenly there's a new pattern, and we just have to get used to it. You know?'

He nodded.

'So all those rules that made sense in the old days, when the girl might end up pregnant – well, they just don't any more. So perhaps we have to start thinking about things in a different way. Try to be less possessive. Willing to share a bit more.'

Did I know what I was doing? You probably think I must have. But all I was conscious of at the time was the wonderful sense of floating free – so high, now, that the day-to-day world, with its dull calculus of cause and effect, was completely lost from view. So when he kissed me, then slipped his hand under my dress and unhooked my bra – deftly done, I noticed – I wasn't startled or taken aback: it simply seemed the natural next stage in my serene progression through the stratosphere.

'This isn't very comfortable, is it?' I murmured. 'Shall we move?'

I led him into my room, shut the door, then stood by the bed, waiting for him take the first step – to indicate, somehow, what was required of me. Very slowly he unbuttoned my dress, lifted it over my head, removed my underwear. Some faint radio signal from planet earth told me to cover my breasts and my pubis, but even that seemed too assertive. So when he started taking off his own clothes, I just stood there, open to his gaze, watching as he unhurriedly opened himself to mine.

I'd seen Greek statues, so I sort of knew what to expect. But the particularity of his body – the constellations of moles and birthmarks; the bony shoulders; the shadowy imprint of his ribs on his pale skin – awed me. And the startling darkness of his groin, the dense chocolate-brown curls, the baby mouse pink-grey of the genitals, the way they seemed to move independently of him, like a primitive sea creature, the last vestige of some earlier stage of evolution…

'You're lovely,' he said. And he came towards me, kissed me softly on the mouth, then picked me up and laid me on the bed. As he started to stroke me, hands moving at a tantalizing snail's pace over my breasts and belly, I found myself half-listening for Sadie, imagining her coming in and lying on *her* bed, making an unconscious mirror image of the phantom threesome...

And then there was nothing but sensation.

It was dark when I awoke. I was wet and sore and had a headache. I patted the bed next to me. It was cold and empty. I put on my dressing-gown and peered out of my room. No light anywhere, except the bilious glow of a streetlamp coming through Sadie's window. She wasn't back yet. And Adam, obviously, had left.

In a panic, I blundered out to retrieve the note I'd stuck on the door. It wasn't there. He must have seen it on his way out and removed it. I went back to my room and flicked on the light switch. The sheets were a bloody tangle. Had Adam noticed? Did he realize he'd taken my virginity? I bundled them up, shoved them in the wardrobe, then went out and collected a fresh set from the airing cupboard. I was surprised by my own matter-of-factness. What was wrong with me? Something momentous had just happened, and I was behaving like a robot.

As soon as I'd made up the bed, I ran a bath and soaked myself clean. Afterwards, when I went to my chest of drawers to get a new pair of pyjamas, I found, lying on top, a page torn from a notebook and folded in two. I opened it and read:

Thank you. That was fabulous. A

I re-folded it and slipped it under a pair of knickers. Then I made myself a cup of tea and went to bed.

In the morning, Sadie still hadn't returned. I knew that the earliest she'd be back now was lunchtime, so I dumped the stained sheets in a cold bath and pummelled them till the water was tinged with pink. Then I wrung them out, wrapped them in a towel and took them to the launderette. When I got home I emptied the ashtray, hoovered and dusted the sitting room, opened the window to let out the tell-tale smell of stale marijuana fumes. By the time Sadie finally came in, just as I was about to make myself some supper, there wasn't a scrap of evidence to suggest that Adam had been there at all.

'Hullo, sweetie. Good weekend?'

I nodded.

'Do anything exciting?'

'Not really. How about you?'

'Oh, the usual complications. Trying to explain chap A to chap B, and actually not seeing why I should have to.'

I managed a smile. 'Do you want something to eat?'

She shook her head. 'I'm going to have a bath. Followed by a hot milky drink. And then fifteen hours' sleep.'

By the next morning – astonishing, thinking about it, how quickly and seamlessly it happened – we were more or less back to normal. My brief encounter with Adam had been so extraordinary – so totally disconnected from the rest of my life – that it soon retreated into the same dreamlike realm as the phantom threesome. The only tangible reminder of it was Adam's note, which I stumbled on every morning when I got dressed. I held out for a week or so, then tore it up, telling myself I was just being careful, in case Sadie ever chanced to look in my drawers. But the true reason, I realize now, was that seeing it made it harder for me to preserve the illusion that the whole thing had taken place in a kind of never-never land, where I wasn't really responsible for what I'd done.

A couple of weekends later, Sadie told me that Adam was coming to stay, and asked – in the sweetest possible way – whether I would mind absenting myself for the night, so that they could have a proper, long overdue talk. I went home to my parents, and spent the entire time worrying. What if Adam, in the course of their conversation, decided to tell her what had happened? Even if – true to her principles – she accepted it, she would know I had lied to her, and probably never trust me again.

But on Sunday evening, when I finally let myself in, heart thudding, she rushed to the door to give me a big hug.

'Oh, there you are, sweetie! I've been feeling awful about sending you away like that. But it's been really great. We've talked things through, just like you said we should, and everything's fine. Better than ever. So thank you.'

'I'm really glad.' And I was. But, now that the danger was past, I was also aware of a twinge of disappointment mingled with my relief. Some small schoolgirl part of me, I realized, had been secretly hoping he'd tell her he was leaving her for me.

'And it turns out I was right,' she said. 'He has been sleeping with other girls. Well, one girl, anyway.'

'Who?'

'He didn't say. And I didn't ask him. He doesn't know the names of any of my chaps, either. But the important thing is, we've cleared the air. And now, when we're together' – she shivered – 'it's just fantastic!'

It was a few weeks after that that I began to suspect I was pregnant.

Sorry, I'm going to have to stop there. The next bit's just too painful.

11

ROY BATLEY

OK. But if this is just another travel brochure for the Swinging Sixties – on your left, the Abbey Road studio; on your right, the UFO Club – count me out. Far as I'm concerned, the sixties lasted exactly three years, from 66 to 68. And yes, during that brief moment, some of us were stupid enough to believe that if we just pushed really hard, we could drive all those hoary old monsters that been messing things up since the year dot – capitalism, war, racism, the class system, jealousy – back into their cave and roll a rock across the entrance. Or rock a roll. Then, flip flip flip, Bobby Kennedy, Martin Luther King, Czechoslovakia, Charles Manson, the whole house of cards came tumbling down. I know a lot of journalists and TV people have done very nicely, thank you, out of trying to put it up again, but I'm not going to join them on the gravy train.

Ditto if this is a dewy-eyed lovefest for Adam Earnshaw. All the guy had to do, apparently, was disappear mysteriously at the age of twenty-two, and people were falling over each other to say what a huge musical talent we'd lost. Well, I'm not going to pretend I agree with them. I never liked the music much – all those fey, *oh, I'm so deep* lyrics – and I didn't like the man, either. In fact, I found him a royal pain in the arse. And I'm not just saying that because, one way or another, he more or less ruined my life.

Don't get me wrong: it wasn't that he was ever *rude* to me. Just the opposite, in fact: if anything, he was *too* bloody polite, *Hello, Roy, How are you?*, *What have you been up to?*, then pretending to be interested in the answers, like he was the queen or something, graciously giving some member of the lower orders the time of day.

It never fooled me, but you should have seen him with the poor little rich girls that used to flutter around him, the way their faces lit up when he actually condescended to pay them some attention. *Oh, wow,* they'd murmur afterwards, *he's so perceptive!* You'd think some passing god had got off his chariot to talk to them. You wanted to yell, *For Christ's sake! Don't you realize what he's doing? Oldest trick in the book!*

But of course there was no point. They'd just say it was sour grapes, that I had a chip on my shoulder, because Adam was an Oxford posh boy, and I was a working class kid from Birmingham. Which was bollocks. I was prouder of my dad than any of them were of theirs. Most of *theirs* had sent them away to school when they were seven or something and forgotten about them. Mine wasn't just my dad, he was my best friend. He'd build models with me, take me fishing, and when I was older we'd go down the pub together. And even though – apart from the war – he'd spent his whole working life in a factory making machine tools, he didn't stand in my way when I said I wanted to go to art school.

'It's your life, son,' he said. 'But don't forget that old story about spots and leopards. Whatever anyone tells you, you'll always be who you are and they'll always be who they are.'

A lot of times since then I've wished I'd taken more notice of him.

I didn't really know anything about art school: I just thought it sounded better than having to get a job. It turned out, when I got there, that there wasn't actually much art being done, but there was a hell of a lot of music. Pretty much everyone I knew was in a group. Mine was called The Guts, and by early 67 we were already starting to make a bit of a name for ourselves around Birmingham. One night, some zonked-out folkie with long hair and a lisp heard us and said, *goth, you thould twy to get a wecord deal.* She mentioned a few names, including Tate Finnegan at Wheatsheaf. We sent him a demo, and a few days later he phoned me, asking us to come down to London. We'd no idea what to expect, so we Brylcreemed our hair and put on jackets and ties. The instant we saw him – mane down to his shoulders; *Stop me and Turn On* t-shirt – we knew we'd made a mistake.

'Shit, man,' he said, laughing. 'You all look like you're going for an interview at Dow Chemical.'

The upshot was that he liked a couple of our tracks – particularly *(Four*

Minutes to) Lights Out – but felt we still weren't ready to make an album. He said that if we gave him a one-year exclusive deal, he'd try to get us a few gigs and some airplay on one of the pirates, before they were closed down. And he offered me a sort-of part-time sort-of job, working for Wheatsheaf Records. The idea was that I'd be an informal A & R man, pointing him in the direction of up-and-coming Brummy bands, while at the same time learning something about the music business.

His office was a second-floor room split in two by a plywood partition, plus a bit of storage space on the landing. He sat on one side of the partition, I sat on the other. My half was more or less bare. His was plastered with pictures, most of them old black-and-white photos: not just the obvious subjects – blues singers in smoky bars; a Mississippi steamer; a turn-of-the-century jazz band marching through New Orleans – but family snaps, portraits of Sitting Bull and Geronimo, blurred shots of oil prospectors, coal miners, gold diggers, buffalo hunters, all staring blankly at the camera.

My first day there we went through the dozen or so acts he'd signed already. When we got to the last one he said,

'And this dude's *numero uno.* Freak called Adam Earnshaw. You ever hear of him?'

'No.'

'Kind of like Jamie Penhaligon. Only without the gimmicks.'

'Who's Jamie Penhaligon?'

He sucked his teeth. 'Well, take a listen to this, anyway.'

He wound a tape on to the machine and played a couple of tracks. *Cookie-cut Kid*, if I remember right, and *Mr Morris.*

'What do you think?'

I shrugged.

He pushed the flap of his ear with one finger – *Listen harder* – then spun the tape back and re-played it. College boy stuff. I'd no idea what the first song was trying to do at all, except tell us how clever Adam Earnshaw was. *Mr Morris*, obviously, was supposed to be about someone like my dad, but I didn't believe a word of it.

'You think he's ever even met someone who works on an assembly line?' I said.

He tapped his forehead. 'I think he *imagined* something. Anyway, get used to it, man. A year from now, you say you know Adam Earnshaw, ladies going to be lining up in the street to lick your dong.'

It was meant to be a summer job, but come September I couldn't face returning to art school, and Tate wasn't any keener on going back to answering his own phone, making his own tea and delivering demos to radio stations in person. So we agreed – without ever spelling it out – that we'd keep going as we were, a day at a time. I was shit-scared about breaking the news to Mum and Dad, but when I finally did, Dad just said, 'Well, you're doing what you want. And getting a regular pay-packet for it. Not like all these youngsters who think the world owes them a living. So good luck to you.' I didn't tell him the pay-packet consisted of a few quid now and then when Tate could manage it, and that I was sleeping on other people's floors, cos I couldn't afford a place of my own.

Which brings me, *dah-dah*, to the bit I expect you've been waiting for: Sadie Long. I don't know who else you've been in touch with, but it's a fair bet someone along the way will have mentioned my – I can't think of the right word, my *thing* with her – and I'm guessing that's why you bothered to track me down, in hope of picking up a few tasty morsels. In which case, sorry, you're going to be disappointed. If what you heard is that I behaved like a prize twat, then I can only plead guilty as charged. But that's pretty much as sensational as it gets.

It started the first time I met her, soon after I'd begun working for Tate. I was sitting in the office one afternoon, sweating over the typewriter, when he pushed open the door and waved this apparition inside: blonde and brown-eyed, wearing a cream silk dress, and looking about twenty degrees cooler than the rest of us. It was like the TV screen suddenly shattering, and someone from that other, out-of-reach world – Julie Christie, say – stepping through the splintered glass into your living room, turning from black-and-white to colour in the process.

'Here he is,' said Tate. 'Say hello to Sadie, Roy.'

I raised a hand. 'Hello, Sadie.'

'Tate's been telling me all about you.' The curve of her cheek made me think of an eggshell. 'You're obviously doing a fabulous job here, keeping everything running smoothly. And from what he said, your music sounds really fascinating too. I'd love to hear it sometime.'

I raised my eyebrows at Tate.

'Sure,' he said. He went back out on to the landing and started rummaging in the cupboard where we kept the demos.

'Has he signed you to the label?' I asked.

She laughed. 'Oh, no, no, I'm not a singer. I'd love to be, but I haven't got the ability, I'm afraid. Tate and I are just friends.'

'Just good fronds.' That was me back then: trying to be the Brummy John Lennon. 'Can't leaf each other alone.'

She laughed again, as if she meant it. 'Gosh, so many talents. Comedy, music. I can't keep up with them all.'

'OK,' said Tate, returning with an EMI tape box. He slipped out the spool and looped it up on the office Ferrograph. 'Here we go. *Lights Out.*'

She listened carefully, frowning slightly with concentration, looking past my shoulder towards the window. When it was over she turned towards me and said,

'God, that's amazing. I kept expecting to see a mushroom cloud out there, erupting over the rooftops. And the siren at the end, that was a really brilliant touch. It gave me goose-pimples.'

'Should be popular with the Ministry of Defence,' I said. 'If we manage to release it before they blow us all up.'

'Do you ever perform it?' she said. 'On your own, I mean? Without the rest of the group?'

'No.'

'But *could* you?'

I shrugged. 'Well, that depends. Sitting at home on the bed I could.'

'Only some friends are having a party on Saturday. Would you come along and play it for them? I know they'd really love it.'

'When Sadie says friends,' said Tate. 'She's talking about people like Rufus Strange and Mick Jagger.'

'Well, that sounds good,' I said.

So, five days later, there I was, standing outside one of those big white wedding cake houses in Chelsea, clutching a Gibson guitar that Tate had magicked up from somewhere. The front door was open, and groups of people were trickling inside. I waited for a likely-looking group – three men and two girls, so out of it that they wouldn't notice they'd picked up a hanger-on – and followed them in.

The place was my idea of a palace: stone columns, marble floors, big mirrors in swirly golden frames. We traipsed up a massive staircase, past a row of portraits that looked outraged to see someone like me there, and into a room the size of a dance hall. It was full of Kings Road paisley and satin, silk scarves, psychedelic dresses, Vidal Sassoon haircuts. I waited by the door, watching the fashion parade and listening to the drawly voices, wondering how long it would be before someone asked me what I doing there. But nobody paid me any attention at all, and after a couple of minutes I started to make my way through the crowd, looking for Sadie. I'd had nothing stronger than a cup of tea all day, and looking at all those posh shiny faces, pink and goggle-eyed with dope and champagne, was like being trapped in the Chamber of Horrors. I heard my dad murmuring in my head: *This isn't your world, son.* No, but that wasn't the point, was it? I wasn't here to join the club, I was here to teach the buggers a lesson.

'Ah, there you are!' A tap on my shoulder. As I turned, I smelt a whiff of perfume. Even in the midst of that over-packed monkey house, she was as fresh and unruffled as ever. She leaned up to kiss my cheek, then laid a hand on my arm and said, 'Come and meet Suzy. This is her party.'

She led me to the end of the room, where a pair of French windows opened on to a balcony looking out on the street. A bird with long red hair was leaning on the balustrade talking to a guy who looked like he'd walked on to the wrong film set. He couldn't have been more than twenty-five, but he was dressed like a man in his forties: suit, tie, carrying a new-looking black Samsonite attaché case.

'Sorry to interrupt, sweetie,' said Sadie. 'But this is Roy. You remember –'
'Yes, of course.' Big smile. 'Hullo, Roy.'

I nodded and took her hand. Suit-and-tie man melted away without a word.

'Thanks so much for coming,' said Suzy. 'Sadie's been telling me all about you. Don't worry. Nothing but good things. Specially about your song.

I'm really looking forward to hearing it for myself.' She laughed. 'Well, if *looking forward* is quite the word. Given what it's about.'

I shrugged. 'Nice place you've got here.'

'Well, it's not *mine* exactly. But my parents are away –'

'Oh, are they? Well, it's a bit poky, of course, compared to where I grew up. But I don't mind slumming it for an evening.'

She laughed again. 'Yes, she told me that, too. That you're a bit of a comedian.' She glanced at Sadie. 'How are we going to do this?'

'Just find a spot for him. The minute he starts to play, people will listen. You'll see.'

'OK.' She turned to me again. 'You want a drink or something first?'

'Afterwards maybe.'

They led me to a sofa, then stood either side as I launched into *The Sound of Silence*. It turned out Sadie was right: ripples of quiet began to spread through the room, and by the time I'd finished, more or less everyone was watching me. I flicked my eyebrows at her. She nodded. I started in on *Four Minutes*.

I know my friend
It seems like this can never end
The girls, the cars, the yachts, the bars
But while you play
The party's just one slip away
From lights out

In the original version, I'd had *The girls, the cars, the drugs, the bars* – but Tate told me that with *drugs* in there, no broadcaster would touch it, not even Rufus Strange. And I have to say that with this audience, in Suzy whatever-her-name-was's house, *yachts* worked a treat. I could hear people clearing their throats and shuffling their feet as it hit them. They listened to the rest without a sound. At the end there was a brief *Is that it?* pause, then a surge of applause. One girl was so wasted that she forgot where she was and started to scream, hands on cheeks, like a teenybopper on *Top of the Pops*.

'Phew,' said a tall bloke, shouldering his way towards me. 'That was…

Yeah.' He shook his head, running his stubby fingers through his thick dirty hair. He flexed his neck, sniffed, wiped his nose with the edge of his hand, then made a clenched fist salute and punched the air with it.

'I'm The Make,' he said.

I glanced at his outfit: jeans, the jacket from a linen suit that must have cost two hundred quid, and a black t-shirt that looked like an oil-rag.

'Yeah,' I said. 'And I'll bet you're the Spend as well.'

He shivered, like a dog stung by a pebble, then started to laugh. 'You're quick. Quick as a fucking Blue Streak.' He'd chewed the edges off his cut-glass accent, so it came out as a kind of mumble. He made a gun with his finger, pointed it at me, then at his own head. 'But really, that song, it's forensic. Goes straight for the jugular. And I tell you, listening to it, I suddenly got this idea.'

'First time for everything,' I said.

'Oh, fuck.' But he was shaking with laughter. He turned to the people behind him and said to no one in particular, 'You hear that? This guy's our secret weapon. Wrap him up in Christmas paper and drop him on Whitehall and the fuckers won't know what hit them.' He caught sight of Sadie making her way towards us and nodded at her. 'Yeah, you're right. Incredible song. I've just been telling him, it's given me a thought. Something we could do.'

'Yes,' she said, smiling at me. 'It was amazing amazing amazing.'

'Can I have your number?' said the Make. 'And then tomorrow, when you've escaped the *beau monde*, I'll give you a ring and we'll have a chat about it.'

'Sorry, I don't have a number.'

'He could phone you at the office, couldn't he?' said Sadie. And without waiting for a reply, she turned to him and said: 'Wheatsheaf Records –'

'Hang on, hang on.' He reached into his jacket and pulled out an old fountain pen, so red and mottled it looked like he'd been keeping a bruised finger in there. 'OK.'

She dictated the number. He wrote it on the back of his hand. Then he nodded at me and said, 'OK, I'll be in touch.' He pointed the imaginary gun at me again, then turned and barged his way out through the press of people.

'Come and have that drink now,' said Sadie. 'You've earned it.' She laid her fingers on my arm and led me over to a table cluttered with booze. 'Here we are,' she said, handing me a glass of champagne, then grabbing one for herself. 'Take our minds off Armageddon for an hour or two.'

'Armageddon hungry,' I said.

'Really?' She glanced round. 'I don't know if there is anything –' And then she got it and laughed. 'Honestly,' she said, prodding me. 'You never stop, do you?'

'That bloke,' I said. 'Why is he called The Make?'

'Hugo Makeweather?'

She raised her eyebrows, as if it might mean something to me. I shook my head.

'He used to be just Hugo when I first knew him. Then he went to Cambridge and got involved with the International Socialists. That's what *they* call him, for some reason. So now he wants everyone to.'

'The International Socialists?'

'I know.' Her mouth twitched. She nodded at my drink. 'You want something to go with that?'

'Like what?'

She put a hand on my shoulder and lifted herself on tiptoe to peer over the heads of the other people. After a couple of seconds she spotted who she was looking for and waved. The man we'd seen out on the balcony started to weave his way towards us.

'Roy, this is Olly. Commonly known as Doc.'

'What's the matter?' I said. 'Have I suddenly sprouted a third ear or something?'

Sadie laughed. 'Some doctors, you know, can make you feel better even when you were perfectly OK to begin with.'

Suit-and-tie man smiled. I suddenly saw that the right side of his face was disfigured by acne scars, as if someone had started to make him up for a Hammer Horror and got called away halfway through.

'I liked *Four Minutes*,' he said. 'Very raw.'

'That's not the word I'd have used.' I made an explosion with my hands. 'Sizzle sizzle. Totally fried.'

'Can you show us your selection?' said Sadie.

'Sure,' he said. He balanced his case on one hand and clicked it open with the other. Inside, neatly arranged like a salesman's samples, were bags of grass, slabs of dope wrapped in foil, cushiony little packs of white powder, a box of syringes, strips of rubber tubing. Sadie raised her eyebrows at me.

'No, thanks,' I said. The truth is I didn't know what half the stuff was, and I didn't want to look like an ignorant pillock. 'The only heroin I touch now is the fifty-four vintage. Cheeky, I find, but with a *soupçon* of class.'

She laughed. So, to my surprise, did suit-and-tie man.

'Can I just have one of your specials?' she said.

He pulled a leather cigar case from his pocket and tapped out a fat cigarette.

'Thanks.'

He reached for a lighter, but she waved it away. 'No, I'll save it for later.'

He offered me the cigar case. I shook my head.

'It's on the house,' he said.

'Honestly,' said Sadie, 'you don't know what you're missing.'

I took one. It was as perfect as if it had been made in a factory, but no Gold Flake or Senior Service ever smelt like that.

'Ta,' I said.

'A pleasure.' He closed up his case. 'And if I can ever be of help, just ask Sadie for my number.'

He turned and melted back into the crowd. Sadie said,

'It's a bit noisy in here, isn't it? Would you like to see the rest of the house?'

'Long as you don't expect a tip.'

'Why? Don't you think I'm worth it?'

'I left my wallet in the Rolls.'

She laughed. 'Oh, OK. Well, come on.'

She guided me out on to the landing, past the row of disapproving portraits, up the next flight of marble stairs. At the top were more pictures, a big mirror, a set of chairs with scrolled backs. One of them was broken. I shoved it with my foot.

'This lowers the tone a bit, doesn't it?'

She pulled a face. 'They can't bear to part with them, the poor things.'

'They could get a flunky to mend them.'

'Not with The Make's friend the taxman helping himself to all their money.' She pushed open a door in a heavy carved lintel. 'Here we are. This is their room.'

I followed her in. The air was hazy with dust, and smelt faintly of wood polish and wilting flowers. Ahead of us was the largest bed I'd ever seen, smothered in a wrinkly old bedspread. The only light came from a long window facing the street.

'This is better, isn't it?' said Sadie.

'Than what?'

'Being downstairs with all those people. Now I can thank you properly.'

She walked over and closed the door. On her way back she started undoing her blouse. For a confused moment I thought she was just trying to cool down. But then she kept going, two buttons, three, four, until there was a strip of skin running from her throat to her waist. When she reached me she took my hand, slipped it under the loose silk and laid it over her bare tit.

'Shouldn't you lock that?' I said, nodding over her shoulder.

'No one ever comes in here. Except Suzy's parents. And they're away, as she said.'

'Well, mightn't they come back?'

She shook her head. 'They're in South Africa.' She put her cigarette and a box of matches in an ashtray on the bedside table. 'Where's yours?'

I gave it to her. She laid it next to hers, then turned and kissed me lightly on the mouth, brushing my lips with her tongue. Her hand moved down my belly and began unbuckling my belt.

Some bloke I met once told me that sex is controlled by a bit of our brain that evolved millions of years before we could speak. Maybe that's why it's so hard to talk about. But I've got to try, otherwise you won't understand.

I'd slept with a few birds back in Birmingham. One of them, Debbie, had even become a sort of on-off girlfriend. But this was a totally different experience. With the others, having sex – even when they were really into it – was just a part of what they were doing. Somewhere in their heads you knew they were thinking about shopping, or going to work, or the last guy they'd done it with. With Sadie, for those fifteen or twenty minutes, it was what she was. She didn't exactly forget I was there: she couldn't, because my pleasure and hers were the same thing. But she seemed to fold in on herself, like the petals on a flower. I could see the concentration in her face, the way her eyes fluttered shut, like someone listening to a piece of music, determined not to miss a single note. It was – here they come, those words everybody uses – indescribable, unforgettable, beyond anything.

Afterwards she lay quite still for a minute or two, saying nothing. Then she raised herself on one arm and kissed me again.

'Right. Time for the specials.'

We lit up, then settled back on our pillows. After two, three drags, time suddenly seemed to buckle and stretch. What Sadie was to sex, this stuff was to dope. It cut me adrift, carried me to a landscape of weird shapes and shadows, where the sky was brilliant with stars I'd never seen before. Only I wasn't really watching the stars: I *was* the stars, a huge silky ribbon of light spread out across the universe, blown by the breath of creation.

Fuck: *that's* indescribable, too.

From miles away, from a different world, I heard Sadie stub out her special.

'OK?' she said.

I nodded. I was still there, eyes closed, living my star-life. But she rolled towards me and started crab-walking her fingers across my thigh.

'Oh, my,' she said. 'You are an eager boy, aren't you? Another triumph for Doctor Olly's Magic Elixir.' She giggled. 'Guaranteed to restore your manhood in seconds flat. Though *flat* isn't really the *mot juste*, is it?'

In one quick ballet movement she vaulted on top of me and drew me inside her. And then *this* world and *that* world finally merged, and our bodies broke free of their three dimensions, and folded the stars into themselves.

Yeah, it really is impossible to write about. But what you have to get is: it was the most intense experience of my life.

We lay side by side again for I couldn't tell you how long. Then, suddenly, she gave me a peck on the cheek and said,

'There. Thank you. Right. Better go back down, I suppose, and see how everyone's doing.'

And she swung her legs over the edge of the bed and started gathering up her clothes.

So, OK, yeah, I was obsessed. I'd gone to a party and ended up in a fairy story. Not the princess-in-pink and sparkler wand kind: the kind where the world suddenly seems to tilt like a heeling ship, and you've no idea what you'll find round the next corner. But there it was: someone had opened the door to the secret room, and I'd gone inside, and now all I could think was: when can I go back again, and take up where I left off?

In those early days, I was sure that it had been as mind-blowing for her as it had been for me, and she was just sitting there, waiting for my call. But I didn't have her phone number – and, since I didn't have her address either, there was no point ringing enquiries. It seemed pretty much a dead cert, anyway, that she'd turn out to be ex-directory.

I could have asked Tate, of course, but I didn't know exactly what his relationship with her had been, or whether it was officially over. So I sat tight for a couple of days, until he had a lunch date, and then went through his desk. His address book wasn't there. Either he'd deliberately hidden it, to prevent me finding it, or he'd taken it with him, to impress whoever he was meeting with all the big-shot operators he knew.

I was a bit surprised, to be honest, that *she* didn't call *me*. But then I thought, maybe it's a class thing: in her world, the man's always expected to make the first move.

And then, one morning at the end of that first week, when Tate was out doing a recording session, the phone rang, and a man's voice I half-recognized but couldn't put a name to asked to speak to me. I told him that's what he was doing.

'Roy, this is The Make. We met at Suzy's party. How you doing, mate?'

It sounded fake, like he was trying to speak a foreign language.

'I'm just dandy,' I said.

'Great. I said I'd call you, remember?'

'Yeah, I remember.'

He laughed. 'Oh, fuck, you're not going to give me a hard time again, are you?'

I said nothing.

'Cos I want to talk to you. About this idea I had. Wait till you hear what it is.'

'I'm waiting.'

He sniffed. 'The Four Minutes to Lights Out Concert.'

And it all started to gush out, like shaken-up champagne: we'd have this huge venue, Isle of Wight maybe; people would come, not just from all over the country, but from Europe, New York, San Francisco; there'd be whole villages of tents, laid out like a Sioux Indian encampment; there'd be a craft fair, and stalls distributing leaflets and free drugs. And, at the heart of it all, seventy-two hours of non-stop music, from local bands like ours up to big names like Pete Seeger. 'It doesn't matter how well known you are, how many records you've sold. The only thing that counts is that you're committed to the cause. To peace. So what you reckon, man?'

What I reckoned was that he sounded like a druggy posh boy with a rich fantasy life. But – as things stood – he was also my best chance of re-connecting with Sadie, so I said,

'Yeah, interesting.'

'You taking the piss?'

'No.'

'And at ten to midnight on the last day, you and The Guts come on and play *Lights Out*. And then, at four minutes to, everything goes quiet. And as the clock strikes, there's this massive explosion.'

'A real live bomb?'

'Fireworks.'

'That'd look like we were celebrating the end of the world.'

'A mushroom cloud, then. With strobes picking it out in psychedelic colours.' He hesitated. 'Dynamite, yeah?'

'Yeah. Have you talked to anyone else about it?'

'Couple of people. Sadie. She thought it was a fabulous idea.'

'Did she? Can you give me her number, by the way? Can't seem to find it.'

He reeled it off from memory. I scribbled it down, wondering what exactly *his* relationship with her was.

'But I thought you could have a word with Tate Finnegan about it,' he said. 'See if he's interested.'

'Better for *you* to.'

'I don't really know him.'

'Sadie, then.'

'You work for the guy. And it's your song.'

'OK, I'll give it a go. Phone me again next week.'

After we'd rung off, I sat there, staring at Sadie's number, picking up the receiver, dropping it, picking it up again. I was still dickering when I heard Tate coming in.

'Any calls?'

'The Make,' I said.

'The what?'

'Bloke calls himself The Make. Friend of Sadie's.'

He thought for a second, then gun-barrelled his finger at me.

'Oh, yeah, I know, guy drives a hearse. What did he want?'

I told him. I'd expected him to laugh, but he listened quietly, frowning with concentration. When I'd finished, he said,

'And who pays for it?'

I shrugged. 'We didn't discuss it.'

'Well, get the dude in here. We'll talk.'

'If you want. But it'll only encourage him.'

He shook his head. 'You're making the same mistake I did, man. When I first got here, I looked at guys like that, I thought, they're just fucking lapdogs. Took me a while to figure out: *they're* the people who used to rule the goddam world. You know what his old man is? Or was?'

'No.'

'Till a couple years back, last Governor of the something-or-other Islands. Now the independent Republic of something-or-other. So it's in the guy's blood. He needs his own colony to run, just like Daddy. Once he's found it, I'm telling, you, he won't give up. He'll work his ass off till he has the union jack flying over the banana trees, and a bunch of natives dancing around singing *Thank you, Bwana.* And this could be it. Great news for you. And maybe some of our other acts could hitch a ride, too.'

'Yeah, if someone doesn't drop a bomb first.'

I waited till he'd gone home, then finally steeled myself to call Sadie's number. Almost immediately, a girl answered.

'Sadie?' I said.

'No, she's not in, I'm afraid.'

'You know when she'll be back?'

'Sorry, no. Can I give her a message?'

Prim and stuck-up. 'You her secretary?' I said.

She laughed. 'It feels like that sometimes. But no, just her flatmate.'

'OK,' I mumbled. 'I'll try again.'

And I did – that afternoon, several times the next day, several more the day after. Usually there was no reply, but on the third evening, I finally got the same girl again.

'Are you sure I can't give her a message?' she said.

'Just tell her Roy rang.'

'Roy – ?'

'Just Roy. She'll know.'

'And has she got your number?'

'She should.' But I gave it to her, just in case.

'I'll make sure she gets it.'

Answering machines were almost unheard of in those days – at least, I'd never heard of them – so over the next week I waited by the phone pretty much all day, every day. *Nada.* Right, I thought: it's that prim cow. She doesn't like my accent, thinks I'm not good enough for her posh friend. So when The Make finally called, after fixing up a time for him to meet Tate, I said,

'Have you seen Sadie lately?'

'Yeah, at the weekend. Why?'

'She OK?'

'Seemed fine.'

'Only I've been trying to phone her, but I can never get through.'

'Well, you know Sade. Busy busy busy, propping up the fashion wing of the military-industrial complex. Maybe you should drop her a line.'

'I don't think I've got her address.'

'Oh, OK. Here.'

I wasn't going to write, of course – prim bird was probably intercepting Sadie's mail – but that evening I took the office A to Z street directory and set out to find the place. It was tucked away in a little square at an angle to the Kings Road. It wasn't a huge house like Suzy's – but it was newly painted, and the cars on the street outside said *Money lives here.* And not just money: class, too.

There were three buzzers by the door. I pressed hers and waited. Nothing. I rang again. Same. I turned and left. OK, I thought, you've escaped me this time. But you can't go on doing it forever.

It became a routine: every day after work I'd tube down to Sloane Square and have another go. There was never anyone in. But then, one weekend, I finally got lucky – if you can call it luck. Instead of waiting till evening, I went immediately after breakfast. And, just as I was approaching the square, there she was, walking towards me. I knew her instantly, even though she was still a couple of hundred yards away and her face was half-hidden behind a big pair of sunglasses. But she didn't recognize me until I veered into her path and said,

'Oh, hullo, Sadie.'

Even then, it took her a second. Then she smiled and plucked off her shades.

'Oh, Roy! How lovely to see you!'

'Yeah, you too.'

She reached her face up and kissed me on the cheek. Jesus, that moment: the smell of perfume and shampoo; the warmth of her skin; the vision – I could picture it exactly, every mole and fleck and freckle, the shadow of her groin, the swell of her tits, the small, coconut-ice-pink nipples – of what lay beneath her summer suit, a fraction of an inch from me. I backed away, trying to conceal my sudden, out-of-control hard-on.

'What are you doing here?' she said.

'Oh, you know. Just moseying.'

'Oh, yes. The famous Saturday morning London mosey. Well –' She stepped to one side, getting ready to edge past me.

'I was hoping we could meet sometime,' I said.

'Yes.' She was already on the move again. 'Let's fix something up. Give me a ring.'

'I did. I'm always ringing you.'

'Are you?' She stopped and looked back over shoulder, pulling a funny-sorry face. 'Oh dear, how awful of me. It's just there are always so many messages. And it's easy to lose track.'

'I'm free now,' I said.

'Are you? Well, I'm not, I'm afraid.' She paused. 'But anyway...'

And she spun round and walked on quickly towards the Kings Road.

I was gobsmacked. She hadn't been unfriendly exactly, but the message was clear: *don't even think about it*. Why? What had I done? She hadn't complained when we were in bed together, so what – or who – had changed her? The Make? Tate? I couldn't believe either of them would go behind my back like that. Which left me, again, with her snotty cow of a flatmate.

One night, after I'd had too much to drink, and smoked a lot of not-quite-right shit that I'd got from a bloke in a pub, I decided to go round and settle it, once and for all. It was pouring with rain, and by the time I got there I was soaked to the skin. I leaned on the buzzer, and almost immediately someone let me in. I ran up the stairs, two at a time, psyching myself. When I reached the top landing, the door of the flat was open, and a school-marmy looking bird in glasses was peering out at me. I asked her where Sadie was. She said she didn't know. Then I lost it, yelled at her, accused her of I don't know what, which just made her primmer than ever, all raised eyebrows and don't-take-that-tone-with-me-young-man. I was so angry that I almost knocked her out of the way and insisted on searching the flat. But then, somehow, I kind of half-saw how I must look to her, and it scared me. So I just left.

The next morning, I woke with my head coming apart at the temples and a mouth like the Gobi Desert. When I remembered what I'd done, how close to the edge my Sadie obsession had pushed me, I just wanted to go to sleep again. But I couldn't. In the end, I was only able get out of bed by making a solemn promise to myself. No more calls, no more visits: you have to stop now, before you do something really daft.

And for weeks afterwards, I actually stuck to it. I began hitting clubs, going to gigs, meeting Brummy mates for a drink. I even found a pop-crazed bird called Dilly who was happy to spend the time of night with me – and, while we were doing it, I almost managed to get Sadie's closed-up flower face out of my head. The next weekend I went home, and – in the pub – gave my dad a heavily edited version of the Sadie saga, and we had a good laugh about it. When I got back to London, I remember thinking:

you couldn't have done that a couple of months ago. You must be pretty much cured.

Then, a few days later, The Make came swaggering into the office, stinking like an after-match locker room. The Four Minutes to Lights Out Concert was really taking off, he said: they had a dozen acts signed up for it now, including Adam Earnshaw.

'Oh, great,' I said.

'Yeah, I know. But Tate thinks it'll broaden our appeal, show we're not just a one-trick pony. And man, you should see Adam working a room. He's incredible.'

'I'd rather not, if you don't mind.'

He looked oddly at me, but didn't follow it up. 'Anyway, I've got a favour to ask. What we need to do now is get some big-name, hard-line folkies on board. So I'm going down to talk to Mayburn Ellis at the weekend.'

'Tate paying you to do all this stuff?' I said.

He shook his head. 'I've got my own money.' He saw my expression and went on, 'What's wrong with that? If I'm using it to work for the revolution?'

'You ever check with the blokes who're slaving their arses off to *earn* you that money what sort of revolution *they* want?'

'They're not going to have *any* sort of revolution, are they, if we don't get rid of the fucking bomb?'

I shrugged. I wasn't going to argue with that.

'Which is why Ellis is so important. Trouble is, he's *so* hard-line, Tate says, he probably won't want to have anything to do with us. So I was wondering if you'd strengthen my hand by coming with me?'

'How's that supposed to help?'

'I just think it would be better.'

'What, so's you've got a genuine member of the proletariat to get you through the door?'

He shook his head, hissing through his teeth. 'Sharp as fucking ever.'

That Saturday, he picked me up bright and early outside the office. He was driving a black ugly monster of a car, with a wrinkly radiator and an arse like the back end of a dowager duchess sagging over the rear wheels.

'Where's my uniform?' I said.

It took him a moment to get it. Then he laughed and said,

'I told you, man, this is the revolution. It's us bourgeois scum who have to do the chauffeuring now.'

'Yeah. But you still own the cars.'

'Well, what was I supposed to do?' he said, as we glided out into the traffic, 'It was just sitting in the garage at home. My old man never drove it. So I thought, what the hell? If you're on the *Titanic* and someone hands you a first class ticket, you might as well use it.'

'This isn't a ticket,' I said. 'It *is* the bloody *Titanic.*'

We didn't talk much on the way out of London. But as we started to hit the Essex marshes, he suddenly said,

'I hear you've been getting the Sadie treatment.'

It was so out of the blue that I didn't know what to say.

'Don't worry,' he said. 'It happens to the best of us. But it's tough, if you don't know the rules.'

'What rules?'

'She meets you, she fucks you, she drops you.'

I suddenly got this weird picture of hundreds of blokes all over London, mooning around with long faces feeling the same way I did.

'Yeah,' I said. 'Well, no one told me. But I finally sort of figured it out for myself.'

'We all do, in the end. All except Adam Earnshaw, apparently. You hear about him?'

I felt like someone had just poured itching powder all over my skin. 'No.'

'He seems to have the magic key. You know she went to a party with Tate? Some place in Wiltshire?'

'No.' Why hadn't Tate mentioned it to me?

'Well, she met Earnshaw there. Buckled at the knees. Fell down in a dead faint. And now he's more or less moved in with her.'

'They're *living* together?'

He nodded. 'I know. I wish I knew what his secret was.'

'His industrial-size prick.'

He laughed. 'Remarkably, I gather that isn't it.'

'Then they like playing fairy folk together. He puts on his little green hat. And she prances about in a see-through nightie while he sings to her.'

He snorted and looked sharply at me. 'God, you're a cruel bastard, you know that?'

But I didn't feel cruel: I felt cratered. My Uncle John had been on the North Atlantic convoys, and he told me once what it was like to be torpedoed: the thump; the judder; the way the ship seemed to stop dead suddenly, like a harpooned whale. This was kind of similar. I could just about handle the idea that I'd been screwed over, when Tate and The Make and God knows how many other poor buggers had had the same experience. But to know I'd lost out to an airy-fairy Oxford git like Adam Earnshaw – that felt like a mortal wound.

'Stop a minute, will you?' I said.

He pulled over. I got and stood on the verge, trying not to puke. I retched a couple of times but didn't bring anything up.

'Sorry,' said The Make, as I climbed back in. 'Didn't mean to do that to you. I assumed you probably knew. I thought it would be pretty much the talk of the Wheatsheaf office.'

I felt winded. I couldn't speak.

'Are you OK?'

I made a *cut* gesture with my hands.

For the rest of the way, we didn't talk about it again. And by the time we arrived, I'd more or less got my bottle back. Enough, anyway, to be able to get through an hour or two in somebody else's house without making a tit of myself.

Mayburn Ellis lived in one of those picture postcard little places that look like every Yank's image of England. The Make had sketched out a rough map on the back of an envelope, but – instead of driving straight to the house – he left the car a quarter of a mile away in the market square.

'Somehow don't think it'd be the greatest idea to turn up in a Daimler, do you?' he said.

'We could always tell him we'd nicked it. What are we looking for?'

'The Old Bakehouse.'

We found it easily enough, down a small side street that would have been too narrow for the car anyway. The Make bashed on the door. It was opened by a bloke with thick glasses and swept-back grey hair, wearing slacks and sandals and an open-neck blue shirt. My dad would have taken one look at him and said, ah, a member of the do-gooder party. He remembered people like that, Dad did, coming up to Birmingham during the Depression and trying to get everyone to go to lectures about the death of capitalism.

'Hullo,' said The Make. 'I'm Hugo.'

'Yes. Come in, come in.'

'And this is Roy.'

'Oh, hullo, Roy.' The whole of his upper lip moved when he spoke, like he was a ventriloquist's dummy. 'You're the *(Four Minutes to) Lights Out* chap, aren't you?'

I nodded.

'Hugo sent me a tape,' he said. I waited for him to go on, at least say whether or not he liked it. But instead he just murmured, 'Did you have a good journey? How did you get here?'

'We hitched,' said The Make.

Cheeky sod, I thought. 'Yeah,' I said, 'some bloke in a bloody great Daimler brought us pretty nearly the whole way.'

'Really?' said Ellis.

'No, he's pulling your leg,' said The Make. 'People in those sorts of cars don't stop for subversive-looking scruffs like us.'

'Yes, that's what I was thinking,' said Ellis.

'You have to watch him,' said The Make, nodding at me. 'He's a bit of a joker.'

Ellis glanced from one to the other of us, as if we were a comedy duo and he couldn't follow our sense of humour. Then he said,

'Well, how about a cup of tea?'

He led us back through the living room into the kitchen. It was sweltering, with a big iron cooker belting out heat. On the table were mugs, biscuits, milk, a teapot.

'Sit down,' said Ellis. He poured tea for everyone, then settled back in his chair and folded his arms. 'Right, *j'écoute*, as the French say. I always like that: *I listen.*'

'All right,' said The Make. 'Well, I'll tell you how this all began. I happened to be in the same room as this bloke' – jerking his thumb at me – 'when he played *Lights Out*. And listening to him, I had this kind of epiphany, you know? I thought, here we've got the authentic voice of the people, someone saying to our lords and masters, hey, don't think we're stupid, cos we're not. We can see exactly what's going on. And we're not going to stand for it any more.'

Ellis nodded.

'Only the problem was, of course, he was singing to twenty people in a poky little room, so our lords and masters weren't listening. And that' – smacking his palm against his temple – 'is when it hit me. What we needed to do was get musicians from all over the country, all over the world, together in one place, all saying the same thing, at the top of their voices, in front of an audience of thousands. And then the buggers would *have* to listen.'

'Well, yes, I can see...' murmured Ellis. 'Forgive me, I don't doubt your enthusiasm. Or your intentions. It's just that there are such powerful forces at work at the moment. And in my experience, it's all too easy for them to seize control of something like this, without anyone realizing it till it's too late – so they can exploit it for their own purposes.'

I wanted to say, *Yeah, yeah, yeah. But first we need to stop the bomb, don't we, before it stops us? Time enough to deal with that other stuff afterwards.* But obviously The Make hadn't brought me along to offer an opinion. As I started to speak, he shut me up with a wave of his hand.

'They won't seize control if I'm in charge,' he said. 'That's a promise.'

Ellis smiled, then slipped his fingers behind his glasses and rubbed his eyes. 'Believe me,' he said. 'I'm not trying to pour cold water. But if you want my support, I'm afraid I shall need more than a promise. The enemy is at the gate. He's through the gate. And I won't be party to anything that might bring him comfort.'

'OK,' said The Make. 'This is how I see it working.'

And out it gushed again. But this time there was no mention of free drugs or strobe lights: most of it was about cooperative principles, contracts, how there'd be a strict ban on money from record companies or commercial broadcasters. Only at the very end did he talk about the music.

'And then, as the *pièce de résistance*, we'd have *(Four minutes to) Lights Out.*'

Ellis thought for a moment, then nodded. Neither of them looked at me. I felt like a discarded bus ticket. I got up and said,

'I need the toilet.'

Ellis jumped visibly, as if he'd forgotten I was there. 'Oh, oh, upstairs,' he said. 'Straight ahead of you.'

They wouldn't miss me for at least half an hour, I figured – more than enough time to have a quiet smoke. But when I got out into the hall, I could hear music coming from somewhere. I tiptoed up to the landing, to be greeted by a man's voice leaking through a half-open door: *This is big beautiful Radio One. The home of great music.* He sounded as happy about it as if he'd just won the pools. Taped to the door was a handwritten sign: *Ministry of Lily. Keep Out. Authorized Personnel Only.*

A kid. Right, I thought, no sweat: change of venue. A quick piss, then back downstairs. Just as easy to smoke in the street. There wasn't anyone around. And even if there was, in a place like this, they wouldn't know what a joint looked like.

But the squeaky floorboards did for me. As I was coming out of the bathroom, Radio One suddenly went silent and a girl appeared from the Ministry of Lily. She was sixteen going on twenty, overweight, wearing a mini-skirt that didn't do her legs any favours. Her face was white with make-up, all except a dark mole at the corner of her mouth.

'Which one are you?' she said. 'Roy or Hugo?'

'Roy.'

She smiled, jutted her hip. 'You're the one who works for Wheatsheaf Records?'

'Yeah. But only part-time. I'm also a flying ace and a brain surgeon.'

'Honestly?' she said, tugging her hair.

'No. Who are you?'

She pointed to the sign on the door.

'OK. Well, I'm not authorized. So –'

I started towards the stairs. She called after me,

'Do you know Adam Earnshaw?'

I stopped and turned.

'He came here once.' Her tongue darted out and started probing the mole, as if she thought she could lick it away. 'Will you give him something for me?'

'I never see him.'

'Well, make sure he gets it, anyway. I keep writing to him.'

That rang a bell. Poor kid. 'Oh, yeah,' I said. 'I think I've forwarded a few things that came to the office.'

'But he never replies.'

'Yeah,' I said. 'I know the feeling.'

'What, with a girl, you mean?'

I nodded. 'And not just any girl, as it happens, but –'

'*His* girl?'

Fuck me, I thought. *It must be written all over my face.*

'Yeah,' I said.

'You mean *Carrie*?'

'Who's Carrie? No, her name's Sadie.'

She looked thrown. 'Oh. Is she very beautiful?'

I nodded. We stared at each other for a few seconds. Then she said, 'We could be like *Strangers on a Train*.'

I went blank.

'Don't you know that?'

'Never heard of it.'

'I'll show you.'

She went back into the Ministry of Lily. Stuck to the wall was a poster for *Bonnie and Clyde*, showing Faye Dunaway and Warren Beatty shooting the bejesus out of anything that moved. *They're young. They're in love. And they kill people!*

The girl burrowed under the mattress of the unmade bed and pulled out a paperback: *Strangers on a Train*, by Patricia Highsmith. The cover showed a moody picture of a man holding a gun standing behind a seated woman. It was so well-thumbed that the paper was starting to shred round the edges.

'Here.'

'You expecting me to read this now?'

She actually laughed. One up for me.

'No, but you *should* read it. It's really neat.'

'*Neat*? You American or something?'

'My cousin is.' She pointed to the poster on the wall. 'She sent me that.

So anyway' – turning back and nodding at the book – 'what happens in it is, Guy and Bruno meet on a train and swap murders. Bruno kills Guy's wife. Guy kills Bruno's dad.'

'God, whatever happened to *Goldilocks*? And *Old Mother Hubbard*?'

Another laugh. I was cooking with gas.

'We could do the same,' she said. 'Only it wouldn't be murder. It'd be kidnapping. You kidnap Adam for me. And I kidnap this Sadie for you.'

I'll be honest: it never occurred to me that she could be serious. But, all the same, I did have a sudden weird feeling that something had just crawled out of a jar and it would be hard to get it back in again. So yeah, I won't deny it, it was probably stupid of me to say:

'I don't think we ought to be talking like this. Not even as a joke. But I'll tell you what: why don't I just give you their address, and then you can write to him direct?'

But God's truth, that is all I did.

You'll know everything else from the papers, or from Sadie – I'm sure she couldn't wait to give her side of the story. All I'd say is, don't take it all at face value. She's a world-class twister, that one.

But there was just one strange little – what's the word? Postscript? Coda?

Nine months later, I'm a guest of Her Majesty, doing twelve months for possession at Winsbrook Open Prison. One afternoon, I'm told I have a female visitor. When they take me out to meet her, I find – of all people – Prim Girl waiting for me. She asks me how I am. She says she doesn't bear a grudge against me and feels bad about what happened. She tells me Sadie's doing fine.

When she goes, she leaves me some biscuits and an old copy of *The Scene*. And there, in the middle, is a two-page spread on the Four Minutes Festival, with a picture of The Guts, minus me, on stage in the pouring rain, with a huge mushroom cloud erupting behind them.

12

OLIVER DOCKRILL

(Alias *Doctor Olly*; *The Doc*; *The Big Guy*; *Your Local Travel Agent*; *Cosmic Filth*)

You didn't expect me to reply, did you? You thought I'd be too ashamed. Hence, I assume, the offer of anonymity or a *nom de guerre*. Well, you needn't have worried. I feel no shame at all. And I'm perfectly happy to appear in your – what's it going to be, exactly: you don't say? A book? – under all or any of the monikers above, which between them cover pretty much my entire career. So to any guys or gals out there who remember me: a big hi, from *delete as applicable*.

Long time ago, life has begun. And for billions of years after that, slowly, painfully, a step at a time, it evolved. The cost was immense: whole species went to the wall; stronger individuals saw off weaker individuals, denying them the chance to procreate; each organism was itself a battlefield, in which millions of other organisms fought it out to the death. But if, at the end of this torturous, long-drawn-out process, you happened to be one of the survivors, you were perfectly equipped to…well, survive.

And then, *ba-boom*: the 1960s. And all of a sudden, the human race, at least in the West, succumbed to a kind of collective madness, and decided for some inexplicable reason to throw down the weapons that countless generations of ancestors had endured so much to put into its hands. It didn't matter who you fucked, what genes mixed with yours: having healthy kids and raising them as decent citizens wasn't a biological necessity any more, it was a consumer choice. It didn't matter what you sucked or licked or ingested, sending your immune system into meltdown or releasing a plague of chromium-plated cockroaches in your brain: some clever medic would pump you full of something to yank you back from the precipice. Or not.

But you can't just suspend the laws of nature by an act of will. Turn yourself from lord of creation into defenceless prey, and – in no time at all – a newly-mutated predator will have sniffed you out. And just as well too, because that's the only way that natural selection can reassert itself. All those ODs, suicides, bad trips – yes, I profited from them. But so did *homo sapiens*, because it helped to weed out the runts and the inadequates, and make the species stronger.

Little Roy was a natural runt, the end product of the Christ knows how many millennia that the Batley clan had been cringing, scrawny and half-starved, at the bottom of the heap. In all that time, the first decade when a specimen like him could have got anywhere near a woman like Sadie Long – except as a foot-stool – was the 1960s. Before then, a Tate Finnegan or a Hugo Makeweather would have simply lumbered out of the trees, thumping his chest, and little Roy would have scampered back into the bushes, squealing.

So when Sadie told me what he'd been doing (pretty stupid, by any standards), and asked me – for a very satisfactory consideration – to help, I didn't hesitate. To operate as I did back then, you had to be adept at playing both sides of the fence, and it was the easiest thing in the world to tell my pet sergeant in the Drugs Squad that, if he got a search warrant for a certain West End premises at a certain time, his efforts would be rewarded. And not just with your average long-haired pop singer, but with a particularly nasty bit of work, who was bent on making trouble for the government.

Actually doing the deed was child's play. Little Roy was pitifully nervous before The Make's big party – largely, I suspect, because he knew Adam Earnshaw was going to be there – and wanted a pocket full of my specials and a stock of uppers to see him through. Then it was just a matter of giving Detective Sergeant X a brace of Polaroids: Roy Batley (*he's the one you're after*) and Adam Earnshaw (*on no account touch him*).

Bingo.

Adam Earnshaw, of course, was a natural runt too. But in his case, I wasn't the chosen instrument. Nature had to find another means.

And, as things turned out, evidently she did.

13
SADIE LONG

People talk about picking up the pieces. Personally, I'm not sure how helpful that is. Sometimes I think it's better just to let the pieces lie where they are. Nothing's permanent, and the less attention we pay to them, the quicker they can start the transformation into the next stage of their being: the knife that cut you to rust; the stone that bruised you to a beautiful rain-shaped pebble. But each of us has his or her own journey to make, and if it would really help you on yours to know about Adam Earnshaw and me, then I'll do my best to explain what happened. Ten years ago, I have to say – five, even – I wouldn't have done: I was still too angry. But now, finally, I've come to see anger for what it is: a poison – worse than alcohol; worse than drugs – that can make you sick, and eventually kill you. So, though it wasn't easy, I had to learn to let it go. If I hadn't, I wouldn't be here now.

I'm sure you've spoken to lots of other people, but I'm not going to second-guess what they said about me. Maybe – I hope they have – they've managed to put *their* anger behind them too. But if they haven't, I shan't waste time trying to defend myself against them. That would just be to descend to their level. In the end, you're going to have to decide who you think is telling the truth.

Incidentally, FYI: since my divorce, I've been Sadie *Long* again. That probably doesn't seem terribly important to you, but it is to me!

You'll have the bare facts, I imagine: where and when and how Adam and I met. If not, they're all in the public domain, and easy enough to come by. What's harder to convey is who, exactly, we were back then. Certainly it wasn't a meeting between me as I am now, and Adam as he *would* be now, if he's still out there somewhere. Or as I *hope* he would be now, anyway. For all the pain he caused me, I couldn't bear the thought of him still being trapped in the peculiar hell he made for himself – and for all us other poor moths, who flew too near his flame.

You're very coy about yourself, I notice. You've really told me nothing – not even your age, so I don't whether you're old enough actually to *remember* the sixties. My hunch, though, is that you're not. Something in the way you write, like a stranger asking directions. Besides, if you *had* been around at the time, you'd be retired now, and wouldn't have to be trying to earn a crust – if that is what you're doing – by collecting people's reminiscences of Adam Earnshaw.

So I'm afraid, when I introduce to you the young Sadie Long, you're going to think her terribly naïve. And – no point denying it – I was. I went to London straight after school, without even the decompression chamber of three years at university to prepare me for the reality of being a grown-up. And when I got there, I was just dazzled. Everywhere I looked, there was so much beauty, so much colour, so many new things to take delight in. It seemed a crime not to spend every single moment revelling in it all. You know that poem by William Blake?

> *He who binds to himself a joy*
> *Does the winged life destroy;*
> *But he who kisses the joy as it flies*
> *Lives in eternity's sun rise.*

Well, that was more or less my motto. It still is. The mistake I made, in my innocence, was to assume that everyone else – and especially chaps – felt the same way. Since the year dot, men – or so I believed, anyway – had wanted nothing more than to have a good time, sleeping with any girl who took their fancy, and only complaining if she got pregnant and they found themselves trapped into marriage. But for my generation, it seemed to me – and lots of others – that wasn't a problem any more. Thanks to the pill, *everyone*, boys *and* girls, could have a good time, without having to worry about the consequences.

And quite a lot of chaps seemed as keen on that arrangement as we were.

But every now and again you'd meet one who wasn't – and that's where the trouble started. You couldn't tell just by looking at them: they all had long hair and wore nice clothes, like the sort of boys you saw on *Top of the Pops.* But as soon as you'd slept with one of them, all that would go, and out would come the grunting cave-man. *You mine now. You my woman.* If you kept your wits about you, they'd usually see sense in the end. But occasionally you'd find one who wouldn't – and then things could become very unpleasant indeed.

I don't, incidentally, want you to get the impression – which a few people I can think of might have tried to give you – that my life was just a progression from one bed to the next. I only ever slept with chaps that I liked and found attractive. And always it was an extension of some lovely moment we'd spent together – dinner at a restaurant, or an evening dancing. That, or else simply an acknowledgment – a token of appreciation, like a bunch of flowers or a box of chocolates.

You're thinking: gosh, she was a slow learner. And yes, oh dear, how right you are! But you must remember the world I was in. Even by the standards of 1960s London, the fashion industry was a self-absorbed hot-house, with its own rules and ways of doing things. To begin with – and I'm not being homophobic here: it's just a fact – a lot of the chaps who worked in it were gay. That was a real education for me. My father was a dear lovely man, but he shared the prejudices of his generation – which included an ill-concealed contempt for what he called "queers". And of course, incredible though it seems now, homosexuality was still actually against the law when I started out. So to find myself surrounded by chaps who made no secret of being *that way inclined* (isn't it awful? That's what we used to say when I was at school), who even dressed and acted the part, quite openly – well, it took some getting used to.

But then, when I *did* get used to it, in no time at all we became friends. They were such good company, so amusing, so quick to sympathize if you'd taken a bit of a knock. One chap in particular, a stylist called Ken, soon turned into my sort of unofficial best-buddy-and-confidant-in-chief. We'd spend hours together drinking after work, making each other laugh, commiserating over the behaviour of this or that unreasonable fellow who had wronged one of us (or, in one case, both of us!). So I never felt – as perhaps I would have done otherwise – like a square peg in a round hole. Whatever was happening in my life, there always seemed to be someone else who was going through the same thing. And who would help me – when necessary – to pick myself up, dust myself down and start all over again.

And then, in the summer of 1967, an American record producer I knew, Tate Finnegan, asked me to go to a party with him at a house called Sibley Park in Wiltshire. He was a big, loud chap, who said *fuck* every other word and loved terrorizing the poor old Brits by playing the wild backwoodsman. But once you got to know him, as I had, you realized he was the sweetest man in the world: thoughtful, a wonderful lover, and with an intuitive understanding of the rules of engagement that would have shamed a duke. We'd seen each other a few times, but now – though he was much too delicate to say so – it was obvious that he was ready to move on. And the trip to the country, I suspect, was all part of his strategy: he'd signed Adam to his label, and saw him, I think, as a natural next step for me, after he had bowed out. Very few men, in my experience, would have been that considerate. I could have gently pointed out that I didn't really need his help in finding a replacement – but I didn't want to hurt his feelings, so I stayed *schtum*!

But for all that I had some inkling of what Tate was up to, nothing could have prepared me for my first encounter with Adam. There you are, on a summer evening, sipping champagne in the grounds of an English country house. Out on the lake, silhouetted against the glow of fairy lights from a little island behind him, a man in a boat starts to sing. From the first note, you know you're in the presence of something extraordinary.

Up until then, I'd always been a bit snooty about folk music. It sounded so fusty and earnest. And the people who liked it…you mustn't think I'm *blaming* them: of course I know they couldn't help the way they'd been born; but they never seemed to make the best of themselves. It was as if they *wanted* to look ugly. But this chap, sitting there in his little dinghy, was the opposite of ugly: he looked like an ethereal water sprite. And when he launched into *Scarborough Fair*, it was so full of love and loss and yearning that it appeared to be gushing up from his own experience.

And then he started on his own songs. They were all about other people – a girl who picks up a hitchhiker, a man with a dead-end factory job, an unhappy teenager – but, again, they felt so completely authentic that it was as if he'd taken up residence inside their heads. Or inside *my* head. It made my heart thud and snatched at my breath. How did he *know* these things – about me, about himself, about the girl he was singing about?

At the end, he stood up, wobbled on the boat for a moment, then clambered ashore. The whole scene seemed not-quite-real: a moment from a dream, or from a film director's version of an Arthurian legend. Tate Finnegan went down to the water's edge – in my memory I see him moving in slow motion – put an arm round Adam's shoulder, and guided him through the stunned crowd towards me. *Sadie, meet Adam. Hello, Adam. Hello…Hello…*

Sometimes you read about scientists in the wilds of Siberia or somewhere stumbling on an odd lump of rock in a crater and doing the tests and finding that it's the remains of a meteorite from outer space. Well, this was like that. Adam *looked* like other men – a head; two hands; two feet; the usual equipment (I soon discovered!) – but you only had to be with him for two minutes to realize that he came from somewhere else entirely. Or that, anyway, is the way I felt that night. I told him I really loved his songs. We talked about them. He seemed startled, then ridiculously grateful. He said I was the only person he'd met who actually understood what he was trying to do. And then, in a great rush, he said that wasn't a coincidence, he didn't believe in coincidences, it was destined in some way, part of the magic of the evening. Well, you can imagine, that sent a shiver down my spine. Especially since, all around us, watching us wistfully, were fifty or sixty gorgeous girls, any one of whom would have given anything to be standing where I was, listening to Adam Earnshaw saying those things to *her*.

'Shall we see if we can find somewhere quieter?' I said.

I led him to a marquee on the far side of the lawn. It must have been put up in case of bad weather, but – thanks to the balminess of the evening – it was completely empty, except for a line of trestle tables. As we went inside, Tate Finnegan stationed himself by the entrance, to make sure no one followed us. I put my arms round Adam and reached up on tiptoe to kiss him. He turned his face and murmured in my ear:

'Is that what *you* think?'

'What, about coincidences?'

He nodded.

'Yes,' I said.

This time he let me kiss him. Then I took his hand and drew him down on to the grass. Most men at that point, I knew, would have been interested only in getting inside my pants without further ado. But it was obvious that, in this case, quite a lot of further ado was going to be required. So I lay beside him with my head on his shoulder and my arm draped chastely across his stomach. For a few minutes he was completely quiet: I think he may even have been asleep. And then I felt him twitch – and all of a sudden he was talking.

I can't remember everything he said: it came out in choppy little bits, like a series of short messages spliced together on a tape. But the gist has stayed with me. Or perhaps I should say *gists*, because there were a lot of different themes, all jumbled up: his loneliness as a child in Africa; his fear of the landscape; his mother's sweetness and his father's disapproval; his longing to escape to England; his fantasy – a killer, this one – of getting off the plane and hearing a perfect stranger say, *Welcome home.*

'Oh!' I whispered. 'Is it too late for me to say it now?'

He shook his head.

And that was when we made love for the first time. I don't know why, but he insisted that we should do it under one of the tables.

'What's the matter?' I said. 'You think there might be a nuclear attack?'

'You never know.'

We woke in the dawn, cold and stiff. Almost immediately, the monologue resumed: how baffled he'd been by what he'd actually found in England; the hurt and confusion and guilt he'd felt; how, nonetheless, he'd continued to hope, to believe, that life was leading him homewards, towards his heart's desire.

At which point he broke off to gaze at me, stroking my hair. And then bent over and kissed me.

What was a girl to do?

*

This is a bit of a cliché, I know, but it happens to be true: if you succeed at anything in Britain, people will be queuing up to try to knock you off your perch. That's certainly what happened to me. At least I was spared what the poor loves have to endure now – but still it was bad enough: gentlemen of the press taking photos at 3.00 a.m.; made-up stories about orgies (one of them, as you may remember, involving novel uses for the contents of a Fortnum's Christmas hamper); anonymous tittle-tattle in the gossip columns. For a few months, in late 67 and early 68, I seemed to have taken over from Marianne Faithfull as the press's fallen-angel-in-chief.

So it's inevitable you'll have heard all kinds of awful things about me – what a bitch I was, and how I didn't even try to make the relationship with Adam work. But honestly, it isn't true. I'm the only one who knows what it actually felt like, and I can tell you: I *did* try. Harder than I'd ever done, with any man.

I could give you loads of examples, but perhaps the weirdest was something that happened right at the start of our relationship, the morning after we first met. While it was still early, and nobody else seemed to be around, Adam suggested a walk. I thought he might be worried that someone would be arriving soon to take down the marquee, and he wanted to go somewhere we could fool around without the risk of being walked in on, so I said yes.

But instead of going into the woods as I'd expected, he skirted the lake and then – after stopping for a couple of minutes to roll a joint – led me up a rutted track towards a sad, abandoned-looking church built high on the ridge of a hill. As we got closer I started to hang back. He turned and tugged my hand.

'Come on.'

'It's a bit lugubrious, isn't it?' I said. 'Can't we go somewhere a bit more cheerful?'

He shook his head. 'This is important.'

We set off again. But my legs seemed to get heavier with every step, and by the time we reached the entrance to the graveyard I was close to outright panic.

'I'm sorry,' I said. 'Places like this give me the creeps.'

'They give everyone the creeps. That's why we came here.'

But his voice sounded funny, and I could feel him shaking. I could have broken free and made a run for it, but I was too much under his spell. So I let him drag me past the off-its-hinges gate and on to a crazy paving path squidgy with moss and weeds. All around us was a jungle of grass and nettles and brambles. Here and there you could just see the arm of a stone cross, or the top of a weathered headstone, leaning out of the greenery at an odd angle. It was as if they were in pain – wounded animals gasping desperately for breath as the greenery smothered them.

Adam turned suddenly, grabbed me to him and kissed me.

'What are you doing?'

He said nothing, but started to undo my poor crumpled dress. It was farcical: his hand was trembling so much that the zip got stuck, and he had to jerk it back on track and start again.

'Adam!' I said. 'We can't do it here!'

'Yes, we can. We're going to.'

He was – well, I don't need to give you a blow-by-blow account: you know what a chap does to a girl in a situation like that – and pulling me towards the ground. But it was a clumsy performance. Somehow our legs got tangled and we both fell over on to a thick cushion of grass between a pair of graves. On the way down, I caught a glimpse of a lichen-covered name: *Sophia* somebody, eighteen-something to 1918.

'For God's sake, Adam!'

He moved his quaking fingers on to a very intimate part of me. It felt about as erotic as being rubbed by a bunch of twigs.

'This is silly,' I said. 'Let's just go back and –'

'No!'

'Why not, for heaven's sake?'

'Because we're free.'

'What on earth are you talking about?'

He hauled himself on top of me, waving a hand towards the graves. 'I'm not going to let them intimidate me any more.'

'Well, they seem to be doing a pretty good job at the moment,' I said. 'Just give me a minute.'

And – rather than just pushing him off, as most girls would have done – I did. He thrust and ground and grunted like a complete novice, until he'd recovered the wherewithal to gain admission. But only after a fashion: more slipping in while no one was looking than making a grand entrance. Once there, he pumped away to the bitter end, but I can't say it was a terribly satisfying experience. He, however, seemed rather pleased with himself.

'There,' he said, as he rolled off me. 'We did it.'

But that didn't stop him dragging on his clothes in a mad rush and beating a hasty retreat.

I should have asked him what exactly he thought we'd done – but he seemed to have some arcane knowledge of the world, to possess the secret of life and death itself, and I didn't want to reveal my own ignorance by quizzing him about it.

People would tell me that he was, as they put it then, *fucking with my mind*, and I suppose he was. But he was also – ably assisted by copious quantities of dope – fucking with his *own* mind. That's what's so sad. Because it meant that, without realizing it, one stone at a time, he was building a kind of mental Colditz for himself. And in the end it was so impregnable, so escape-proof, that he couldn't get out, and no one else could get in.

Not, of course, that I saw any of this at first. I was too much in awe of him. And he, in a funny, unexpected way, seemed rather in awe of *me*, or at least of my world; so when he came to see me in London, and later on moved in with me, he was always pretty much on his best behaviour. There was still the occasional odd moment – like, for instance, when we came upon three chaps swaggering down the Kings Road in scarlet tunics they must have bought from I Was Lord Kitchener's Valet, and for some reason he was so shocked that he had to cling on to some railings to stop himself falling. But most of the time he seemed – well, almost ordinary. One surprise was that I thought I was going to have a battle with him over his appearance, but it turned out he was perfectly happy to let me take him shopping and buy him new clothes, standing there patiently, like a big docile horse being re-shod, as I unhooked a shirt or a pair of trousers from the rail and held it up against him to see what it looked like. And he was lovely with my friends, too – quite happy to perform for them, if I asked him to, but never playing the rock star prima donna, or (which I feared more) the wild-eyed mystic. For a while, except when I was working, we were almost inseparable.

And it wasn't just the sex, though that was part of it: we went out a lot, too, to parties, art shows, concerts, or just walking in the park and talking about books, history, music, the tradition of courtly love, or anything else that had found its way into one or other of our heads. I won't pretend I didn't enjoy my work, but a fashion model wasn't expected to have a mind of her own, and it was a huge relief to be with someone who recognized that I did. So Adam and I were both of us insatiable – not only for each other's bodies, but also for each other's company, and the extraordinary, exhilarating sense, whenever we were together, of being in a shared world, where we could cross boundaries and roam where we pleased, and never knew where the day might take us. *The two halves of an amulet*, that's what he called us.

But then, about six weeks after he came to stay with me, I got the first glimmer of what was to come. We were in my bedroom one evening when we heard the phone ring in the sitting room. A minute later my flatmate, Rachel, knocked on the door and said it was for me.

'Who is it?' I said.

'Roy Batley.'

The last person in the world I wanted to hear from. 'Oh, Gawd,' I said. 'Tell him I'm not in.'

After she'd gone, Adam said, 'Roy Batley? The bloke who works for Tate Finnegan?'

I nodded.

'Why is he ringing you?'

I shrugged. Adam shifted his weight on to one elbow and peered into my eyes. It was like being caught in an X-ray machine.

'He's just a pest,' I said. 'He won't take no for an answer.'

'So what's the question? Will you go out with him?'

'Something like that. I have tried, you know, to tell him…As politely as I can…But he doesn't get the message. It's his background, I think. His upbringing. Where he comes from, everything has to be spelt out. In neon lights.'

'Well, you must have said something to encourage him.'

'I didn't. All I did was to ask him to play that song of his once, *Four Minutes* or whatever it's called, at a party at Suzy's. And it obviously gave him the wrong idea.'

Adam was still staring at me. I felt myself starting to blush.

'All right!' I said. 'I went to bed with him, OK? Just that once. Before I met you. That's it. So just forget about him. That's what I'd do, if only he'd bloody leave me alone.'

Adam rolled over and lay on his back, looking up at the ceiling.

'Oh, come on,' I said. 'You must have known I've had previous lovers.'

He said nothing.

'What,' I said, 'you'd rather I'd been an ice maiden, would you, keeping myself pure for you?'

He let out a long juddery sigh, as if he was about to start crying.

'Honestly,' I said, 'Roy Batley is nothing. Absolutely nothing. Except an almighty bloody nuisance.' I shook him gently, then leaned over and kissed him. 'OK?'

He turned his head away. 'I'm not good at this.'

'No, I can see.'

'I mean, I knew, of course, you must have...But I didn't know any of them. I couldn't *visualize* them.'

I was on the point of telling him about Tate Finnegan, then thought, why rub his nose in it? So instead I said,

'Why does it matter, anyway? What's past is past. The only people here now, in case you hadn't noticed, are you and me.'

Not the hint of a smile. I shook him again.

'Oh, come on, sweetie.'

'The trouble is, it doesn't feel like that,' he said. 'The past being past, I mean. I see it around me all the time.'

It was true: you *did* get the sense that the past was somehow a living presence to him. His memory was extraordinary: if I told him something, however slight or incidental, it seemed to lodge itself in his head, and stay there, long after I'd forgotten it. That was part of his power: the feeling that he knew me, somehow, better than I knew myself.

'Well, I'm sorry,' I said. 'I am what I am. I can't change it, can I?'

'No, *I'm* sorry,' he said. His eyes were closed, but I could see tears forcing their way between the lids. He reached for my hand. 'I'll try to be better.'

And he did. And for a month or two after that, things went more or less back to normal – though sometimes I'd catch him watching me with a wistful look in his eyes, and guessed he was imagining me with someone else. It upset me, and made me a little bit angry. But he never said anything about it, so neither did I.

But then, at the start of October, he had to go back to Oxford. I remember the next few months as a kind of surreal drama – moments of normality punctuated, more and more insistently, by *motifs* lifted straight from the bumper book of dreams: feelings of helplessness and dread, the mad collision of different worlds. When, years later, I finally got round to telling a therapist about it, even she had to admit that there was something *uncanny* about that period of my life. Nowadays, I'm more inclined to think of it as the working out of other people's karma.

To begin with, I just felt lost. And I mean that literally: a ship without a compass, not knowing whether to turn to port or starboard. So when I wasn't working I was almost always at home, comforting myself with hot milky drinks and waiting for Adam to call. And he *did* call most days. But it was never enough: he always sounded constrained and remote – much further away than the sixty miles that actually separated us – and then suddenly, in the middle of a conversation that neither of us had managed to kick-start into life, we'd hear the *beep beep beep* telling us he'd run out of money. And then there was only time for me to blurt out what I really *wanted* to say – *I miss you so much. I wish you were here* – before he had to ring off.

It feels funny to be writing this, because nowadays I'm quite happy to be on my own for days – and nights! – at a time. But young Sadie was a very physical person, and really needed to be *with* someone just in order to feel alive. I was constantly *cold*, I remember. Even after a scalding bath, going to bed by myself was a purgatory. I felt as if I were laying myself in my own coffin.

> *The grave's a fine and private place*
> *But none, I think, do there embrace.*

That was a poem Adam had introduced me to. And it fitted the bill perfectly.

I did my best not to let what was happening seep into my professional life, but if you look at any of the shots of me from that period you can see that it was a lost cause. In picture after picture I'm staring out at the camera with a kind of sullen vacancy, as if I'm in a state of shock after witnessing a horrible accident. Thankfully, that was exactly the effect a lot of the photographers were after, so they probably didn't notice. But stylist Ken did. And one day, when we broke for lunch, he took me aside and said,

'What's wrong?'

'Nothing.'

'Oh, come on. You're walking around with a hundredweight bag of cement on your shoulders. Those stuck-up pardon-my-Frenches may not be able to see it. But to anyone who loves you it stands out a mile. If a bag of cement can stand out a mile.'

I managed a watery smile. And then I told him.

'Well, you know what I think?' he said. 'I think you should find yourself a gentleman friend. Or three.'

'Adam's my gentleman friend.'

'No, Adam's your *boy*friend. But Adam isn't here, is he? And there's plenty of chaps who are, and wouldn't mind slipping into his brogues every now and again. I can see them looking at you. Like dogs ogling a string of sausages.'

'What a disgusting image!'

'Careful: you came dangerously to laughing there.'

'I can't,' I said. 'You know, what you're saying. I mean, Adam…He's not –'

'Why should he ever know? Honestly, you'd be doing us all a favour. You'd be doing *him* a favour.' He touched my cheek. 'Take it from me, he'd be as thrilled as the rest of us to see a bit of colour back here.'

I did hold out for a few days. But then Ken confronted me again:

'So, have you done what I suggested?'

I shook my head.

'No, I thought not. I've seen cheerier-looking corpses. Well, I'll give you forty-eight hours. After that, I'm going to start walking up and down with a sandwich board saying *Lady to Let*.'

So I succumbed. And Ken was right: it did make things better with Adam. Now when I talked to him I wasn't thinking about sex the whole time, fighting the urge to tell him to get on a train immediately and hotfoot it to my bed. That side of my life was taken care of. Which meant I could give my full attention to what *he* wanted to talk about: a gig he'd done at Poor Tom's Folk Club, or the trouble he was having getting to grips with *The Changeling* or *Hamlet* or *The Allegory of Love*.

But then things started to get more complicated. It wasn't the fault of the two chaps I was seeing: they were both lovely, and very understanding. It's just that it became much harder to make plans and stick to them. With the best will in the world, you can't always allow for traffic jams, flat tyres, last-minute phone calls from your parents. With the result that sometimes I'd tell Adam to ring me at home at such-and-such a time, and when he did, I still wasn't back. My excuses started to sound more and more threadbare, even to me. I hated lying to him, and sensing the growing gulf it was creating between us. Once I almost broke down and told him the truth, but – remembering his reaction to Roy Batley – I bit my tongue.

And then there was Roy bloody Batley himself. I'd tried everything I could think of, but he still wouldn't leave me alone. He'd already terrified Rachel, turning up drunk one evening and demanding to know where I was. Now, more or less every weekend – and sometimes during the week – I'd find him hanging around the place when I went outside. The first time it happened, he subjected me to an embarrassingly unconvincing *Good Lord, fancy meeting you here!* But even he wasn't dense enough to think he could get away with that twice, so he switched tactics, and began lying in wait and spying on me from the other side of the square. Usually there were too many people around for him to risk approaching me, and he'd just turn away abruptly, in hope – I suppose – that I wouldn't notice him. Once, though, he started to follow me towards the tube, and I only managed to throw him off by hailing a cab.

Work, Adam, Chap A, Chap B, avoiding Roy Batley: that, for I don't know how long, became my life. It was no more than a juggling act: a good day was when I went to bed having kept all the balls in the air; a bad day was when I'd dropped one or more of them. And then, one weekend in the middle of it all, Adam phoned to say he was coming to see me. He sounded strained and preoccupied. I hastily rearranged the chaps, sent Rachel home to stay with her parents and prepared myself for the worst.

And things were certainly uncomfortable for the first hour or so after he arrived. He didn't want to go to bed with me; he could barely bring himself to touch me. He didn't want a drink. He didn't – pretty much unheard of, this – reach for his trusty Golden Virginia pouch and roll us a joint. He found it hard even to sit still, but kept getting up and prowling round the flat, picking things up, putting them down again. If I asked him a question, he just shrugged. Sometimes he'd start to say something himself, before abandoning it mid-sentence and lapsing into gloomy silence.

And then all of a sudden he wheeled round, grabbed the back of a chair to steady himself, and blurted out that he knew I'd been sleeping with other men.

'Who told you that?' I said.

'It doesn't matter. It's bloody obvious, isn't it?'

'Well, I think at least –' I began, but he held up a hand to stop me.

'Don't, don't,' he said. 'Listen, I'm a mess. I've got all these ideas floating around from, you know, mediaeval love poetry and Victorian novels and Jacobean tragedy and fuck knows what. And I can't square them with –' He waved his hand despairingly. 'But I know I've got to try. Because we're the –' He put his fingers together, making an inverted heart. 'And the one hope, the only hope, is that we're honest with each other.'

Tears were pricking my eyes. I said nothing.

'So, me first: I've slept with someone else too.'

Odd: I told myself there was no reason he shouldn't be, it was what I'd expected, and yet it still gave me a queasy pang, like the twinge of a muscle I hadn't known existed. And for an unbearable moment I suddenly saw the world that he and I had shared, not as a paradise lost, but as a paradise forfeited.

'Who?' I said.

He shook his head. 'I'm not going to tell you. And don't you tell me who your *beaux* are, either.' He ran his fingers through his hair, then held his hand up again. 'I don't want to know.'

'OK.'

'But just admit it. They do exist. You do have *beaux*.'

'I don't like that word.'

'Pick your own, then.'

'Friends. I have a couple of friends, who keep me company when I'm lonely. But I don't love them. I'm not in love with them. I'm in love with you.'

We were both crying now. I hugged him and whispered,

'We aren't like everybody else. I'm the other half of the amulet, remember? We aren't going to let this break us apart, are we?'

He shook his head.

'Come on, let's go into the bedroom.'

We did. And afterwards I lay there feeling, for the first time in weeks, that perhaps the different elements in my life weren't at war with each other after all. Maybe we were among the pioneers, Adam and I – forging, for the first time in history, a new kind of relationship between men and women, based on openness, frankness, an unflinching acceptance of the reality of desire. In the future, everyone – or at least everyone who was brave enough – would live like this.

Of course, looking back, I can see I was being naïve. But at the time I really believed it, which meant I was blind to the warning signs that someone older and more experienced would have noticed. The first was that Adam seemed oddly reluctant to come to the flat. I thought perhaps it was because he associated the place with the earlier phase of our life together, and felt we should mark the new dispensation by starting afresh. It was difficult for me to visit him in Oxford – he had a mad landlady, who patrolled the premises like an elderly terrier, snarling at girls and nipping at their ankles – so we tended to meet at b and b's or little hotels, where we would check in under the name (don't ask me why: it was his idea) of Mr and Mrs Elvin. In order to avoid being recognized, I took to wearing shades, whatever the weather, inside and out. Even then, a suspicious-looking owner would sometimes stare at me with an *I'm sure I've seen that girl somewhere* expression, but no one ever came right out and challenged us.

But however far we removed ourselves from our day-to-day lives, he never seemed completely able to relax. There was always a kind of wariness about him, some hidden constraint that I kept bumping into but could never identify. Once, when we were in bed together and he was just reaching the critical moment, I saw him violently scrunch up his eyes suddenly, as if he couldn't bear to look at me. Afterwards I said,

'What's the matter? Is something hurting?'

He shook his head.

'Or were you imagining I was someone else? Your girl in Oxford? Or should I say *girls*?'

He said nothing.

'Come on,' I said. 'I don't mind. I just want to know.'

'We said we wouldn't tell each other, didn't we?'

'Oh, yes, that's right! You've looked at the contract and that's what it says, clause four, article (a).'

'It's what we agreed.'

'Yes, all right. But I'm not a lease or a bill of sale. I'm a girl. And I want to know who you were thinking of.'

He turned away from me. I pummelled his bare shoulder.

'Tell me!'

He got up without a word and padded off to the bathroom. When he got back I was weeping. He didn't seem to notice, but sat on the edge of the bed and started to get dressed. I pulled him down next to me.

'I'm sorry,' I said. 'I didn't mean to snap at you. It's just I feel so desperate. I didn't know...I didn't realize...How horrible it is. To feel jealous.'

'It's what we have to deal with,' he said. And then, without even looking at me, he stood up and started groping around for his socks.

And that was the start, the moment when the world of dreams began to take over my life. The opening salvo came one evening the following week. I'd just got home after a gruelling shoot, and was rummaging in my bag for the keys, when I noticed a figure standing in the shadows next to the front door. *Oh, my God,* I thought. *This is all I need: Roy Batley.* But then, as I turned, I glimpsed the pudgy, unlined blob of the face and caught a powerful whiff of *Oh! de London.*

'Are you Sadie Long?' she said.

I didn't reply. As she stepped out into the light from the streetlamp I saw that she was no more than sixteen or so, though she was dressed to look older.

'You are, aren't you?' she said.

I still said nothing. She suddenly lunged towards me, thrusting her hand into her bag, then pressing it against my ribs. Inside it I could feel something round and hard.

'This is a gun,' she said.

I stared at her. She was deathly pale, except for two streaks of eye-liner and a dark mole at the corner of her mouth. Was this a joke? A crazy way of asking for a penny for the guy? Or was I so tired I was starting to hallucinate?

'What do you want?' I said.

'How much money have you got?'

God, I thought, a junkie, at that age.

'How much do you need?'

'Enough for a taxi.'

'A taxi where?'

'Soho.'

Even worse: she must be selling herself to support her habit.

'I can give you five bob,' I said. 'But I think you should phone your –'

She rammed the bag against me again. 'Shut up! You're coming *with* me!'

'Why?'

'Shut up, I said!' She was trembling. She glanced up at the flat. 'Is he in there? Adam?'

Everything suddenly reassembled itself into a different pattern.

'Adam?' I yelled. 'What do you know about Adam?'

My rage startled her. She took an involuntary step back. I went after her, grabbed her wrist, smashed it against the wall. She screamed and dropped her bag. It fell with a muffled thump. No gun, obviously.

'Are you the little slut he's been sleeping with?' I said.

She said nothing. I dragged her whimpering out into the light again. Her face had frozen over with shock. I squeezed her bruised wrist. She *oohed* with pain.

'No! I'm just…It's just…I like him.'

'What, you're a fan, you mean?'

She nodded.

'How did you find out where I live?'

She didn't answer. I gave her another squeeze.

'Ah! No, stop it!' She was sobbing now. She wiped her nose on the back of her free hand. 'Someone told me.'

'Who?'

She said nothing.

'All right,' I said. 'We're going upstairs, and I'm going to phone the police.' I yanked at her arm. 'Come on.'

'OK! OK! It was someone called Roy Batley!'

I leaned closer to her. The sense of being in a nightmare was turning my legs to lead.

'Roy Batley? *He* told you to do this?'

'We were going to help each other. I was going to take you to him. And –'

Suddenly I needed all my strength just to stay on my feet. She must have felt the slackening of my grip, because without warning she broke free, snatched up her bag, and set off down the street. After fifty yards or so she paused just long enough to look back over her shoulder and yell, 'You won't keep him!'

It was pointless even to think about going in pursuit: I was drowning in treacle.

I plodded upstairs, clutching the banister like an old woman. Rachel was huddled in front of the gas fire, holding a mug of something in both hands. As I came through the door she glanced up and murmured *Hullo*, then went back to thinking about whatever it was she was thinking about.

'Are you all right?' I said.

She nodded.

'Well, I'm not.'

She turned towards me. Some semi-detached bit of my mind noted that it seemed to be an effort for her to meet my eye. But the rest of me was too distracted to wonder why.

'Why?' she said. 'What's happened?'

'What *hasn't* happened?'

'Oh dear. Sit down. Do you want me to get you something? Some wine, or –'

I nodded and slumped on to the sofa. She went into the kitchen and came back with a glass of Chablis. Another signal from the observation post in my head: *look, she hasn't brought one for herself.*

'So,' she said, returning to her chair, 'tell me.'

'Someone just tried to kidnap me. At least, I think that's what she was trying to do.'

'What!?'

'With the aim of delivering me to Roy Batley. So, presumably, that he could have his wicked way with me.'

She clapped a hand over her mouth and stared at me, big-eyed. She didn't know if I was joking or not.

'It's like something out of The Goon Show. The not-funny version.'

'So what did you do?'

'I knocked her bag out of her hand. The one with the supposed gun in it.'

'Gosh, that was brave of you.'

'Not really. She was just a kid. A schoolgirl in civvies, that's what she looked like. But that's not the end of it. Because *she* seemed to have an unhealthy interest in *Adam*. That was more or less her first question: was he here? I even wondered whether maybe she was his secret lover. Because he's always been very cagey about her. And that would explain why, wouldn't it, if she's under-age? Though frankly I'd have hoped he'd have better taste.'

This time I couldn't just file it away for future reference: her response was wrong. No sympathy, no conspiratorial snickering. I stared at her. It was like watching a house collapsing: one moment a blank façade, the next a chaos of cracking and buckling. She gasped, shook her head, started to sob.

'Ah,' I said. Of course: this was the world of dreams, and had its own inescapable logic. '*You're* the secret lover.'

She was hunched over now, her head in her hands. But she managed a nod.

But even that couldn't explain the full depth of her despair. There had to be one final twist of the knife.

'Don't tell me,' I said. 'And you're pregnant.'

The house had collapsed, all right. Up until then, Rachel had been more or less the only stable point in my life: I'd asked her to share with me because we had separate worlds, and I knew – or thought I knew – that she would always be a non-combatant in mine. Now it turned out that behind my back, and no doubt in my own flat – the flat that had always been my shelter from the storm – the prissy, butter-wouldn't-melt-in-her-mouth little bitch had secretly betrayed me with Adam. And *he*, of course, had betrayed me with her. With *her*: a girl who'd been born middle-aged, and looked like a provincial librarian.

I could have gone under. I think I probably would have done, if it hadn't been for heroic Ken, who swooped yet again to my rescue.

'Honestly,' he said. 'You look like death warmed over. What's happened? Tell Uncle Ken.'

So I did. It took twice as long as it should have done, because I was crying so much.

'Right,' he said, when I'd finished. 'It's no good just dissolving in an embarrassing patch of wee on the carpet. You're better than that. You're Sadie Long. You're one of the most life-enhancing people I've ever met. God, listen to me. *Life-enhancing.*'

I laughed, for the first time in days.

'And you're strong,' he said. 'You're going to fight.'

So I did. The next day I sat Rachel down at the kitchen table and said, 'So, how far gone are you?'

She looked startled: we'd hardly spoken since she'd admitted she was pregnant. 'Two months.'

I resisted the temptation to work backwards and figure out when they must have slept together.

'And what are you going to do?'

She shook her head: *I don't know.*

'Have you told Adam?'

'No. I can't decide…Do you think I should?'

Thank God for that, at least. 'No, absolutely not.'

'But it is his. I mean, don't you think he has a right –'

'It would destroy him.'

'But he might want to keep it.'

'What, and get married, and settle down with you, and take a job in a tax office?'

She started to cry. I felt myself relax slightly.

'You can't have it,' I said. 'We're going to have to get rid of it.'

'But how…I mean, it's against the law –'

'If you could have only waited. It'll probably be legal in a few months. But you simply couldn't keep your hands off him that long, could you?'

She dropped her head on to her arms and heaved almost silently.

'There are still doctors who'll do it,' I said. 'Of course, a good one'll be expensive. And you can't really run home and say, *please, Mummy and Daddy, can I have an abortion for my birthday*, can you?'

She beat her fists on the table like a little girl.

'But I can lend you the money, if need be. The main thing is, you've got to be quick.'

I knew a couple of other girls who could have suggested someone, but I didn't want to have to explain why I was asking. So in the end Rachel got the name of a doctor from the creepy owner of the language school where she worked, who – it turned out – had extensive experience of arranging abortions for clueless female students.

On the day she went in to have it done, Adam phoned. So far I'd stuck to my resolve to act as if nothing had happened, but that morning my feelings were so jangled that for a moment I started to weaken. Then I got a grip on myself. To tell him now would be to squander my trump card. Much better to stick to my plan, and keep it as a last resort.

One down, one to go: Roy Batley. I did think about reporting him to the police, but Ken advised against it. The only actual threat I'd received was from the crazy girl who'd accosted me at the front door, and I didn't have her name – and, even if I had, it would have been just my word against hers. And, strange as it may seem now, *stalking*, as an offence, didn't even exist back then – so I really had no choice but to take the law literally into my own hands.

Just for the record: I haven't done drugs for years. But in those days everyone did, and – like all my friends – I had a regular supplier: a chap called Doc Olly, who sold the best dope this side of Marrakesh. I'd introduced Roy Batley to him, and knew they'd had some dealings since. It was, in fact, when Doc mentioned that – after a bad experience with someone he'd met in a pub – the miserable Batley was now getting all his hash from him, that the scheme suddenly appeared, fully formed, in my head.

It was common knowledge (though I was a bit hazy about the details) that Doc not only had some big-name clients, but also a couple of connections in the Met who – as long as he was discreet about it, and provided them with information when required – allowed him to operate more or less with impunity. So I explained my problem to him, and suggested that the powers that be might be interested in getting their hands on a rabble-rousing young loudmouth like Roy Batley – whose only claim to fame was a noisy anti-war song – and making an example of him. Doc thought for a moment, then nodded. He named a sum. I agreed – on condition that that was where my involvement ended. He nodded again. 'Leave it to me.'

For a week or so everything went quiet. And then, one evening, when I was about to leave for a party at my friend Hugo Makeweather's house, Doc phoned me.

'Are you heading to The Make's tonight?'

'Yes, I was just on my way out.'

'Don't.'

'Oh, God, you're not dragging him into this –' I began, but he'd rung off.

I phoned The Make, said I had a headache and wouldn't be coming.

'Shit, man, that's terrible. I can give you something guaranteed to take it away, if you can get yourself here. Course, it might take your head with it.'

I laughed, but it made me feel like a traitor. 'I think I'd better just stay in bed. Can you explain to Adam when he arrives?'

'Yeah, OK. But Adam, without you: it's going to be like having a one-legged chicken hopping about the place.'

Of course, if we'd had mobiles then, I could have called Adam myself and warned him not to go either. In which case, at least half a dozen lives might have turned out differently.

Or not. Perhaps however much we try to outwit it, karma, or whatever you want to call it, always finds a way.

This part is hard to write. Don't misunderstand me: it's not that I regret what I did, or feel guilty about it. Guilt is such a useless emotion anyway: all it does is make you – and everyone else – miserable. And you have to remember: I was fighting for survival. If I were in a similar situation today

I might, with the benefit of experience, handle things a bit differently – but the result would still be the same. Pain, as a wise man once wrote, is just part of life: what we have to try to avoid is *suffering*. So yes, this hurts. But I shan't allow it to *harm* me.

I went to bed early that evening and fell asleep almost immediately, soothed by the thought that my problems with Roy Batley would soon be over. At some point during the night I was woken by the sound of somebody moving about in the sitting room. Rachel had gone home for a few days to recover from her operation – heaven knows what she told her parents – and the only other person who had a key was Adam. But if it was Adam, why was he out there rather than in here with me? In my half-asleep state, a horrible idea suddenly hit me: what if Roy Batley had given the police the slip and broken in to take his revenge?

I put on my dressing-gown and tiptoed out into the hall. The sitting room door was closed, but underneath it I could see a pencil-line of light. With one hand on the key – so that if necessary I could pull it shut again and lock myself in – I eased it open and peered through the crack. The lamp was on, and Adam was lying on his back on the sofa, with his coat spread over him like a blanket and one arm flung across his eyes.

'What are you doing here?' I said.

The sound startled him. He kicked out and sat up abruptly.

'Why don't you come to bed?'

'They said you weren't feeling well.'

I smiled. 'Well, I'm fine now.'

He pulled his knees up, then leaned forward and hugged them. 'Do you know what happened?'

'Where?'

'At the party.'

I shook my head.

'Roy Batley was arrested. For possession of drugs. Just Roy. No one else. And he thought it was me who'd tipped off the police. As they were taking him away he screamed at me, "You toffee-nosed, stuck-up cunt! You set me up, didn't you?"'

'Don't use that word.'

'It's what he said.'

'And *did* you set him up?'

'No, of course not.'

Not *of course not, I wouldn't,* but *of course not, I know who did.* We stared at each other.

'What else could I do?' I said. 'He's been making my life a complete misery.'

He shook his head. 'You know what he'll think? He'll think it's because of his background. And he'll go to his grave believing that's why he was singled out. Because he got above himself, so the nobs slapped him down. And stooped pretty low to do it.'

'Ah, what, so you're saying I behaved like the most frightful little sneak, are you?'

'That's how it'll appear to him.'

'And to you, apparently.'

He said nothing.

Something tipped in that moment. Until then, both of us had been prepared to fight our own instincts, to lie, to endure jealousy and anguish – anything, to keep our relationship afloat. And now, suddenly, we weren't. It was as if the secret garden where we had known and loved each other had bit by bit been eroded and reduced, until now even the very heart of it had vanished under concrete. A day earlier, perhaps we could both of us have acknowledged it, and parted as – friends? No. But at least as two people who could still have a conversation without shouting.

But I was feeling wounded and angry and misjudged.

'Well, when it comes to sneaking, I don't think you're in a much of a position to talk. Sleeping with Rachel behind my back. Betraying me with my own flatmate. I'd say that's a little bit worse than arranging for a criminal to be shoved behind bars.'

He stared at me, as if the words made no sense to him at all.

'Did you honestly think the silly cow would keep her mouth shut? She couldn't wait to crow to me about it.' I teetered on the edge of delivering the *coup de grâce*, then stopped myself. The abortion was my nuclear weapon – and some instinct made me think I should keep it in the bunker for possible future use. Instead I said, 'If she'd at least been beautiful, I could perhaps have understood. But to think of you with a dowdy bitch like that, who couldn't get a man to sleep with her if she paid him. And then touching *me* afterwards…'

He shook his head, then shrugged on his coat and went out into the night without a word.

And that was it. The pieces were too scattered, too hopelessly fragmented. Even if it were possible to gather them all up and stick them back together, you'd end up with nothing more than a lifeless imitation.

Which is why I decided to leave them exactly where they were.

14

PIP RANDALL

What an odd request. You must be either remarkably astute or remarkably ignorant. Sorry if that sounds rude – but ignorance, I find, is pretty much the order of the day now. No one seems to understand any more what a vicar actually *does*. Over the course of a career like mine, you meet thousands of people. And most of them – contrary to the sitcom stereotype – aren't spinsters sitting around a vicarage tea-table, talking about flowers and knitting: they're human beings at the limit, facing the crises that polite society turns away from in embarrassment: grief or sickness or despair. You never *forget* these poor struggling souls: by some slow geological process of accretion, they become part of your own life. But, as time goes on, they do lose their individuality, dissolving bit by bit into the great undifferentiated mass of affliction. And there's no reason why a troubled young musician should resist that process, any more than anybody else.

But yes, as it happens, I *do* remember Adam Earnshaw. Perhaps it's because, not long afterwards, I read in the paper that he'd disappeared. Under the headline was a newsprint picture of a smiling, clear-complexioned, bright-eyed young man holding the neck of his guitar like a staff. That image has stayed with me ever since. It's a sort of visual hair shirt, constantly reminding me – whenever pride and self-satisfaction come a-calling – of my failings. Because I can't throw off the feeling that if I'd only seen more clearly what was needed, he'd still be with us now.

I make excuses for myself, of course. One of them was that I was very young. St Frideswide's was my first living, and I'd only been there a few months. The Church wasn't suffering the kind of unstoppable lemming exodus that we're seeing today: indeed, looking back, it seems to have been going about its business like the good folk of Pompeii in AD 78, oblivious to the acrid portents of destruction on the horizon. Nevertheless, it was beginning to feel the impact of never-had-it-so-good complacency, and the seductive Milk Tray Assortment of sixties hedonism: drugs, sex, music, fashion, *me*. If we were to remain *relevant* – very much the word of the moment – we somehow had to find a different approach.

For me, that meant, above all, being *visible*. My predecessor – a lean, unworldly character from a nineteenth century novel – had spent most of his time in his own study, classifying his collection of flint arrowheads and fragments of pottery. Even his services were an encounter with the past, full of arcane references that meant nothing to most of the congregation. But with his retirement, the big old vicarage was sold off, and a small modern replacement built in a corner of the grounds. The aim, of course, was simply to save money; but I was determined to make it symbolize something more: a new start in the relationship between the church and the parish. I wanted to bring the gospel into the present, make it part of the day-to-day life of the community – which meant rolling up my sleeves, and getting involved in whatever was going on.

And that's how, one afternoon in early 1968, I found myself pushing a car with a flat battery along Church End. It was an evil-tempered pre-war Wolseley, built like a tank. The owner, a young chap who – to the best of my knowledge – had never set foot in St Frideswide's, kept jumping out to push with me, then jumping in again to try to get the engine to fire. But every time he let in the clutch, the villainous old brute juddered to a halt, and I wasn't strong enough to shift it on my own.

And then, suddenly, I sensed someone next to me. I glanced side-ways: a tangle-haired waif of about twenty, wearing a stained ex-army greatcoat and carrying a moth-eaten knapsack with a missing strap. A few years before, you'd have called him a tramp, but now the word that sprang to mind was *hippy*. He was pale and scrawny, but our combined weight was just enough to heave the car into motion. As we started to pick up speed, I was surprised to see the expert way he braced his beanpole arms to get maximum purchase. After twenty seconds or so, the Wolseley gave a mulish lurch and spluttered into life. The driver leaned out and flashed us a thumbs up, then drove off before it had a chance to stall again.

I turned to my fellow-pusher. 'Thank you.'

He nodded.

'You saved the day. You're obviously an expert at this. I don't think I know you, do I?'

He shook his head.

'I'm the new vicar here. Pip Randall.'

I held my hand out. He took it.

'You local?' I said. 'Or just visiting?'

'Visiting. Well, no, not really.'

I waited for him to explain. But he just stared at me, brow furrowing, then relaxing, then furrowing again, as if he had trouble bringing me into focus. Drugs, presumably. I'd read about the wildfire spread of LSD, but never seen the effects with my own eyes.

'Are you all right?' I asked.

He said nothing, but looked up at the rough grey face of St Frideswide's.

'Would you like a cup of tea or something?'

He seemed not to hear me. 'How old is it?'

It took me a second to figure out that he meant the church.

'Oh, well, it's a bit of a hotchpotch. The oldest part's thirteenth century. But most of it's Victorian.'

'And how old are you?' As he heard himself say it, it must have awakened some dim childhood memory that it's rude to ask someone's age. He flushed and mumbled, 'Sorry.'

'No, that's fine,' I said. I studied him for a moment. 'At a guess, I'd say I'm probably ten years older than you are.'

He went on looking at the wall, so minutely that it seemed as if he was trying to count the individual flints.

'Where are you from?' I said.

'Nowhere in particular.'

'No, but I mean, where are you living at the moment?'

He nodded at the ground. 'Here.'

You're in the middle of a game of chess, and your opponent suddenly moves his pawn as if it were a knight. How do you respond? If you're me, you don't promptly remind him of the rules. You don't, in fact, rush to do anything: you slow your breathing and wait for the tell-tale sensation below your diaphragm – a bud opening its petals, is how I've always visualized it – that means you're listening, not with your own ear, but with the ear of God.

'Well, that's good,' I said finally. 'In the end, you're right, it's where we all live. It's the only place we've got, isn't it? And now – this instant – is the only time.'

His gaze flickered towards me. I'd caught his interest, at least.

'What's your name?' I said.

'Adam Earnshaw.'

'And where did you spend last night, Adam?'

He waved vaguely towards the east.

'What's it called? The place you were staying?'

'I don't know. It was in a wood.'

'Haven't you got a home to go to?'

'No.'

Inasmuch as ye have done it unto one of the least of these my brethren, ye have done it unto me. It was a straightforward injunction. But the new vicarage was tiny, and my wife and I had only been married a few months. What would she say if I brought him back with me and told her he'd be staying?

'Well, is there anywhere you can go? Someone who'll take care of you? Your parents, or –?'

He shook his head. 'Can I look in the church?'

'Yes, of course. I'll show you.'

I led him through the lych-gate and across the graveyard, trying not to let him see my unease. A vicar shouldn't be ashamed of his church; but everything about St F's – the smell of damp plaster; the massed ranks of oak pews; the dingy hymn number boards – told you, the moment you set foot in the place, that you were entering a lost world. On the wall was a fragment of a mediaeval fresco of the last judgement, showing a cascade of damned souls, faces contorted with horror, tumbling head-over-heels into a pit of orange fire. Worst of all was a row of nineteenth-century stained-glass windows, which reduced the nave to a dull kaleidoscope of reds and blues. If I'd had my way, I'd have ripped the lot out – but of course, my only hope of being allowed to do that was a violent storm that damaged them beyond repair.

'It's a bit dark, I'm afraid,' I said, as we went in. 'Here, I'll put on the lights.'

'No, don't!'

The ferocity in his voice took me by surprise. I could only imagine that whatever he was on must have made him super-sensitive to glare.

'OK,' I said. 'Don't worry. I won't if you'd rather not.'

He stood there blinking for a moment. Then, as his eyes adjusted, he said,

'Which is the old part?'

I pointed to the three surviving Early English arches. He walked over and touched one of the pillars.

'Where does this come from?'

'The stone, you mean?'

He nodded.

'I don't know. Somewhere local, probably. You didn't lug things further than you had to in the Middle Ages.'

He leaned close and rubbed his cheek against it.

'Are you interested in architecture?' I said.

'I'm interested in…' He was silent for a few seconds. 'I'm looking for something to hold on to.'

I slowed my breathing again. The temptation, of course, was to send the ball straight back over the net: *Hold on to Jesus.* But that was the human response. I had to give God time to answer for me.

'Would it help to talk about it?' I said finally.

'Who was the rock?'

'Sorry?'

'In the bible. Christ told one of his disciples he was a rock.'

'Peter,' I said. 'As in *petroglyph. Petrify.*'

He looked at me oddly. 'You think I should have known that, don't you?'

I was startled – not just at the way he'd shifted the spotlight on to me, but also because he was right. Most kids of his generation, religious or not, *wouldn't* have needed to ask: it would simply have been part of the air they breathed as they were growing up. Nowadays you'd be hard-put to find a twenty-year-old who *did* know.

I laughed. 'That might have been my first thought. But of course, there's no reason why you should, if you didn't go to church when you were a kid.'

'I went a few times. When I was staying with my grandparents.'

'But yes, it's an important moment in the gospel. The reason we're both here, in a way. *That thou art Peter, and upon this rock I will build my church.*'

'Do you believe that?'

'Of course.'

'All of it?'

'God's purpose in the world? The incarnation? The resurrection? Yes, absolutely.'

'And the commandments?'

I smiled. 'All those *thou shalts* and *shalt nots*?'

'Yes.'

What did he want to be absolved of? Drugs? Sex? Pilfering something?

'I do,' I said. 'But things change. Every generation has its own challenges, its own way of understanding what God requires of us. And He knows that. What's important is to remember that the last word is always mercy. There's nothing we've done – any of us – that can't be forgiven. If only we turn to him, and honestly admit how far short we've fallen of His vision for us.'

'What, acknowledge our sins, you mean?'

'Well, yes. That's how they'd have put it in the seventeenth century. But to be honest, I'm not sure how useful the word *sin* is these days. I think for a lot of people it just conjures up some idea of, you know, breaking the school rules. Smoking behind the bike sheds or something.'

I paused, waiting for an answering smile. But I'd lost him: he was looking, not at me, but at something behind me. I twisted round, knowing – even before I saw it – what must have caught his attention: the mural of the damned being flung into eternal torment.

'That's my point,' I said. 'That's how *they* understood it, back when the church was built. But really, hell is just a metaphor. For the place we find ourselves in when we cut ourselves off from God.'

He went on staring at the picture. Then, suddenly, without a word, he hooked his knapsack on to his shoulder and headed towards the door, limping and shuffling like an old man in a hurry. I followed at a distance, taking my time, not wanting to seem too pushy. When I got outside, I found him slumped on the seat in the porch, shivering.

'Are you sure you're OK?' I said.

He nodded.

'Well, all right. But if you change your mind, if you want something to eat, or a bed for the night, just ask someone the way to the vicarage and knock on the door. OK?'

Another nod. But there was something mechanical about it, as if he wasn't really aware of me.

What had I done wrong? What should I have said instead? By the time I reached the road, an answer had half-formed in my head. But then, as I looked back at him, before I could crystallize it into words, it evaporated.

No, I hadn't misjudged the situation. There he was, still sitting in the porch, rolling himself a huge joint with trembling hands. The problem wasn't me: it was drugs.

I spent the rest of the day at home, car half-cocked for the rap on the door. But it never came.

15
HUGO MAKEWEATHER

Hm.
You know what I've been doing? I've been trying to reconstruct the chain that led you to me, link by link by link. And I'm buggered if I can. Shit, I am the original off-the-map man. When the sixties finally ran out of road, and we found ourselves, not in the promised millennium, but in a giant development of executive style homes, most of my friends said, yeah, well, if you can't beat them, join them. What *I* said – partly thanks to Adam Earnshaw, as it happens – was *if you can't beat them, lose them*. So after the Thatcher victory of 1979 I set out to expunge myself from the record, first of the late-capitalist state – no tax code; no National Insurance number – and later of its shadowy Big Brother successor. As I'm sure you've discovered, apart from a few passing historical references, a Google search for Hugo Makeweather will yield absolutely nothing. All the usual stuff – credit score; email address; social media accounts; online shopping history, telling you my taste in ready meals – is conspicuous by its absence. Fuck, it's more than ten years since I even spoke to anyone who knew my real name.

So, yeah: Hm. I did consider not replying at all, and hoping you'd just give up and leave me alone. But then a thought struck me: people have been trying to discover what happened to Adam Earnshaw for God knows how long. You – if you've managed to track *me* down – might actually be the person to do it. So OK: The Make's on board.

Here's a list:

Tate Finnegan
Sadie Long
Rachel Lake
Roy Batley

I'm guessing you must by now have spoken to at least three of them, and that one or more will have given you a graphic account of the wreck of the S.S. Adam Earnshaw in late 67 and early 68. So I'm not going to waste time by going over it again. There's not a lot I could tell you, anyway: I really just caught it out of the corner of my eye. I only came on the scene when Tate hurriedly winched me down to pick up the survivors.

And I'm not simply talking about handing out a blanket or two and doing a bit of minor first aid here. It was an honest-to-God life-or-death emergency, not just for Adam, but for all of us. We were three months away from the *Four Minutes* Festival, and *wham*, thanks to Britain's farcical drug laws, we'd suddenly lost two of our key performers – one of whom was also a lynchpin in our shoestring operation, manning the office while Tate and I rushed around hustling promoters, booking equipment, touting our wares to the doped-out hippies of the underground press.

It was actually a couple of days before we realized the full extent of the disaster. Adam had obviously been shaken by the drug bust – particularly as, when he was being manhandled out of the door, Roy Batley accused him of having organized it – but we assumed that Sadie was busy applying balm to the wounds, and that he'd soon bob up again, none the worse for wear. It was only when he failed to appear for a rehearsal and we phoned Sadie's flat, that she told us he'd walked out a few nights before and she hadn't heard from him since.

'Oh, fuck,' said Tate, clawing at the air like a cornered bear. 'This is all we need.'

We called Adam's landlady in Oxford. She hadn't seen him for more than a week. Tate drafted a telegram to his parents in Africa, then – revealing an unexpected streak of thoughtfulness – decided not to send it, because it would only worry them and make them feel helpless. For the same reason he held off telling the police: once *they* were involved, he thought, there'd be no way to keep the family out of it.

'This is on my tab,' he said. 'I'm not going to dump in anyone else's can, not if I don't have to.'

I shook my head. 'It's just Adam.'

'Yeah, but whose idea was him and Sadie? Mr Nitro, meet Miss Glycerine.'

So we waited it out. Every morning I'd switch on the radio, bracing myself for news of a body being discovered at the side of a railway line or the bottom of a cliff. And at Wheatsheaf – where I'd temporarily taken over office duties from Roy Batley – I'd sit hunched over the phone, jumping every time it rang. And it rang a lot: as well as organizing the Four Minutes Festival, Tate was putting together a tour for Bill Sweet and a couple of support acts, and we seemed to be in non-stop negotiations with hotels and venues and coach-hire firms. By the end of the week, I felt as if I was about ninety per cent adrenalin. So when a strange woman called and asked in a doom-laden voice to speak to Tate, I immediately thought, shit, this is it.

'He's not in at the moment, I'm afraid,' I said. 'Is there anything I can do?'

'Well, it's just...Do you know a Mr Adam Earnshaw?'

My heart went through a gymnastics routine. 'Yes. Why?'

'Well, the thing is...' She had a strong northern accent, and spoke so slowly that I wanted to shriek at her, *For Christ's sake, get on with it, woman!* 'The thing is, he's here.'

'Where's *here*?'

'Buxton. In Derbyshire. Well, near there. We have a farm.'

'Jesus! How the hell'd he get to Derbyshire?'

I could hear her snuffling. She didn't like the *Jesus* and the *hell*.

'I don't know,' she said. 'He came to the door and asked if we could sell him some hashish.'

'Oh, God!'

She didn't like that, either.

'And I told him we couldn't,' she went on, coolly. 'And then he said, did I know where a Dr Horne and his family lived? And I said no, I'd never heard of them. And then he just sort of collapsed. He was weak and, you know, really thin. He'd obviously been sleeping rough. So my husband and I carried him into the house and laid him down on the settee. We asked him what his name was, and he told us, Adam Earnshaw. And then he passed out. So we went through his pockets and found a card with Mr Finnegan's name on it. And this number.'

I scrunched up my eyes, trying to jolt my brain into action. 'Has he woken up yet?'

'No, not yet. I don't think he's very well.'

'Have you called a doctor?'

'We didn't want to. Not until, you know, we'd spoken to –'

'Well, give me your address. And someone will come and get him.'

Massive Tate sank into a chair when I told him, rolling his eyes with relief. I remember thinking: this isn't just professional. Adam means more to him, for some reason, than any of his other acts. So I naturally assumed he'd want to go to Derbyshire in person. But instead he said,

'Why don't you do it? That way, it won't be so heavy for him. Soon as he sees me, all he'll be thinking is pressure, pressure, pressure.' He sighed and shook his head. 'Fuck, how crazed do you have to be to knock on a door in the middle of Hick County, and think you're going to find a candy man waiting to make you a sale?'

It was a tough gig. Tate thought I should go at once – if I left it till the next day, Adam might have recovered enough to make another break for it before I showed up. So I plied myself with bennies and made it to Buxton in four hours flat. It was after dark when I got there, and it took me a while to find the place: a clutter of stone buildings at the end of a rough track. Behind it, menacingly huge, a bare black hill swept up to the starry horizon. The air smelt of mud and wet grass, coal smoke and sheep shit.

The woman must have been watching for me because, as I approached the house, she came out to meet me. Stocky, big-muscled, with a weatherworn patient face that looked as if it was used to having the troubles of the world flung at it. She was dressed against the cold in coat and gloves, and carried a big torch.

'He's in the barn,' she said.

I laughed. 'God, was he that dirty?'

'He could have had a bed, and welcome. But he didn't want to.' She touched her temple. 'I don't think he's quite right.'

She led me across the yard, cutting a path through the darkness with the torch. Adam was lying on his back on a stack of bales, covered in a blanket. The sudden glare made him wince and shade his eyes.

'Here's the fella come to take you home,' said the woman. She shone the beam into my face. Adam stared at me but gave no sign of recognition.

'How are you, Adam?' I said.

'Some and some.' It sounded as affectless as a speak-your-weight machine. I wondered if he was even fully conscious.

'The Make, remember?' I said.

He frowned. 'Yeah.' And then, like an *idiot savant* reciting a list of telephone numbers, he rattled off a random catalogue of facts about me, some of which I couldn't remember telling him: nickname at school; first girlfriend; the college I'd been at at Cambridge.

'Whoa, your memory's incredible,' I said. 'So what you doing up here, man?'

'I was trying to find someone. Get back to something.'

'What?'

He said nothing, but started to stroke some invisible surface. His fingers were torn and scabbed, dotted here and there with drops of still-fresh blood. The woman gave me a half-concerned, half *told-you-so* look.

'OK,' I said. 'Did he have anything with him?'

She kicked at the straw, revealing a filthy old knapsack.

'Right, then.' I turned to Adam. 'Let's go.'

Someone has probably already mentioned my car. Tate called it a hearse. Sadie said she'd heard of champagne socialists, but I was the only Daimler Trotskyist she knew. It was all water off a duck's back. Some of the country's finest workers had spent hundreds of hours putting the thing together. It was a monument to their skill. Who was I to kick them in the teeth?

But that evening it did make me uneasy. The woman had taken in a strung-out vagrant, found a number in his pocket, phoned it – and now a limousine, the kind she'd have seen pictures of the queen getting in and out of, had appeared out of the blue and stationed itself in her farmyard. Tate had given me £20 for her, hoping that it would buy her silence: after

Roy Batley, the last thing he wanted was yet another lurid story in the press about a druggie singer on his label. But now, as I reached for my wallet, I felt suddenly awkward about it. How to avoid it looking like either a bribe from a showbiz mogul or a tip from the people at the big house?

'Here,' I mumbled. 'A small thank you for your –'

'What's that?' she said, flashing the torch at it. 'Oh, no, I don't need money!'

'Please.'

She hesitated, then took it. 'All right, I'll give it to the mission.'

I almost asked, *What mission*? But I was exhausted, and had a reeking, more or less dumb-mute Adam Earnshaw to deal with. The thought of being stuck next to him all the way home was a nightmare, so I thanked the woman again, then yanked open the rear door and shoved him into the cavernous passenger compartment behind the sliding glass screen. He was as pliant and out-of-it as a rag doll. When he was settled in his seat, I gave him – the way you'd slip a dog a bone, to keep him quiet on a long journey – a chunk of Tate's Mexican Gold, a pouch of Old Holborn and a packet of Rizla papers. He studied them incredulously for a moment, as if he thought he might be hallucinating, then fell on them hungrily, and – hands shaking like an old geezer with palsy – started to roll himself a joint.

God knows how many hours – and one benny stop – later, we pitched up in front of Tate's place in Notting Hill. It was still dark, but he'd told me to get there as soon as I could, so I blundered out and rang the bell. After half a minute or so Tate opened the door, naked except for a pair of jeans he hadn't bothered to zip up properly.

'You did say,' I said.

He nodded. Between us we managed to get Adam – fuddled, silent, but unresisting – out of the car and into the hall. Then, taking an arm apiece, we carried him upstairs to the flat – a miniature warren of evil-smelling little rooms inexpertly carved out of two big ones. A door opened, and a half-asleep girl wrapped in an eiderdown appeared.

'This is Patti,' said Tate.

She smiled. 'Hi.' American.

He noticed I'd noticed. 'Patti and me, we go way back,' he said.

'He OK?' she said, nodding at Adam.

'Yeah,' said Tate. 'Far as you can be, if you're Adam Earnshaw.'

'OK.' She yawned, then retreated, shutting the door again.

'Here, man,' said Tate, kicking an old Victorian sofa with his colossal bare foot and sending up clouds of dust.

We laid Adam down. Tate clapped me on the shoulder.

'Right on, man. You did it.' He turned his arm and showed me a blue vein pulsing beneath the skin. 'One of these days I'm going to slit this open, and you and me, we're going to become blood-brothers.'

I hardly saw Adam for the next month. Tate kept him under a kind of benign house arrest, feeding him, ensuring he was well supplied with dope, giving him a guitar, pen and paper and an old tape recorder to play with. And Patti, it turned out, wasn't – as I'd first thought – just the one-night stand *du jour*: she was a key part of the plan, drafted in to act as nurse-cum-prison guard when Tate wasn't there. For a week or so I had the sense that everything was touch-and-go: Tate shuffled round the office as if he were wearing an invisible ball and chain, and twitched violently whenever he heard the phone. But then one morning he came in and said,

'I think it's going to be OK, man.'

'He'll be able to play? At *Four Minutes*?'

'One step at a time, dude. OK's always relative.'

'But he's showing signs of life?'

He nodded.

'Has he told you yet what he was doing? Why he went up north?'

He shook his head. 'I didn't ask. It'll be in the music.' He went into his section of the office and returned with an old photo: a dozen or so smiling men striking oil, dwarfed by the huge black geyser they've just sprung from captivity. 'That's what Adam does,' he said. 'Finds stuff none of the rest of knew was down there. Shit, I don't think *he* knows it's down there. But he's drilling again. And he's started to hit pay dirt.' His forehead wrinkled and he looked past me, blank-eyed. 'Synchro-fucking-nicity. Two days before Bill Sweet gets here.' He reached into his hip pocket and pulled out a wad of notes. 'Take this' – unpeeling one, and pinning it to the typewriter with his finger – 'and buy a bottle of Black Label, OK? Leave it on my desk. You know Bill. He'll be expecting it.'

Actually, I didn't know Bill: I'd hardly even heard his music. Blues was something I'd always felt I *should* like, but never really could. I was committed to the revolution – still am – and to me the music seemed dangerously *counter*-revolutionary. All that misery, all that fatalism, felt like no more than a kind of opiate, a way of controlling the poor and the dispossessed, making them passively accept that their lives were shit, blinding them to the possibility of change. And, in keeping with the smoky monochrome mood, the people peddling it – or so I imagined – were all just down-home grandads wearing ill-fitting Goodwill suits and outsize shades to shield them from a hostile world.

So when Bill Sweet finally flew into Heathrow, and Tate – after leaving him to crash at his hotel for a few hours – brought him into the office, I was completely unprepared for the apparition that breezed through the door: a twenty-eight carat dandy, sporting a hand-made shirt and a bespoke cashmere jacket, with a matching silk handkerchief folded in the breast pocket.

'Bill, this is the Make,' said Tate.

'OK.' He moved his head slowly, like a wine-taster sampling a new vintage. 'Not sure as I ever met a Make before.' He turned to Tate and smiled. Two of his upper teeth were missing. 'Always something new, huh?'

'Bill's just been telling me that he wants to see Stonehenge,' said Tate.

'Really?'

'Yep.' The smile widened. 'Funny thing: always did. Ever since I was little. We was cleaning out my auntie's house after she passed away, and I found some pictures. Guess it must've been some old magazine or something.'

'So how far is it?' Tate asked me. 'He was thinking maybe we could go now.'

'Oh God, no,' I said. 'You'd need to allow a day. There and back.'

Bill Sweet chuckled. 'Oh, OK. I didn't realize. Some fella in New York show me a map and' – holding his thumb and forefinger half an inch apart – 'seems like it's right here.'

'It *would* be in the States,' said Tate. 'But over here, you have to remember, fifty miles is a big deal. A hundred, and you expect to start seeing little green men.'

Bill Sweet laughed. 'OK. Have to be another time, I guess, then, won't it?'

Tate touched his elbow. 'Come on, man. There's something I want to play you.'

They went into Tate's part of the office and closed the door. I heard the chink of glasses, the rumble of laughter, the wordless music of their conversation: Tate's speed-fuelled jabber, counterpointed with Bill Sweet's *what's-the-hurry* bass line. And then a pause and the click of the Ferrograph – and suddenly, out of nowhere, a jangling, frenetic burst of guitar, so utterly unlike anything I'd ever heard that it brought me out in a sweat. Chains, that's what it made me think of: the chains they used to weigh a hanged man's corpse on the gibbet, sent thrashing and rattling by a wild gale. On and on and on it went, until I was on the point of stuffing my fingers in my ears. And then, surging in over the top, so sharp that it seemed to razor your skin, came a long twisting howl of despair. You didn't wonder who or what was making it: it was disembodied, the voice of the gale itself. Only as it climaxed with a sob, and then subsided into a soft keening lament, did I catch the characteristic breathy *timbre*, and realize that I was listening to Adam Earnshaw.

I got up and stationed myself close to the thin partition. The singing had stopped, and the guitar – released again from any constraint of rhythm or melody – had turned into a chaotic, fibrillating jumble, careering out of control towards disaster. And then *wham*, the apocalypse – followed by a last few discordant individual notes, like pieces of a shattered window tinkling to the ground.

Silence. For once, not even Tate seemed to have anything to say. I waited, holding my breath, until a sudden cacophony of horns in the street outside broke the mood. And then, at last, Bill Sweet cleared his throat, and murmured:

'Yep, always something new.'

It stayed with me, that track, for days. Not musically (it was so complex and disordered that I couldn't have repeated a single bar), but as one of those moments – like, say, when you unexpectedly witness a fight or a car crash – when the surface of life suddenly splits open, and you glimpse the darkness beneath the skin. And just because it was so outside the normal run of things, it didn't even occur to me to wonder why Tate – a man who did nothing without a reason – should have played it to jet-lagged Bill Sweet so soon after he got here. Which meant I was completely taken by surprise when, the following weekend, Tate said,

'You free Monday?'

'I'm *here* Monday, aren't I?'

He shook his head. 'What I'd like you to do is drive Bill to Stonehenge.'

'Why?' I waved at the pile of letters and invoices on the desk. 'We're running out of time here. Why can't he just go on a bus tour?'

'That's OK, dude. I'll take care of that shit. Monday's the only rest day the guy has, and he's bushed. Plus: I had a *eureka* moment. Adam's going along too.'

So: the trip to Stonehenge. God knows when I last even thought about it. But the video's still there, amazingly, tucked away in some long-neglected bit of my brain. All I have to do is blow off the dust and press *play*.

A steel-grey November day, with a vicious east wind scouring the sky and slicing the last leaves off the trees. The Daimler's sclerotic heater barely managed even to take the edge off the chill, so stately Bill Sweet was swathed in a rug, like some elderly royal on her way to court. At the other end of the rear seat, wedged as tightly into the corner as he could squeeze himself, sat Adam – dough-pale, mussy-haired, shivering in his outsize army greatcoat, with his hands in his pockets and his face half hidden by the turned-up collar. They made such an odd couple that I found myself constantly glancing from one to the other in the rear-view mirror, trying to figure out why Tate had put them together.

For the first forty minutes or so, neither of them spoke. But as we reached the last circle of hell, as my father used to call it – the long tentacles of between-the-wars semis reaching out along the Kingston bypass, clutching at the countryside beyond – I heard Bill Sweet saying,

'This all look kind of strange to me. All them bitty houses. But I expect it look just like home to you, huh?'

Adam shrugged.

'You wasn't raised in these parts?'

'I grew up in Africa.'

He said it quite unselfconsciously – not even looking at Bill Sweet to gauge the response, but staring out of the window.

'The British just can't keep their hands off other people's countries, I'm afraid,' I said.

Bill seemed not to hear me.

'I never seed Africa,' he said. 'Pretty hot down there, I guess.' He chuckled. 'No wonder you shivering like that.'

Adam made a noise that might have been a desultory laugh or a sickly cough. 'Yeah.'

And that was it, for at least another hour. From time to time I'd see Bill glancing at Adam out of the corner of his eye, but he didn't speak again until we were almost at Salisbury Plain. Then Adam suddenly looked out of the window and murmured,

'Oh, shit!'

Bill Sweet stared at him, shaking his head. 'Oh, man, he got you good, don't he?'

I saw Adam's lips move, but couldn't hear what he said.

'I know what he like,' said Bill Sweet. 'He been in and out of me ever since I was a naked-faced boy. But it harder for you. Cos round here they don't know nothing about him. They don't *want* to know, cos then they have to deal with the facts of life. Everything with a little bit of sugar, that's what *they* want, so it taste better. So they say there ain't no such thing. And when you say you seed him, they just think you crazy.'

Adam was staring at him now.

'Where *I* come from, everybody know he's real. Or they used to, anyways. You could meet him on the road or out in the fields. And when you did, you knew you must've done something bad and left the door open. And that's why he there. Cos he looking around, trying to find a way in that door 'fore you can shut it again.'

Adam shunted himself up straight, took his hands out of his pockets, started nervously knitting the purple-with-cold fingers together in his lap.

'Only you know what my mother used to say?' said Bill Sweet. 'She say, sometimes God *want* you to let the hellhound in. Because He know *you* strong enough to fight him. You going to hurt, it going to be so bad you cry out loud. But the badder it is, the more it going to make the other folks feel good. Cos when they hear it, they know you going through that shit for *them.*'

What was he talking about? Something to do with the devil, obviously. Beyond that I hadn't a clue. But I could see Adam nodding gravely.

'And that where the blues come from,' said Bill Sweet. 'Not here' – touching his head – 'but *here.*' He laid a hand over his heart. 'That why I calls *you* a blues singer. It ain't the chords, it ain't the notes. It the *feeling.*'

Adam gazed at him for a few seconds more, before turning to look out of the window.

'A woman?' said Bill Sweet.

Adam hesitated, then nodded.

'Or maybe there more than one. Betty Sue done you wrong. And you done Billie Jean wrong. And now' – sniffing, and putting a finger under his nose – 'you thinking, that smell I'm smelling, that the hellfire, being stoke up ready for me.' He saw Adam's startled expression and chuckled. 'You wondering how I know? Ain't no trick to it. Like I say, I been there. Looking at you now, it like looking in the mirror when I'm twenty. 'Cept for the colour, of course.'

Adam said something, but again I couldn't catch it.

'That what we are,' said Bill Sweet. 'Ain't nothing we can do about it. We the battlefield. That what we was put here for. We ain't never going to make the world right. The world *always* be wrong. And we ain't never going to make *us* right. But we telling the truth, and that what –'

He stopped suddenly, craning his head forward to see out of the windscreen. I followed the direction of his gaze. There on the horizon, like a mouth full of broken teeth, was the dark jumble of Stonehenge.

'That it?' he asked.

'That's it,' I said.

Adam slumped back in his seat, as if he were taking cover from a sniper.

'What the matter?' said Bill. 'You don't want to see?'

Adam shook his head.

'You scared they gonna come down on top of us, that it?'

'I don't know what they are.' He was trembling so much that it came out as a kind of machine-gun stutter.

'I heard it a church of some kind,' said Bill. 'Or a what they call it, a temple.'

'I don't think anyone knows,' I said. 'Some people believe it might have been used for human sacrifice.'

Bill shook his head. 'Phew, that heavy.' He pressed his face to the window. 'Well, all I can say is, whatever it is, they must've wanted it real bad. They didn't have no machines, not as I understand it. Didn't have pretty much of anything. Just' – stretching his hands out in front of him – 'these.'

Adam didn't respond. But after a moment he dragged himself up straight again, and sat scowling apprehensively out of the window as we drew closer. When I turned into the car park, he suddenly said,

'Have you heard of the Olduvai Gorge?'

'Older what?' said Bill.

'Olduvai Gorge,' I chipped in. 'In east Africa. It's where we all came from originally.'

'What, like the Garden of Eden, you mean?'

'My father's done a lot of work there,' said Adam. 'On early hominids.'

'That's primitive human beings to you and me,' I said.

'*I* know what he saying.' He turned to Adam, then pointed at the giant stones. 'And you think this like that?'

Adam nodded. 'The bones. The bits of skull. The artefacts. They all terrified me. Because I could never really know what they meant. To the people themselves. The people who left them behind. What it actually *felt* like to live those lives.' His mouth was dry: you could hear the gluey click of saliva with every word. 'My father said, *Don't be stupid. They're dead and gone, and that's all there is to it.* But I couldn't believe that. And I thought they must be angry with me. For looking at them like that. Touching them. Treating them as nothing more than objects. When I got to England I thought I'd stop feeling like that. But...'

I glanced in the mirror. From the anguish in his face – one eye scrunched up, and his mouth lopsided, like a stroke victim's – I could only guess that this was something he'd never dared tell anyone before, and he was desperate to know the response. Not mine – I think he'd forgotten I was even there: all that counted was Bill Sweet's.

'Well,' said Bill, after a long pause. 'That all part of the battlefield, I guess. But we better do something about it. Come on.'

He got out of the car. Adam hesitated for a few seconds, then scrambled across to follow him. For a long time they stood side by side, looking at the massive arches, blackened by rain and silhouetted against the scratched-pewter sky. Then Bill put an arm round Adam's shoulder.

'They not angry. They happy we still thinking about them. Let's go see.'

Slowly he started to lead Adam towards the stone circle. The whole thing felt as alien to me as witnessing someone else's dream, so I stayed in the car and watched them perambulate round the perimeter, pausing every now and again to stroke one of the uprights, and – as far as I could tell – speak to it. When they'd completed the circuit they stopped for a minute or two, then made their way between two of the pillars to the very centre of the complex. They were so still that, as the daylight leached away, they began to look like part of the structure.

At last they turned and sauntered towards the car again. I switched on the headlamps to guide them. As they stepped into the light, I was startled to see that Adam had a faint smile on his face.

And all the way back to London he slept as peacefully as a babe.

At Bill's suggestion, instead of returning to the Wheatsheaf office, we all went straight to his hotel. Someone – he seemed a bit unclear who – had arranged for some women who wanted to meet him to come to his room, and we were welcome to join them.

I dropped him and Adam at the entrance and went to park the car. By the time I got upstairs, the party was well under way. As soon as the door opened, I was hit by a wave of laughter and a powerful fug of smoke and whisky fumes. The only light came from a single lamp in the corner. At first I couldn't see Bill and Adam at all, but after bumping and stumbling through the crush of creatures without a face, I finally found them next to the curtained window.

Each of them was with a girl. Bill Sweet's, a sumptuous brunette in her early twenties, was leaning close, gazing with bright admiring eyes as he talked, as if she was afraid of missing something. And Adam's – Adam's was younger, tall and doe-eyed, with the look of a just-out-of-school kid who couldn't quite believe where she was. As I watched he stroked a finger slowly down her cheek and neck. And she shivered and flushed, laughing at the brazenness of her own desire.

Two days later Tate told me that, after all, Adam wouldn't be playing the Four Minutes to Lights Out Festival.

'Why not?'

'Something about the blind leading the blind.' He shook his head. 'I figured the trip with Bill would psych him up. And I guess I was too successful. Cos now he wants to go to the States and tour with Bill.'

To me, I'll be honest, it didn't feel like much of a loss. Adam wasn't one of our star acts. And there'd always been something detached about him, as if most of his attention wasn't on the life-and-death struggle facing our generation, but on some arcane question that the rest of couldn't even see – and wouldn't have given a shit about if we could. If he'd lost his nerve suddenly, so what? It didn't affect the rest of us. We'd be able to manage perfectly well without him.

And we did.

We didn't save the world, of course. But, hey – I'm still on the case.

16

EMMA SCOTT-NELSON

Thank you for your message to Sir Tim, which I am answering on his behalf. He asked me to say that, so far as he is concerned, the disappearance of Adam Earnshaw is ancient history, and he has nothing to add to the statement he made to the press at the time.

Best wishes,

Emma

17

CAROL WINTER

You, I'm guessing – whatever else you are – are not a journalist. And I, of course, am (yes, still at it, though like pretty much every hack and his dog these days, I've more or less emigrated to the internet now). That means I know instinctively how a story needs to be trimmed and filleted, bones removed, unsightly protuberances cut away or patted into place, leaving a simple tale of good guys vs bad guys that the punters can take in at a glance. Which I suspect is what you're trying to do here – with me as bad-guy-in-chief. Only – forgive me if this sounds rude – a pro would have done it better. The tone you want is, *hey, this is your once-in-a-lifetime chance to be heard!* – whereas *your* message has a distinct whiff of the *I have to warn you that if you choose to remain silent, it will be interpreted as an admission of guilt.*

If you used the same approach with Tim Bruce, it's no wonder, frankly, that he refused to help. Why on earth should a knight of the realm take time from preening his collection of classic cars to justify his behaviour half a century ago? But with me, as it happens, you're in luck – because I'm glad finally of the opportunity to set the record straight. Just one proviso: if you change, remove or add so much as a word, you'll be hearing from my lawyers.

Don't get me wrong: I can see the logic here. It's appealingly simple: *this is a woman who went on to bare-knuckle brawl her way through four decades in Fleet Street. And the infamous Sadie Long/Adam Earnshaw story – which appeared while she was still at university – was her declaration of intent: a deliberate act of provocation, designed to grab the attention of as many readers as possible, and damn the consequences.*

The only problem is, that isn't true. I was as surprised as anyone by the impact we had – and, for a couple of weeks, convinced that I'd made a terrible mistake, threatening Tim Bruce with bankruptcy, and blighting my own prospects of a career in journalism. I was still in my second year at Oxford, remember, and – at that point – I had only the haziest conception of the English libel laws. It never even occurred to me that I was, in effect, venturing completely unprotected into a minefield.

Tim, you'd have thought – since he was actually *studying* Law – should have had a better idea of what we were letting ourselves in for. But he, like everyone else – including me, I'm afraid – quickly fell victim to my lippy over-self-confidence. Which is odd, thinking about it, because normally his judgements were spot-on. But, when we met, he'd just broken up with some poor unsuitable girl from Cowley, and – as a result – was in an uncharacteristically subdued and self-questioning mood. The first time he came to my room, I showed him my portfolio of clippings from the newspaper I'd edited in sixth form – the letter I'd received from the Prime Minister; the picture of me and Sandy Shaw together by a pedestrian crossing, promoting my *Road Sense for Schoolkids* campaign – and he appeared completely engrossed, leafing through them for perhaps twenty minutes, just occasionally muttering, *God, that was a bit of a coup, wasn't it?* or *You've obviously got a talent for this stuff.* And the impression must have stayed with him, because more than a year later – long after our brief fling had fizzled into nothing – he left a note in my pigeonhole, asking if I'd be interested in meeting to discuss a new magazine he was starting.

I was. To understand just *how* interested, you have to realize that both my parents were teachers, and – having coached me through the 11-plus and sent me to a half-decent grammar school that eventually got me into Oxford – expected me to repay the compliment by following in their footsteps. To me, that felt like the kiss of death – and journalism seemed to offer the only chance of escape. It was, at least, a profession – and one that they respected. If I could make enough of a mark to get myself a job when I left university, or a place on a trainee scheme, I knew they wouldn't stand in my way.

Tim suggested we meet for lunch in a garlic-scented little French place with chequered tablecloths and a chalked-up menu – not grand, like the

Restaurant Elizabeth, but fairly sophisticated by my standards. He ordered some wine, then – with effortless charm – turned the spotlight on me, teasing out everything I'd done since we'd last seen each other, saying how much he'd enjoyed a couple of pieces of mine in *Cherwell*. And then – at exactly the right moment, just after the arrival of our first courses – he refilled my glass and said,

'So let me put a proposition to you.'

Even today, after all these years, that conversation still feels like one of the most momentous turning points of my life. It was as if, up until then, I'd just been part of a huge herd milling blindly along the bottom of a deep valley. We really had no idea where we were or where we were going: all that kept us on the move was a series of slogans – Love! Peace! Change the World! – which we believed simply because everyone else did. And now, suddenly, here was someone who'd climbed up to the top of the cliffs looming above us, and surveyed the actual landscape. It would take me hours to reconstruct everything he said – even assuming I could remember it all – but the essence of it was this:

1. *There wasn't going to be a revolution.*
2. *But that didn't mean that things would simply go back to the way they'd been before. A whole generation had tasted freedom – and they were no more prepared to return meekly to tugging their forelocks than to be told what to do and think by a bunch of granite-faced commissars.*
3. *At the heart of that freedom was choice. What they wanted, above all, was to be able to decide for themselves how to dress, what music to listen to, what films to see – how to live their lives.*
4. *And the time was coming – and soon – when they would realize that, far from being their enemy, the market was actually their best hope. It was the market, after all, that had already given them Carnaby Street, the Beatles, pirate radio. For thousands of years, unscrupulous demagogues and boggle-eyed madmen had been promising the millennium – and now, for the first time in history, popular capitalism was actually starting to deliver it.*
5. *And for anyone with the vision to see that, and to seize the opportunities it created, the sky was the limit.*
6. *Which was where the new magazine came in…*

I was mesmerized. I pushed my plate away, lit a cigarette, blew a smoke-ring across the table.

'OK,' I said. 'I think I'm beginning to…'

He nodded: *Go on.*

I shook my head. 'You've obviously thought it all through. And I haven't. So join up the dots for me.'

'Well, at the moment, everything's like this,' He karate-chopped the air with his hand. 'All divided up. Along the most predictable lines. There are papers that talk about fashion and music – but most of them are just patronizing pap, aimed at very young, none-too-bright girls. At the other end of the scale you've got *Oz* or *The International Times*. Great for giving you the low-down on the arcane outer reaches of the counter-culture. But not much good if you've just met the dishiest bloke on the planet, and are trying to decide what to wear to impress him.'

I laughed.

'What you want – what you're crying out for, if you did but know it – is something that will do both those things: treat you as an intelligent human being, who cares about the world; and recognize that you're a consumer, too, who wants to have a good time. Without finger-wagging, without talking down, without judging. Because it's *OK* to want to have a good time.'

'It makes sense, when you put it like that,' I said. 'But has anyone actually done any research on it?'

He shook his head. 'Wait for the research, and it'll be too late. Everyone'll be trying to do it. The prize goes to the chap – or the girl – who can see what's happening before anybody else has noticed.' He refilled both our glasses. 'Look at the late Radio Stella. *Strange Sounds*?'

I nodded. 'Yeah, of course.'

'Well, I met Rufus Strange once. And I'm telling you, a less prepossessing character would have been hard to imagine. The sort of bloke who was never any good at games at school, and tried to ingratiate himself by fooling around and putting on funny voices. If I hadn't known who he was, it would never have occurred to me that you could make a fortune by sticking him on the radio in the middle of the night and letting him play music no one had ever heard of. But the Major could see it – and had the guts to trust his own hunch. Result: Rufus Strange is now one of the highest-paid DJs in the country.'

'Who's the Major?'

'Oh, it doesn't matter. My point is, we can do the same with the magazine. The timing isn't ideal, I know. I'd have preferred to wait till we'd both gone down. But speed is of the essence. And I've got a bit of money. From my parents. So –'

'And what do you see my role as being?'

'Editor.'

I felt fuddled. I wasn't used to drinking at lunchtime, and the collision of alcohol and adrenalin was disorientating. I half-closed my eyes. That was the test: could I actually *see* this unborn magazine, feel the paper, smell the ink? Or was it destined to remain lodged in Tim Bruce's head, a canny business idea incapable of taking flesh?

'What would we do for an office?' I said.

'I've seen a little place off the High. Just a desk and a phone, but it would do for the moment.'

'And have you got a name?'

'I was thinking of *The Scene*.'

And suddenly there it was, blossoming in the grey nothingness behind my eyelids: the title in squiggly psychedelic orange; the text artfully broken up with dramatic black-and-white images, like stills from a silent film; the use of different fonts and layouts – the words on one page confined in regular columns, and on the next blowing free, like leaves in an autumn gale – to suggest different moods. And, at the bottom of the first page, in the severest black typeface: *Editor: Carol Winter.*

I opened my eyes. 'It sounds very exciting,' I said.

'I wouldn't interfere' – he smiled – 'well, *over*-interfere, on a day-to-day basis. I'm the Major, not the station manager. But there is one writer I'd like you to meet. An American chap called Peyton Whybrow.'

'OK.'

And the die was cast.

*

I assume you know who Peyton Whybrow was. But the Peyton Whybrow I'm talking about isn't the ageing *enfant terrible* of his apocapleptic (his word) later years, after the drugs had set up a one-party state in his head, but the enigmatic young lion of the late sixties, when he was busy establishing himself as one of the most original journalists on either side of the Atlantic. It's hard for me to convey the impression he made then. If your idea of a hack – as mine was at the time – was of a booze-raddled loudmouth with dandruff all over his collar and nicotine-stained fingers, Peyton didn't fit the bill at all. He was short and slight, dark-skinned and black-haired (the legacy, supposedly, of a Choctaw Indian great-grandmother), and given to wearing old-fashioned, well-cut jackets he'd picked up in a second-hand shop. He was taciturn, almost to the point of self-effacement, so you began to wonder if there was a mouth at all behind his heavy moustache. And when he did finally break silence, speaking in a slow courtly drawl, he chose his words with fastidious care, like a jeweller trawling through his tray of gems for something with exactly the right shape and colour. The effect was like finding yourself in the presence of some minor character from a Jacobean revenge drama, who had strayed somehow on to the wrong stage, and was watching from the shadows, waiting for the protagonists to start disembowelling each other.

I've encountered some eccentric writers since then – but none, I have to say, whose style seemed, at first glance, more at odds with their personality. At the end of our first meeting, he left me with a couple of samples of his work, and – as I started to read – I remember letting out an inaudible gasp. How could someone so guarded and self-enclosed reveal himself so recklessly on paper, use such antic language, pursue such wild flights of the imagination into the stratosphere? I was so startled that I found myself wondering if the real writer was a kind of Cyrano de Bergerac, who – for reasons I couldn't guess at – had allowed his drab friend to claim the credit for his brilliance. It sounds an absurd idea now, I know, but it was only after I'd spent several more hours in his company that I completely laid it to rest. At which point another thought began to obsess me: what would it be like to go to bed with him? Would he still, even between the sheets, hang back, playing the role of third gentleman, watching proceedings from the wings? Or would the membrane between the man and the writer finally rupture, making him dissolve in a paroxysm of grunts and yelps? (In case your eye starts dancing ahead at this point, I should tell you that I never found out.)

After talking it over with Tim Bruce, I commissioned an atmospheric meditation from Peyton about a party at a country house in Wiltshire. And then, for issues two and three, a couple of follow-up pieces: one on the US underground scene (San Francisco vs New York: different drugs, different music), and the other an American take on British politics (predictably a lot about class, although from an unusual Old South, mint-julep-and-magnolia-blossom slant). They added a distinctive, high-octane infusion to the mix – articles on summer fashion, student travel, birth control, as well as music and film reviews and relationship advice – which helped to make our first few outings sell-out successes (and, within months, collectors' items).

But with the fourth issue, Tim thought we should keep people on their toes by doing something different.

'You know Tate Finnegan?' he said.

'Record producer?'

He nodded.

'Only by repute.'

'He's a friend of Peyton's. He's helping to organize a three-day peace festival in June. And my idea is, why don't we take that as our theme? Devote the whole magazine to it? The timing would be perfect.'

'I wouldn't have had you down as a CND supporter,' I said.

He laughed. 'That isn't the point, is it? The point is that there are thousands of people who are. And they deserve some serious coverage.'

'How would it work?'

'Here, I've jotted down a few thoughts.'

He handed me a sheet of paper. Scribbled on it, in soft pencil, I saw:

Interviews: Performers. Adam Earnshaw?
"Living Under Canvas: a Survival Guide." (Approach Black's for advertising?)
Something on Roy Batley and the law on drugs? (A debate, maybe? Two sides of the same spread: against, the police view; for, a user?)
As a centrepiece, an extended essay by Peyton – reportage, mixed with a wide-ranging reflection on the state of the youth movement.

'Hm,' I said. 'Why did you single out Adam Earnshaw?'

'He's a friend of mine. Well, sort of. And Tate's his manager, and keen to promote him. And Peyton's an admirer. So…That's what we've got, with this whole thing. An almost perfect convergence of interests. *They* are guaranteed a huge amount of publicity. For which *we*, in return, receive privileged behind-the-scenes access – demonstrating, beyond doubt, that when it comes to having its finger on the pulse, *The Scene* is way ahead of the competition.'

I wasn't entirely convinced: I was bothered that it might make us look too grandiose and self-important, and that – if we abandoned our winning formula too soon – readers would start to give up on us. But Tim seemed absolutely certain – and I already knew him well enough to realize that he had a kind of sixth sense about these things that you ignored at your peril. So I decided to keep my reservations to myself, and put all my energies into making the idea work.

And – in fairness to Tim – if everything had gone according to plan, I'm sure it would have done. What derailed it wasn't some flaw in the concept itself, but life suddenly producing a wild card that no one could possibly have foreseen: the news, almost at the last moment, that Adam Earnshaw wouldn't be appearing at the festival after all. Not only that: he'd left Oxford, and seemed to have become a kind of vagrant.

I was too removed from the court of King Tate to hear the details, but from what I did manage to pick up, it was obvious that Adam had suffered a major breakdown. Tough for him, of course, and a setback for Tate, but – aside from the disappointment of not being able to run the interview we'd planned with him – not, on its own, a major problem for us. What *made* it a problem was Peyton.

I wish now that I'd pressed Peyton more, forced him to explain just why he reacted as he did. But when he was working on a story he was like a highly-strung thoroughbred, and I worried that – if I tugged too sharply on the bit – I might spook him. You don't, though, have to be much of a psychologist to see that there must have been an element of identification involved. Like Adam, he had a natural sympathy for people who felt marginal, misunderstood, out of place. And the reason, in both cases, wasn't hard to find. Peyton was a double-outsider: a southerner in an America dominated by the west and east coasts; and an American in a Britain that – just beneath the anodyne surface – seemed riddled with cruel taboos and conventions that no one who hadn't been born here could hope to grasp. And Adam, for all his apparent Englishness, was paradoxically in a similar position: an innocent abroad, constantly grazing his shin or stubbing his toe against some invisible obstacle or other. Unpicking the chain of events that – as Peyton saw it – had led to Adam's dramatic self-imposed exile, would expose the coldness at the heart of British life for everyone to see.

Exactly how he managed to piece the story together, I don't know. But – though both of them always denied it – I can't help suspecting that Tate Finnegan, wittingly or unwittingly, must have got him off to a flying start by filling him in on the background and giving him the key names. Once he had those – well, Peyton was always good at disarming people, insinuating himself through the door, then sitting there, grave and attentive, more like a confessor than a hack, while they gradually unburdened themselves to him. The result was a more or less flawless bit of investigative journalism.

I imagine you've read it – but just in case you haven't, it traces Adam's collapse unequivocally to his tortured on-and-off affair with the model Sadie Long. She emerges as the villain of the piece: a manipulative, self-obsessed upper-class bitch, who ruthlessly used every man she came into contact with for her own gratification, and then cast herself as the victim when things went wrong. If that didn't work, she used her establishment connections to clear up the mess for her.

But with Adam Earnshaw, she quickly found herself out of her depth. She enjoyed the kudos of being in a relationship with him, but wasn't prepared to pay the price for it. An unworldly visionary, with a hotline to the collective unconscious – Peyton made a lot of Adam's supposed sensitivity to the dead – but with impossibly romantic ideas about women, he was baffled and deeply hurt by her duplicity and infidelity. She tried to force him to adapt – and when he couldn't, rather than making the effort to change herself, she threw him out. A rock, that's how Peyton described her: an unyielding rock in a stormy sea, surrounded by treacherous reefs, where the frail bark of Adam Earnshaw – having failed to find a safe haven – eventually simply broke up.

OK, I realize you must think I was being reckless. I think so too. But, in my own defence, I was operating in far from ideal circumstances. Peyton only filed his piece the Sunday before we were due to go to print; and, as luck would have it, Tim Bruce was away that weekend, at someone's birthday bash. No fax or email in those days, of course, and – though I did manage to speak to him briefly on the phone – he didn't have time to listen to the whole thing. In the end, he said,

'Well, it does sound a bit incendiary. But we're not going to make a name for ourselves by playing safe. If you're happy with it, go ahead.'

Seventy-two hours later I walked into the office to discover a letter from a firm of solicitors representing Sadie Long, saying that they were taking action against us for libel.

I won't give you a blow-by-blow account of the next few weeks: suffice to say, they were gruesome. The spectacle of a group of cocky youngsters who thought they were God's gift to journalism getting their come-uppance provoked a tidal wave of *Schadenfreude* in the established press, who had a field day at our expense. Which meant, of course, that we had to conduct our increasingly desperate battle for survival in the full smarting glare of publicity – so adding a hearty dollop of humiliation to the legal mulligatawny into which we'd dropped ourselves.

To his credit, Tim remained scrupulously professional, resisting the temptation to throw me to the wolves, and insisting that, as publisher, he took full responsibility for *The Scene*'s content. To begin with, he even appeared reassuringly confident: *Don't worry: they're soon going to realize they've picked on the wrong chap. I'm an Oxford lawyer, for God's sake; I'm not going to be intimidated by a bit of sabre-rattling.* But as he started to do his homework – consulting several friends of his father, including a judge – it grew more and more apparent that we actually didn't have a leg to stand on. If the case came to court, it was almost certain that Sadie Long would win, and we would be lumbered not only with substantial legal costs, but also with damages – which, given her public profile, were likely to be enormous. That wouldn't just mean the magazine having to fold: it could ruin Tim, and quite possibly lead to our both being sent down.

The toll on Tim was visible. Every time I saw him, he looked paler and more drawn. His eyes began to change, too, taking on the milky blankness of a blind man's, as his mind progressively withdrew from the external world altogether and devoted itself entirely to legal and financial calculations. While he still stopped short of blaming the whole disaster on me, he became moody and unpredictable, prone to sudden outbursts of snappishness. When, for instance, I suggested we might launch a public appeal for contributions to help us fight the case, he said *That's the most stupid idea I've ever heard*, and stormed out, slamming the door.

Odd how the sense of powerlessness alters one's perceptions. I know, rationally, that something like normal life must have continued – we still, after all, had essays to write and tutorials to go to, and were even half-heartedly preparing for an issue five that seemed increasingly unlikely ever to see the light of day – but, looking back, I have no recollection of any of it. My only lasting impression of the whole period – I can feel it again now, flooding in, as I write this – is of an ever-deepening sensation of dread in the pit of my stomach. You're on a plane; the engines have cut; the pilot can't restart them. He's no longer even telling you not to panic. In total silence – apart from the poison-gas hiss of the air conditioning – you watch from the window as the ground billows up towards you…

And then, miraculously, inexplicably, at the last moment you feel the nose lifting again.

I still don't know exactly what happened: Tim was always uncharacteristically cagey about it. It was only by chance, in fact, that – the day after we received a letter setting the date for our court appearance – I discovered he was still battling with the controls, valiantly trying to find another way to avert disaster. As I was climbing the stairs to our third-floor eyrie, I heard him talking on the phone, and was immediately struck by the unexpected tone: tentative, diffident – even (a word you'd never usually associate with Tim Bruce) *ingratiating*. When I got to the landing I hesitated, straining my ears.

'You're a pal,' he was saying. 'Can you put me on the list to become a blood brother?'

Not, I thought, a conversation I should just walk in on, so I decided to wait outside until he'd finished. But he must have heard me, because after a moment he said, *Hang on a second*, and opened the door. When he saw me, he spun back to the desk, snatched up the receiver, said, *Sorry, I have to go*, and rang off.

'I can come back later,' I said.

'That's OK,' he said. 'The deed is done.'

'What deed?'

He just shook his head.

'Nothing I should know about?'

'Not at the moment. We'll see.'

That *Not at the moment* gave me a tiny flutter of hope. In the next few days, as I dealt with a flurry of phone calls and a sombre meeting with our own solicitors, I clutched it to me like a hot water bottle – grateful for the background warmth it gave me, but fearful of examining it too closely, in case it turned out to have a leak.

And then, one evening the following week, just as I was leaving the building, I saw Tim barging his way towards me through a crowd of tourists. He was smiling, and moved with the loose-limbed cricket-player's grace I remembered from when I first knew him. In his hand was a bunch of roses.

'Here,' he said, thrusting them at me. 'Come and have dinner with me.'

I was too flabbergasted to say anything. I took the flowers and held them under my nose. Instantly, the choking traffic fumes vanished in a waft of sweetness.

'I would suggest the Elizabeth,' he said. 'But it might be a bit conspicuous. If someone saw us, they could put two and two together, and decide it came to seven. So how about the Luna Caprese?'

'Yes, I…OK. But what's going on?'

'I'll explain when we get there.'

I'd only been to the Luna Caprese once before – as the prelude to a one-night stand with a hooray Henry (why did I have such a weakness for them?) who'd run out of conversation before he'd finished his prawn cocktail. Even then, for a girl who'd grown up in austerity Britain, it had seemed – despite the growing sense of impending catastrophe – impossibly, theatrically glamorous: flickering candles; brilliant Mediterranean colours; a *corps de ballet* of attentive waiters, flamboyantly dressed as Italian fishermen. Now, walking in, I felt like Katharine Hepburn in *A Philadelphia*

Story. A smiling *Maître D* who knew Tim by name greeted us at the door and showed us to a table in the window. When he asked if we wanted an aperitif, Tim ordered champagne. As the man left, I leaned across and said,

'What *is* this?'

He glanced round. But the couples at the neighbouring tables were far too interested in each other to pay any attention to us.

'We're off the hook,' he said.

'What?'

'It's all over. Bar the grovelling.'

'How?'

He smiled, eyes crinkled, lips pressed together: *I did it.*

'An out-of-court settlement?'

He nodded. 'But we don't have to pay anything.'

I shook my head, completely at a loss.

'I decided to go and see her,' he said. 'Tate Finnegan arranged it, bless him. And we managed to reach an understanding.'

'You mean,' I said, reckless with relief, 'you went to bed with her?'

'What on earth makes you say that?'

'Well, that's the currency she usually prefers, isn't it?'

Instantly I regretted it. He started to blush, and his jaw hardened, turning his smile into a grimace.

'See? That's exactly what the poor girl's up against, that idea about her, that she's just some sort of a horrible heartless nymphomaniac. And –'

'Sorry, I –'

'No, that's what I thought too, until I met her. She's actually not like that at all. She's very sweet, very vulnerable. She wouldn't for a moment pretend to be a saint. But she doesn't think she deserves the kind of out-and-out character assassination she got from Peyton. And I happen to agree with her.'

I shrugged. 'Fair enough.'

The waiter brought our champagne. 'Are you ready to order, *signore*?'

We quickly scanned the menu. To save time, I simply picked whatever was most expensive. Tim followed suit, then chose something from the wine list with a grand-sounding name. The waiter retreated, smirking.

'So,' I said, as we clinked glasses, 'what do we have to do?'

'Apologize.'

'That's it?'

'She's not after money. She isn't vindictive. She doesn't want to close us down. She actually likes what we're doing – apart from, you know –'

'God, maybe she *is* a saint.'

He laughed. 'But there is one other thing. And it's a bit tricky. I'm not quite sure how to handle it, to be honest.'

'You have to marry her?'

He blushed again. Two blushes in one evening: unheard of.

'That wouldn't be so bad,' he said, laughing. 'No, this is – well, it's effectively a piece of black propaganda. Something about Adam.'

'What, a lie?'

'Not a lie. But not the sort of thing you just mention casually over dinner. A bit of a bombshell, actually. She thinks if people knew about it they'd be more sympathetic to her. And she's right. But she doesn't want it to be traceable to her. So our job is just to slip it quietly into the bloodstream, without –'

'What, get it into the gossip columns, you mean?'

He nodded. 'But the problem is, none of them will touch it with a bargepole. Unless we can give them some rock-solid evidence.'

'Why, what's he supposed to have done?'

He looked round furtively again.

'If you don't tell me in the next fifteen seconds,' I said, 'I'm going to faint.'

He turned back, and beckoned me closer. 'Apparently' – he was so close I could feel his breath on my cheek – 'he screwed Sadie's flatmate behind her back. Got her pregnant. And the girl had an abortion.'

'Christ.'

He nodded.

'Well, yes, I can see, that does –' I paused, letting the enormity of it sink in. 'Always assuming it's true, of course.'

'She swears it is. But the trouble is, we can't even say that, can we?'

'Did she tell you the other girl's name?'

'Rachel Lake,' he mouthed. 'But obviously that's *sub judice* too.'

'The doctor she went to? The date?'

He shook his head. 'But I could probably get them.'

'Try. And if you can, I'll do the rest.'

He raised his eyebrows. 'You think you can?'

'It won't come cheap,' I said. 'There'll be a substantial entertainment bill.'

'Still less than the cost of a court case, I take it?'

I laughed. 'If you're lucky.'

Our food arrived. We fell on it with the abandon of a couple of condemned prisoners reprieved from the gallows. We swilled down our wine, ordered another bottle, and followed it up with a couple of *grappas* apiece.

And then – though I can barely remember this bit – we went back to his place, and, for the last time, tumbled into bed together.

The final act. And here – yes, I do actually still feel a tiny spasm of guilt. The plan itself was flawlessly conceived and executed: a master-class in journalistic strategy, though I say so myself, of which I remain – with good reason, I think – quite proud. But it's true that I didn't take full account of the human cost until it was too late.

I'm not going make myself feel even worse by dwelling on the details. So, to cut a long story short: Tim discovered that the operation had been done at a practice near Wimpole Street. Immediately, I set out to worm my way into the confidence of the nurse there – a gaunt, haunted-looking woman in her thirties called Annette. *The Scene* was hoping to run a piece on the impact of the new abortion law, I said, and my friend Rachel Lake had suggested that I should talk to her – on condition, of course, of complete anonymity.

It was my first experience of something I've seen countless times since: the way people – particularly lonely, troubled people – respond to the faintest glimmer of interest from the press. You expect them to be suspicious, to start pulling up the drawbridge – and instead they welcome you in, luxuriating in the attention like cats in a patch of sunshine. I'd prepared myself for a long siege, and it was more or less all over in twenty minutes. Before I left, I pretty much had Annette's life story: the alcoholic father; the Catholic Irish mother who made her uncomfortable about what she was doing. It's just your job, I told her. Wasn't that what the concentration camp guards said? Oh, come on, I said, that's hardly the same thing, is it?

She was quiet for a moment, and then she said, Thank you. That makes me feel better.

When I left, I suggested meeting for a drink. She leapt at it. That evening, I borrowed a little Fi-Cord tape-recorder from a chap – yet another hooray Henry – who'd been two years ahead of me at Oxford and was now working for the William Hickey column on the *Daily Express*. I hid it in my bag, and fixed the mike in place with Sellotape. After her second glass of white wine, she made a not-very-funny joke about her employer, then started spluttering with laughter at her own indiscretion. I decided to take my chance.

'One thing,' I said. 'Rachel was always very cagey. About who the father was. She didn't ever say anything to you about him, did she?'

Her eyes narrowed with the effort of remembering.

'Only rumour had it,' I said, 'that it was a bloke called Adam Earnshaw. Who's actually quite a well-known musician.'

She looked up suddenly, waving a finger at me, as if she were trying to snag a wisp of something she'd seen floating in the air.

'Yes,' she said, 'that was it. He's the fellow. Just before we put her under, it all came out. She was very upset about it. Wished she'd told him. And the doctor said, well, you should have thought of that before, shouldn't you?' She shook her head. 'He's cruel, that one. When it was over, she clutched my wrist and said, was it a boy or a girl? And I said, stop torturing yourself, you don't need to know that. And she said, yes I do. All right, I said: it was a boy. And – I've never seen anything like it – she just howled and howled and howled and howled and howled.'

As easy as that. All that remained now was to return the Fi-Cord to William Hickey man, give him the tape – and wait. It was only a few days before our patience was rewarded:

Anyone who read Peyton Whybrow's fulsome tribute in The Scene *last month must have gained the impression that soulful one-man-band Adam Earnshaw is the next best thing to a saint. Alas, my spies tell me that the reality is rather more complicated than that. His knightly (or should that be nightly?) behaviour seems, in fact, to have left at least one young lady of previously blameless repute in a delicate and all-too-familiar dilemma. But*

good news, if nothing else, for certain members of the medical profession.
Every cloud has a silver lining, I suppose.

And within a month – though the name *Rachel Lake* never actually appeared in print – the whole sordid tale was common knowledge. Leaving, one assumes, not a few teenybopper hearts in pieces.

So all right, if you like: *Mea culpa.* But it would have got out anyway, one way or another. It just so happened that, in the event, the finger on the trigger was mine.

And at least, as a result, *The Scene* survived to fight another day.

18

CHARLEY GIBB

Well, OK. But it's a real shame you didn't think about doing this a few years back, when Bill was still here. Cos you'd have been a whole lot better off talking to him. He'd been all over – England, Germany, Sweden. And me, I never went anyplace, 'less you count Newport, Rhode Island. So fact is, when Adam showed up in America, I never met anyone like him before. And I don't believe I ever truly figured him out. Whether that was just the accent, or what it was, I don't know. All I can tell you is, when Bill come to tell me Adam walked out and disappeared, well, I'm surprised. But I'm not *sur*prised, if you know what I mean. Cos a lot of the time, seem to me Adam wasn't never really there in the first place.

I expect you think that's cos I never talked to a white fellow before – not like that. But it ain't so. I knew white folks when I was growing up – and you didn't know if they was going to buy you a beer or tell you coloured folk ain't welcome and you better beat it, now, quick, 'fore something bad happen. And then later – we're talking about the sixties now, civil rights time – there was a lot of college kids down from the north, come to take a stand with us. Or, leastways, seems to *them* that's what they doing. Clean white shirts, very polite, very respectful. Oh, man, were they respectful. One time, we're playing this little town out by the shore, and the police says there's too many of them – white college kids, I'm talking about; cops thought they might make trouble, that's what they told us, though they didn't look much like trouble to me. So they moved us on, and we ended up playing a church a few miles away. And when we seen all those white faces in the audience shining up at us, Bill Sweet, he there with me then, he leaned over and say, Good thing we're here, Charley. If we was still there by the ocean, I reckon these folks be expecting us to walk on water.

But Adam, he wasn't like none of them. Sometimes you're driving some-place and you look at him, you can see, he feel really lost. He just stares out the window at the cars, the homes, the juke houses, the stores, the big fields – like someone put him down on the moon, and he don't know how he got there. He looked whiter than any white guy I ever seen – and so thin you think when you open the door, he going to blow away like tumbleweed.

When we was just starting out the tour, I tell Bill, I say to him, you wrong about this fellow. He ain't strong enough. But Bill said, wait till he pick up his guitar. And he was right. Least, to begin with. Soon as he start to sing, Adam's right at home, just like you was sitting with him on your own porch. Cos you and him, you're both talking the same. Both talking music. You put *his* fingers up 'gainst *my* fingers, and that old guitar, it won't know the difference. And when we were playing together, *that's* when he finally opened his mouth. He asked me all kind of questions, where I was raised, who learned me this or that or the other. I showed him some licks, he picked them up just like that, like he been doing it all his life. I never knew nobody that could ever do that like he did. You play something, and *phew*, it come right back to you, near as a slick of paint on a wall. I say to him one time, you do a deal with someone to play like that? He look at me like he don't know what I'm talking about. But I think he knew.

So anyways, that how we get along. I come in and I find him sitting there, just looking at a blank wall like he dreaming, and I know better than to say, How you doin'? I just sit down, and pick up my guitar, and he do the same. And pretty soon it's all there, everything we thinking, everything we *feeling*, going forward and back, back and forward between us.

But then the change come. I seen it with my own eyes. We finish the tour, and that night there's a party in Bill's room. Only thing is, Adam ain't there. And that's funny, cos normally he like to come along, choose something sweet from the lady tray. So I go to his room and he just laying on the bed, with his arm over his eyes, like he's trying to shut the world out. Usually, you go anywhere near him, he's in a cloud of smoke. But not tonight. No smoke, no pills, no bottles.

So I say, you not joining us? Then I notice there's an envelope next to him, and a what you call that thing, a newspaper clipping, laying right there on top. I say, What is it, man? You had bad news or something? He don't say nothing. So I sit down and I try to get a look at that clipping, you know, before he realize. I can't see much, just his name, and something about a lady and *a member of the medical profession.* So I say, what is it, someone sick? And he say, yeah, *I* am. I say, you take something? But he shook his head. So I ask if he want me to call a doctor. And he says no, not that kind of sick. Must be some kind of sick, I say. I'm like the plague, he says. You mean the clap? I say. You caught a dose? Worse, he say. I spread destruction, wherever I go. Hey hey hey, I say, shaking him. That's crazy talk. Let you and me go have a drink. That'll make you feel better. But he say, no, please, I can't. Just leave me. So I leave him. Oftentimes since then, I think maybe I should have stayed. Held his hand and said a prayer with him. But what's done is done.

Next thing I hear , he got a few shows on his own, over at St Louis, Cincinnati, towns like that. So I tell myself, *phew*, it's OK. That's what I tell the bit up here, anyways, in my head. But there's another bit of me, didn't matter what I said, wouldn't believe it. *That* bit thinks when I go in his room that night, the devil already there, saying, remember the deal we made? Well, it's payback time. And a week later, when he disappeared, that bit's saying, told you so. Them other folks, the folks said it was drug dealers or little green men or I don't know what, they didn't see him laying there on the bed, with the sins of the world on him. And I did. And I still think that's what it was, all these years later.

That it? OK, well nice talking to you.

No, the pleasure's mine.

19

ANDREA WHYBROW SCHUYLER

I guess you must be one of the people who didn't realize my dad passed away. Seem to be a lot of you out there: I still get mail for him pretty much every week. Most of it I send back *addressee deceased*, but in your case, I figured he'd have wanted me to respond. Only that meant going through his papers, and for a couple of months there I just didn't have the time. So please excuse the delay.

Here, finally, anyway, is what I was looking for: a piece Dad did about Adam Earnshaw's disappearance. It was intended for *The Scene*, but in the end they didn't use it. The previous article he'd done on Earnshaw had led to a libel suit, and they didn't want to risk repeating the experience with a whole gamut of potential plaintiffs, most of them American. I can't say I blame them. Quite a lot of the information he used had been told him in confidence – and though in some cases he changed people's names to conceal their identities, it wouldn't have been difficult for a hard-nosed investigator to uncover the truth.

In the end he approached *Rolling Stone* with the project. But by then the story was no longer news – and, without that hook, or any sensational new information, the editor didn't feel Adam Earnshaw was a big enough name to justify devoting the space to him. So it finished up languishing in a file.

Just a little bit of background: Adam Earnshaw was always something of an obsession for my father. He used to talk about the guy endlessly, right up to the end. When my sister and I were growing up, he'd play us *Standing Stone* again and again, trying to convince us the man was a genius. Maybe we were just snotty teenagers, determined not to be impressed, but we never got it. And he'd shake his head and say, *You would if you'd heard him live.*

But the music was only part of it. The other part was the mystery of what happened to him. And Dad was always convinced that those two things were connected somehow, opposite sides of the same coin. Whatever the explanation was, he couldn't believe it was just some random accident. That would be too banal. It would be *bad art.* Life, fate, whatever you want to call it, would have made more of an effort for Adam Earnshaw. Come up with something that, at the deepest level, made a satisfying objective correlative to his strange talent. And that, I think, affected the whole way Dad approached the subject. He was always such a romantic.

Anyway, here's the article. I hope it is some help. Please let me know how you get on.

20

PEYTON WHYBROW

I get to St Louis – 90 degrees and humid; the Mississippi a lazy giant alligator twitching in its sleep – at 4.00 p.m. on July 14 1968, less than seventy-two hours after Adam Earnshaw vanished. I'm here courtesy of Tate Finnegan, who bought my plane ticket and gave me my orders: to find Adam, if I can, and get him back on track before the story leaks out and the tour has to be abandoned. Why me? I'm familiar with the area, and Tate trusts me. Plus I'm a journalist, so I'm used to talking to strangers.

But I know I don't have long. Wheatsheaf have paid for Adam's room at the Indian Springs Motel for another three nights, just in case he comes back unexpectedly. But after that, they're going to have to start cancelling gigs, and officially report Adam as a missing person. And then – this is what they're really dreading – the inevitable headlines. *Was junkie folk singer slain by drug dealers? Killed by the CIA? Abducted by aliens?*

The first day-and-a-half I concentrate on simply trying to gather the known facts. To start with, I track down as many of the people who were actually there that night as I can: the owner of the bar; the sound guy; assorted kids, strung out and puzzled-looking, but willing enough to talk. My job – not easy – is to play down the significance of what happened, while at the same time extracting every detail I can. This is what I finally manage to piece together:

On July 11 1968, after a successful tour supporting bluesman Bill Sweet, Adam Earnshaw is booked to appear at a student hangout in St. Louis called Maggie's Bar. He isn't a household name in America, but his reputation is growing. This gig won't do it any harm. Rock stars fill arenas; soulful troubadours play smoky, sawdust-on-the-floor places like

Maggie's. Word gets about. By the time the doors open, the line reaches half-way down the street. More than fifty people are turned away. Scuffles break out. Someone calls the police. There are a few arrests, mostly for possession of cannabis.

Inside, doped-up, adrenalin-fuelled kids squeeze in, pushing chairs and tables out of the way, then sit in tight huddles on the floor, waiting for their guy. Only their guy isn't there. He was due to sound check at six-thirty, but hasn't showed. After half an hour, Maggie calls his motel. Sorry, ma'am: he's not answering.

You've only got to look at Maggie – burly; thick-armed; thirty-some-thing; hung with hippy beads – to see she isn't given to panicking. But she's worried. She tells the sound guy, Jeremy (yes, that really is his name), to put on *A Gift From a Flower to a Garden*. For the first few tracks, the audience assume they're just being got in the mood, and sway along, trance-like, to Donovan's hymns to gulls and magpies. But when they get to the end of side one, and Jeremy flips the LP over, they become restive. A big tangle-haired fellow at the back – a football player dressed like a scarecrow – yells, 'We didn't come here to listen to a record!' A moment later, three or four voices chorus: 'Where's Adam?' A girl shouts: 'How'd we even know he's here?'

Somebody lobs a lighted joint on the stage. People watch mesmerized as it lies there smouldering, the cardboard roach slowly uncoiling as the paper burns away. Then a guy throws his beer. Jeremy gathers up his stuff and scuttles for cover. For a moment, the evening is poised on the edge. Then Maggie appears on stage, a galleon under full sail.

'Guys! Listen! I just want you to know: Adam Earnshaw is in the build-ing. He'll be on in a couple minutes.'

Order is restored. But the mood's broken. Beneath the silence in the room, you can still feel the sharp edge of resentment. When Adam Earnshaw finally shuffles on, stooping like an old man, there's only a murmur of response. Several people mention the strange look in his eyes. *Like a zombie. Like a sleepwalker. Like a guy who just came through the wrong door and can't figure out where he is.*

He circles the stool, then sits down, settles his guitar on his knee, gri-maces as if he's trying to remember something, and starts in on a song that no one in the audience has ever heard before. His voice struggles to reach the low notes, and, to a bunch of mid-western college kids, the refrain – *Gog and Magog, help me now; Rise up again and help me now* – means nothing. At the end, there's a patter of applause. Respectful, but only just.

If he'd been alert to the impression he was making – or cared about it – he'd have switched tack at this point: made a self-deprecating little joke – *You can tell what kind of a mood I'm in, can't you?* – or launched into something more accessible. But the next song is even less of a crowd-pleaser than *Gog and Magog*: a jangled train wreck of chaotic rhythms and splintered melodies called *Night of the Snake*. The lyrics are hard to follow, but seem to be about a guy who hallucinates a giant serpent emerging from the speaker on his radio. They eye each other. He hears the snake saying,

> *You're foolin' yourself, man*
> *I ain't what I seem*
> *Not a trip, not a dream*
> *I'm the price that you pay, man*
> *The crack in the wall*
> *Goin' to make your house fall*

The crowd give it maybe a minute before they decide they've had enough. There's a lot of coughing and shuffling. A pasty-faced girl at the back calls out: 'Play *Annabelle, Dancing!*' And instantly the refrain starts to spread though the crowd: *Annabelle, Annabelle, Annabelle!'*

There are conflicting accounts of what happens next. Does he get up, as if he's leaving, and then sit down again? Rub his eyes with the back of his hand, as if wiping away tears? Or merely sigh and shake his head? The one thing everyone agrees on is that there's a pause – perhaps as much as half a minute – before his fingers start picking their way through the intro to his best-known song.

A couple of people clap. He begins to sing:

> *Annabelle*
> *Tripping through the daisy ring*

Taking wing
Sweet and wild
Fairy child
Annabelle
Lying on the sward –

'Grassy sward!' yells a girl close to the front. She's right – as you'll know if you've heard it. Without those two syllables between "the" and "sward", the line doesn't even scan.

Adam Earnshaw stops playing, gets up, rests his guitar against his chair, and walks off. And that's it. As he pushes aside the curtain and disappears into the shadows, we move from fact into the realm of hearsay and conjecture. Because – at this point, at least – there is no credible evidence that anyone ever sees him again.

*

Before we go on, I need to declare an interest. Despite what you just read, I'm not a camera. (No one is, of course, but that's the illusion with journalism, isn't it: your Man-in-wherever-it-is is no more than a sort of Arriflex, poked out the window on to the world, and what's in front of you is a transcript of the film.) As you'll be aware if you've followed my zigzag trail through earlier issues of *The Scene*, I knew Adam Earnshaw – not well, but enough to realize I'd never met anyone like him. For me, he was a kind of saviour, the last best hope of a generation that had lost its bearings, seen them swept away on a strobe-lit sea of drugs and sex and consumer goods. Not exactly a Messiah, striding ahead, leading us to the sunlit uplands: more a kind of lightning rod, channelling the 30,000 volts of shit that would have reduced anyone else to a French fry, and somehow managing to stay functional with it – or just *about* functional.

And without him, we've had to take the shit for ourselves. And look where that's gotten us. Of course, you can say we'd have fucked up anyway, Adam Earnshaw or no Adam Earnshaw. But speaking for myself, ever since he vanished, I've been careful to keep out of the way of storms. And part – a big part – of the reason I wanted to find him was the longing to feel insulated again – to know that I could venture out in the rain without ending up frazzled like a bug on a zapper. So there's a lot at stake for me here.

OK: back to the story.

*

Of course, there are other people I could talk to, if I could find them. How about the scarecrow man in the audience, for instance? Or the pasty-faced girl who wanted *Annabelle, Dancing*? But the meter's running, and I don't have time. So late afternoon the second day I decide to call it quits, and drive out to the Indian Springs Motel. It's one of those spreadeagled, single-story places that suddenly erupted all over the country in the 1950s: thirty identical rooms, each with its own entrance and parking space, and an air conditioning unit hung out the window like a colostomy bag. I pull up in front of the reception and peer through the double door. A round-faced motherly-looking woman in her fifties sits at the desk, sucking on a ballpoint pen as she pores over some paperwork.

'I'll be with you in a minute.'

'That's OK. No rush.'

She finishes what she's doing, then lays down the ballpoint and beams at me. A gold crucifix at her throat glints in the light from the entrance. Pinned to her blouse is a plastic name tag: *Leanne Kaiser*.

'How may I help you?'

'Just wondering if I could ask you a couple questions?'

She laughs. 'You can try. I may not know the answers.'

'Adam Earnshaw. The English guy who was staying here?'

She nods.

'Well, he's a friend of mine. He's gone missing before, so we're not too worried about him. But still –'

She shakes her head. 'I wish there was something I could tell you, honey. But I was here when he checked in. And that's the only time I ever laid eyes on him.'

'Was he with anyone?'

'No.'

'And nobody saw him after the concert?'

'Not as I know of. But I can ask around, if you want. Spread the word. And call you if I hear anything. What's your number?'

'I don't know it, I'm afraid. But it'll be in the phone book. I'm at the Thunderbird Lodge. Room 22.'

'I didn't ought to help you, then. Not if you're staying at the Thunderbird. They're the competition.'

'OK, I'll move.' Why hadn't I thought of it before? This was where he'd been. Who knew what traces he might have left behind?

She laughs. 'No call for that. I'm just giving you a hard time, sweetie.'

'No, really,' I say. 'One good turn deserves another. Do you have a room for tomorrow?'

She checks the bookings and nods. 'Room fifteen. What's the name?'

'Peyton Whybrow.'

She writes it down, then looks up and says,

'Where's your momma, Peyton? She must miss you something terrible.'

I laugh. 'Which is *his* room?'

'Fourteen.'

I hesitate. 'There isn't any way you could let me see it, is there?'

She shakes her head. 'Sorry, honey. According to this' – tapping the book with her pen – 'he's still a guest here. Which means I can't let *no* one in, not without his permission. And if he don't come back, and we have to call the police – well, they're going to want everything left just the way it was, aren't they?'

'I wouldn't –'

But I've lost her attention. An elderly couple is hobbling into the lobby, dragging a huge suitcase.

'Well, hi there,' she says. 'May I help you?'

'See you tomorrow,' I say, and walk out into the sauna heat to find room fourteen. From the outside, it's more or less indistinguishable from its neighbours, except that the curtain's closed. There's still a tiny crack, through which I can just make out the dim bulk of the bed. Otherwise all I can see is my own reflection, super-imposed on a watery mirror image of the parking lot.

I shut my eyes, try to open my mind. If it was Adam standing here, I know, time would suddenly loosen its grip and he'd be able to *feel* something. That was his gift. He arrives in England with a mental map that's all wrong. Try as he may, he can't find anywhere marked *home*. But that doesn't make him close in on himself: it leaves him preternaturally alert – not only to the echoes of the past, but to whoever happens to cross his path in the present. If he can't be the someone he thought he was, he can be *anyone*. His sixth sense means he's able – maybe unconsciously – to snatch things from the air and give them form in himself.

But I can't. I can't feel anything. Room fourteen is just a room. I give it a few minutes, then open up my stifling car and drive back to the Thunderbird Lodge. When I get there, there's a message waiting for me from Tate Finnegan in London, asking me to call him collect. I run to my room and grab the phone. He must have news. Maybe even from Adam himself. Just a few seconds, and this weird, sea-sick, trapped-in-a-nightmare feeling could be over.

But the moment I hear Tate's voice, I know it isn't.

'Where is it with you, man?'

'I'm here. That's about it.'

'No leads?'

'Nothing you don't know already. He was obviously pretty fucked-up when he came on. But no surprise there. Might just have been bad dope. Or all-purpose paranoia.'

'Shit.' He exhales through his teeth. 'I'm starting to feel like some old lady keeps losing her dog in the park. I'm telling you, he shows up this time, I'm putting him under twenty-four hour guard.' He hesitates, clears his throat. 'Ghosts. Ghosts and chicks. They're what trip the guy out. You figure he thought there was a ghost the place he was staying?'

'Indian Springs? It's about as haunted as a piece of Tupperware.'

He's silent for what feels like a minute. Then he says,

'Well, I don't know, man. But if you find anything, call me. Any time.'

After he hangs up, I lie on my bed, thinking. Maybe it's just the mention of ghosts, but the room feels unsettled, as if the walls of the room have suddenly become porous. I keep half-expecting Adam to appear out of nowhere, like Jesus to his disciples, and tell me what happened. He doesn't, of course. But it's not a restful idea to have thrumming through your brain. So: time to do something practical.

I head for the bar and launch an all-out assault on a club sandwich. It turns out to be too much for me, so I wrap it in a napkin and put in my bag: in a place like this, you never know when you're going to run into a hungry dog. Then I open my notebook and try to figure out the basics:

On the day he disappeared, Adam checked in to the Indian Springs Motel around 3.00 p.m. Maggie's was no more than a fiftee- minute drive away, but – despite being due there at 6.00 p.m. – he didn't actually show until some time after 8.15. Why not? Did he just set off late from the motel? (His door opened directly on to the parking lot, so none of the staff saw him leave.) That would have been out of character: even at his most chaotic, he tended to be morbidly punctual. Did someone intercept him? And/or did he stop somewhere of his own accord? If so, why? To score some dope? To eat something? If we knew that, it might give us the answer – or at least a clue – to where he went afterwards.

It's a laborious job, but I decide to cruise all the restaurants between the bar and the hotel. Most are just the ubiquitous junk factories you find anywhere: Wendys, McDonalds, Arbys, Bob Evans. It's hard to imagine Adam setting foot in any of them, so I focus instead on the sprinkling of little family-run ethnic places. None of them reports serving anyone like Adam Earnshaw on the night of the gig.

But – with almost my last throw of the dice – I do turn something up. At La Mesa – billed as *East St Louis's premier Mexican dining experience* – I find a young waiter who, at around 9.30, decided to escape the steamy reek of guacamole and re-fried beans for a few minutes to get a breath of fresh air. While he was standing on the street he noticed a red Corvette – itself an unusual sight in that neighbourhood – speeding erratically out of town. He couldn't see who was driving, but had the impression there were two people inside. He tried to make out the licence plate, in case something was up, but it was moving too quickly.

Have you told anyone else about this? I say. He shrugs and shakes his head: Nobody asked me.

Good, I say. Please don't. At least for the moment. And I give him ten bucks. I don't know if it's enough to buy his silence, but he looks happy.

It's late, but I find a drug store that's still open and leaf through a copy of *The St Louis Dispatch*. When I get to page five, my heart gives an electric jolt: *Body found in river.* But two lines are enough to tell me it isn't Adam. And there are no stories featuring a red Corvette.

'You here to buy, son? Or you just passing the time of day?'

I look round. The burly guy behind the counter is scowling at me. I put the *Dispatch* back, then walk over and ask for a couple packs of Zig Zag rolling papers. He knows what they're for, and doesn't like it. But he still takes my money.

*

In the morning Leanne from Indian Springs hasn't called me, but when I go to check in I still take her some flowers. She flushes and says,

'Oh, no need for that, honey.'

'Hey,' I say. 'You're the best friend I have here. I appreciate it.'

She doesn't know what to do with that, so waves it away with her hand.

'I do have something for you, though,' she says. 'I just got a call, not twenty minutes ago. From this one gal.' She pauses, looks round the lobby to make sure we're not overheard. Then, dropping her voice, she says, 'Only you have to be careful. Tell her you don't got nothing to do with the police. She's scared of getting into trouble, see.'

'Why might she get into trouble?'

She blushes. 'Thing is, Peyton, sometimes one of our gentleman guests is lonesome…Wants a lady to keep him company. And he'll ask for a suggestion. Can't say I'm too happy about doing it, but…' She reaches into a drawer and pulls out a card showing a pouty brunette wearing a tantalizingly unbuttoned blouse and no bra. *Cindy. Call 733 9978.*

'And what, this Cindy's saying that Adam –'

'Uh-uh.' Her blush deepens. 'I guess he wouldn't have no need for that, would he? No more than you. No, it's something she saw. She'll maybe tell you herself. But only if she trusts you. She says to meet her at Maggie's Bar at eight. And then she'll see.'

'Maggie's? That's not a hooker's hangout is it?'

She shakes her head. 'I guess that's the point.'

I wave the card at her. 'This what she actually looks like?'

She smiles. 'Pretty much. Anyways, you're checking in, right?' She reaches for a key. 'How many nights?'

I pay for two. She gives me the key.

'By the way,' I say, 'sounds like a crazy question, I know, but this place isn't supposed to be haunted, is it?'

She doesn't seem surprised. 'You afraid of ghosts, honey?'

'Not me. But he was. Adam.'

'I saw one one time. When I was little. Out at my uncle's, by Cahokia Mounds. If you're looking for ghosts, that's the place to go. But I never heard of anything like that here.'

I nod. 'Well, thank you.'

I park in front of number 15 and let myself in. It has that cheap motel smell of stale smoke and air freshener and dead skin – mingled, in this case, with a whiff of Mississippi ooze. There's lots of *faux* wood, and a picture above the bed of a mounted cowboy silhouetted against the setting sun. The unloved carpet is blotched with coffee stains (I hope it's coffee), and there's a black cigarette burn close to the bedhead. You wouldn't have to be particularly crazy to find it all pretty depressing.

I want to be at my best for Cindy, so I lie down and try to nap. But I'm too uptight to let go of the controls, so – after twenty minutes or so – I roll myself a monster j-stick, like one of the gargantuan brutes Adam used to make. Maybe, I think, by a kind of sympathetic magic, that will create a bond between us, tune my mind to his, give me a sudden flash of insight, or even beam an image of where he is into my head. But unlike Adam, I'm only a dabbler; and the unaccustomed chemical overload unleashes a gargantuan panic attack, making me gibber at every stray noise, and sending me scuttling to the door three times a minute to check that it's locked. In the end, I drift into an odd half sleep, half hallucination, in which the horizon becomes the rim of an outsized eyeball, blank and lustreless, and veiled over with death.

*

I arrive at the bar just before eight. The place is packed, but I soon spot her, tucked away in a corner with a Coke in front of her. She's tried to blend in with the hippy/student clientele – tie-dyed t-shirt; jeans – but that only makes her styled hair and make-up more conspicuous. As I get closer, I can see a man sitting next to her, his whole body twisted towards her. He's around forty, prematurely bald, with big shoulders and arms like sides of beef. A truck-driver? A longshoreman? Not a peace child, anyway. I can't hear what he's saying, but from his expression it's urgent, maybe angry.

'Excuse me,' I say. 'Are you Cindy?'

She glances up, bends the lipstick into a brittle smile. 'Oh, hi, hi. You're the guy Leanne –?'

I nod. The hulk turns and glowers at me.

'Pardon me, fella,' he says. 'I was here first.'

'I can come back,' I say.

'Why don't you do that? In maybe a week?'

'No,' says Cindy, so quietly that I have to lip-read it. She glares at him, her face bruised with rage.

'What's the matter?' says the hulk. 'This faggot's money better than mine?'

He grabs her arm. She pulls away and – when he won't let go – pummels his hand with her fist. People near us are starting to stare, but he takes no notice, and jerks her closer with a violent yank. She gasps, and I hear a catch in her throat, as if she's about to cry.

'Is there some problem here?' asks Maggie, lumbering up like a speeding rhino.

'This guy,' says Cindy. 'He keeps bugging me.'

Maggie leans over the hulk. 'OK, sir. Please leave.'

'Why? I've as much right to be here as anyone else.'

'Not if you're harassing another customer.'

He says nothing, but clenches his hands and exhales noisily through his nose. Maggie touches his shoulder.

'Out,' she says. 'Now. Or I'm calling the police.'

I clutch the edge of the table, bracing myself for the eruption. But to my surprise he levers himself heavily to his feet and heads towards the door without a word, squeegeeing the sweat from his forehead with his fingers.

'You OK, ma'am?' says Maggie.

Cindy nods. Maggie turns to me and laughs.

'Thought I'd seen the last of you,' she says. 'But I should have known better, shouldn't I? Seems like any time there's trouble, there you are.'

She saunters back to the bar. Cindy waits till she's out of earshot, then says,

'Sorry about that.'

I shake my head and point at the hulk's empty seat. 'OK if I sit there?'

'Sure.'

I settle myself next to her. It's swelteringly oppressive, despite the best efforts of a couple of noisy air conditioning units. I can feel her body pumping out heat like a radiator.

'Some guys are just shitheads,' she says. 'He sees me on the street and follows me in here. I tell him I'm meeting someone, but he won't take no for an answer.' She looks shyly at me. 'You know what I am. Huh? I guess Leanne told you?'

'She showed me your card. You're very pretty.'

She bites her lip as if I'd hit her.

'I'm quitting soon,' she says. 'I'm going to be moving out to Olympia to live with my sister. And starting college. But a guy like that, he looks at me, and all he sees is a piece of merchandise. Like if he has the money, I just have to go with him. Period.'

'Yeah, that's a bummer,' I say.

She smiles, more openly this time. 'You seem nice, though.'

I smile back. She drops her gaze.

'Leanne says you know this guy that disappeared, Adam whatever-his-name-is.'

'Earnshaw.'

'And you're trying to find out what happened to him?'

She says it with a little smile that makes me think, maybe she's going to be a prick-tease, try to drag this out. So I say,

'Yes. But I'm up against it. I don't have a lot of time.'

'OK.' She studies me closely. Finally she says, 'I think I saw something that could help. Only I have to be real careful. It's tough for girls like me round here. The cops are always trying to run us out of town. Except when they want a slice of pie for themselves. So if I tell you –'

'I promise,' I say.

She looks at me some more.

'OK,' she says, 'I'm going to trust you. Maybe it's the wrong call, I don't know. I can be pretty stupid about guys.' She tugs her lips down ruefully: sad clown. Then she brightens again. 'But what the hell?'

'You want another drink?'

She lifts her glass. 'No, this is fine.'

I say nothing, giving her space.

'So what it was,' she says, still looking at her Coke, 'is the night your friend went missing, a john picks me up downtown, we're driving to his hotel, we're stopped at the traffic light' – nodding towards the street – 'out there. And while we're waiting, I see this red Corvette parked out front.'

My heart starts tap-dancing. 'A Corvette? You're sure?'

She nods. 'I always liked Corvettes. That's why I noticed. And the door's open, and this young guy, long hair, could have been your friend, he's talking to someone inside. I figured it was a girl. But it might have been a guy. It's just I remember thinking, some people have all the luck. I'm stuck in a big ugly Chevy with this fat middle-aged slob. And she has her own beautiful car, and is picking up a guy looks like a rock star. Nice work if you can get it.' She pauses, stares into the middle distance, re-running the moment in her head. 'No, it *was* a girl. I'm pretty sure.'

'So he did get in?'

'Yeah. He looks over his shoulder, like he thinks someone's following him. And then he jumps in and slams the door and they take off. Real fast. You know, tyres screeching, all that shit.'

'You remember what time this was?'

'Round nine-thirty?' She pauses. 'So, is it worth something?'

'Well, it might be. I mean, obviously if we could trace the car. Find out where it went, whether it showed up on the cops' radar. But the trouble is, I can't –' Too late, it suddenly hits me what she meant: she could have been working all this time, so talking to me is costing her money. 'How about twenty bucks?' I say.

She pulls a face.

'Fifty?'

She thinks about it, shifting her head from side to side, yes, no, yes, no. Finally she says,

'OK.'

'All right. But I'll need to change a travellers cheque.'

I open my bag and take out the American Express wallet. Maggie looks oddly at me – guys like me in bars like hers don't normally pay for sex, which must be what she thinks I'm doing – but she shells out the money. When I get back to the table Cindy wrinkles her nose and says,

'Yuck. What's that smell?'

She points at my bag. I pick it up and sniff. She's right: it stinks like a garbage can. I peer inside and see the remains of the club sandwich, disintegrating in the heat.

'Oh, God, I'm sorry,' I say. 'I forgot.'

'It's making me feel nauseous.'

'I'll go dump it someplace.'

She nods and smiles. 'You coming back afterwards?'

There's an unmistakable invitation in her eyes. I can't say I'm not tempted. But life is too complicated already.

'No,' I say. 'I better be going.'

I hand her the fifty, thank her again, and make for the door.

I have a lead, but it doesn't take me anywhere. To track down every red Corvette in Missouri would require access to the police vehicle register – and if I go to the police, there's no way I can tell them what I know without (a) implicating Cindy, and (b) risking the story of Adam's disappearance leaking out. This is my problem: I'm trying to operate at breakneck speed, but I have one hand tied behind my back. I'm hazy about the law, but phrases like *obstruction of justice* spring to mind, and images of spending the night in a cell smelling of piss and vomit, surrounded by drunks, while Tate Finnegan in England makes a long-distance attempt to rustle up a lawyer for me.

And it's not just the Adam situation that's frustrating: Cindy's left me feeling antsy too, and I'm struggling with the urge – despite my better judgment – to go back and see if she's still at Maggie's. Sleep is out of the question: I need to do something decisive. And as I turn into the Indian Springs parking lot, and see in front of me the line of blank doors and windows, sulkily guarding their secrets, I suddenly realize what it is. I go into my room, splash water on my face, brush my hair, change my sweaty shirt, then head for the lobby to try my luck with whoever's taken over from Leanne.

To my surprise, nobody has: she's still there. She looks up, smiles when she sees it's me.

'Well, hello. How'd it go?'

'It was good. Thank you.' I glance at the clock. 'Boy, they work you pretty hard, don't they?'

'Mary Beth called in sick. So I said I'd stay on.'

'Whoa, they're lucky to have you. I hope they appreciate it.'

She nods. 'This way I have Saturday off, so I can see my grandson.'

'Do you want me to sit in for you for fifteen minutes? So you can take a break? If it's just a matter of picking up the phone and saying, *Good evening, Indian Springs Motel*, I could probably just about handle it.'

She laughs, but there are tears in her eyes. 'Oh, that's real sweet of you, honey. But no, it wouldn't be right.'

'How about a drink, then?'

She nods at the Coke machine. 'I wouldn't say no to a Seven Up.'

I get us one apiece.

'You better lock your door, Peyton,' she says. 'Else I might I come right in and kidnap you. Take you home and adopt you.'

I laugh. 'Sounds good to me.'

Neither of speaks for a moment. Then, as if she can see what I'm working round to and wants to save me the trouble, she says,

'You know what you was asking? About seeing your friend's room? The manager's not here now. So I reckon I could let you. Just as long as you promise not to tell him. Or move nothing.'

'Word of honour. I can sign something in blood, if you want.'

She laughs. 'Just the word of honour's fine.' She hands me the key, then quickly looks away, as if she's trying to fool even herself about what she's done.

I take a towel from my room and use it to grip the handle of number fourteen, just in case the police ever become involved. Once inside I shut the door behind me and stand there for a few moments, absorbing the atmosphere. Even with the curtains closed, it's not completely dark: there's enough light filtering in from the parking lot to make a faint pattern of blacks and greys, like the image on a print starting to take shape in a developing tray. The air is stale, heavy with the smoke from long-dead joints, and the rotting-fruit smell of clothes that have missed their appointment with the Laundromat.

With my elbow, I switch on the light. God, the banality of the place, the *ordinariness*. A bed, just like mine. It's made up, but of course that doesn't mean Adam didn't sleep in it that night: the maid must have come in and fixed the room before anyone realized he was missing. On the bedside table is a creased copy of *The Woman in White*. I've seen it before: Adam took it everywhere with him, and it's so well used that the cover has started to disintegrate.

A guitar – nothing to say whether it's the one he played at Maggie's – leans against the wall in its fat Michelin man case. Next to it a bag lies open on the chair. It's full of rumpled, unwashed clothes. Holding my nose, I poke gingerly beneath the top layer, but all I find is more of the same. I ease open the drawers in the *faux*-wood chest. There's nothing in any of them, except a packet of spare La Bella guitar strings.

The door to the bathroom is half open. I flick on the light, jumping as the electric fan suddenly whirrs into life. The towels are all fresh, and there's a powerful whiff of days-old air freshener. The only sign of Adam's presence is a battered toilet case next to the sink. Inside are an old pre-war ivory-handled cutthroat razor; shaving brush; soap; toothpaste; a couple of unused condoms.

As I go back into the bedroom, I notice something I'd missed before: a tiny black triangle sticking out from beneath the edge of the bedspread. I stare at it for a moment, memorizing the exact position, so that I can put it back in precisely the same place. Then – my muscles aching with adrenalin – I carefully lift the fabric.

A notebook, with a hard shimmery cover like watered silk, and a ballpoint pen bookmarking a page towards the end. I pick it up and open it:

Gobelin

> *Take the path between the trees*
> *Softly, now, the hounds are close*
> *Past the castle, up the hill*
> *~~Beyond~~ Behind the silken-threaded oak*

Here you escape the watcher's eye
Where the hunters cannot follow
Only the robin and the swallow

There's nothing to say when he wrote it, of course: it could have been years ago. But even so, reading it, I feel a vertiginous undertow, dragging me back to the fatal final hours before Adam vanished. I see him sitting there, hunched over the little table, forehead ridged with concentration. And that image keeps cross-fading with the mediaeval hunting scene he's describing, hung – here's how I visualize it – above some massive old stone fireplace.

What if he *did* compose it then? What does that tell us? That he foresaw his own disappearance? That he *planned* it? On the face of it, that seems to be contradicted by the pen in the notebook – assuming that's how he left it – which suggests he saw the lines as unfinished business, and intended to go back to them.

But perhaps – it suddenly hits me – that was all part of the plan. This is his final attempt to turn life into art – and it's *his* life this time, not someone else's. The half-completed song embodies its own meaning. The singer walks into the tapestry, takes the path between the trees, vanishes behind the silk-threaded oak – and we see him no more. But did he mean to get lost there, or was it a mistake?

I collect my own notebook from my room and copy the lines into it. Then I put everything back the way I found it and return the key to the lobby. To my relief, Leanne is on the phone, so I just drop it into her hand, mouth *Thank you*, and skedaddle into the hot night.

I've taken a shower, gotten into bed, and am trying to distract myself with some late-night trash-TV when there's a knock on the door. I check my watch: it's after midnight. In the time it takes me to pull on some clothes, a fantasy has woven itself in my head: it's Adam, exhausted from days of wandering the back-roads of Missouri, longing for the comforts of his motel room. But when he hears I'm here, he holds off just long enough to come and put me out of my misery.

I squint through the spy-hole. Not Adam: a girl. The foreshortened features are a grainy blur, and it takes me a moment to rearrange them into Cindy's face. In the midst of my disappointment I feel a surge of excitement. I must have lingered in her mind the way she did in mine. No point fighting it now: it was obviously meant.

I unhook the chain and open the door. She stands there, arms crossed in front of her, shivering despite the electric-blanket warmth.

'Hi,' I say. 'Come in.'

She does, but only far enough for me to close the door behind her.

'How did you know where to find me?' I ask – then guess the answer just as she's about to tell me.

'Leanne,' we say in unison.

She's still hugging herself shyly. I wonder if she sees this as a commercial transaction, or just r and r, but it seems churlish to enquire. *Sorry*, I hear myself explaining to Tate. *I didn't find Adam, but I did spend a hundred bucks of your money on a hooker.*

'I know it's late,' she says. 'But you said you didn't have much time. And I found something out.'

'About Adam?'

'About the Corvette. Well, *a* Corvette. Seemed like you didn't want to talk to the cops. So I called this detective I know. He was working late.' She blushes. 'We did a deal.'

I start to speak. She holds a hand up.

'I don't want to talk about it.' She can't stop shivering. 'If you take a ride with me, I'll tell you what he said.'

'Can't you tell me here?'

She shakes her head. 'There's a place I want to show you.'

No wonder she ogled the Corvette: she drives a beat-up old Falcon, with a dented fender and a door that rattles like chattering teeth. I'm crazy with impatience, but she doesn't seem in a hurry to talk, so I hold my tongue and watch the landscape slipping by. To begin with it's the usual jumble of electricity pylons and business parks and vacant lots, but after fifteen minutes or so the buildings start to crowd more tightly together, and through the spaces between them I can glimpse the outsize silhouettes of ships tied up in the docks. And then, suddenly, we're on the bridge heading out of the city, watching the reflected streetlights bleeding into the river, feeling its slow reptile movement beneath us, its monstrous imperviousness to our mayfly lives.

'How far we going?' I ask.

'Not far. You see the sign to Collinsville?'

'Yes.'

She still seems reluctant to talk. We drive on in silence. I press my face against the window, straining to see anything that will give me a clue to where we're heading, but every time something recognizable – a gas station; a house; a line of trees – starts to take shape, it's bleached out by the dazzle of oncoming headlights. Eventually we turn off the highway on to a narrow country road.

'Are we there?'

'Almost. See anything?'

I crane my neck and peer through the windshield. As my eyes acclimatize, I can make out ahead a series of hill-sized bumps – scores of them – extending across the landscape almost to the horizon. At their centre, dominating the whole site, stands a much bigger, flat-topped pyramid. The effect is startling, as if a fleet of alien spacecraft had appeared out of nowhere and deposited itself, more or less at random, on a patch of American soil.

'God, what's that?' I say.

'Cahokia Mounds.'

Out at my uncle's, by Cahokia Mounds. When Leanne said that, it just seemed like a throwaway line. Now, suddenly, it's become the soundtrack to a horror movie.

'It's some old Indian place,' she says. 'They found a load of bodies there.'

'Bodies –'

'I'm talking about *old* bodies, from way back when. Ancient. And some of them are pretty weird. Like they'd been sacrificed or something.'

'Jesus.'

'Anyways, what this cop said was, the night your friend went missing, a couple kids came out here to make out. On the way they passed another car, pulled right off the road.' She waves towards the nearest mound. 'Just about there someplace. They didn't notice the model, but it was red, and looked kind of sharp and sporty. They went on a ways, then pulled off themselves and started necking. But after a couple of minutes they heard a loud noise coming from behind them, close to where they'd seen the other car.'

'What, like a gunshot?'

'No, more like a kind of howl. At first they thought it must be a coyote, but then they figured, no coyote ever made a sound like that. It was human. Either someone having weird sex, or else, you know…Being murdered or something. So they drove like crazy till they found a phone booth and called the cops, and the cops sent two guys in a cruiser. The kids said they'd meet they them there, but when they got back, the red car had gone. But the cops took a flashlight anyways and went up on the mound to look. There was no one there – no body, no trace of blood. But they did find a pair of silk panties. And just a couple feet away, some scraps of paper they figured were probably tabs of acid.' She pulls the car over. 'You want to see?'

'OK.'

We cross a strip of parched grass, then scramble up the side of the mound. It's no more than fifty feet high, but enough to see the breath-taking scale of the place from the top: the dark lines of monumental earthworks stretching away before you, fainter and fainter, until they finally merge with the charcoal grey of the night. Clearly, constructing the whole complex must have required an almost unimaginable effort by thousands – perhaps tens of thousands – of people. What were they trying to achieve? I can't begin to imagine. The whole place feels strangely mute – a giant with its tongue cut out, so that it can never betray the true reason for its existence.

A giant. What made me think of that? *Gog and Magog, rise up and help me now.*

'Kind of creepy, huh?' says Cindy. She's so cold that her breath comes in unsteady judders. I put an arm round her. She presses close, resting her head on my shoulder.

'There's a lot of weird people out there,' she says. 'Jesus knows, I met most of them. But would *you* want to do it here?'

'No.'

'Me neither.' She's quiet for a moment. 'You seen enough? You ready to go?'

'Sure.'

Neither of us speaks again till we're back on the highway. Then I ask, 'Did he say anything else?'

'Who?'

'Your cop.'

She shakes her head.

'The trail just goes cold at that point?'

'What trail? There isn't one. They have nothing to investigate. End of story.'

'You didn't tell him about Adam, then?'

'Nope. I didn't think you'd want me to.'

'Thank you.'

We're both silent again. I don't know what she's thinking about, but I'm freaked out, crazy with lack of sleep, barely thinking at all. Hallucinations are clawing at the edge of my field of vision. If I don't make a mighty effort to get my mind straight, I'm going to lose it.

So what on earth happened that night? Or what, anyway – given what I know now – is a reasonable conjecture?

When Adam walks out of the concert, a girl in a red Corvette picks him up. Whether it was pre-planned, or she just saw an opportunity and took it, it's impossible to say. But, either way, the chances are she's some kind of groupie, looking for a bit of excitement with the limey troubadour.

What then? Do they go back to his hotel – or head straight for Cahokia? Again, there's no way of knowing. But Cahokia, evidently, is a popular nookie destination for local kids, so she may have had it in mind from the start to bring him here. What she probably didn't realize was that these kinds of places – ruined houses; prehistoric monuments; abandoned sites – obsessed Adam, and could send him hurtling off the rails. Clearly, that's something she discovers soon enough…

'You know what?' Cindy says. Her voice sounds tight, all of a sudden, as if there's a hand round her throat. 'I'm leaving tomorrow.' She glances at the car clock. 'Actually, today. I called my sister. Told her I'm coming.'

We're across the bridge now, and heading through the wasteland beyond the docks.

'You mean for good?'

She nods again. 'I just decided. That creep in the bar. And then talking to you. And then sucking that greasy cop's dick, to get some information out of him.' She shakes her head. 'I'll wait tables, I'll do anything. I'm just not doing that any more.'

Well, good. But that seems presumptuous, somehow, a judgment I'm not qualified to make. So I say nothing.

'Don't you approve?' she says, flicking a sideways look at me.

'Of course I approve.'

She nods. Silence again. But it isn't just neutral now: it's a palpable presence, filling the car with unborn hints, questions, suggestions. What am I expected to do next? Just give her another fifty and send her on her way? Invite her into my room? Or simply buy her a meal at an all-night diner, and – if I can keep awake – listen to the story of her life? Finally, as we turn into the Indian Springs parking lot, and I can't put it off any longer, I say,

'You want to come in?'

She switches off the engine, then turns and smiles at me. I smile back. She leans across and kisses me. Her mouth tastes of spearmint, and I can smell perfume on her skin. My body feels like Frankenstein's monster, jolted into life by an alchemical rush of electricity.

'Don't worry,' she whispers, moving her lips to my ear. 'I'm starting over. So –'

I pull away, groaning. 'No.'

Not the toughest decision I've ever made. But close.

She stares at me. Even in the dimness I can see her cheeks darken with anger. My tired brain tries out a few phrases: *I'd really like to, honestly, but… In a few days you'll be glad we didn't…It's not the way to start your new life, fucking another guy you hardly know…*They all sound crass. In the end, I get out of the car and take a fifty from my pocketbook.

'Here.'

'Fuck you.' She's almost in tears.

'Come on. It's not the same.'

She hesitates, chewing her lip, then reaches out and plucks the bill from my hand. Then she starts the engine, and – without looking back at me – drives out of the parking lot, heading for downtown.

*

I call Tate the next day, tell him what I've found out.

'So where'd he go after that?'

'I don't know.'

He makes a weary sound through his teeth. 'Well, if he doesn't show up by the end of the week, man, nothing for it, we're going to have to go to the cops.'

Adam doesn't show up by the end of the week. Wheatsheaf cancels his motel room and calls in the police. He migrates from being a private grief to – for a few days – a page two story. The cops follow up several leads, including the red Corvette, but all of them peter out. After six months, the detective in charge of the case says he's ninety-nine per cent certain Adam is dead, probably by his own hand. Within a year, that's become the accepted story.

And maybe it's true. Maybe today or tomorrow or the next day a body will be dredged out of the Mississippi, or discovered lying at the bottom of a gravel pit. Or someone walking in the woods will come upon a red Corvette with a blood-spattered windshield, and half a head, buzzing with flies, caked to the wheel. Mystery solved.

It's possible. Anything is possible.

But I won't be surprised if, in the end, the mystery *isn't* solved – or, at least, not in a way that allows the police to write, definitively, *case closed* on the Adam Earnshaw file. Because to me – crazy as I know this must sound – there's something else going on here. Something more like a poem, or a myth, with its own rules, its own logic.

The simple truth, in my view, is that Adam had reached the end of the road. Day after day, he had been strapping himself to the electric chair, because he didn't know what else to do – and it had more or less burned him up. And then, just when he was so frail he could barely function, the contradictions that had always threatened to tear him apart fell on him with renewed fury.

You have to feel sorry for the girl, whoever she was. She can't have understood the part she'd been chosen to play. *Let's drop some acid and go fuck on Cahokia Mounds.* How could she know what she was unleashing? Let's just hope she got out of it with her sanity intact.

And as for Adam – poor beautiful tormented Adam – I don't even want to think about the forensic details. Perhaps there weren't any. Perhaps what we're dealing with is something else altogether, something more like *transfiguration*.

That's how I like to imagine it, anyway. He takes the path behind the silken-threaded oak – and on the other side, he finds his heart's desire.

21

MAEVE RAMAGE

OK. In answer to your questions:

When was it? 11th July 1973, five years to the day after Adam disappeared.

Where was it? The lake at Sibley Park.

Whose idea was it? I honestly can't remember. I'm not sure I ever actually knew. I've a feeling it might have been Sadie – which, all things considered, would have been pretty weird. Perhaps she wanted a chance to show the rest of us that she hadn't just survived the break-up with Adam, but had become a bit of a superstar.

Who was there? I'm not good at numbers. Maybe twenty of us, mostly from the music world: Tate Finnegan – unmistakable in jeans, a collarless white shirt, and the top half of a dark suit; assorted sound engineers, record producers etc.; plus me and Stevie, Rufus Strange, and a singer called Carrie Bateman who'd known Adam in the early days. Well, she wasn't a singer at that point: she was living in a commune, and pregnant with her first child. The father – she showed me a picture of him: a beanpole of a guy, with a long straggly beard – must have been as mild-mannered as she was, earnestly agreeing to look after the goats while she went off to mourn a former lover. I couldn't imagine Stevie doing that for me.

There were also a few people from Oxford. Most conspicuous was Tim Bruce, just returned from his Caribbean honeymoon with Sadie, the pair of them looking like the centre-spread from a fashion magazine, her in a gorgeous silk waistcoat and flares, him in a linen jacket and polka-dot shirt. (That's stuck in my mind, because, looking back, they're the only figures I see in colour. That can't be right, I know, but it's how I remember it.) Then there was a girl called Mel something-or-other, who'd hitched down from Cowley. I never figured out *what* she was doing there, but it turned out that she – no, no, I'll get to that later. And then there was a sad-looking guy called Roddy, an art historian or something, who'd been at college with Adam. He showed me a photo, too: a very recognizable him and an almost unrecognizable Adam, together with an older woman and a young girl with her arm in plaster, all smiling at the camera. 'This is us. Our very first day at Oxford.'

'Who's that?' I said, pointing to the girl. 'Your sister?'

He nodded, then swallowed, his eyes brimming with tears.

'Oh, I'm sorry. Did something happen to her?'

He nodded again. 'She died. A road accident.'

'How awful.'

One person I *didn't* see, to my surprise, was Peyton Whybrow. I asked Tim Bruce where he was. *Oh, he's gone back to the States. Really*? I said. *I thought he was more or less a permanent fixture at the magazine? Sadie felt it was time to move on*, he said. *Push The Scene in a new direction. Less counter-cultural navel-gazing, more fun. And I thought she was right.*

So obviously the article Peyton had written about her and Adam still rankled.

What happened? What *didn't* happen? No, that's ridiculous: there wasn't a murder or a flash-flood or an earthquake. But still, it was pretty dramatic, for such a sombre occasion.

For a start, Mr Toad (since you've been in touch with Stevie, you'll know who I mean) had laid on food and copious quantities of drink, and seemed to have decided to get the ball rolling by polishing off most of a bottle of gin before anyone else arrived. For most people, the result would have been slurred speech or an inability to walk in a straight line, but the effect on Mr Toad – I recalled it only too well, from the summer we'd spent there – was to convince him that he was absolutely irresistible to women. The sad truth was that – in an attempt to keep up with the times – he'd actually made himself look even more ridiculous. No more paisley shirts: instead, he was wearing a red tank-top darkened with sweat. And in place of the familiar floppy pop-star hair, he sported a cascading, outrageously baroque *coiffure* that made him look like one of Louis XIV's mistresses.

I tried to stick close to Stevie, but he'd been drinking himself on the way there – we hadn't had a gig for over a year, and booze was the only way he could cope with his sense of failure, and his jealousy at the fuss people were making over Adam Earnshaw – and after half an hour or so he'd stomped off to try his luck with dopy Carrie Bateman. As soon as he'd gone, Mr Toad saw his chance and swooped, and within two minutes he was fumblingly trying to unhook one of the straps of my overalls.

Point of information: my relationship with Stevie had been going steadily down the plughole since we'd finished our last album, and – in an attempt to deal with my pain and confusion – I'd joined a women's consciousness-raising group. According to our leader, Miriam, who'd survived three years in a hippy house in Hashbury, the mistake we'd all made was to fall for the male myth of the sexual revolution. Actually, she said, there hadn't been a revolution at all: free love had been free just for the men, and it was the women, as always, who'd had to pay the price – if not, thanks to the pill, with unwanted pregnancy, then with emotional and physical collateral damage. And the only way finally to break the age-old cycle was to see the situation for what it was and stop behaving like victims.

So I punched Mr Toad in the stomach.

I'll never forget the look of disbelief on his face. He reeled, stumbled, struggled to regain his balance – and then his legs folded under him, and he went down.

Everyone, of course, was staring at us. Roddy and Mel, who were talking only a few yards away, hurried to Mr Toad's aid. I didn't want to have to explain myself, so I walked off quickly, slapping my hands. But I'd only gone twenty paces or so when I began to feel really bad. *You didn't need to do that. He's just a pathetic little inadequate. You could have told him to fuck off. That would have been enough.*

I spun round, intending to go back and say sorry. But Mel was already on the ground next to him, cradling his head in her lap and stroking his hair. If I intruded now, she'd probably attack me.

'It's OK,' said a voice at my elbow. 'I saw what happened. You were well within your rights.'

I turned: Rufus Strange.

I shook my head. 'It was a shitty thing to do.'

'He was asking for it.' He slipped his arm through mine. 'Why don't we take a stroll? Everyone's so pissed, by the time we get back, they'll have forgotten about it.'

He led me across the lawn and into the stable yard, where we'd be hidden from view.

'God,' I said, 'talk about a trip down memory lane.'

'Why?'

'This is where we lived,' I said, showing him the two little side-by-side cottages. 'Stevie and me in this one. And Adam in here.'

I peered in through Adam's window, half-thinking, for one crazy second, that I'd see him sitting there, hunched over his guitar. The place looked deserted, the Swedish chairs grey with dust, the orange-and-black rug reduced to a dingy blur by the dirty pane.

'God,' I said, 'this is really weird.'

His reflection nodded at me in the glass.

'Us then and us now.' I shook my head. 'Jesus.'

'Yeah, I know, it's been hard,' he mumbled apologetically. 'I have tried to get you on. But Auntie isn't like Stella. The producer always has the last word about what we play.'

'It's not your fault, Rufus. Why would they want to play us? We can't even get gigs any more.'

'It's just fashion, I'm afraid.'

'That's what Stevie says. But it isn't just that. *I* wouldn't book us, the way he is now. If you want to see a guy screaming abuse at his wife and then throwing up, go down the pub. It's cheaper.'

He laughed and put his arms round me. 'I'm sorry, Maeve.'

My whole life had become an act – and now, just for a moment, I didn't have to keep it up. God, the relief! I hugged him back, resting my chin on his shoulder. We were so intertwined that, when we heard footsteps approaching over the cobbles, we didn't manage to extricate ourselves in time.

'Oh, there you are,' said Stevie. He stopped a few paces from us, legs spread wide to steady himself. His face was a gargoyle leer. Obviously Carrie had given him his marching orders. Good for her: I wouldn't have thought she'd had it in her.

'I was just showing Rufus the nymph and swain quarters.'

'Were you, indeed?' He glared at Rufus. 'Decided to try playing for the other team, have you? And thought you'd get a bit of practice in with my wife?'

'Oh, for Christ's sake, Stevie!' I said.

'Don't worry,' said Rufus. 'I've heard a lot worse.'

'I'll bet you have,' said Stevie. 'In the toilets at Piccadilly Circus. Wouldn't you be more comfortable inside? Here, let me open the door for you.'

He edged stiffly towards it, like an old man struggling to keep his balance, and tried the handle. It was locked.

'Ah. Well, perhaps Mr Toad would let you use one of his bedrooms. He's got enough of them, hasn't he? And I dare say they're all full of chintz and swags and flounces. Right up your street, I'd have thought.'

'Right,' said Rufus quietly, touching my hand. 'I'm going back.'

'Oh, please,' said Stevie, 'don't let me put you off. She can't bring herself to fuck me any more. Straightening out a queer is probably just what she needs.'

Rufus said nothing, but shook his head and kept walking. Even a few months ago, I'd have explained that he'd been trying to comfort me, told Stevie to go after him and apologize. But now I knew it was pointless. However carefully I chose my words, he'd find a way to turn them against me.

'I'm going too,' I said.

He grabbed my wrist. I tried to pull free. He tightened his grip.

'Please let me go,' I said.

He started dragging me back towards the cottage. How had I got myself into this situation? Miriam would be furious with me. Her first rule was: *Take control.* That meant: *Never put yourself in a vulnerable position. Always make sure you have a safe place to go to. Never let him manipulate you into being alone with him when he's drunk.*

'Look,' he said. He twisted me round and pressed my face against the window of our old house. Inside, it was as decrepit and neglected as Adam's. But the familiar shapes of the sofa and the ladder-back chairs and – just visible in the half-open door into the kitchen – the big pine table where we'd eaten so many meals together, worm-holed through the intervening years, like a needle finding a nerve. They belonged to that other reality, when the man standing next to me – reeking of alcohol and Players Number 6, pinioning my arm and making me shake with fear – had been my true love, and I'd trusted him more with my own body, my own oddities and desires, than I trusted myself.

'What?' I said, struggling not to cry.

'That's it,' he said. And then, suddenly, he was crying himself. He pulled me to him, squeezing so hard that it hurt, and started sobbing in my ear,

'Oh, God, I'm sorry, I've been such a stupid cunt.'

One strategy you have to look out for, said Miriam's voice in my head, *is when he apologizes. 'I'm going to be better from now on, I promise. It'll be just like it used to be again.' He probably even believes it himself, that's what makes it so dangerous. But it's just another way of trapping you in a relationship that doesn't work, and can* never *work.*

And she was right. I knew it was hopeless – that we'd passed this point on the less-and-less-merry-go-round God knows how many times, and that the false dawn always started to fade within hours, or even minutes. But still, as I clung to him, digging my fingers into his flesh, the temptation to say, *Yes, yes, let's try again*, was almost over-whelming. What stopped me, in the end, wasn't my own strength, but the sudden, startling sound, from the direction of the lake, of a wistful guitar intro – so powerful, so evocative of the golden age, that for a second I felt as if I was back in 1967, waking from a long-drawn-out nightmare.

'Fuck me,' said Stevie, pulling away. 'What's that?'

'Don't you recognize it?'

He nodded. And then, from the spirit world, we heard Adam's voice:

> *'Rainy Friday, Mr Morris*
> *Takes his lunchbox, leaves the assembly line*
> *In the street the kids are drifting*
> *Going nowhere*
> *Blowing like litter*
> *Don't they know we fought a war for them?'*

At eight he's down the Leg of Mutton
Usual, Ted? No, that's all right, I'm buying
Snuffing at the smell that's wafting
Sweat and polish
Fags and bitter
Telling him he's finally at home.

Stevie and I looked at each other. Then, without a word, we headed towards to the music. I don't know what was going through his mind, but mine was a jumble of free associations: a lurching boat; a summer evening, smelling of dope and perfume and cut grass and tobacco plants; a firmament of Japanese lanterns strung through the trees of a little island – *the* island, where Stevie and I had once gorged ourselves on smoked salmon and chilled white wine, before making love and falling asleep in each other's arms and then making love again.

We came out by the lake just in time to hear the last bars of *Mr Morris*, and the opening of *I Am a House*. Tate must have put together a special tape, so that the songs appeared in the order Adam had sung them on the night of our party in 1967. The speakers were under the drinks table, concealed by an overhanging white cloth, giving the impression that the sound was coming from a discarnate being hovering above the water. Everyone else seemed to find it as eerie as I did, standing in complete silence and staring off into nothingness, as if they weren't sure where they should be focusing their gaze. A few people were fighting tears, and Sadie – who I'd always thought had a heart of flint – was weeping openly, dabbing her eyes with a frilly handkerchief, while Tim Bruce distractedly rubbed her back.

We listened through *Oxford Blues* and *Cookie-cut Kid*, everyone sealed away in their own thoughts. And then Tate clicked off the tape recorder, clapped his huge hands together and started to speak. I can't give you his whole speech – although I can tell you that, for the only time ever in my hearing, he didn't use the word *fuck* once – but a few phrases have stayed with me, and I can remember the gist:

OK, people. I knew Adam for three years, less time than it's been since he disappeared. And you know what? I'm prouder of what he and I achieved together during that short interlude – that's kind of what it feels like now, just an interlude – than I am of anything I ever did.

And that's a bit weird – because, of course, Adam was the unlikeliest freak ever. He didn't belong in the underground scene, probably didn't belong anyplace at all. But thinking about it now, that seems kind of the point. It was just because *he didn't belong that he brought something to it, gave something to it, that nobody else did, nobody else could have done. And now he's gone, it's gone too.*

What that something is will be different for everyone. Because that was his gift – to get inside all our lives, see the world through the eyes of every one of us. And without him, the world has shrunk, grown colder, because we're on our own again.

So let's all just take a moment to remember him in our own way.

It wasn't just Sadie: pretty much *everybody* was crying by this point. Without anyone suggesting it, we all started to assemble in a circle. To begin with, people were self-conscious and awkward: Carrie moved nimbly out of the way to avoid ending up next to Stevie, and Mr Toad, still with Mel in tow, stationed himself as far away from me as he could, glaring fiercely in my direction. But soon, everyone had found a place, and we all started groping tentatively for our neighbours' hands. The spontaneous sense of unity had an odd effect, reducing the whole group to silence, and synchronizing our breathing, as if we were all part of one organism, directed by a single nervous system.

'Great,' murmured Sadie, after a minute or two. 'Let's all just stay with this, shall we?' And then, a few seconds later, 'Come on, everyone. It'll be more powerful if we say it together. *We miss you, Adam, wherever you are.*'

'We miss you, Adam, wherever you are.'

We bowed our heads. I shut my eyes. Adam floated into the darkness, hunched over our kitchen table, a giant joint in his hands. His face was fuzzy, but he seemed to be smiling at me – as if, after all, whatever had happened to him, he was somehow OK.

'Oh, fuck,' said Stevie. He made no attempt to keep his voice down, and – erupting into the silence without warning – it sounded shockingly loud.

I opened my eyes. 'What?'

'This is ridiculous.'

He yanked himself free and reversed out of the circle, shaking his head.

'Why?' I said. 'Because it's about Adam? And not you?'

'The whole thing, it's just fucking crap.'

'Could you be quiet, please?' called Sadie, icy-voiced. 'You're spoiling the mood.'

'Come on,' I mouthed, beckoning him back. But he ignored me, and – making a megaphone with his hands – bellowed at Sadie:

'Have you any idea what complete tits you all look?'

Out of the corner of my eye, I saw Tate and Tim Bruce starting to move in our direction. They'd only taken a couple of steps before Mr Toad barged past them and began barrelling towards us himself – his arms jerking furiously like the wings of a cartoon chicken, and with Mel, solemn-faced with sympathetic anger, half-running after him.

'We'd better go,' I said.

'Why? We've as much right to be here as anyone else. I need another drink. If they want to behave like a bunch of fucking morons –'

He broke off. Mr Toad was upon us. 'Get out!'

He gave Stevie a violent push. Stevie stumbled, regained his balance, and launched a lumbering, drunken-bull counter-attack. But Mr Toad stood his ground, and Stevie was left swaying from side to side, jabbing the air impotently with his fists.

'You've got two minutes,' said Toad. 'Then I'm calling the police.'

You could see it in his face, the set of his shoulders, the splay of his feet: this was the payback for the months of mockery and humiliation he'd suffered at our hands. Emboldened by booze, and – miracle of miracles – the admiring gaze of a not-bad-looking girl, he was finally letting us know that he wasn't going to stand for it any more.

'You can do what you like, you fucking little aborted foetus,' said Stevie.

'God!' said Mel, lunging forward. 'What a horrible thing to –'

Toad laid a hand on her arm. 'You go in' – nodding at the big house – 'and dial 999.'

'Is that all right?' she said. 'I mean, just swanning in like that?'

'Of course it is. It's mine. There's –'

'What, this? All of it?'

He nodded. 'There's a phone in the hall.'

She stared at him for a moment, then darted off. I jangled the car keys and grabbed Stevie's elbow.

'Come on.'

'Why should I?' he said, shaking me off. 'We knew Adam fucking Earnshaw better than any of these cunts.' He prodded me with his foot. 'Specially you. What, did you think I didn't know, you bitch?'

Mr Toad stiffened, glancing from Stevie to me and back again. What he didn't realize was that this was just a regular staging-post on the endless circular journey, and that in three hours – if he hadn't refuelled in the meantime – Stevie would be sobbing and muttering, *I'm sorry, I'm sorry, I don't know why I said those things.*

'Well, I'm going, anyway,' I said.

If he's going to end up dead in a ditch or a police cell, said Miriam in my head, as I started across the lawn, *that's his choice. You can't protect him from himself.* Your *job is to protect* you. But still, I knew that if he called my bluff, I couldn't just drive off and leave him. I'd give him fifty paces. If he hadn't come after me by then, I'd have to go back.

Forty-five, forty-six, forty-seven. And then, thank God, I heard him stumbling in pursuit.

When we reached the front of the house, I stopped and looked back. There, spread out behind us, were all that remained of Adam Earnshaw's life: a mute tape-recorder; a table littered with glasses and half-empty bottles; a handful of people, standing around alone or in pairs, puzzling over a world that – for some reason they couldn't figure out – had failed to keep its promise.

Not with a bang, but a whimper.

OUTRO

We're back at the bar we saw at the beginning. It's dark now, the sky tattooed with stars, the air humming with the sound of crickets. The flashing Double D and the neon beer signs in the windows are almost lost in the blackness, giving the whole place a forlorn, lonely, makeshift feel, as if it's just a figment of someone's imagination and might vanish at any second.

In the parking lot, our man is still in his car. Remember him? Walter? On the seat next to him lies his empty satchel. The pile of papers is on his knee. He sits huddled, hugging himself against the cold, watching the door. In the darkness, he seems little more than a blur.

After a few seconds the door opens, releasing a blast of country music into the night. Three men come out, laughing. The door swings shut behind them and – sailors making their way along a heeling deck – they lurch towards their pick-up truck.

Still Walter sits there. After another minute or so the door opens again and he stiffens. This, obviously, is the person he's been waiting for: the seventy-something woman with the corkscrew hair. Her head's tilted at an odd angle, and as the glow from the Budweiser sign catches her, we see why: she's talking urgently into a mobile phone clamped to her ear. She hurries to the Corvette, fumbles keys from her bag, gets in, switches on. Walter keeps quite still until she's left the parking lot. Then he starts his own car and eases it into her wake.

For ten minutes they wind in tandem along an unlit country road. Then the woman slows and turns off down an almost-concealed track. Ahead we can see the blank face of a house cut into the hillside. Odd silhouettes – a periscope, maybe? An air vent? – jut from the rock above it. To one side are the remains of a vegetable garden, now more or less reclaimed by the surrounding wilderness.

Walter pulls off on to the verge. He watches the woman park the Corvette and walk towards the house, triggering a security light. He waits until she's disappeared inside, then gets out and sets off after her. But he's only gone a few yards when the front door opens again and the corkscrew-hair woman re-emerges. As the security light flicks back on, we see that next to her, clutching her arm, is another, squatter woman who walks with a stick.

Walter stops dead. Then, as they start to hobble slowly towards him, he beats a quick-march retreat, the sound of his footsteps drowned out by the chorus of crickets.

He ducks into his car, reverses as far as the road, then backs into the entrance to a field, from where he can see without being seen. After a couple of minutes the Corvette passes him. He follows it. Soon the unbroken walls of forest hemming the road start to give way to a more open landscape. Lights show through the trees. We come to a gas station, a business park, a small shopping mall.

At the next junction the Corvette turns into a large car park. A sign by the entrance says: *Hamer-Kossow Medical Center.* Dominating the horizon is a white modern building, a confection of horizontal lines and lit windows, like a giant cruise ship in port. The Corvette manoeuvres through the maze of parked cars and noses into a space near the entrance. As the two women get out – for simplicity's sake, let's call them Corkscrew and Stick – there's no sign that they know they've been tailed. Without even a glance behind them, they limp towards the entrance.

There's a constant trickle of visitors and staff going in and out, so it's easier for Walter to blend in. In fact, no one appears to notice him at all. Even in the glare of the interior there's something oddly indistinct about him – as if he's negatively charged, and the bright light that has robbed other people of their shadows has left *him* with nothing else. He flits after the women along a wide, rubbery-floored corridor, past a café, a little shop, clusters of elevators, through a door marked *Magnolia Ward.* He lingers in the hall, pressing himself against the wall as two nurses walk by. They pass close enough to brush his sleeve, but neither of them challenges him.

Emboldened, he slips into the ward, and catches the two women up just as they reach the door to a private room at the far end.

He doesn't follow them in: that would be pushing his luck. But through the clear plastic panel in the door, he can see and hear what's going on. On the bed lies a white-haired, heavily-bearded man, his eyes half-closed, one withered arm wired to a bank of monitors. One side of his mouth is pulled down, saliva oozing over the purple lip. Next to him stands a nurse in pale blue scrubs holding a chart.

'Jesus!' says Stick. She's thickset and heavy, wearing jeans and a rumpled sweater. She leans over the bed, head bowed, her body skewed to one side, as if she's compensating for a damaged knee.

'I'm so sorry,' says the nurse. 'It was a couple hours ago. Hit him just like that.'

'Is he conscious?' asks Corkscrew.

'Hard to say *what's* going on in there,' says the nurse. 'Even the doctors don't really know.' She turns, so the patient can't see her face. 'But I'm afraid,' she mouths, 'they don't think he's going to make it. Which one of you is –'

'Her,' says Corkscrew, pointing at her companion.

'Only a while back, it sounded like he was trying to say something. Like he was asking for someone. His *son*, maybe? That could have been the word. Does he have a son? Cos somebody better call him, if he –'

'No,' says Stick. 'Looking after *him*, that was enough. He was always sick, up here' – tapping her temple. 'And for years we were on the road the whole time, just a couple weeks here, a month there, before we'd have to move on. No way I could have handled kids, top of all that.'

'There isn't …I don't know, someone from a previous relationship, maybe?'

Stick glares at her.

'OK, I was only asking.'

Stick leans down and strokes the patient's beard with the back of her hand. Her eyes brim with tears.

'God,' she says, gazing at him again. 'If you could just see him…The way he was when I met him…The most beautiful thing I ever saw.'

The nurse smiles. 'Yeah, I'm sure.'

'But that guy died a long time ago. They destroyed him. And it was stupid old muggins here had to pick up the pieces.'

'Who?' says the nurse. 'Who destroyed him?'

'All of them.' She can't say any more. She clamps a hand over her lips, trying to stifle an animal moan that still manages to seep out between her fingers. Corkscrew takes her wrist. As she gently pulls it away, we see a mole at the corner of Stick's mouth.

'Come on, Lil,' says Corkscrew. 'Let's go get something to eat in the café. Cup of coffee. That'll make you feel better.'

Stick is still howling, but she doesn't resist. Slowly they edge towards the door.

'You two sisters?' asks the nurse.

'Cousins,' says Corkscrew.

After they've gone, the nurse makes a note of the instrument readings on her chart. Then she follows the two women out into the corridor.

Walter sees his chance. Checking that no one is watching him, he slips into the room. As he approaches the bed, the camera suddenly swivels. Finally we're looking through the old man's eyes.

Through *my* eyes.

'So,' I say, 'you ran me to earth.'

He gawps. 'Are you really–?'

I nod. Walter shivers and hugs himself. He looks towards the door. 'And was that–?'

'Yes,' I say. 'That's her. That's Lily. Don't be too harsh. You could say she and I deserve each other. Both of us crazy, in our own way. And without her, I wouldn't be here at all.'

Walter hesitates. 'So was it…Did she…did she actually realize? What she was doing back then? Or –'

'Yelling for *Annabelle*? Driving me to the Cahokia Mounds? Yes, she realized. If she was going to pick up the pieces, I had to be completely broken first. And I was. I was totally shot.'

Walter is silent for a moment, thinking through the implications. Then he says,

'Fifty years. *More* than fifty years. I mean, for God's sake, what were you–?'

'Hiding out. Lying low. I needed taking care of.'

'And the music? What happened to the music?'

I touch my scalp. 'It's still in here. Along with everything else. Hundreds of songs no one will ever hear.'

He shakes his head. *What a tragedy.*

'*You* could have heard them. If I hadn't been such a fool. Left this so late.'

'What do you–?' He breaks off suddenly. 'Hey, what is this? I thought you couldn't speak?'

'I can speak to you.'

'How?'

'Don't you know?'

Walter shakes his head. Miraculously, for the first time, we can see him clearly now: pale skin, beaky nose, blue eyes, uncombed hair. The resemblance to the young me is unmissable.

'No, of course you don't know,' I say. '*I've* had years to think about it. But you...' I pause. 'So what did you conclude about me?'

Walter shrugs.

'Be honest. What kind of a person am I?'

'You're...Porous.'

The patient nods. 'Yes. A good word for it.'

'No borders, no lines of defence. Anybody who can inhabit other lives like you do has to be constantly open to everyone. Not just the living, but the dead. So you even converse with ghosts. You –'

He breaks off, eyes widening.

'You're getting there,' I say.

His eyebrows shoot up. He points a finger at his chest. 'Me?'

I nod.

'No, that's bullshit. Look, I can show you.' He reaches for his wallet. 'My driving license. Here–' He riffles through the compartments, then stops as he realizes they're entirely empty. 'I had it! Just now! I know I did! I'm Walter–I'm Walter–'

'Walter who?'

'Walter–' His face stiffens. That fatal hole in his memory is finally bringing it home to him. He starts gnawing on a knuckle, trying to hold panic at bay.

'*Walter* was as far as I could get,' I say. 'It's what I would have called you, if I'd had the chance. What I *do* call you.' With my good hand I tap my head. 'In here.'

'Christ.' He slumps on to the edge of the bed. He stares unseeing at the panel of monitors, trying to assimilate what's he's just heard. Finally he says, 'So I'm...all I am is something you thought up? An invention?'

'Not an invention. A speculation. What you would have been. *Might* have been.'

Walter shakes his head.

'I know,' I say. 'You probably feel cheated. But you were a free agent. All I did was set you in motion. It was your choice to come after me. That's what I was hoping you'd do. And I'm so glad you did. So grateful.'

'So...so all those people? Cat and Tate and Carrie and Rufus Strange. Roddy and Sadie and Rachel–' For a second he can't go on.

'I know,' I say. 'Rachel must be the hardest for you.'

But he doesn't want my pity. It just makes him more furious. 'All the fucking trouble I went to, finding them. Wheedling with them. Saying, please tell me about Adam Earnshaw–'

'It wasn't wasted. They were free agents too. I didn't load the dice. They could have refused to talk to you. Tim Bruce did, didn't he? They all spoke in their own voices, told the truth as they saw it. And you did a great job. Peyton came close. But you actually found me.'

He hooks his hands under the side of the bed, trying to hold on to existence.

'Of course you're angry,' I say. 'If I'd known...If it had been up to me, I promise you, you'd have been more. But this was the only life I could give you.'

The despair on his face, the abjectness...Unbearable.

'I'm so sorry,' I say. 'I screwed up. But you saw what it was like back then.'

He doesn't respond.

'So.' I can't put it off any longer. 'What's the verdict? On your poor God-forsaken old father? Can you...Can you let me go in peace?'

Walter gets up and starts towards the door. But after a few steps he stops again. He stands there, staring at the floor. Then he turns and walks back to me.

For a few seconds he embraces me, weeping. I try to hug him back, but my useless arms refuse to obey orders. I manage to say, 'Thank you.'

And then his grip loosens, and he starts to fade. And soon all that is left is empty air.

ACKNOWLEDGEMENTS

I prepared myself for my journey back to the sixties by relistening (and in some cases listening for the first time) to a wide range of music, re-viewing films and TV programmes, and reading widely. Two books, in particular, were instrumental in helping me to recapture the atmosphere of the time: Rob Young's *Electric Eden*, a superb cultural history of the world Adam Earnshaw finds himself in; and Joe Boyd's evocative, entertaining and beautifully-written memoir of his life as an American-in-Britain record producer, *White Bicycles*.

I'm indebted to a number of people who read and commented (always positively!) on the manuscript: Roger Bilder, Andrew Hilton, Sarah LeFanu, Ellen Pasternack, Dominic Power, Matthew Scott, David Stoll and Paul Willetts. I am also deeply grateful to Derek Johns and Louise Greenberg, who – both as agents and as friends – have been stalwart supporters, not only of this book, but of all my work. Especial thanks, too, to Lee Oser, for his generosity in reading the text so astutely (and quickly!), taking time he could ill afford to talk to me about it, and then promoting it more widely.

I am grateful to Jamieson de Quincey and her colleagues at Senex Press, who have been a pleasure to work with.

And finally, I want to thank my family: my wife Paula, for her unflagging patience, love and support; and our sons Tom (a brilliant critic, who read and made helpful suggestions about several versions of the manuscript) and Kit, for their active interest and encouragement.

JAMES WILSON has written six previous novels: *The Dark Clue*, *The Bastard Boy*, *The Woman in the Picture*, *Consolation* (all published by Faber), *The Summer of Broken Stories* (Alma Books), and *Coyote Fork* (Slant Books). He is also the author of a prize-winning work of narrative non-fiction, *The Earth Shall Weep: A History of Native America*. His work has been translated into nine languages. He lives in London with his artist wife.